Medillia's Lament III

"The Path That Leads Back Home"

A novel by Jody Clark

DEDICATION

To all my family and friends.
Especially Erica and Owen for their endless support and encouragement

ACKNOWLEDGMENTS

A special thanks to Jeff Sinon for the beautiful cover photo.
You can check out more of his amazing work at:
jeffsinon.com

Chicago – 2011
(Six years after book one ended)

He stares down from a dreary grey sky…
All that can be seen is the ocean far below…
The closer he gets, the more he sees how rough and harsh it is…
The water—pitch black and angry…
The waves—enormous and unforgiving…
The type of waves that could swallow a large boat whole…
He floats even closer and that's when he sees them…
Two people trying their best to swim…
The waves are unrelenting, pounding and pushing them under…
He tries to call out to them, but no words emit from his mouth…
The more he tries to speak, the deeper they sink…
Before going under for the final time, they call out…
"Help her to help us."

Kevin sat straight up, letting out a muffled scream of sorts. Sweat poured down his face, and he quickly looked around as if to collect his bearings. There were no giant waves, no dark ocean, and certainly no drowning people. There were just the familiar surroundings of his living room. With the exception of the glow from the TV, the room was completely dark. He could tell by the cheesy infomercial that it was well after midnight. A glance at his watch confirmed it—3:15am.

Kevin looked down the darkened hallway. He wondered if Julie heard him scream, and if she did, would she even care at this point? He knew she was getting increasingly bothered by his absence in their bed. Ever since the dream returned, he spent nearly every night sleeping on the couch. Well, *attempting* to sleep was more like it. Most nights were spent tossing and turning, which is why he chose the couch. The last thing he wanted was to disturb Julie's sleep. Actually, the last thing he wanted was to have to explain his dream to her, especially considering he couldn't even explain it to himself.

Kevin clicked off the TV then reached down to the floor, grabbing the crumpled blanket. He buried himself beneath it, but his eyes remained open. His mind and body were torn between being completely exhausted and not wanting to fall back into the dream again. It took a few hours, but the exhaustion eventually won out. It was just after sunrise when Kevin finally fell into a dreamless sleep.

By the time Julie awoke and entered the living room, he was curled into a tight ball and was snoring loudly. It was cute the first couple of times she saw him sleeping on the couch. If the TV was still on, she'd turn it off. She remembered pulling the blanket up around him and laughing at the stream of drool flowing from his mouth. But now, as she walked by the couch, it was obvious that the novelty had worn off. It was more annoying than cute. She had lost track of how many nights he hadn't come to bed lately. And if he did come to bed, it was always short-lived. She also lost track of how many times she awoke in the middle of the night to him being gone.

Whenever she did make a comment, his responses were always the same: "I fell asleep watching the game," or "I was watching a movie and ended up crashing on the couch."

After a while, she just gave up on saying a word. His sleep pattern wasn't the only thing starting to get on her nerves. From day one, their communication had always been top notch, but lately it was becoming non-existent. He was moody—and Kevin was never moody. That was usually reserved for his brother. Kevin and Julie were going on their fifth year of marriage, and she couldn't help but wonder if their flame was starting to flicker.

She thought about yanking the blanket off him and forcing him to talk to her; to explain what the hell was going on with him—with them. The longer she contemplated, the louder his snoring became. But like always, she decided against a confrontation. Instead, Julie grabbed her sweatshirt and duffle bag then headed out to the gym for her daily workout.

***

Across town, John was also getting ready to leave the house. Although, he wasn't going to the gym or even to work. For the past few weeks, his morning ritual consisted of lounging at the local coffee shop. Some days he would spend the entire morning there. Mostly, he would just drink his coffee while he people-watched. Sometimes, especially lately, he would just stare off into space. What he would never do, however, was anything work related: no sketches, no plans, no paperwork, no thoughts of woodworking at all.

John always made sure to mute his phone. There was nothing worse than a phone call interrupting his act of sitting on his ass. On that particular morning, he made the mistake of looking down at his phone. He had three missed calls and one voicemail, and that was just from the morning. There were other missed calls and messages from earlier in the week as well. Most of them were from the same person. John had no intention of calling him back, but he did decide to torture himself by listening to the latest voicemail. It was from his newest customer, Mr. Gilpatrick.

"John, this is Brent Gilpatrick. I've left numerous messages and I've even stopped by your shop. I'm not gonna lie, I'm starting to get quite irritated! You promised the custom-made hutch would be ready by Saturday… *last* Saturday! My wife's surprise party is tomorrow night. The hutch needs to be delivered by tomorrow morning at the latest! Understood?"

3

The good thing about John's talent was it attracted a more high-end clientele. Unfortunately, most of them were impatient and uppity pains in the ass. Mr. Gilpatrick was no exception. But to be fair, he had a right to be upset. John had been putting this project off for weeks now. Usually, he could use the excuse that he was juggling too many projects at once, but this really wasn't the case. Currently, Mr. Gilpatrick was his one and only customer. John's demand was still high, but over the past few weeks, he found himself unmotivated and uninspired. He began turning down one potential customer after another. John felt guilty; not enough to call Mr. Gilpatrick back, but he did get off his ass and headed over to his shop.

***

For the longest time, Kevin and Julie had no problem working seven nights a week together at the Wild Irish Rose. If they needed a night off, one of their friends would fill in. Either that, or John would volunteer his services. There was a part of him that still felt connected to the Wild Irish Rose. Not to mention, he still felt like he owed Kevin for mentally and physically bailing on him in the beginning. It wasn't until recently that Kevin and Julie decided to hire a couple of part-time bartenders. It didn't allow for extended time off, but it did provide them with a break here and there.

It was late afternoon when Julie swung by the bar. It was one of her nights off, and she claimed to be there just to check on things, but what she was really checking on was to see if Kevin was there. She hadn't seen or heard from him since she left the house earlier that morning. She called and left several text messages to no reply. This wasn't like Kevin. However, over the past few weeks, it was becoming more and more apparent that Kevin wasn't himself. Julie couldn't help but take it personally.

As she walked through the front door, she was curiously greeted by her two bartenders, Cat and Devon. "What?" Julie asked, as both girls laughed and shook their heads at her.

Cat gave the bar a wipe down and said, "We just find it funny that you hired us so you guys could get away—"

"Yet you both end up here on your night off," Devon said, laughing.

Julie thought for a second. "Wait, Kevin is here, too?"

Both girls smiled and motioned towards the back.

When Julie opened the office door, Kevin was face down on the desk snoring. Normally, she would have given him a gentle nudge to wake him up, but seeing as he hadn't returned any of her messages, she chose a different method. She gave the door a slam and watched Kevin spring up, nearly falling out of his chair.

"What the hell!" he yelled, wiping the drool off his cheek.

"What the hell is right," she said. "What are you doing?"

"Just taking a quick nap. I'm exhausted."

No shit! Maybe that has something to do with you sleeping on the couch every damn night!

That's what she wanted to say but didn't. She decided on a softer approach.

"Well, you should probably head home to shower and change. We're meeting them at six."

"What? Meeting who?"

Julie let out an exasperated sigh. "Pam and Jared. We're supposed to have dinner with them tonight, remember?"

"Shit. I thought that was next week."

"Nope. Tonight."

Kevin yawned and gave his back a crack. "I think I'm gonna take a raincheck."

"Are you kidding me?"

The argument that ensued was short but most definitely not sweet. It ended with Julie slamming the door and storming out of the bar. By the time she reached the sidewalk, her nerves were shot. The worst part was she still had no clue why Kevin was acting like this.

Desperate times call for desperate measures, and if she couldn't figure out Kevin's behavior, she knew there was only one person who could. John hadn't been by the bar much at all lately, so she crossed her fingers and walked next door. When she saw the light on, she let out a sigh of relief, composed herself, and entered.

John had his back turned and didn't see Julie enter, and due to the loud Led Zeppelin music blaring out, he didn't hear her either. He had just finished applying the final coat of polyurethane and was apparently celebrating by playing a mean air guitar. Julie remained quiet until the song had ended.

"Looking good," she called out.

"Jesus Christ!" John yelled, spinning around. "You scared the shit outta me."

Julie smiled. "And by looking good, I meant the hutch, *not* your guitar playing. I'd hold off on that rock-star dream if I were you."

"Ha ha, smartass." John pressed the lid onto the polyurethane then wiped his hands and asked, "What's going on?"

"Not much. Haven't seen you around in a while."

"Aw, Jules, do ya miss me?"

"Of course."

"Yeah, right," he said, laughing. "I was actually in there about an hour ago for a Coke. How are the new chicks working out?"

"Good. Really good."

"So what are you doing here then? I thought the whole point of hiring them was so you and Kevin could have a night off to do married people stuff."

She shrugged and looked away. "That was the plan."

"Uh oh," John said with a grin. "Trouble in paradise?" Before she could answer, he joked, "Well, it's been what, five years now? Ya can't expect the honeymoon phase to last forever." He started to laugh at his own joke but stopped when he saw tears running down Julie's cheeks. "Jules? Are you crying?"

Embarrassed, she swiped them away. John moved forward and

6

wrapped his arms around his sister-in-law. The tightness to which she clung to him told him just how serious it was. He pulled up two chairs and sat listening to her vent about what was going on. When she finished, he leaned back and responded.

"I swear I'm not trying to be insensitive, Jules, but… but it really doesn't sound *that* bad. I mean, does it really bother you that much that he occasionally falls asleep on the couch?"

"Occasionally? It's been almost every night for the last few weeks. And it's been even longer since we've had—"

"Whoa, whoa, whoa! That's a little too much information, Jules."

"I know it all sounds silly and insignificant to you, but trust me, John, there's something going on with him. He barely acknowledges me, and when he does, he's snippy. For the past month, he's just been so… distant. Maybe you're right. Maybe the honeymoon phase *is* over. Maybe he's bored with the marriage… with me."

"Oh, Jules, I was totally joking. I'm sure he's not—"

"Maybe he's having an affair."

"What? No way! Kevin would never. Trust me, he loves you more than anything. I know I haven't been around the bar much in a while… I guess I've been in my own little funk, but I'm sure he's just going through some sorta funk, too. It's probably just the moon, or maybe the planets are aligning in some weird way." John's attempt to lighten the mood failed to resonate with Julie. He looked into her sad eyes and sighed and said, "I'll talk to him."

"Would you really?" she asked, a bit more hopeful.

"Yeah, I will. I promise."

Just then, the front door swung open.

"Oh, shit," John mumbled under his breath. He then put on a fake smile and stood up and said, "Mr. Gilpatrick, how are you? I was actually just about to call you."

Mr. Gilpatrick saw through John's bullshit and gave him a dubious glare.

"I was just showing my sister-in-law your wife's present."

He motioned over to the large and beautifully ornate hutch. The fresh coat of urethane caused it to glisten beneath the shop lights. For the moment, it was enough to curb Mr. Gilpatrick's irritation.

"Wow. It's… it's perfect. But it would have been nice for you to have returned my messages, ya know? Some would call that being professional."

John wanted nothing more than to smack the uppity look off his face, but ultimately, he knew Mr. Gilpatrick was right. He had dragged his feet on this job. So much so, he missed his original deadline; a deadline he should have easily hit. He deserved everything that came out of Mr. Gilpatrick's mouth. But still, it would be nice to smack this rich prick in the face and send him hightailing it out of there in his BMW… or Mercedes… or whatever type of yuppie-mobile he drove.

Halfway through their exchange, Julie politely excused herself and headed home. When she gave John a hug goodbye, she whispered in his ear, "Don't forget to talk to Kevin, okay?"

"Don't worry, I will," he whispered back.

John would eventually fulfill his promise, but it wouldn't be that night. By the time Mr. Gilpatrick left, John was beaten down and exhausted, and he certainly wasn't in any mood to talk to his brother. After chastising John further about his lack of communication and about missing his deadline, Mr. Gilpatrick insisted on a ten percent discount. He sarcastically called it an *unprofessional late fee.*

John fought with every inch of his being not to tell this smug asshole where he could shove his late fee. He also thought about taking a baseball bat and smashing the hutch right in front of Mr. Gilpatrick. He thought about it but didn't do or say a word. Instead, he promised he would deliver it in the morning, and after Mr. Gilpatrick finally left, John locked up and headed straight home.

He spent the entire ride mumbling profanities to himself. He loved working with his hands, he really did, and seeing the end result of a project was always satisfying. But more and more lately, it seemed like his customers were nothing but rude and ungrateful assholes.

Despite Mr. Gilpatrick's demeanor, and despite John's recent lack of motivation, he knew he needed to get back into the swing of things. As he lay in bed that night, he promised himself that tomorrow would be a different day. His plan was to wake up early and haul the hutch over to Mr. Gilpatrick's house. He also had a few leads on some new customers and planned on reaching out to them as soon as the hutch was delivered.

Like most things in his life, tomorrow morning didn't exactly go as planned. He did wake up early. And he did deliver the hutch. But that was pretty much where his aspirations ended. As usual, he found himself at the coffee shop. The only thing different than most days was he got his coffee to go and decided to take a ride. Over the next hour, he aimlessly drove in and around Chicago. He had no specific destination in mind, but subconsciously, he knew exactly where he needed to be.

As if on autopilot, his truck rumbled to a stop just outside the gates of St. Boniface cemetery. Over the years, John made it a point to visit his girls at least once a week. But as he sat there in his truck, he couldn't remember the last time he was there. It was at least two or three weeks—maybe even a month. He chastised himself for spending hours doing absolutely nothing at the coffee shop. As he walked through the gates, he felt guilty for showing up without any flowers. He felt even more guilty when he noticed there was not one flower around their headstones. Usually, even if John hadn't visited in a while, there were still plenty of flowers placed by Kristen's parents. But ever since her parents retired down to Florida, it was up to John to keep up with the flowers. He pushed the guilt and anger aside, put on a smile, and then knelt on the soft grass.

"How are my favorite two girls doing? I'm sorry it's been so long since I've visited. And I'm sorry I didn't bring any flowers. I wasn't really planning on coming here today… it just sorta happened." John looked over at Kristen's headstone and smiled. "I know, I know, nothing in life just sorta happens. I'd be lying if I said I've been too busy to visit. The truth is… I haven't been feeling like myself lately. Been feeling lost… and, well… a bit hopeless, to be honest with ya. Don't worry, Hannah, Daddy isn't gonna start drinking again. I promise."

John began picking at some of the rogue weeds that had sprung up since his last visit. He then focused on Hannah's stone.

"The Cubs are off to a good start so far this summer. Maybe this will be their year," he said, winking at her stone. "I really miss watching the games with you, kiddo. It's not the same without you. Don't get me wrong, I like watching with Uncle Kevin, but you're a much better snuggler." As he joked, he could hear his daughter's giggle as clear as day.

"Speaking of Uncle Kevin, I should probably swing by and see him after this. Apparently, he's having a rough month as well. He probably just needs some wise advice from his big brother. You're rolling your eyes at me, aren't you?" he said to Kristen's headstone.

John spent the rest of the morning there with his girls. He talked about a little bit of everything with them. He even told Kristen about his latest customer, Mr. Gilpatrick. Of course, he had to apologize several times for letting out colorful swear words in front of Hannah.

Before leaving, John promised them his next visit would be sooner than later. He then hopped into his truck and headed to the other end of town to fulfill his promise to Julie. He could have just called Kevin to see if he was home, but it wasn't like he had anything better to do that day.

After three quick knocks, he stepped back and waited. A few moments later, Kevin opened the door, looked curiously at his brother, and said, "What are you doing here?"

"What? Can't I swing by and see my brother?"

"You can. It's just you haven't done it in weeks… maybe months."

"That's not true. I came over for Julie's birthday party, remember?"

Kevin smirked. "That was two months ago."

"Really? Hmm, I could have sworn it was a couple of weeks ago." John also smirked as he walked past his brother and headed towards the kitchen. "Got anything to drink?"

"Yeah, there should be something in the fridge. Just don't touch my last can of Coke."

As soon as Kevin uttered those words, he heard the pop of a tab, followed by a refreshing exhale from John. "*Ahhhh*. What was that you say?" John asked, standing in the doorway with Kevin's last can of Coke in his hand.

"Never mind," Kevin said, shaking his head. "What brings you by?"

John shrugged. "Just seeing if you wanted to hang out… maybe hit the batting cages?"

"You came all the way out here to ask me that? You could have just called."

Kevin and Julie lived on the opposite end of the city as John, and on multiple occasions, John would make comments like: *Why the hell did you guys move so far away? It takes forever to get across town. The traffic sucks ass!*

"Eh, I just happened to be in the neighborhood, that's all."

Again, Kevin shot him a look of disbelief. "Come on, John, you're a shitty liar. What's on your mind?"

John entered the living room and plopped himself into Kevin's reclining chair.

"By all means, make yourself comfy in *my* chair. You already drank my last frickin' can of Coke."

Although he said it slightly sarcastic, John could sense there was more than a hint of annoyance in Kevin's tone.

"Holy shit, she's right. You really are a moody son of a bitch."

"Who said that? Julie? Did she send you here to talk to me?" Before John could reply, Kevin continued with, "Well, you can save your breath… I'm fine."

"Yeah, I can see that," John said, smiling.

"If that's the only reason you came, then you can—"

"You do realize she thinks you're having an affair, right?"

Kevin's tone softened. "What? She does?"

"Are you?"

"What? An affair? God no!"

John also softened his tone. "Seriously, Kev, what's going on? She said you've been moody and distant... and she said you've been sleeping on the couch a lot."

Kevin shrugged. "I just fall asleep watching TV sometimes, that's all."

John finished off the Coke and placed the can on the table next to him. "C'mon, Kev, you can't bullshit a bullshitter. Seriously, what's going on?"

Kevin let out a resigned sigh then slumped down onto the couch. He knew he needed to get this off his chest.

"It's been weeks since I've slept, like, *really* slept. And when I do finally fall asleep, I keep having the same dream—nightmare, actually. I wake up in a cold sweat... hands shaking... heart pounding."

For a quick second, John thought about making fun of his brother for stressing out over a silly dream, but he didn't. John knew all too well just how exhausting and stressful dreams could be.

"That's why you've been sleeping on the couch?"

"Yeah. I didn't want Julie to worry. But obviously that theory didn't work."

"What was the nightmare about?"

Kevin leaned back on the couch, covering his face with his hand. "You're gonna think I'm crazy. I mean, just thinking about it now, it seems so harmless and silly, but..."

"But while you're in it, it seems real... and scary as hell, huh?"

Slowly, Kevin nodded in agreement. "It's pretty much the same every time. It starts off with me floating above the ocean... and it's dark, like, really dark... not the sky, but the water. It's pitch black. And the waves are gigantic. Up ahead of me, I see two people trying to swim, but the waves keep pounding and pushing them under. I want to try and help them, but I can't move… I can't even speak."

John nodded along. "I think we've all had those types of dreams before."

"But it doesn't feel like a dream. Even when I wake up, it feels so real."

John's mind recalled the dream he used to have about Kristen and Hannah… of them in the fog-covered playground, disappearing on the swing set. He never told Kevin about his strange dreams and nightmares, but he thought this might be a good time to mention them. Maybe it would help Kevin realize that he wasn't the only one in the world who had life-like nightmares. Before John could say a word, Kevin spoke.

"I just wish I knew how to help them."

"Who?"

"The two people in my dream."

"Do you recognize them?" John asked.

Kevin lowered his eyes to the ground and took a long pause. Finally, he looked up at his brother and said, "Um, no. They've always been sorta faceless."

"Faceless?" John asked, fighting back his laughter.

"Not literally. Just too blurry to tell who they are. It's always been like that."

"Wait… what do you mean *always*? How long have you been having this dream?" Kevin hung his head and looked away. "Kevin? How long?"

"I used to have it all the time when we were younger."

"How much younger?"

Kevin made eye contact with John and replied, "Back when we were at the O'Neils' house."

"Since then? How come you never told me?"

Again, Kevin looked away. It took a second, but John was able to

13

answer his own question. *Of course Kevin didn't tell me. He was too busy looking out for me... he was always too busy looking out for me.*

"You've been having this same dream all these years?"

"No. It went away for the longest time... most of my life, actually. But in the last few weeks... it's come back... hardcore."

"And you've never told anyone? Even our hippy-chick shrink?"

Slowly, Kevin shook his head no.

"Jesus, Kev, you shoulda told me. You shoulda told me when you first started having it."

Kevin shrugged. "It was just a stupid, silly dream. Besides, you had a lot going on back then. I guess I always felt like I needed to be the strong one."

Normally, a comment like that would have sent John into a defensive rage, but over time (in particular, the last few years), John came to appreciate just how much Kevin had done for him. He thought back on all the times that his life was either falling apart or spiraling out of control, and Kevin was right, he was always the strong one. John made it impossible for him not to be. Over the next few minutes, John apologized for being so needy over the years and for not always being there for his brother. In true Kevin fashion, he played it off like it wasn't that big of a deal.

Kevin kept repeating, "It's just a stupid, fucked up dream, that's all. It's meaningless. Does Julie really think I'm having an affair?"

"Relax, bro. I reassured her that you were not having an affair."

"Did she believe you?"

"I think so, but..."

"But what?"

"At the very least, she thinks now that the honeymoon phase is over, you might be having second thoughts. And she mentioned something about it was probably because she had put on a few pounds."

"Are you kidding me?" Kevin said, standing up.

John smirked. "Yeah, I am kidding... about the fat part anyway.

But she does think you're having second thoughts."

"What the fuck! This isn't funny, John."

"I know. I'm sorry."

"You better have reassured her that none of that is true!"

"I did. But she needs to be reassured by *you*, not me. Just tell her about your reoccurring dream. What's the big deal?"

"This coming from the guy who never completely let Kristen in. I mean, did you tell her about your past, or your fears, or your deepest thoughts... ever?"

John's demeanor saddened, and he looked Kevin straight in the eyes and answered, "No... but I should have. I absolutely should have. And so should you."

"I know, I know, you're right. I just wish I could figure out why I keep having it. And I really wish I could figure out what they're trying to tell me."

John couldn't help himself. "These faceless drowning people talk to you? Like, words or just gurgling sounds?" His joke was met by a stern glare from Kevin. "I'm sorry, bro. I don't mean to make light of it. I know exactly how real dreams can feel, but at the end of the day, they're just dreams. Come on," John said, standing up. "Let's go hit the batting cages. That'll take your mind off things. And after that, come back home and take a long hot shower. I'll cover for you guys at the bar tonight. Why don't you take Julie out for a nice dinner and explain everything to her."

As Kevin followed John out the door, he smirked and said, "Since when did you become the wise older brother?"

"I've always been that... minus the wise part."

They both laughed as they climbed into John's truck. Kevin clicked his seatbelt then said, "And by the way, the faceless drowning people don't make gurgling sounds. They just keep repeating the same phrase over and over."

"Let me guess," John said, grinning. "If you build it, he will come."

"Ha ha, smartass. No, that's not what they say. They just keep repeating the phrase, *Help her to help us.*"

"Who's her?"

"No idea."

"Maybe it means if we help Julie with something, she'll get us season tickets to the Cubs?"

Kevin shook his head. "Don't quit your day job to be a therapist. You'd be the worst one ever."

"You are not wrong, my brother. You are not wrong."

It had been a while since they had done anything together, so they took full advantage of their time at the cages. There was no talk about Julie, or business, or anything serious. And there wasn't another word mentioned about Kevin's strange and unsettling dream. They spent the entire time at the batting cages trying to outhit one another. Even though they both had less than stellar performances, they still felt a little bit better than when they started.

2

Once again, John found himself driving around with no real destination in mind. And once again, his subconscious knew exactly where he needed to be. It wasn't long before he found himself driving by his old therapist's office. He couldn't remember the last time he was in that part of town. It had been five years since his last session.

For whatever reason, he found himself pulling up and parking in an empty space directly in front of her building. He had no intention of going in and continued telling himself it was a mere coincidence he was driving in that area to begin with. He also came up with reason after reason why he shouldn't go in and see her.

She's probably not even there, he thought. *And if she is, that must mean she's with another patient. And even if she was free, I don't even have an appointment. Although, she has seen me before without one. Of course, that's back when I was a fucking mess… rock bottom.*

He had reason after reason why he should just head home, yet as the entire conversation was going on in his head, his feet had different thoughts. The next thing he knew, he got out of his truck and entered the building.

"What the hell am I doing here?" he mumbled to himself.

He repeated this over and over until he came face to face with her office door—more importantly, with the FOR LEASE sign, which hung on the door. Out of all the reasons he came up with, not one of them involved her not being there anymore. In true John fashion, he made it all about himself.

Why didn't she tell me she was changing locations? Did she change her phone number, too? Was she purposely trying to avoid—

A loud crash interrupted John's self-absorbed thoughts. It was quickly followed by a shriek and a woman yelling out, "Oh no!"

John recognized the voice and immediately knocked and turned the knob. "Hello? Everything okay?" he called out, opening the door.

It wasn't until he fully stepped into her office that he was able to assess the situation. Hope stood in the back corner staring over at him with a frustrated and helpless look.

"John? John Mathews? What are you doing here?"

With a smirk, he said, "I heard there was a cleanup on aisle six that needed tending to." He then looked down at the smashed fish tank. Plastic castles and colorful pebbles were strewn across the soaked floor. "Any casualties?" he asked, bending down for a closer look.

"Thankfully, no. The last fish died a few months ago, and I haven't had a chance to get any new ones yet."

"Got a broom and a mop?" John asked, picking up some of the larger pieces of glass and throwing them into the garbage.

"You don't have to help, John. It's my mess. I'll clean it up."

"Eh, it's okay. I'm an expert at cleaning up messes… especially broken glass."

What John really should have said was he was an expert at *making* messes, and Kevin was the expert at cleaning them up. Although, to his credit, it had been a long time since he had made a mess that Kevin had to clean up. Hope pulled out a broom, dustpan, and a Swiffer mop from the closet and aided John in cleaning everything up.

"At least it wasn't your trusty ole lava lamp, Doc." He looked over to where the lamp usually sat. When it wasn't there, he gazed at Hope and hesitantly asked, "Uh oh… don't tell me you broke that, too?"

"No," she said with a wry smile. "I already packed it away."

Hope motioned to the floor behind John. He turned and saw not one but three boxes.

"Lemme guess, Doc, you're moving up to the big time? To a bigger, ritzier office up in the rich part of town, huh?"

"Yeah, right," she said, laughing. "I'm actually... calling it quits."

Hope's response caught him off guard. "What? As in retirement? You're not that old, are ya, Doc?"

Mentally and physically, Hope felt like she was well beyond retirement age, but the truth was she had just turned fifty a few months earlier.

"I'm sure I'll have to get some sort of a job to pay the bills, but as of now, I'm calling it quits from this profession."

John was still surprised, but the more he thought about it, the more he completely understood. This woman spent day after day and year after year listening to people bitch and moan about their problems. Or in John's case, she sat there listening to him *avoid* his problems.

"Good for you, Doc. Good for you. You deserve it. Especially for putting up with people like me all these years."

"Eh, you weren't so bad," she said, grinning.

"Ha. You're a horrible liar, Doc."

"Speaking of years, how long has it been? Three... four?"

"Five. Five years, Doc. Late April of 2006, to be exact."

"Wow. How did you remember that?"

"It was the day after the Brewers spanked the Cubs sixteen to two."

Hope laughed. "You remembered the exact date of your last therapy session based on a baseball game?"

"Well, yeah. I was very depressed the day after and figured I could use a little pick-me-up session with my favorite shrink."

"Ah, I see. Lucky for you, you don't base all your therapy sessions on losses by the Cubs."

"No shit, Doc. I'd be broke for sure."

Again, she laughed. "I can't believe it's been five years. If I remember correctly, the last time you were here you were going on and on about a certain new woman in your life."

John finished the last swipe of mopping and quietly said, "Jain."

She could tell by the way he said her name that the relationship had either ended or was on rocky ground. John paused and pointed out it was the former not the latter.

"We broke up years ago."

"I'm sorry, John. Would you like to talk about it?"

He laughed. "Thanks, but that's okay. I didn't come here to talk about my problems. I just happened to be in the neighborhood and thought I'd pop in to say hi."

It was Hope's turn to laugh. "You're a horrible liar as well."

As usual, John knew she saw right through his bullshit answers. And as usual, John stubbornly held his ground.

"Seriously, Doc. I was just passing by, that's all. Besides… you're officially retired, remember?"

"I'm retired as your therapist, but not as your friend. Come, sit," she said motioning towards the familiar futon.

John thought for a second then smirked and joked, "Well, if this is just a friendly chat then maybe *I* should get the comfy chair this time."

Hope looked over at her Papasan chair, grinned, and said, "Sure, sit wherever you'd like."

"I was only joking, Doc… but if you insist." He plopped himself into her chair. "Ohhh, now *this* is comfy!"

Hope continued grinning as she sat across from him on the futon. John watched as she squirmed back and forth trying to get comfortable.

"See, I wasn't exaggerating before," John said. "You should never have gotten rid of that old leather couch you used to have."

"I can't believe you remember that. That was forever ago."

It was forever ago, and although hazy, John remembered being a scrawny teenager and sitting on the large brown leather couch. He remembered not saying a word as this strange hippy-chick shrink tried to get him to open up to her about the O'Neils. But now, as he sat across from her, he couldn't help but smile, knowing Hope had only grown stranger and hippier over the years. Of course, he meant it in the best way possible. The truth was both brothers had grown quite fond of their wacky shrink; just as she had grown quite fond of them.

"So, what happened with you and Jain," Hope asked, still trying to get comfortable on the futon.

"Just sort of ran its course, I guess. It didn't end horribly. I mean, we don't hate each other or anything. Certain circumstances just got in the way, that's all."

"Ah, I see."

"That's it? Aren't you gonna ask me what the circumstances were? Or how I feel about that?"

Hope laughed. "This isn't a therapy session, John. We're just talking as friends. If you want to tell me, I'll listen, but I'm not going to pry."

John was used to being on the defensive and having her answer his questions with a question. He wasn't sure he was comfortable with this *talking-as-friends* thing. What he *was* comfortable with was her Papasan chair. It enveloped his body and was worn in all the right places. He thought about being a wiseass and taking off his shoes and going barefoot like she used to do, but seeing as he knew how much his feet reeked, he decided against it. After a quick moment of silence, he began talking to her about his relationship with Jain.

"I met Jain two years after the accident and one year after I was completely sober. Up until she walked into the bar that night, I'd been concentrating on getting my business off the ground and living one day at a time. And to be honest, up until that point, I didn't really think I would fall in love again or even be in a serious relationship ever again. And then Jain entered my life. It just happened naturally. We got along, we had similar interests, and I found myself feeling those sparks… sparks that I didn't think I'd ever feel again. And even though I took it slow, I was never able to fully commit. Emotionally *or* physically, to be honest with you."

Hope was still trying to get comfortable on the futon. "I can only imagine how hard it was to allow that intimacy to return."

"Don't get me wrong, we kissed and whatnot, but I never touched all the bases, if ya know what I mean, Doc."

She smiled and shook head back and forth.

"But seriously, even when we did kiss or get physical, it had to be at her place. I couldn't dream of doing something like that in the house I used to share with my wife."

"And how did Jain handle that?"

"She was patient and understanding... as much as anyone could be in that situation. But eventually, I think it started to become a problem. Well, maybe not a problem, but definitely something that needed to be talked about. And as you know, Doc, talking isn't one of my strong suits. Babbling. Now babbling I can do all day long."

"Oh, I know."

"Anyway, one night while we were out to eat, she gently brought up a few things that were on her mind. Basically, we had *the talk*. She wanted to know where I saw the relationship heading... if I could ever see us living together, yada yada. Don't get me wrong, she did it in a respectful way, but... but unfortunately, I didn't really have any answers for her."

"What happened?"

John smirked and said, "You know, I did what I do best... I danced around the subject and eventually changed the topic. I know what you're going to say, Doc, my communication skills suck ass."

Hope laughed. "I don't think I was going to be that colorful... or harsh. But from the outside looking in, I can sympathize with both of you. Intimacy, living together, and even thoughts of marriage are all difficult emotions to sort through. Especially after losing a spouse. But from her point of view, I can understand why she would want to know where things were heading."

"Oh, I absolutely understood her point of view," John said. "She had every right to ask those questions to me. Like I said, I just didn't have the answers. I guess I just assumed I could keep dancing around the subject and avoiding it until I did find the answers."

"And?"

"I was only able to avoid it for another two weeks. That's when she was offered a huge promotion and job down in Houston. Once again, we went out to dinner and had *the talk*. She gave me her best pitch and suggested that moving out of Chicago and getting a fresh start was just what we needed for our relationship to go to the next level. She was so excited talking about us going house shopping together in Houston."

"And you didn't share that same excitement?"

"I wanted to. I really did. But apparently, I didn't have a very good poker face on that night, and it wasn't long before she knew exactly where my heart was. To her credit, she was so sweet and understanding about everything. And at one point, she even suggested that maybe she should turn down the job and stay in Chicago. There was no way I was going to let her do that. And in her heart, she didn't really want to do that either. Besides, there was more to it than just moving from Houston to Chicago."

Sympathetically, Hope nodded. "When did this all happen?"

"About four years ago. It was towards the end of 2007. And believe it or not, I haven't even gone on a date since then. Pretty pathetic, huh?"

"No, not at all, John."

Hope didn't tell him this, but it had been an even longer stretch for her.

"It was four years ago, yet I've been thinking a lot about Jain lately… the whole situation, actually."

"Anything specific?"

John shrugged. "What if… what if I screwed up? What if she was the *one*… the one I was supposed to be with?"

Hope paused, carefully thinking about her response. Finally, she said, "This might come as a shock to you, but I don't have a lot of experience when it comes to serious relationships. That being said, this is how I look at it: I believe when you meet *the one*... the one you're meant to be with, you'll know."

"But what if I'm too stupid to know?"

Hope laughed. "It has nothing to do with how smart or stupid your brain is. It's all about your heart... you'll know when you know."

Skeptically, John leaned back and shook his head. "I don't know about that, Doc. The first time I laid eyes on Jain... I thought for sure we were meant to meet, ya know? I felt it in my head *and* in my heart. Like, destiny... or fate... or something. I guess I shoulda known better. It was all for nothing."

Hope laughed, shaking her head.

"What?"

"You still don't get it, do you? Just because someone doesn't *stay* in your life, it doesn't mean they were never meant to enter it."

He dismissed her comment with another shrug. "I don't know. I suppose that's one way of looking at it."

"It's the only way, John. It's the only way. Just remember, you'll know when you know."

Like many times in the past, John's head was spinning from all the back-and-forth banter with his therapist. He needed to take the focus off himself. "Anyway... enough about that. So, you're really calling it quits, huh?"

"From this profession anyway. Maybe I'll try my hand at something new, but I have a feeling I'm a little too old for that now."

"Pfft! You're never too old for new beginnings, Doc. Age is just a number."

As Hope allowed his words to soak in, she found herself cracking a smile.

"What's so funny?" he asked.

"All this time I thought I was pretty good at giving advice... as it turns out, it must be whoever sits in that chair."

John laughed and nestled himself deeper into the Papasan chair and said, "It really is comfortable."

"And this one really is *not!*" Hope said, standing up. "My apologies for making you sit on it during all those sessions."

"Eh, it really wasn't that bad." John pulled himself out of the chair. "We can switch, if ya want?"

"That's okay. I really should get back to packing up," she said, looking around the room. "I've been procrastinating for weeks now."

Good to know I'm not the only one procrastinating this month, John thought to himself.

"I can give you a hand, if ya want?"

"I appreciate that, John, but I'm sure you have better things to do than to help your wacky hippy-chick shrink pack up."

John froze. Her comment caught him off guard.

I never actually called her that name to her face, did I? No. I know I didn't. So how did she know? And just like that, the answer came to him. *Fucking Kevin.*

Before he had a chance to say a word, Hope giggled and said, "I've been called worse. Besides, it kind of has a groovy ring to it."

John shrugged and slightly blushed. He then spent the rest of the afternoon helping his former therapist pack up her belongings. The boxes fit nicely into the back of her Subaru Outback, and John used his truck for the chair, futon, and the rest of the random furniture. After everything was loaded into their vehicles, he looked around at the empty office. "I still can't believe you're done… like, done, done."

All of her items might have been packed up, but the room was far from empty. It was still full of all the conversations from the patients that had previously come through her doors. John knew if anyone deserved time away, it was her. She deserved it just for listening to *his* problems over the years, never mind everyone else's. Some of his most uncomfortable moments were spent in this room. Most of the time, he hated being here, but now… he hated the thought of it being empty. It saddened him to know that he'd never have another session with her ever again.

He followed her back to her house and insisted on unloading everything himself. He figured it was the least he could do. After she thanked him for the fifth time, she told him to be sure and say hi to Kevin for her. And just like that, the only therapist he'd ever known was now officially retired.

3

Even though he promised himself to get back into the swing of things, John found himself falling into the same old unmotivated routine. Over the next couple of days, he did absolutely nothing work related. He never called those potential customers back, nor did he even step foot into his shop. He stayed up late and slept in even later. The coffee shop around the corner was as far as he made it from his house. And even then, it was less about people-watching and more about just sitting there, mindlessly staring into space. If it weren't for an urgent voice message from Kevin, he might not have ever left his neighborhood. John would have been content with just calling him back, but at the end of the message, Kevin made it a point to emphatically tell him to come see him in person. It took him a few hours to get motivated, but eventually, John made his way down to the Wild Irish Rose.

"Well, look who finally made an appearance," Julie said, looking up from the bar.

"Yeah, I guess I've been keeping a low profile lately."

"No new projects?"

"I have a few things on the horizon, but..." John shrugged off the rest of his response. "Anyway, is Kev here?"

"If you wanna call it that," she said, rolling her eyes. "He's in the office. Is everything okay?"

"I don't know, you tell me. He left me a voicemail saying I needed to come down ASAP."

"See, I told you he's been acting weird lately. Did you ever talk to him for me?"

John could tell by her question that Kevin had yet to tell her about his dream or anything else, for that matter.

"Um, no, not yet."

Julie let out an exasperated sigh.

"I'll talk to him right now. I promise."

"Just a warning... he's in an extra grouchy mood today."

"Eh, I'm sure it's nothing. Probably that time of the month," John said with a chuckle.

Julie was not amused. She cocked her head and shot John a look.

"Bills! That time of the month to pay bills," he clarified with a smirk.

Julie didn't return his smirk. Instead, she mumbled *idiot* under her breath and walked away. She wasn't normally this sensitive about John's sarcasm or his inappropriate humor. Not at all.

Jeez, John thought to himself. *She really is stressed about Kevin's behavior. Either that, or maybe it's her time of the month as well.*

If that were the case, then John would rather take his chances dealing with Kevin. He headed towards the back of the bar, but before his hand grasped the doorknob, he heard what appeared to be a chair angrily getting kicked over. No matter who he dealt with, it seemed like a no-win situation. John was tempted to bolt, but his curiosity got the better of him. He couldn't remember the last time Kevin was angry enough to toss around furniture. It might have been when the Cubs were swept out of the playoffs by the Dodgers in '08. Of course, more times than not, it was John who was the cause of Kevin's anger.

When all was quiet in the office, he knocked twice and slowly opened the door. Sure enough, one of the chairs was knocked over, and Kevin was sitting in the other one with his head in his hands. John did what he does best in these types of situations. He used sarcastic humor. "You do realize the Cubs came back last night and won in extra innings, right? Besides, if we tossed around furniture every time they lost then we would…" John paused mid-sentence when he realized Kevin was also not in the mood for his humor. "Okay, okay, fine. What did I do this time?"

After letting out a frustrated sigh, Kevin finally looked up at John and said, "It's not you… or the Cubs. It's our asshole landlord."

"Sid? Since when is Sid an asshole? I like Sid."

"I like him, too, but if you recall, Sid sold the building last month."

John had always left the financial stuff up to Kevin and Julie. He pondered a second then said, "Oh, yeah. I think I remember you mentioning that. But didn't you say the new landlord was going to still honor our existing lease?"

"He is. But our lease is up soon—very soon."

John picked up the thrown chair and sat on it backwards.

"Um, okay. So we negotiate a new one with him. I really don't see what the big deal is. Personally, I think you need to switch to decaf. Either that or score yourself some Xanax."

Kevin stared blankly at his brother but didn't offer a retort. Instead, he handed him a piece of paper.

"What's this?"

"Our new proposed lease agreement. And those are the other twenty pages," he said, motioning to the pieces of paper strewn across the floor. "That page is all you really need to know."

John squinted and quickly began to scan the agreement. It wasn't long before his eyes widened.

"Holy shit! That's our new monthly price?"

Kevin shook his head. "Nope, that's *my* new monthly price. That's just for the Wild Irish Rose, not your space. Keep reading."

John's eyes returned to the paper. As Kevin watched him continue reading, he internally began to count backwards. *Three… Two… One…*

Right on cue, John shot up from the chair. He crumpled the paper, tossed it to the floor, and exclaimed, "That's highway robbery! There's no way we can afford that. How much does he think we make anyway?"

Kevin shrugged. "What are we gonna do?"

"I have no idea. What does Julie think about this?"

Again, Kevin lowered his head into his hands and slumped deeper into the chair.

"Dude, she's our business partner, and more importantly, she's your life partner. And I'm assuming you haven't told her about the dream either? What the hell is going on with you keeping all these secrets from her?"

"I know, I know! I'm obviously gonna tell her, but right now, the last thing I need is a goddamn lecture from you, okay? Okay?"

Kevin was always cool, calm, and collected, so the fact that he was this angry and frazzled caused John to lay off any sort of lecture. Once again, John straddled the chair and sat back down.

"It'll all work out. It always does. Maybe the three of us can go talk to the new landlord. I'm sure we can work out a deal that everyone is happy with."

Kevin stood up and began pacing around the small office. "Between you and me, John, I'm not sure I want to work out a deal."

"What do you mean?"

"I mean I'm not sure I want to own a bar anymore."

Assuming he was joking, John started to laugh.

"I'm serious. I know it's only been eight years, but... but I think I'm burnt out."

John would have been a hypocrite if he said anything other than *I totally get*. He tried his best to lift Kevin's spirits. He told him about his own funk lately, and even mentioned that he had an impromptu session with their shrink.

"You went and saw Hope? I haven't seen her in forever. Maybe I should go see her, too. Maybe she can make sense of—"

"Too late, bro. She's officially done."

"What?"

He explained to his brother about Hope's early retirement and how he'd spent the other day helping her pack up her office.

"Wow, I can't believe she's calling it quits. She's not even that old."

"She's been doing it for over twenty-five years. Hell, I'm surprised she lasted that long without getting burnt out." John laughed and said, "Besides, you're much younger than her, and you've only owned this place eight years, yet you're ready to call it quits, right?"

Kevin started to reply but realized his brother had a point. John turned his attention to the papers scattered across the floor. He then looked up at Kevin and noticed how worn down and exhausted he was.

"I'm sure you don't need me to tell you that you look like shit… so I won't," John said with a sarcastic grin.

Kevin didn't respond. In fact, he didn't even give his brother the familiar disapproving glare. That's when John knew how serious it was.

"Look, I really wouldn't stress out about this landlord thing. It'll all work out. But my advice to you is the same as it was the other day: Talk to your wife! And for God's sake, get some sleep!"

John picked up the papers and stacked them onto Kevin's desk. He gave his brother a pat on the back and left.

4

Less than a week into her retirement, Hope was going stir crazy. She'd always been a workaholic, and even when she wasn't working, she was volunteering or out scouring used bookstores. She never owned a TV, so when she was home, she loved to be curled up on her tiny couch or in bed reading. She assumed once she retired that she'd have even more time for those things, but that was not the case. She attempted to catch up on her reading, but in the week following her retirement, she barely read five pages. She didn't even leave her house the entire week—not once. Even worse, she was still wearing the same clothes as day one.

It wasn't a case of missing her job. She really didn't miss it one bit. And it wasn't even a case of being bored. It was more like being stressed out. At first, she found herself racking her brain trying to think what she was going to do next with her life. But her thoughts soon began to go from her future to her past. Now that she'd recently turned fifty, she couldn't help but analyze her life's accomplishments—or lack thereof. Helping people with their problems and issues had always been her forte, but figuring out her own was a different story.

In one short week, she went from being bored to being stressed and depressed. It wasn't just her mind either; her body felt weak, and it ached in places it never ached before. It got to the point where she knew she needed to do something about her overall well-being. She decided to start with her physical health, so she made an appointment with her doctor.

Most people would be ecstatic getting a clean bill of health, but Hope was adamant that something was wrong with her. So much so, she convinced her doctor to send her to get extensive blood work done. The next day she went to the lab in the hospital, and it was there she received a huge surprise. Ironically, her surprise had nothing to do with the blood work. It happened less than twenty seconds after entering through the hospital doors.

"Hope? Hope Simmons?"

Hope stopped mid step. She hadn't heard that voice in nearly thirty years. Slowly, she turned to her right, and standing with a big smile on her face was her old college roommate, Robin. They, along with Darcy and Dee, lived together during Hope's junior year. Robin was a year older, and after she moved out and graduated, they never saw each other again. It wasn't for lack of effort on Robin's part. When she left, she gave Hope her contact information and told her to reach out anytime. Hope's self-esteem was at its low point back then, so she just assumed Robin was being polite. In her heart, she knew Robin was one of the most genuine people she'd ever met, but still, Hope never reached out. They only knew each other for that one school year, but Robin was the closest thing to a best friend Hope ever had in college—maybe even since.

"Robin?" Hope said, still shocked and wide-eyed.

Robin continued grinning as she rushed over and gave Hope a big hug. "Holy shit. How long has it been?"

"A long time," Hope said, starting to blush for no real reason. "Do you still live around here?"

"Me? No. I've been living down in Springfield for the last twenty years or so. I'm just here to see my grandmother."

"Is she okay?"

"Yeah, she's fine. She's ninety-five and still going strong... for the most part anyway. She's just having a minor procedure done today, and

I told her I'd come sit with her for a few days. She really doesn't have any family around here anymore."

Hope thought about her own grandparents. They also would have been in their mid-nineties.

Robin looked over at the clock. "Speaking of which, I'm running late. I wanna see her before she goes in for surgery."

"Oh, of course. I'm sorry."

"No reason for you to be sorry. You didn't make me late. I'm here for a few days… let's catch up."

"Um, yeah… sure."

Robin pulled out her phone and punched in Hope's number.

"Perfect. I'll give you a call later." Before she rushed off, Robin looked back at Hope and said, "It really was great running into you again."

"You too," Hope said, and watched Robin head for the elevators.

***

True to her word, Robin called Hope later that afternoon and set up a dinner date for that night. Hope was never the most social person in the world, but over the past ten years, her social life had become nonexistent. That being said, she was excited to catch up with Robin. They met at a casual neighborhood restaurant right around the corner from Hope's house. Ironically, it was the first time she'd ever been there. Robin wasted no time ordering a glass of wine. She laughed as she watched Hope pass on alcohol and order an ice water with lemon.

As soon as the waitress walked away, Robin said, "Still straight as an arrow, huh?"

Hope blushed and shrugged.

"I'm just kidding, Hope. I always envied you for marching to your own beat and never caring what others thought."

"You envied *me*? I cared what others thought… just not enough to stop being me."

"Exactly! And that's why I envied you, and that's why we were friends."

Hope continued to blush and said, "To be fair, you didn't really care what others thought either."

"Eh, that's not true. I tried my best to be my own person, but there were plenty of times I went along with the crowd."

Hope smiled. "Not as much as Darcy and Dee did."

Robin nearly spit out her drink, and they both burst out laughing.

"I don't think anyone went along with the crowd as much as those two," Robin said.

Hope giggled. "I wonder whatever happened to them."

Robin took a sip of wine then matter-of-factly stated, "Dee is on her third husband and has five kids… plus two or three step-kids."

Hope's eyes widened. "Holy Brady Bunch. Really?"

"Yup. And I think her oldest is in their mid-twenties and her youngest just started kindergarten."

"Wow," was all Hope could muster.

"And wait until you hear about Darcy. She lives in New York City and has been married to the same guy for over twenty years. No kids, but get this, she does hair and makeup for Victoria's Secret. You know, for runway models and stuff."

Again, all Hope could say was, "Wow." After letting it all sink in, Hope asked, "How do you know all of this? Do you girls still stay in touch?"

Robin laughed. "Noooo. I'm what you call a Facebook creeper. Although, technically, we're not even friends on there. But their profiles are public, so I'm able to creep away without them knowing. I thought about friending them, but…"

"But what?"

"Thirty years might have gone by, but at the end of the day, they're still Darcy and Dee. Ninety percent of Dee's posts are overly dramatic drivel. Let's just say when her and her husband… or her and her kids have an argument, they do it on Facebook for all the world to see. And don't get me started about Darcy's posts. They're full of lingerie-clad supermodels, or worse… lingerie-clad pictures of Darcy trying to look like a supermodel."

Hope gritted her teeth, cringing.

"Exactly! The pure definition of cringeworthy."

Both women looked at each other and cracked up laughing. Their laughter was so loud it caused the people around them to stare over. Hope and Robin didn't even notice. With her straw, Hope pushed the lemon wedge down to the bottom of the glass. She watched it float back to the surface. She then looked over to Robin and said, "Hard to believe it's been thirty years."

"I know. It's crazy how time flies." Robin watched Hope continue to poke at her lemon wedge. "I tried looking you up, too… on Facebook. Heck, I even tried searching for you on Myspace years ago."

Hope shrugged, blushing slightly. "I never really got into the whole social media thing. Like, not at all."

Laughing, Robin said, "Yeah, that's what I assumed."

"I know, I know, I'm super boring."

"Nah. You probably have the right idea. Social media is a huge time-suck, and most of the time it's pointless… yet I seem to continue to waste one or two hours a day on the stupid thing."

The two old friends continued bantering about their college days and some of the more comical memories of Darcy and Dee. It wasn't until their dinners were served that they finally got into what each of them had been up to over the years. Robin went first. She spent her twenties working for a travel agency, mostly international travel.

"I know what you're thinking, Hope. What's a Psych major doing working in the travel industry?"

Before Robin could explain her choice, Hope stepped in. "I wasn't thinking that at all. Actually, I was thinking how cool that sounds. I bet you get some groovy discounts on travel."

"Totally!" Robin said, face beaming.

Hope listened as Robin recited place after place she had been to. Besides visiting her uncle in Germany, the only real vacation Hope had ever taken was when she rented a cottage up on Lake Michigan… by herself.

"I did the travel agency thing until I was nearly thirty. That's when I met my husband. Well, I should say, my ex-husband."

Hope sympathetically looked over at her friend and said, "I'm sorry it didn't work out."

"Don't be. We made it nearly fifteen years. That's better than most people nowadays. Not to mention, we were lucky that it didn't end horribly. We're still civil to each other."

"That's good."

"Yeah, it is. I have no regrets. Besides, he blessed me with two amazing kids."

"You have two kids?"

Hope listened intently as Robin talked about her family. Hope was envious, but ultimately, she was happy for her old friend. At one point, Robin pulled out her phone and showed Hope countless pictures of her two kids.

"Ugh," Robin said, closing her phone. "You know you're getting old and pathetic when you finally get a few days away from your kids, and you spend it showing off pictures of them."

"Not pathetic at all. I bet you're a great mother," Hope quietly said.

"Thanks. But to be honest, most of the time I don't really feel like I am. Do you know my son had the nerve to call me uncool? Me… uncool."

Hope smiled.

"And just the other day, my daughter said I was too old to understand her boy troubles. Does she not get that boys haven't changed one iota in thirty years?"

Again, Hope laughed and said, "I wouldn't be too hard on yourself. I'm sure you didn't go to your mom for advice on boys when you were her age."

"No, no I didn't. But... but I'm way cooler than my parents were. Despite what my kids say."

Hope nodded in agreement. "I still think you're pretty cool."

"Why, thank you, Hope. As are you! And you're still easy as ever to talk to. But enough about me, I want to hear what you've been up to the last thirty years."

Hope's smile faded and knots formed in her stomach. There was no way her boring life could compete with Robin's. Hell, her life couldn't even compete with Darcy and Dee's. Hope didn't reveal how she had always wanted a husband and children of her own. She briefly went into detail about her longest relationship. He was also a therapist... and a workaholic. These two things in common carried them for most of their relationship. The real turning point came when he told her he was seriously thinking about moving down to Tulsa to be closer to his family.

Just like when they were roommates, Robin listened attentively and reacted in such a sweet and positive way that even Hope thought her life was better than it actually was. Robin focused on Hope's career.

"I knew it, I knew it, I knew it! I knew you'd become a successful therapist. I'd like to think I had a hand in that. I mean, I did give you plenty of practice back in the day. I bet I came to you daily... and you always gave me great advice."

Blushing, Hope said, "I don't know about daily. And I'm sure it wasn't always great advice either. I didn't really have any real-life experience back then. To be honest, I'm not even sure I have much real-life experience now."

"Yup, you haven't changed a bit. Still as modest as ever and still blind to your gift."

"My gift?" Hope said, rolling her eyes.

"You've always had the ability to put people at ease… the ability to get people to open up to you. More importantly, you get them to open up to themselves… to see the truth inside themselves. So yes, that's a gift, my friend. A rare and beautiful gift."

Hope's face continued to turn bright red, and she did her best to fight back tears. What Robin just said was one of the sweetest things Hope had ever been told. Never once had she thought of herself in those terms. She was simply a therapist. She listened to people's problems and did her best to navigate them through whatever they were dealing with. She never thought of herself as anything special, and she certainly never thought of herself as having a gift.

As a matter of fact, the older she got, the more she thought the exact opposite. It wasn't a gift she had; it was more like a curse. It started with her parents and somehow filtered down to her. But unlike her parents, she wasn't cursed with mental issues. Her curse was forever being alone… forever being single…. and never finding her soulmate. And more importantly, never finding her true purpose. It certainly wasn't from a lack of trying. Over the years, she read various self-help books and had immersed herself in more philosophies, cultures, and religions than she could keep track of. Despite her exhaustive searches, the answers eluded her.

"I'm so glad we ran into each other," Robin said, snapping Hope out of her thoughts.

"Me too. This was really…"

"Groovy?" Robin said with a wink and a smirk. "I'm just kidding, Hope. But *groovy* used to totally be your go-to adjective."

"I didn't say it *that* much, did I?"

"Well… Darcy and Dee did turn it into a drinking game. Every time you said the word groovy, they'd take a shot."

Hope's eyes widened and she covered her mouth and said, "Is that why they were always drunk? Oh my gosh. I never knew."

It wasn't until Robin burst out laughing that Hope realized she was still as gullible as they come. Throughout the rest of their dinner, they continued to catch up on the past thirty years. Hope talked about the passing of her grandparents, and although tempted, she never mentioned her father's death. Nor did she talk about her wild and crazy Applewood trip back in college. Besides, the details of that trip were hazy at best. Over the years, Hope had suppressed her memories of that week in Maine with her father. There were even times when she thought the whole thing was just a dream—a weird and strange dream.

After the bill was paid, they headed out to the sidewalk in front of the restaurant. "Here," Robin said, handing Hope a business card. "A bit pretentious, I know, but it has all my contact information on it."

Hope glanced down at the card and saw the words Real Estate Agent after Robin's name. "You're a realtor?"

"Yeah. Like I said earlier, I took time off from the travel gig to raise my kids, and by the time I was ready to go back to work, I wasn't really feeling it anymore and decided to try something new. I got my real estate license a couple years ago. I'm licensed all throughout Illinois, so if you or anyone you know needs a reliable agent, I'm your girl!"

"I think it's great you're out there trying new things," Hope said, continuing to stare at the card. "Maybe I should consider doing something like that."

Robin laughed. "I'm only jumping rock to rock because I still have no clue what I really want to do with my life. But you, my friend... *you* are a therapist through and through. There are hundreds of people out there who are better off now because of you."

Hope's face turned redder than it had the entire night. The two old friends embraced in a long hug and went their separate ways. Hope remained in a good mood even after she got home. She was so glad to have reconnected with Robin. This time, she promised herself to stay in touch. It was only a three-hour drive down to Springfield, and now that she was technically retired, she had plenty of time to take as many road trips as she wanted. She was already looking forward to hanging out with Robin again and was excited to meet her kids. She still couldn't believe all the kind words Robin had to say about her. They were only roommates and friends for a year in college, so it blew Hope's mind that she had so many long-lasting memories of her.

For the first time in a long time, Hope fell asleep with a smile on her face. Unfortunately, that's not how she would wake up. Just as she fell into a deep sleep, her mind took her back to a place she hadn't seen in thirty years. Although, the dream didn't start off familiar at all. She found herself barefoot, walking across soft wet grass. The fog surrounding her was so thick that she could barely see her own hand in front of her face. The only things that gave away her location were the smell of salt air and the faint sound of a foghorn in the distance. She knew she was in Applewood. Although short, she spent the entire dream aimlessly walking around what she assumed was the park overlooking the lighthouse. After the third and final blare from the foghorn, everything went quiet. And then it happened. She heard a voice. Her father's voice.

"It's time to come back, Hope. It's time."

She spun around to see where he was, but he was nowhere to be seen.

"Dad? Where are you?" she called out. The next thing she knew, she was sitting up in bed; her breathing was heavy, and her body was soaked in sweat.

Over each of the next three nights, she had that same dream. Although the locations in Applewood were different each night, her father's message was the same. The fourth time she had the dream, it took place at the Great Blue Heron Inn. She was curled up reading a book in her favorite room of the inn. Floor-to-ceiling bookshelves surrounded her as she read. Just as she turned the page, her father's voice called out from behind the chair.

"It's time to come back, Hope. It's time."

When she finally opened her eyes, her breathing was no longer heavy nor was she sweating. She didn't necessarily consider it a nightmare. They weren't scary or unsettling. They were just dreams.

But they did get her thinking quite a bit about the next phase of her life. Subconsciously, her father's voice and message continued to echo through her head. From an early age, Hope believed that everything happens for a reason. And whether it was a person or a moment, no matter how brief or insignificant it seemed, there was most definitely a reason for it. Unfortunately, over the years, life had worn her down, and she had now become jaded to her original philosophies. Part of her still believed there was a reason why people entered each other's lives, but she was having a hard time believing that she was included in this.

Hope spent her entire career—actually, her entire life trying to let people know just how special they were. Ironically, she never believed the same about herself. She never once considered herself special, and she certainly never thought she had a gift. Over the next month, however, all of that would change. Little did she know at the time, but she was about to make a decision which would allow her to discover her true gift and purpose. Not only that, but her decision would allow her to find out the truth about her parents—and about the island of Applewood.

As much as Hope enjoyed her dinner with Robin, it would prove to be the high point of her social life. It didn't take long for her to slip back into her old ways. She went to bed early and slept in late, and she very rarely left the house. The only form of a social life she had was communicating back and forth with doctors. Even though her bloodwork came back normal, she was adamant there was something wrong with her.

She saw doctor after doctor, but they all said the same thing: "There is absolutely nothing physically wrong with you."

As demented as it sounds, she would have been happy being told that she had some type of cancer or even some sort of rare disease. At least then she'd have a definitive answer. Most of the doctors told her it was all in her head or that it was probably stress related. And they politely hinted that she should think about seeking a therapist. One idiot doctor even chalked it up to menopause. Hope was becoming more and more frustrated with each and every silly diagnosis.

After a while, she didn't have the energy or motivation to follow up with any of the doctors. She didn't really have the energy for anything other than sleeping. The only semi-active thing she did was donate most of her belongings that John had hauled out from her office. Though, even that wasn't really being active. Goodwill did all the work. She placed a call, and they sent a truck out and picked most everything up: a couple small bookshelves, end tables, the futon, and yes, even her comfy Papasan chair.

The only thing she kept from her office was one of the large cardboard boxes. It contained her crystals, dreamcatchers, lava lamp, and finally, her teddy bear. The box remained tucked away in the corner of her bedroom. Normally, Hope would have taken care of it right away, but between her failing health and her lack of motivation, the box just sat there untouched.

It wouldn't be until late one night that she found the urge to go through it—3am, to be exact. She had just awoken from that same mysterious dream. This time, she was sitting on the riverbank of the Willows. The current was barely moving, and she focused in on a lone leaf being slowly carried down the river. Just then, her father's voice spoke to her. It was louder and more adamant than before.

"It's time to come back, Hope. It's time."

She opened her eyes and reached over, turning on the lamp beside her bed. *Why do I keep having this dream*, she thought. *What does it mean?* She placed her hands over her face, shook her head, and muttered, "Maybe the doctors are right… maybe it is all in my head… maybe I do need some mental help."

As she continued to think and mumble to herself, her eyes focused on the cardboard box in the corner of her room. Biting down on her lip, she crawled out of bed and knelt in front of the box. She only made it as far as the top item—her teddy bear. Out of all the items in the box, the bear was the oldest and most sentimental to her. Around the bear's neck, hung the seashell necklace her father had left for her years ago.

Before she knew it, she was sitting crisscross on the floor with the bear sitting on her lap. She was tempted to place it on the nightstand or maybe on her bed. Instead, she decided to place it with the rest of her parents' memories—in her mother's antique chest. In the beginning, Hope clung to and embraced the memories of her parents. But as time moved on, she began to consciously push them from her mind. As a matter of fact, years ago when she bought her house, rather than place the chest at the foot of her bed, she instructed the movers to put it downstairs in the basement. The irony of her doing the exact same thing as her grandfather was not lost on her. Over the years, Hope's philosophy had turned to: *out of sight, out of mind* and *keep the past in the past*. Of course, this was the exact opposite of what she preached to her patients. Again, the irony was not lost on her.

After thinking long and hard on it, Hope stood up and made her way down to the darkened basement. It was much smaller than her grandparents' basement, and although it lacked tools and a workbench, it still had the same old musty smell as she remembered as a child. And even though she was a full-grown adult now, the cobwebs and creaky stairs still creeped her out.

Besides the oil tank and furnace, the only other thing in the basement was the chest. It sat alone in the far corner, and there was nearly an inch of dust that had accumulated over the top of it. Hope began feeling guilty for ignoring it all these years. It had been so long since she had actually opened the chest or had even thought about her past. She almost felt as if it was all just a dream: her mother's diaries, her father's tattered notebooks… her trip to Applewood. Hope had indeed become the master of suppressing her past.

With her teddy bear in one hand, she used the other to slowly turn the key and open the chest. It wasn't slow enough, for clouds of dust filled the air, tickling Hope's nose. So much so, it caused her to sneeze nearly ten times in a row. When her sneezing subsided, she peered inside the chest. The first thing that caught her eye was her father's leather jacket and satchel. Just one touch and smell of them brought her back thirty years to that strange and hazy week in Applewood. The more she rummaged through the contents of the chest, the more she felt guilty for neglecting each of these sentimental items of her parents.

The next thing she knew, tears were running down her cheeks and falling onto the cold concrete floor. She began to reach for her father's old notebooks but stopped short. She wasn't ready to revisit the past yet, so instead, she nestled the teddy bear into her father's leather jacket, closed the lid, and then headed back upstairs—*Out of sight, out of mind. Keep the past in the past.*

Throughout the next few days, even though the chest remained in the basement, thoughts of its contents and thoughts of Applewood lingered in Hope's mind. Leading the way were thoughts of Applewood. She found herself waking up in the middle of the night thinking about the island... the lighthouse... the Willows... and of course, her father.

She thought about Janice and the Great Blue Heron Inn. Still to this day, Janice was one of the sweetest and most understanding people Hope had ever met. Maybe it was her kind eyes or her non-judgmental demeanor, but either way, she felt like Janice completely understood her. Ultimately, it was the frequency and powerfulness of these thoughts and dreams which led Hope to make a life-changing decision.

5

On the third ring, Robin answered the phone. "Hey, Hope! I must admit, I wasn't sure if I'd ever hear from you again. I left you a couple of messages but..."

"I know. I'm sorry for taking so long to return them. I guess I've just been going through some things."

"It's okay. No need to apologize. Is there anything I can do to help?"

Hope paused. "Actually... I think there might be."

As soon as the call ended, Robin went into action. Before Hope had a chance to reconsider her big decision, Robin had sold Hope's house—above market value. This, combined with her large savings account, would allow her to put her new retirement plan into motion. Hope remembered when her grandmother sold her house. She couldn't believe how little she took with her. Ninety percent of her belongings were either left there, given away, or taken to the dump. Hope didn't understand it at the time, but now, forced with the same situation, she completely got it. Luckily for Hope, she had remained a minimalist throughout the years, so she hadn't really accumulated anywhere close to what her grandmother had. As a matter of fact, everything she ended up keeping fit perfectly into her Subaru Outback. She had one of her neighbors help her load the heaviest item last—her mother's chest.

If it weren't for Robin throwing her a two-person going away party, Hope would have left Chicago with little to no fanfare. Besides a few professional acquaintances, Hope didn't really have anyone she needed (or wanted) to say goodbye to. That, in and of itself, was a little depressing. There were, however, two people she knew she needed to pay a visit to. So, on the eve of her departure, with her car packed full, she made her way to a place she had yet to ever step foot in.

***

Hope wasn't the only one with Applewood on their mind. Even though he promised himself multiple times, John had yet to return any phone calls to his potential new customers. When he wasn't spacing out in the coffee shop, he was spacing out on his couch watching mindless TV. Today's guilty pleasure was the *Antique Roadshow*. The episode focused on classic baseball cards. John couldn't believe how much some of these were worth.

It piqued his curiosity so much that he decided to go dig up all his old cards. They'd been safely packed away ever since they moved into the house years ago. He headed straight for his bedroom closet, but his eyes never made it to large plastic bin in the back corner. Instead, he found himself focused on a shoebox. It was the same one that he had placed all the photos he took in Applewood years earlier. It also included some of the photos of his parents that Mary had given him, plus the newspaper article about the plane crash.

Before he knew it, he was going through each photo and reminiscing about his dream-like couple of weeks on the island. What was underneath the shoebox grabbed his attention. It was the *Medillia's Lament* manuscript William had written. Fondly, John flipped through the pages. He only knew William for a short period of time, but like Applewood, it also seemed like a dream. He never made it to his bin of baseball cards. He carefully placed the manuscript and shoebox back where they were and closed the door. John was so caught up in reminiscing that he decided to drive down to the Wild Irish Rose and have a Coke with extra ice in honor of his old friend. It had been days since he'd made an appearance down at the bar. Seeing as he hadn't heard anything from his brother or Julie, he assumed everything was back to normal with them. He assumed wrong.

John sat on the far-left stool at the bar, and as Julie placed his Coke in front of him, he looked around and asked, "Are you working by yourself tonight?"

"Don't get me started," she huffed.

"Uh oh, what's going on?"

He asked out of politeness, not really wanting to hear her response. Julie spent the next five minutes venting about Kevin's moody and irritable behavior. It was obvious that Kevin hadn't communicated a thing to her.

"You did talk to him, right?" she asked. Before he could respond, she quietly said, "Do you think he's sick?"

"What?"

"He doesn't sleep… he hasn't been eating right… and I think he's lost weight. Don't you think he's lost weight?"

Not wanting to get involved in their marital problems, John was intentionally vague. "Relax, Jules. He's not sick… he's not having an affair… I think he's just going through some stuff."

"What kind of stuff? Like a mid-life crisis?"

He laughed. "Jules, he's too young for one of those."

"Then what is it?"

"I'll talk to him again. I promise." John tried to soothe her worry, but in his head, he was questioning why the hell he left the house in the first place.

"Pfft, like that'll do any good," she said, walking away.

John took a sip from his Coke then shook his head and mumbled, "Fuck me. And this is why you shouldn't leave the house, John."

His plan was to finish his Coke then get the hell out of there and head back home to his couch. But as usual, life had other plans for him. Moments later, Hope entered through the large oak door of the

Wild Irish Rose. She paused and slowly took a good look around. Bars were never her scene, but she knew how much blood, sweat, and tears the brothers had put into the place. John's beautiful craftsmanship combined with the cozy ambience that Kevin had created caused a proud and beaming smile to appear on her face. As she made her way up to the bar, she didn't notice John sitting off to the left.

Julie could tell by the way Hope was looking around that this was probably her first time there. In true Julie fashion, she politely greeted Hope. "Hi. Welcome to the Wild Irish Rose. What can I get ya tonight?"

Hope's eyes danced across the rows of colored bottles lining the shelves behind Julie. She had no intention of ordering any of them, but the way the bar lights were illuminating the bottles made it hard to look away.

"Um, could I just have a ginger ale, please," Hope finally said.

It wasn't until she spoke that John looked over to his right. He would have recognized that voice anywhere. At that very same moment, a waft of patchouli hit his nose. It was a smell he'd recognize anywhere as well.

"Doc?"

Hope turned to her left and saw John staring at her with a bemused smile.

"I'd say your job finally drove you to drink, but I don't think a ginger ale counts as drinking."

Hope grinned and said, "Trust me, if I were a drinker, my job would have driven me to it a long time ago."

Without missing a beat, John replied, "If dealing with me never drove you to drink then nothing will."

Hope let out a chuckle as she accepted her ginger ale from Julie.

"Thank you, dear."

"Make sure this woman doesn't pay for a thing tonight," John said in Julie's direction.

"That's very kind of you, John, but you don't have to do that."

"Trust me, Doc, I owe you more than just a few ginger ales. If it weren't for your help, this Coke would be mixed with a whole lotta Jack right now."

"I appreciate the compliment, but I think you're giving me too much credit. You did all the work. I was just the voice trying to guide you."

"An annoying voice at times," John said with a smirk. "And I still hate the way you always answered my questions with a question, but… but make no doubt about it, Doc, you were there for me when I was at my lowest."

Listening to their exchange, Julie had her assumptions of who this woman was, but just to be sure, she gave John a look.

"Oh, I'm sorry," John said, looking at both women. "Julie, this is my long-time shrink. Doc, this is Julie. AKA, my sister-in-law. AKA, Kevin's better half."

Warm smiles filled both faces as they reached out and shook hands.

"Very nice to finally meet you, ma'am."

"Please… I feel old enough as it is. You don't need to call me ma'am… or Doc," she said, grinning in John's direction, which caused him to grin back. "Call me Hope," she said, returning her eyes to Julie. "And congratulations, by the way. Kevin was always one of my favorite patients."

"Hey! What about me?"

Julie rolled her eyes as Hope smiled and clarified her comment. "*Both* brothers were amongst my favorites."

Due to John's highly competitive nature, he was hoping to be ranked slightly higher than Kevin, but he decided not to make a fuss over it. Besides, he was still shocked to see Hope at the Wild Irish Rose.

"Speaking of Kevin, is he here?" she asked, looking around.

Julie's cheerful expression faded. "No idea," she said, shrugging. She forced a smile at Hope then politely excused herself to take care of some of the other customers.

"Is everything okay with Kevin?" Hope asked John.

"Yeah, he'll be fine. Just going through some stuff, that's all."

Hearing this, Hope couldn't help but feel concerned for Kevin. Even worse, for the first time since she retired, she felt guilty for not being there for a patient—especially Kevin. Her curiosity got the better of her, and she asked, "What's going on with him?"

John could see the concern on Hope's face and quickly pointed out, "Don't worry, Doc, I've got everything under control with Kev. You don't have to worry about us anymore. Besides, you're officially retired now, right?"

"I am," she said, taking a seat next to John. "That's actually why I stopped in. I wanted to say goodbye to you two in person."

"Goodbye? What does that mean?"

Hope went on to tell John that she had sold her house and was leaving town in the morning. She explained she had always wanted to travel and that it was time for a change of scenery. If anyone deserved to take time for themselves, it was her. But there was a part of him that was saddened by the news. Even though it had been years since his last session with her, it was comforting to know she was only twenty minutes away if he needed her.

"Wow. Well… good for you, Doc. Good for you. Do you have a specific destination in mind?"

Hope knew exactly where she was headed to but didn't want to get into the backstory behind it. She shrugged and said, "Just travel around, I guess."

John smiled to himself. He couldn't help picturing her roaming around the country in an old beat-up hippy van. Before John had a chance to ask her another question about her road trip, Kevin entered the bar.

"Aw, look who's here," Hope said, gazing up at the front door.

John turned around and saw Kevin making his way towards the bar. As if sensing their eyes on him, Kevin stopped and looked over at

John and Hope—more so at Hope. Taken aback, a look of surprise came over his face.

"I know, right?" John called out, grinning.

Kevin stole a quick glance over at Julie then headed over to John and Hope. For a split second, Kevin thought this might be a setup. John must have convinced her to come and check on him; a therapy house call, if you will. Just as Kevin began to curse his brother out under his breath, John spoke up and filled him in on what was going on.

"You're really leaving town… tomorrow?" Kevin asked.

He was happy that Hope was finally taking some time for herself, but like John, he was saddened that she would no longer be within reach, if needed. Throughout the next hour, they each talked about what had been going on in their lives since the last time they had seen each other. Hope didn't say a word about her failing health. Kevin never brought up his reoccurring dream. And both brothers avoided talking about their growing lack of motivation towards their businesses. In other words, the hour was spent on small talk. Towards the end of their conversation, when John went to the bathroom, Hope jotted down a few names on a napkin and handed it to Kevin.

"What's this?"

"Just some recommendations… in case you ever need someone to talk to."

At that point, Kevin knew his brother must have said something to her about him. But as he gazed into her kind eyes, he could see the concern in them, which made it impossible to be mad at John or anyone else, for that matter. He gave her a look of appreciation and slipped the napkin into his pocket. Hope used that moment to say her final goodbyes to both brothers. She'd known John and Kevin for nearly twenty-five years, yet this would be the first time they would ever hug each other. After she gave them each a long, heartfelt embrace, she headed out for good. None of them said it out loud, but they each knew this was probably the one and only time Hope would set foot in the Wild Irish Rose.

After she left, the brothers sat in silence.

"I can't believe she came here," Kevin finally spoke.

"I can't believe she's actually retired and leaving Chicago."

Slowly, Kevin nodded in agreement. John didn't really want to get into it, but he figured while he was there, he should check on his brother. "How are things going?" he asked.

Kevin shrugged. "As good as it can for someone who's in the middle of a midlife crisis."

"Oh, God," John said, rolling his eyes. "Dude, neither of us are old enough to be in a midlife crisis. We're just in a little rut, that's all. I take it you still haven't talked to Julie about any of this?"

"What am I supposed to say? Hey, honey, I know this bar was my big idea, and I know how much you love being an owner of it, but I don't think I want to do this anymore. Oh, and by the way, I have no idea what I want to do instead of this place. Is that what I'm supposed to say to her?"

John had no response.

"Not to mention, we've been trying to get out of our apartment and buy a house... and eventually start a family. But there's no way that's going to happen without the bar."

"You don't know that. Either way, I think you should talk to her."

"It doesn't matter anymore... I think I've already made up my mind."

"What's that mean?"

"I've decided to go ahead and sign the new lease next month."

"Are you kidding? That rent hike is ridiculous."

"I know, but I'd rather pay extra rent than to have no business at all."

For the first time all night, John looked at his brother—like, really looked at him. Julie was right, he did look like he'd lost some weight. And the dark circle around his eyes told John that he wasn't sleeping at all.

"You're not still having that reoccurring dream, are you?"

Kevin paused and answered, "Um, no. It wasn't really that big of a deal. I feel stupid for even mentioning it to you."

Normally, John would have sensed Kevin was lying, but seeing as he had his own things going on in his head, John took him at face value. Kevin hated that he was keeping things from Julie, and it even bothered him that he was keeping things from his brother as well. It bothered him, but not enough to do something about it. The bar was getting busy, so Kevin headed over to help Julie. John used that moment for his official escape. He was glad he was there to see Hope, but other than that, he told himself it was probably best to lay low from the bar for a while. He had his own things going on, and he didn't need or want to be in the middle of Kevin and Julie's issues.

6

Bright and early the next morning, Hope climbed into her Subaru Outback and headed east on I-90. She wasn't even outside the city limits and already had tears in her eyes and was second-guessing herself. This was much harder than she thought it would be. Ironically, she never fully experienced all that Chicago had to offer, but still, it was the only hometown she'd ever known. What made it even more sad was she knew in her heart that once she left Chicago, she would probably never again return.

By the time she reached Cleveland, her mood had begun to shift. Her tears had long since dried up, and she was enjoying her little road trip. As she drove down the highway with the Grateful Dead blaring out, she found it quite freeing. She'd spent her whole life planning everything out, and she lost track of how many broken New Year's resolutions included her telling herself to be *more spontaneous*.

As hard as she tried, she could barely remember the last time she did this drive. It was thirty years ago but seemed even longer. She did remember how anxious and stressed she was. Not to mention, that was her first-ever road trip, and it was all she could do to follow the atlas and not get lost. This time felt different. She was much more relaxed and even took the time to appreciate the sights along the way. While in Cleveland, she spent several amazing hours wandering around the Rock & Roll Hall of Fame. From there, she made her way up to Niagara Falls. She was so mesmerized and enthralled that she got herself a hotel for the night overlooking the falls. She was quickly getting used to not having a specific itinerary.

Over the next couple of days, Hope used her cell phone more than she had the entire year. She found herself constantly googling interesting sightseeing ideas. From scenic overlooks to roadside oddities, she thoroughly enjoyed her slow trek east. By the time she hit New Hampshire, she was completely relaxed and enjoying her trip— but then it happened. As her car passed over the Piscataqua Bridge, her eyes focused on the large blue sign:

WELCOME TO MAINE – THE WAY LIFE SHOULD BE

And just like that, her heart raced, and the anxiousness returned. That would be nothing compared to the feeling she got after she crossed the causeway and saw the smaller sign, which read:

WELCOME TO APPLEWOOD – MAINE'S MAGICAL ISLAND

One of its wooden posts had rotted away, causing the old sign to lean to the left. Eerily, as she entered the island, she was greeted by a thick fog and light rain. Hope's heart raced even more when she drove through the marina and spotted the Rusty Anchor Tavern. It pretty much looked the same as she remembered it. She'd only been there once, but it was where her father first told her about how he met her mother. It didn't really matter if the story had since been disproven; that week with her father still held a special place with Hope—even if she hadn't thought about it in years.

Less than a mile later, she found herself turning into the Great Blue Heron Inn. It was more to gather her thoughts than anything. She stopped at the very bottom of the driveway but didn't bother going all the way up. The large wooden sign out front was in even worse condition than the Applewood sign. The paint was so faded and peeled you couldn't even tell what it said. Hope didn't feel the need to go any farther up the driveway. The place didn't look to be in business anymore, and even if it was, she was almost positive that Janice was long gone by now, retired or otherwise.

The next familiar sights she came across were the general store and diner. This forced more memories to start coming through. Although tempted to stop, Hope drove past the store and decided to explore the rest of the island and see what other memories came back. Unfortunately, the four-way stop sign was as far as she would get that day. She stared at the small sign with the picture of a lighthouse on it. It was pointing to the right and said: HARBOR COVE PARK.

She put her blinker on then froze. Her hands went numb and began to tremble. She remembered the first time coming to that stop sign with her father. He adamantly refused to let her turn right towards the park. He told her the park was a very special place for him and her mother and that he wasn't ready to revisit it yet. Hope didn't quite understand it at the time, but she did now. Throughout that week, especially their final night, the park had also become special to Hope. It was where she had felt closest to her father, and strangely, to her mother as well.

Slowly, Hope turned off her blinker. She, too, wasn't ready to revisit the park—not yet anyway. The more she thought about it, she wasn't ready for any of this yet. With her head in her hands, she leaned against the steering wheel and thought, *What am I doing here?*

She continued to sit there, thinking and talking to herself. "Okay, Dad, you got me here… now what?" She looked around as if she expected to hear his voice guiding her. The only thing she heard was a loud beep from the impatient car behind her. Startled, she quickly drove straight ahead through the stop sign. She pulled into the next driveway she came across, gathered herself, then turned around and headed back the way she came.

She wasn't hungry enough to stop at the diner, but she desperately needed a bottle of water and maybe a small snack. Just as she parked at the general store, the rain picked up. "Just my luck," she muttered.

Hoping it would lighten up, she decided to wait it out in her car. But after fifteen solid minutes of heavy downpouring, she knew the chances of that were slim. She parked as close as she could to the front door, but still, she was soaking wet by the time she entered the store.

"Another miserable day out there," a voice from her left called out.

Hope turned and saw an older woman with dark black hair and big brown eyes. She looked to be in her upper sixties. Hope offered a polite smile but didn't say anything in return. She ran her fingers through her rain-soaked hair then focused on her familiar surroundings. Hope always believed the fastest way someone could transport themselves back in time was through smells or songs. She was about to experience both.

The place had a distinct smell. The dusty old wooden floorboards combined with the sweet smell of home-baked goods took her right back to the first time she ever stepped foot in that store. It seemed like nothing there had changed one bit: the same products, the same set up—it was like a time capsule.

Hope was a creature of habit, and she went straight for a bag of trail mix and a large bottle of water. She wandered the narrow aisles and eventually came face to face with another familiar sight—the alcohol section. Her eyes went directly to the bottles of vodka. She couldn't help but think of her father. As much as she knew vodka was the main cause of his early death, she'd give anything to be purchasing one of these for him right now.

She let out a sigh and sadly lowered her eyes. "Seriously, why am I here?" she whispered to herself. "This was a big mis—"

She stopped mid-sentence and tilted her ear towards the front of the store. The woman at the counter had a small radio playing behind her. The volume wasn't up very high, but it was loud enough for Hope to make out the song. It was "Can't Help Falling in Love" by Elvis. And just like that, her mind transported her back thirty years; when her father told her that was the first song he had ever danced to with her mother. Hope also remembered how she played that song for her father in the center of Gerrish Falls when he took her busking. As a lone tear formed in her eye, she took the song as a sign; a sign telling her that indeed she was supposed to be here right now. After blinking away the tear, she made her way up to the counter to pay.

"Find everything you were looking for?" the woman asked.

For a brief second, her question caught Hope off guard.

"Um... yes... thank you."

She placed the water and trail mix on the counter, paid, and then started to leave. Before she got too far, the woman called out, "New in town?"

"Um... just sort of passing through. Not sure how long I'll be here."

"Ah, I see. Well, welcome to Applewood. Sorry about the weather, but you might as well get used to it. It's been like this for a while now."

"Thanks," was all Hope said. She started to walk towards the door but stopped short. She turned around and asked, "Are there any hotels or motels... or inns that might have some availability?"

The woman started to laugh but quickly apologized. "I'm sorry... it's just been a long time since I've been asked that question. The island's tourism has dropped considerably over the years. And by considerably, I mean, it's non-existent. Of course, this weather doesn't help either. Your best bet is to go back to Gerrish Falls. There are plenty of options there."

"Thanks," Hope said, and once again started to leave. She reached for the door handle but stopped. Hesitantly, she turned and asked, "Is the Great Blue Heron Inn still in business?"

"I'm afraid not. It's been closed for years now." She then smiled and added, "But the owner still lives there."

"Janice?" Hope asked.

"Why, yes. Do you know her?"

Hope briefly explained how she stayed there for a week back when she was in college.

The woman continued to smile and said, "She's an original, that's for sure. My daughter is actually there right now delivering some groceries to her. Janice doesn't drive anymore and has a hard time getting around, but other than that, she still has all her faculties. And she's still as sharp as a whip."

The thought of Janice still being alive and well gave Hope a comforting feeling.

"You should stop in and see her," the woman suggested. "I'm sure she'd love the company."

Hope shrugged. "Yeah… maybe. Thanks again," Hope said, then finally exited the store.

She remained in the car as she polished off the entire bag of trail mix and drank every drop of water. The past few days of travel were starting to take a toll on her. Her eyes felt heavy, and she knew she needed to find a place to stay for the night. Now that she was in Maine, she had no idea what to do next. Seeing how exhausted she was, she felt it best to sleep on it and tackle her future in the morning.

Although her destination was Gerrish Falls, her mind and hands had a different idea. As she approached the Great Blue Heron Inn, her hands began turning the steering wheel left into the inn. She drove up the long driveway and parked out in front. There was only one other car there, and by the looks of it, she assumed it was Janice's. The back two tires were completely flat, and it looked like it hadn't been driven in years.

The rain had subsided, so Hope was spared from getting even more wet going from her car to the porch. Just like the sign out by the road, the old inn had seen better days. The paint was badly peeled, and there were multiple spots on the trim which were completely rotted through. Even the yard looked different than before. What were once beautiful gardens and flower beds, were now overgrown with weeds and tall grass.

The next thing she knew, she was knocking on the front door. It wasn't until about twenty seconds went by that she began questioning what she was doing there. Over the years, Janice must have had thousands of guests stay at the inn. There was no way she was going to remember a young, awkward, hippy girl from thirty years ago. Knowing this was probably a stupid idea, Hope quietly shut the screen door and turned to leave. But before she made it off the porch, the front door creaked open, and an elderly, yet familiar voice called out, "Hello? Can I help you?"

Hope stopped short of the steps, bit down on her lip, and slowly turned back around. As Hope hesitated with what to say, Janice opened the screen door and squinted for a closer look. It only took a second for her eyes to widen and for the biggest of smiles to appear on her face.

"Well, I'll be," Janice exclaimed, placing her hand over her mouth. "You're back."

"You... you remember me?"

"I may be old and grey and wrinkly, but I haven't gone senile... not yet anyway." Janice stepped fully out onto the porch and wrapped her frail arms around Hope. She whispered in her ear, "Of course I remember you, Hope. I knew you'd come back one day. I thought it would have been a lot sooner than now, but I'll take it!"

After a long embrace, Janice stepped back and looked her up and down. "Wow. You've grown into a beautiful woman. And you barely look like you've aged since the last time I saw you."

This caused Hope to laugh. "I appreciate that. But I just recently turned the big five-o, and trust me, I look and feel every bit of it."

It was Janice's turn to laugh. "Fifty? Why, you're still just a baby. Heck, I was older than that the last time you saw me, and that must have been, what... at least thirty years ago?"

Hope was surprised at Janice's accuracy. "Actually, it's been exactly thirty years," Hope said.

"See, I told you I'm not losing my mind. Well, don't just stand there, come on in. Let's get you warm and dry."

She led Hope into the living room, where there was a small fire burning in the fireplace.

"How sad is that... having the fireplace going in the middle of summer. This weather seems to be getting worse and worse."

"Yeah, it's definitely a big change from Chicago. It was in the low nineties when I left."

"I don't think we've seen it above sixty all summer."

While Hope warmed by the fire, Janice went to the kitchen and made a pot of tea. The next thing they knew, they were talking and laughing like no time had passed at all. Hope did her best to make sure the conversations revolved mostly around Janice and not her. She knew the typical questions were going to come up, but she tried putting them off as long as possible. She began by asking Janice how long ago she closed the inn.

"Hmm... must have been about ten years ago. I figured my early eighties were a good time to call it quits."

Hope was in awe of Janice's longevity—her lifespan as well as her career. It also made Hope feel pathetic for retiring at only fifty.

"Do you miss it?" Hope asked.

Janice pondered and thoughtfully answered, "I don't really miss the day-to-day chores: cleaning, laundry, making beds, doing dishes. But I do miss the guests and the socializing. It's amazing how lonely this house can be without it."

When they hit their first lull in conversation, Janice offered to make Hope some dinner.

"No thank you. I'm not really that hungry... more tired than anything."

"Where are you staying?"

Hope shrugged. "I was going to check out some places over in Gerrish Falls."

"Gerrish Falls? Nonsense! You will stay here."

"Oh, that's okay… you don't have to—"

"It was a statement, Hope, *not* a question," Janice said, winking. Hope started to tell Janice that she had no idea how long she was going to be in town for, but it was as if Janice read her mind. "And stay as long as you'd like."

Hope knew it was no use arguing, and if truth be told, she was secretly hoping that Janice would offer her to stay there. Janice gave her a handful of clean linens and told her she could choose any room she wanted. For sentimental reasons, she thought about choosing her old room, but instead, she was somehow drawn to her father's old room across the hall.

When the bed was made, Hope decided to lay down for a second before heading outside to get her suitcase. A second was all it took. She was out cold. After a while, Janice came upstairs to check on her and saw that she was sound asleep, so she covered her up and shut off the light. As she closed the door, she whispered to herself, "Welcome back, dear. Welcome back."

***

The next morning, Hope awoke to the smell of bacon and eggs. It reminded her of when she used to live with her grandparents back in the day. Her grandmother wasn't the most warm and fuzzy or social person in the world, but she took great pride in cooking for her husband and Hope.

"Perfect timing," Janice said as Hope entered the kitchen. "Grab a plate and help yourself."

"Thank you," Hope softly said.

"I'd say we should go eat in the sunroom, but it hasn't really lived up to its name in a while. Let's do the living room."

Janice popped open a couple of TV trays, and they cozied up to eat their breakfast. Hope was quick to apologize for passing out so early the previous night.

"No need to apologize, dear. You obviously needed the sleep."

Hope nodded. "I think the last three or four days are the most I've driven in my whole life."

"Really? I would have bet anything that you would have grown up to be a world traveler."

"I always wanted to," Hope said, shrugging. "I guess I always put my job first. Married to my career, so to speak."

Hope would quickly regret her choice of words.

"Speaking of marriage…" Janice hinted with a devilish grin.

Hope bit down on her lip and moved her gaze to the floor.

"I know, I know, I'm being a nosy old biddy, aren't I? I'm sorry."

Hope hated talking about herself, especially regarding marriage or relationships. But there was just something about Janice that had always put Hope at ease. She kept her response brief. "It's okay. No… I've never been married."

Smoothly, Janice moved on to the next topic. "So, what is this career that you've worked so hard at?"

"I'm a therapist. I've owned my own practice for about twenty years now."

"A therapist?" Janice said, beaming. "Just like you always wanted."

"Yeah, I guess so."

"That must be an extremely stressful job… listening to everyone else's issues and problems."

"Yeah, it can be."

Now would have been the perfect time to mention her early retirement, but even though she felt comfortable with Janice, she wasn't ready to get into the details of her retirement or of her spontaneous trip to Maine. And she certainly wasn't ready to tell Janice the trip was suggested to her in a dream—by her father. She did tell Janice about her father's passing soon after he left Applewood. But for the time being, Hope didn't mention anything about how he had made up the whole story about meeting her mother on the island.

Janice asked how her grandparents were doing, and Hope sadly informed her that they had both passed away. After breakfast, Hope insisted on doing the dishes, and Janice didn't put up too much of a fuss. Truth be told, she was never a fan of dishes.

"It's pretty grey and dreary," Janice said, looking out the window, "but at least it isn't raining. Not yet anyway. I'm sure you want to head out and explore the island, huh?"

Hope still wasn't ready to revisit her past or certain places on the island, but she politely nodded along with Janice's suggestion.

"But I have to warn you, this place has changed quite a bit since you were here last."

"How so?" Hope asked.

"You'll see for yourself."

Soon after she finished the dishes, Hope took a shower and headed out for the day. She wanted to drive around the island. She wanted to revisit all the places her father had introduced her to, but she just couldn't. The general store was as far as she made it. She parked in the back corner of the lot and remained in her car for the next few hours. Part of the time was spent writing in her journal. She hadn't done it in years but had recently started up again.

When Hope wasn't writing, she was thinking. She was trying to make sense of what she was going to do with her life moving forward. She was also thinking about what she had done with her life so far. She remained in her car for the better part of four hours. This exact scenario would happen for the next few days. She'd wake up, have breakfast with Janice, then tell her she was going to drive around exploring. But she never did. She parked in the same spot at the store and just sat there writing and thinking, and at times, crying.

Her father's voice hadn't come to her since Chicago. She was beginning to wonder if it had ever occurred at all. Maybe she was going crazy. Maybe she was turning out just like her parents. In the overall scheme of things, Janice was right, fifty really wasn't that old. But Hope *did* feel old. Her body ached. Her bones ached. Even her heart felt like it was aching. She was sluggish, highly unmotivated, and even though she was sleeping fairly well at night, she was exhausted. If this was one of her patients, she would have surely diagnosed them with depression. Hope knew all too well that even the best therapists have a hard time facing these same truths about themselves. It's much easier to point out other people's problems rather than your own.

Each afternoon, when Hope returned to the inn, she did something that she never did—she lied to Janice. She led Janice to believe that she'd been driving around for hours exploring the island and taking pictures.

"How's our old lighthouse holding up?" Janice asked. "It must be taking a pounding with all these storms we've had this year."

"I haven't been able to go up there yet. I guess the road has been closed for a while now."

On this occasion, Hope actually spoke the truth. The road really was closed about a half mile in. The only reason she knew this was she overheard someone mention it when she was in the general store the first time. Pretty much everything else she told Janice was a lie. And the more she did it, the more horrible she felt. She hated lying, especially to Janice, but it was much better than the sad and pathetic truth.

Unfortunately for Hope, her lies were about to catch up with her. Late afternoon of her fifth day there, she found herself browsing Janice's bookshelves for something to read. She was hoping that maybe a good book would help snap her out of this depression she was falling into. And yes, by now she knew she was smack dab in the middle of some sort of life depression. She wasn't really browsing books either. All she seemed to be doing was slowly walking around and running her fingers on the spines of the books. Her eyes weren't even focused on the titles.

Halfway around the room, she stopped and turned her head towards the doorway. She thought she heard something. A moment later, she heard it again. Someone was knocking on the front door.

Hope had no idea where Janice was, so she made her way down the hall. About ten feet short of the entryway, she stopped. She saw the doorknob twisting, followed by the door swinging open. A woman in a blue raincoat entered carrying two bags of groceries. With her hood pulled over her head, she peered out from behind the bags. She looked surprised to see someone other than Janice there.

"Oh… hi," the woman said, pushing the door shut with her foot.

"Hi?" Hope said, more curious than anything.

"I'm just delivering Janice's groceries."

Just then, Janice's voice came from the opposite hallway. "Good afternoon, dear." Upon closer inspection, she noticed how soaked the woman was. "Oh, my! You could have waited until the rain slowed."

The woman laughed and said, "That could be another few months."

"Sad but true," Janice said, nodding along. "This weather is just awful."

The woman placed the wet bags on the table next to the door then slowly pulled her hood off. As the woman and Hope looked at one another, Janice realized they had never met.

"Oh, how rude of me," Janice exclaimed. "Charlotte, this is Hope. Hope, Charlotte."

As both girls shook hands, Janice explained that Hope had stayed at the inn thirty years ago with her father.

"And this is the first time I've seen her since then," Janice said with a smile.

Although neither of them said a word, both girls felt a strange sense of familiarity with one another.

"Charlotte and her mother own the general store in town."

That's why she must look familiar, Hope thought to herself. Charlotte was a spitting image of the woman who rang Hope in at the store when she first arrived earlier in the week. She also remembered the woman telling her that her daughter was delivering groceries to Janice as they spoke.

Charlotte laughed at Janice's comment. "Technically, my mother owns it… I'm just helping her out until I get back on my feet. I'm still recovering from my divorce a few years ago. And by recovering, I mean financially, not emotionally. I am much better off without him."

"Amen to that!" Janice said. "Know your worth! That's what I always say."

Hope smiled. She used that exact phrase with her patients more times than she could remember.

"Charlotte is an extremely talented writer," Janice pointed out.

"Ha," Charlotte laughed. "Tell that to the dozens of publishing companies that have turned me down."

"Pardon my language, but… screw them!" Janice emphatically said. "Mark my words, those same companies will one day be kicking themselves!" Just then, the phone began ringing from the other room. "Who the heck is calling me? Would you ladies excuse me?"

After Janice left the room to answer the phone, Charlotte once again gave Hope a curious look-over. She couldn't put her finger on it, but there was just something about her that looked familiar.

"I think it's great that you and your mom run the store together. I love it there. It's so nostalgic. It's like walking into a time capsule from my youth. My grandparents used to take me into a store like that when I was little."

"My mom worked there when she was younger and when the owners retired, they offered it to her. It was originally supposed to be a family business with my older brothers, but one by one, they've all moved onto bigger and better things… things that don't involve living in Applewood. It wasn't my original career choice, that's for sure, but it helps pay the bills."

"Being a writer was your original career choice?" Hope asked.

"Yup. I'm what you call an aspiring novelist… which is just another way of saying a failed novelist."

Hope was quick to step in with some positive reinforcement. "I don't believe that. I don't believe that one bit. I bet you're an amazing writer."

"Thanks... but I wasn't exaggerating when I said I've been rejected by a dozen or so publishing companies."

"It's a tough business, but I hope you haven't given up. I'm sure you have a best-seller inside you somewhere. And when the time is right, the world will see it, too."

Hope always had a way of putting people at ease and building up their self-esteem, even if her own was highly lacking. Charlotte had all but given up on her writing dream, and although she still felt defeated, Hope's comment seemed to perk her up and give her a renewed sense of optimism. Before Charlotte could thank Hope for her kindness, Janice reentered the room.

"Sorry about that. It was my doctor giving me my test results."

Concerned, Charlotte and Hope looked over at her.

"Oh, nothing to worry about. Just my annual physical, and as suspected, everything checked out A-OK. I'm probably going to live forever," she said and winked.

"That's good... especially seeing as you're our best customer."

Janice laughed. "Oldest customer maybe. I'm sure some of your regular fishermen outspend me any day."

"Yeah, but all they ever buy is tobacco and alcohol. That doesn't count."

Charlotte's comment once again reminded Hope of her father. It used to make her cringe, but now she'd give anything to see him with his bottle in one hand and a Marlboro in the other.

"Well, I should get back to the store," Charlotte said. "Let us know when you need another delivery."

"Will do. Thanks again, dear. Be sure and say hello to your mother for me."

"I will," Charlotte said, and then turned to Hope. "It was nice meeting you."

"You too."

Charlotte pulled her hood back over her head and opened the front door. Before she opened the screen door, she looked at the driveway and then back to Hope and asked, "Is that your Subaru?"

Curiously, Hope nodded.

Charlotte laughed. "So you're the one who's been parking at the store all week for hours on end."

Hope knew she was busted. Without making eye contact with Janice, she hesitantly replied, "Um… yes, that was me. I… I…"

"Oh, it's not a big deal," Charlotte said with a grin. "It's just out-of-state plates tend to stick out here on the island… especially Illinois. Don't worry, we won't have you towed. Park there anytime."

Even after Charlotte left, Hope couldn't bring herself to look over at Janice.

"I'll go put these away for you," Hope said, grabbing the two grocery bags and rushing off towards the kitchen.

She crossed her fingers that Janice wouldn't follow her in. She didn't. When Hope was finished, she went straight up to her room. She felt like she was a teenager again, trying to avoid a fight with her grandparents. Except this was different. Hope wasn't trying to avoid a fight; she was trying to avoid pure embarrassment.

She knew she couldn't stay in her room all night, and when Janice called her down for dinner, she knew she needed to come clean. By the time she made her way downstairs, Janice had already set up the TV trays and had a piping hot bowl of soup and a glass of water awaiting Hope.

"Nothing fancy, but I thought soup might hit the spot on a night like this."

"Thank you. Soup sounds perfect."

Janice offered plenty of small talk throughout dinner but never once even hinted at Hope's deceit. At one point, Hope started to wonder if Janice even heard what Charlotte had said earlier. Even after the last drop of soup was finished, Janice was still sweetly carrying on a conversation about the dog she had when she was a little girl. It was a golden retriever. Well, at least that's what Hope thought it was. She was only half paying attention. All the sadness, loneliness, and confusion that she'd been feeling lately began to build up. And no matter how hard she tried to hold it in, it all came flooding out right in the middle of Janice's dog story.

At first, it was just one or two tears escaping her eyes. The real waterworks didn't begin until Janice paused her story and asked, "Hope, are you okay?"

That was all it took for Hope to burst out crying—uncontrollably. What made it worse was she had to watch a ninety-two-year-old woman struggle to get off the couch and come over to console her. On her way over, Janice grabbed a box of tissues off one of the end tables.

"Oh, honey… what's wrong?"

It would still be another few minutes before Hope could compose herself enough to speak a complete sentence, and even then, she was a rambling mess. She did her best to explain everything that had been going on inside her head. She profusely apologized for lying about what she had been doing all week when she went out.

"I… just couldn't bring myself to drive around and revisit all the places he'd taken me to. It's stupid, I know. Especially considering everything he told me was a big lie."

"What was a big lie?" Janice asked, handing her another tissue.

Hope knew she needed to tell Janice the truth. She told her that her father had made everything up about how and where he met her mother. She told Janice about her conversation with her uncle Jeremy, and how he told her that her parents had never even been to Maine.

"For a while after he died, I held onto the memories of being here with him. At the time, it didn't matter to me that he made it all up… and that he lied about the truth behind their love story. I chose to believe the version he told me. It was easier that way, I guess."

Janice sat quietly, letting Hope do most of the talking. It was obvious that it had been building up for years, and she needed to get it all out. She also told Janice about her mother's antique chest and reading through her mother's old diaries.

"Soon after my grandmother gave me the chest, I used it to store all my parents' memories. For the longest time, I was obsessed with every item in the chest: his notebooks, her diaries... heck, even his smoke-filled leather jacket. But then..."

"Then what?" Janice asked.

"I guess I grew up. I stopped holding onto the past and started living in the real world... instead of make-believe. Anyway, I haven't gone through that chest in almost twenty years. At the beginning of the week, you asked me if this place had brought back a lot of memories... but the honest answer is... no. I don't really have any memories of our week here all those years ago. Not vivid ones anyway. It's all hazy. And I know this is going to sound horrible, but I sometimes wish that week never happened. I mean, what was the point anyway?"

In her heart of hearts, she didn't actually feel that way about her father, but over the years, she had become so worn down and jaded that it was easier for her to push those memories deep inside and label them as regrets.

"It's kind of funny, but after I learned the truth that my parents never met in Applewood, I still felt a connection to this place. Pathetic, huh?"

"Perhaps you still do," Janice said. "Why else would you return?"

"Trust me, I've been asking myself that question ever since I got here. Do you realize the only reason I'm here is because my father's voice told me to in a silly dream. Seriously, Janice, what am I doing here? What am I doing with my life? What have I even *done* with my life? Never married... no kids... I'm gonna be an old maid, aren't I?"

At this point, Hope began crying once again. Janice couldn't help but laugh. "Oh, honey. Look at me, I don't have any kids. Do you consider me an old maid? Actually, don't answer that," Janice said, grinning.

Through her tears, Hope said, "At least you've *been* married."

She tried her best to stop crying, but this only caused her to cry even more, which then caused snot bubbles to come out of her nose.

"See, I'm a mess," Hope said, reaching for another tissue.

"No, you're not a mess, dear. You're just going through what everyone goes through."

"And what's that?"

"Questioning life. Its meaning... its purpose... *your* meaning... *your* purpose."

"Do *you?*" Hope asked.

"Do I question those things? Of course I do."

"Have you ever come up with the answers?"

Sweetly, Janice smiled and pushed the hair out of Hope's face.

"Do me a favor... go grab me one of those puzzles over there." Janice pointed to the shelves in the back of the room.

"Um... okay," Hope replied, and then hesitantly walked across the room. "Which one?"

"It doesn't matter. The more pieces the better."

Moments later, Hope returned to the couch with a 1000-piece puzzle. Janice took the box and motioned to the large coffee table in the middle of the room. "Here, pull that closer." When the table was within a foot of Janice, she dumped the pieces onto the table. "Think of life as a puzzle, but instead of a thousand pieces, it's millions of pieces. What would you do first?"

Unsure where this was going, Hope reached over and grabbed the cover. "I guess I would study the picture and slowly start to try and match pieces."

Janice smiled. "Exactly. And that's the same with life... except with life, there's no front cover to go by. Life itself will dictate the picture. I guess what this crazy old lady is trying to say is most of the time we don't see the whole picture until it's finished."

With her tears now fully wiped away, Hope smiled and said, "That's a pretty groovy analogy, but... but it feels like I've spent a lifetime putting pieces together... yet I'm still no closer to seeing what the picture is."

"You will. It'll all come together and make sense to you one day. I promise you."

As Hope stared down at the puzzle pieces, she was still lost and confused but was glad that she had told Janice everything. Janice started to get up and clear their bowls, but Hope wouldn't allow it.

"No, sit. I got it," Hope stood and grabbed the two empty bowls. "Would you like some tea?"

"You read my mind, dear. I would love some."

By the time Hope returned, Janice decided to lighten the mood. "I have something that'll make you laugh." The child-like giddiness on Janice's face caused Hope to smile in anticipation. "I know you claim not to remember much from back then, but do you remember that other couple that was staying here that week with you and your father?"

Hope pondered then smiled widely. "Oh my gosh! The two mushy-gushy lovebirds from down south! What were their names again?"

"Andy and Cindi Henderson."

"Yes!" Hope exclaimed. "Remember all the ridiculous pet names they used to call one another?"

"Remember? How could I ever forget? They're emblazoned in my brain."

They both laughed. "Did you ever see them again?"

"Are you kidding? They celebrated every fifth anniversary right here at the inn. Right up until I closed the place down."

"What? I can't believe they stayed married for that long."

"Yup. And they're still as lovey-dovey as ever... but now with three kids to boot."

"Wow. Good for them."

Janice nodded and said, "As annoying as they were at times, it's nice to see that true love isn't dead."

For the rest of the night, a smile remained on Hope's face. Unfortunately, it didn't carry over to the next day. Now that Hope didn't have to lie about not being ready to drive around the island, she spent her days slumbering around the inn. She found herself leaving the house less and less and started questioning her life more and more.

7

Meanwhile, back in Chicago, Kevin's week wasn't going any better. He still wasn't sleeping, he was stressed out, and he was physically and emotionally exhausted. Unfairly, the brunt of this was directed at Julie, but it was felt by others as well. John was still in his own funk, so he rarely made it into the Wild Irish Rose, but when he did, he usually left just as fast as he came due to the bickering between Julie and Kevin. He left even quicker if Kevin's irritability was directed at him. After leaving, John always managed to feel a twinge of guilt. Kevin had done so much for him over the years, John felt like he should do more to help dig his brother out of this little rut he was stuck in.

John did his best to deal with Kevin's mood swings while at the same time trying to soothe Julie's worry and frustration. The one saving grace was even though Kevin was being a miserable prick to everyone, at least he was doing it sober. He was hard to deal with, but it was a far cry from the dark downward spiral John experienced years earlier.

The only thing worse than constant arguing in a marriage is when the arguing stops because both people have given up and become indifferent. For Kevin, this went deeper than just being stressed out about a new lease. It even went deeper than not being sure if the bar was what he still wanted to do. The majority of his stress stemmed from his lack of sleep. And his lack of sleep stemmed directly from his reoccurring dream. After telling John about the dream weeks earlier,

Kevin began to downplay it by telling him he hadn't had the dream since they talked. Not only was this a lie, but Kevin still hadn't told John about the unnerving new twist that had developed in the dream. On more than one occasion, Kevin wanted to tell him about it, but the right moment never arrived. Usually, it was because Kevin said something rude or mean to John. The latest little brotherly tiff resulted in John storming out of the Wild Irish Rose.

"Well, that was a mistake," John said, shielding his eyes from the late afternoon sun.

He hadn't been by the bar or his own business for a few days, so he decided to check in and see how the *happy couple* were doing. Yup, that was the exact phrase John used. He sat up at the bar and called out, "So, how's the happy couple doing?"

Julie gave him a glare—the likes of which he hadn't seen in years from her. Kevin was a little more verbal with his disgust.

"Fuck you!" This was accented by the raising of his middle finger. "If you're gonna to be a dick, you can leave."

John thought about apologizing but then thought better of it. Kevin wasn't the only one going through stuff, and he certainly wasn't the only one stuck in a rut. John had been lethargic and unmotivated for over a month now, and he, too, was questioning whether he wanted to continue his business or not. Secretly, both brothers were lamenting the fact that their hippy-chick shrink was no longer there for them. They could have easily sought out another therapist, but they knew it wouldn't be the same.

After storming out of the bar, John decided to throw on his sunglasses and take a little walk around the streets of Chicago. As he wandered away from the Wild Irish Rose, he passed by a small park. He paused and focused on one of the benches. It was the same bench that he had sat and talked multiple times with William. Their friendship only lasted a couple weeks or so, but John missed him dearly. Especially times like these. William always listened intently, and always gave thoughtful and wise advice.

Ever since he came across that box the other day, he'd been thinking non-stop about William and Applewood. John continued walking and thinking about his old friend and his magical trip to Maine. The next thing he knew, his feet had taken him directly in front of William's brownstone. He wondered if Rachel still lived there. Actually, he wondered if Rachel was even real. Maybe she, along with everything that happened in Applewood, was all just a figment of his imagination. He began to pace back and forth in front of her steps debating whether to go knock or not. After about the sixth time, John finally decided to walk away.

"Are you coming in or what?" a woman's voice called out.

John looked up and saw Rachel smiling at him through an open window.

"I've been watching you walk back and forth for twenty minutes now. I'm not sure if it'll change your mind or not, but I just made a fresh pitcher of iced tea, if you'd like a glass?"

John smiled through his embarrassment. "Thank you, ma'am. I'd love a glass."

"Well, come on in."

By the time John climbed the stairs, the front door was open, and Rachel pleasantly welcomed him in.

"And I might be a wrinkly old lady, but it's Rachel, not ma'am."

John didn't say a word, but he whole-heartedly disagreed. She looked far from old or wrinkly. Her light brown hair had completely transformed to grey, but other than that, she barely aged since he'd seen her seven years earlier.

"I was just thinking about you the other day," she said.

"You were?"

"Yup. I walked by the Wild Irish Rose and thought of you… and William, of course. He loved going there and hanging out with you all."

"You should have stopped in. My brother would love to meet you."

What John really meant was: *I'd love for you to meet my brother, so I can prove to him that you're actually real.* But the more he thought about it, the more he figured it was probably best if Rachel never showed her face at the bar. If Julie ever found out that William was married, there'd be an awful lot of questions; questions which would force John to tell Julie every crazy and unbelievable thing that occurred in Applewood. Even though John was standing face to face with Rachel, he still found it nearly impossible to believe all that had gone down.

She handed him a tall glass of iced tea then led him into the living room and said, "Have a seat."

The first thing he focused on was the fireplace mantle. It still contained the framed poem William had given to Rachel back at the dance. John smiled to himself. He took comfort in seeing the poem. It was a confirmation that maybe he wasn't crazy. The second thing he noticed was a bunch of packing boxes stacked against the far wall.

"Sorry for the clutter, but I'm in the process of moving."

"Moving? To where?" he asked.

"Savannah, Georgia."

Rachel explained to John that she was moving in with an old friend, who had recently lost her husband.

"I think I'm getting too old and too tired of the frigid Chicago winters. To be honest, I wanted to move a long time ago, but I knew William loved this city. And then he got sick… and then when he passed away, I couldn't bring myself to leave this place. It's hard to explain, but I felt like if I sold the house, I'd be dishonoring him somehow. I'm not sure if dishonoring is the right word, but…"

Softly, John said, "I understand… more than you know."

He didn't go into details about his statement, nor did Rachel ask about it. They had a mutual understanding and that's all that needed to be said.

"So, have you been back to Applewood since I last saw you?"

"No," John said, slowly shaking his head.

"You still have the key, right?"

"Yeah, but…"

"I was serious, John. You and your brother can use it anytime you'd like."

"Thank you, I appreciate that." Not wanting to get too personal, John hesitated but then asked his question anyway. "How about you? Do you ever plan on going back… even for just a visit? I mean, it is *your* house."

Rachel also hesitated before answering. "Applewood will always be my home, and it will *always* hold a special place in my heart, but… but there's nothing left for me there."

They continued talking a little while longer, and when he finished his iced tea, he stood up and said, "I should get going."

Rachel thanked him for coming and walked him to the door.

"I came across his manuscript the other day," John said, grabbing the doorknob. "I only knew him a couple of weeks… but I miss him a lot. I can't imagine how much you must miss him."

Sadly, Rachel smiled and nodded. "I think of him and miss him every day." She watched as John headed out the door. Just when he stepped onto the sidewalk, she called out, "Hey, John… wait one second. I have something for you."

When she returned, she was carrying William's old typewriter. She explained that she was downsizing quite a bit for the move.

"I can't possibly bring all this stuff with me. I remember how excited he was those last few weeks of his life. I don't think I've ever seen him type that fast and for that long. He was so determined to get it finished. It had been years since I saw him that inspired, and I think *you* had a lot to do with it."

"I don't know about that… I didn't really do anything."

"That's the beauty of life. Most of us don't realize how our words or actions truly affect other people. But they do… they do."

At that very moment, a ray of sunlight hit Rachel in such a way that it caused John to take notice: her face, her hair, her smile, her eyes.

Without a doubt, John knew why William had fallen madly in love with her.

Rachel outstretched her arms, and John appreciatively took the typewriter from her. "You do know I'm not a writer. I don't even know how to type."

"It doesn't matter. I'm sure he'd want you to have it. And I know you'll find a good home for it."

"Thank you, Mrs... thank you, Rachel. I promise I'll take good care of it."

As John lugged the old typewriter back to the bar, his thoughts remained on Applewood. So much so, by the time he placed the typewriter into his front seat, his mind was made up. He locked his truck and marched back into the Wild Irish Rose and happily announced, "Just wanna let you guys know, I'm taking a little vacation."

Kevin looked up at him and sarcastically mumbled, "What do ya call what you've been on the last month?"

Julie's comment wasn't any more enthusiastic. "At least one of us is taking a vacation."

Kevin knew her comment was aimed at him. Besides a day trip here and there, the last real vacation they had taken was their honeymoon.

Kevin snapped. "You bitch and moan about us saving for a house, yet you want to go splurge on extravagant vacations?"

Kevin knew his comments were not only mean but were way off base. Julie definitely wanted a house, they both did, but she never bitched and moaned about it. And out of everyone in the world, Kevin knew Julie didn't require extravagant vacations—extravagant anything. She was the most low-maintenance and appreciative person he knew. He wanted desperately to apologize, but his stubbornness and the heat of the moment prevented it. They both just stared and glared at one another, and every single customer up at the bar could feel the tension.

Well, this is good for business, John thought but didn't say. Finally, one of the regulars broke the quiet tension.

"Where ya heading?" he asked John.

"A little island off the coast of Maine," John boasted.

This caught the attention of Kevin and Julie, and for the time being, their demeanors softened.

"You're going back to Applewood?" Kevin asked.

"Yeah, I am. Just need to clear my head for a bit, that's all."

Julie hadn't heard Applewood mentioned in years. Slowly, she turned and looked back at the mirror behind the bottles of alcohol. And there, taped high up on the mirror was the postcard John had given to her when he returned from Applewood the last time. The photo was of the lighthouse with stardust falling all around it. It read:

APPLEWOOD MAINE – HOME TO MEDILLIA'S LAMENT.

Julie's thoughts instantly went to William. She'd forgotten just how much she missed the kind old man. She also remembered the first time he told her about the magical island of Applewood. She was mesmerized and enthralled hearing about the legend of Medillia's Lament.

With a sad smile, Julie asked, "When are you going?"

"I don't know. Tomorrow morning maybe."

Julie came out from behind the bar and softened her tone even more as she gave her brother-in-law a hug goodbye. Sweetly, she said, "Have a safe trip… and call us when you get there, okay?"

For the moment, Kevin and Julie were in complete agreement.

"Yeah, call us when you get there," Kevin yelled out.

"Will do."

After some of the regulars offered their well wishes, John headed out. Seconds later, Kevin hurried out of the bar and caught up to John just as he was getting into his truck.

"You're really going to Applewood, huh?"

"Yeah, I really am," John said, smiling.

"When did all this happen?"

John didn't bother telling him about his conversation with Rachel earlier that day.

"Dunno," John said with a shrug. "Just figured it would be a good place to clear my head. You know, like last time."

You're not counting on that weird and magical shit to happen again, are you? Kevin thought but didn't say. There was still a part of him that was skeptical about all the fantastical-type stuff John had told him after he returned from Applewood the first time. The only part Kevin knew for sure was true was the stuff about their parents. Not only did John provide the old photos and the newspaper article about the crash, but Kevin had done his own research on the matter. He had a friend who was a private investigator, and he dug up plenty of proof that the two people on the plane were indeed their parents. His friend was also able to recover the original documents from the City of Chicago, stating that since there was no extended family or written will, the boys would be placed in the foster care system.

So even though it was strange and highly coincidental, Kevin knew John was telling the truth about their parents. The *other stuff* was a different matter. Did John really talk to ghosts? Did he really meet a younger version of William, which caused him to now be married to the love of his life? Kevin supported his brother and listened intently when John told him of his Applewood adventures, but the truth was Kevin never fully believed what he was hearing. He never voiced his doubts to John, but deep down, he simply assumed his brother had watched *Back to the Future* one too many times. When John originally finished telling Kevin everything that happened in Applewood, they both thought it best to put it in the vault and not breathe a word of it to anyone. Now, seven years later, that's exactly where it remained—in the vault.

Kevin gave his brother a hug and reiterated, "Drive safe… and call when you get there."

"I will."

"How long are you going for?"

"No idea."

The last time John went to Applewood, Kevin felt sick to his stomach with worry. He was so afraid of John's drinking and what he might do being left alone that far from home. He remembered how he desperately wanted to go with him so that he could keep a close eye on him. This time was different. John had been sober for seven years, and Kevin wasn't the slightest bit nervous that he'd start drinking again. He did, however, want to go with his brother to Maine, but it wasn't to keep an eye on him. Kevin needed a place to clear his own head. A place far away from the everyday life of Chicago.

John started his truck then rolled down the window and said, "Hey... go easy on Jules. More importantly, talk to her... like, really talk to her."

Knowing his brother was right, Kevin nodded and waved as John pulled away. He didn't actually apologize to Julie, and he never did tell her what had been on his mind, but he did make a conscious effort to curb his sarcasm and be civil.

John was serious when he told Kevin he had no idea how long he'd be gone. And because of that, he packed much heavier than the last time. He also loaded up the back of his truck with as many tools as possible. If Rachel was going to be nice enough to let John stay there again, the least he could do was check to see if the house needed any repairs.

8

John barely waited until the sun came up to hit the road. He knew this trip would be much different than before. Even though he was in a little funk, his mindset was much better than the last time he made the drive to Maine. He hadn't had a drop of alcohol in seven years, and for the most part, he'd come to terms with the loss of his wife and daughter. He also knew there'd be no magic this time. He remembered the legend stating that the magic of Medillia's Lament only lasted a short while. Surely, the island was back to normal by now. There'd be no Clarence, no Mary, and no Sara and her kids.

His entire trip to Applewood years earlier was the strangest and craziest thing he'd ever experienced, yet the thought of Applewood without them caused him to feel sad. Sometimes, when something is so perfect and so special, you almost don't want to revisit it, for if you did, it might taint the memory somehow. With that in mind, John started second-guessing his decision. It wasn't until he crossed over the causeway and entered Applewood that he knew he was where he needed to be.

It was midday when he arrived, and the weather was overcast and extremely cold for a summer day. The first thing that caught his attention were the many FOR SALE signs everywhere. He barely remembered seeing any the last time. He was glad to see the general store and diner were still open and in business. He would most definitely be frequenting both places.

It had been a long couple of days of driving, so he put off exploring the island and decided to head straight for William's house. John still had the piece of paper with the directions on it that William had given him. He had it but didn't need it. As soon as he entered Applewood, his memory-recall kicked in, guiding him directly to the old dead-end road where William's house was.

Most of the houses on William's road also had FOR SALE signs on their lawn, including Sara's house. Between the tall grass and the many disrepairs, it appeared no one had lived there in quite a while. It looked so run down that it was hard to believe anyone had ever lived there. *Maybe no one ever did,* he thought. Seven years isn't that long of a time span, but to John, it felt like a lifetime ago; like an old dream that was getting fuzzier and fuzzier as the years went on.

When he was done idling in front of Sara's house, he turned into William's driveway. Like last time, one of the first things that caught his eye was the overgrown grass. As soon as he got out of his truck, his attention turned from the yard to the weather. A light rain began to fall, and there was an equally light fog, but what he really noticed was the temperature. It was so cold and raw out; he could have sworn that he saw his breath.

Before heading inside, he gave a quick walk around the property to see how everything looked. The trim he replaced last time had held up, and besides the overgrown yard, the property looked to be in good shape. John smiled as he admired his handy work, especially the gazebo. There were two or three trees, which had been knocked down by storms, but luckily, they all missed the gazebo.

By the time he reached the front porch, his sneakers were completely soaked from the wet grass. As he climbed the steps, he took notice of his previous paint job. It was still in decent shape and was only slightly peeling here and there. If the weather ever cleared, he'd definitely give it a touch up. Reaching into his pocket, he pulled out the key. He still couldn't believe Rachel let him keep it this long. He unlocked the door and entered.

The inside looked the same as before. The boxes of packed items remained stacked against the wall, and a layer of dust had settled on almost everything in the house. It certainly wasn't as thick as the last time he arrived, but it was enough to tell him no one had stepped foot in there since he left. The fact that Rachel had no desire to return home and reclaim their property made John sad. He knew how hard that must be to revisit places which held so many memories. It's the same reason William had avoided a return trip to Applewood. As John looked around the old place, he was reminded of something William once told him: "I think it's time… time to get it fixed up. A place like that… with so many memories… doesn't deserve to be neglected."

There was no way William or Rachel would want this place to be neglected, and there was certainly no way Clarence and Mary would want that either. John had no idea how long he'd be staying, and although he wasn't instructed to do repairs, he knew he needed to do what he could to bring life back to the old house.

His first order of business would be purchasing mouse traps— lots of them. There were droppings everywhere. John was exhausted from his drive and desperately needed some sleep, but the couch was completely covered in mouse feces. For now, the couch was off limits, and he was forced to use one of the upstairs bedrooms. He chose what he assumed was William's old room. The mattress was bare but had little dust accumulation due to the boxes, which were stacked on top. John removed the boxes and brushed away the remaining dust from the bed. He assumed there were sheets and blankets packed away, but he was too tired to search for them. Fortunately, he had his own blanket and pillow with him. He went out to the car and grabbed them along with his suitcase.

It didn't take long for him to fall into a deep sleep. He only intended on crashing for an hour or two, but the next thing he knew, five hours had gone by. He glanced at his phone, which read 5:45pm. It was still raining, and the fog had thickened. He was well rested but starved. He searched online for the hours of the diner and was psyched to see it didn't close until 9pm. It didn't matter what special they were running that night; he could already taste it.

The diner wasn't very busy, but John chose to sit up at the counter. Being a creature of habit, he sat in the same spot as he did seven years ago. There were only a few booths occupied, including Charlotte sitting by herself in the corner. She had a coffee, a half-eaten pie, and was writing in a notebook.

For whatever reason, John found himself continually looking over at her, and whenever she looked up, he'd look away. In his mind, he thought he was being extremely discreet. Charlotte, however, knew he was checking her out, and she also could tell he was an out-of-towner. It was a little obvious, but she didn't think much of it. Besides, she couldn't help but think he was attractive as well. It's strange how that works. If he was ugly, then she would have considered his staring creepy and off-putting. But the fact that she thought he was good looking, made it sweet, cute, and flirty.

This not-so-discreet staring went on for the better part of an hour. Charlotte had the advantage on this one. Her seat was directly facing John, while his seat forced him to turn almost all the way around to see her. Needless to say, his neck was cramped and sore by the time he went back to William's house.

Except for a few sneezing bouts from the dust accumulation on the mattress, John slept well. When he awoke the next morning, it was once again gloomy and cold out, but at least it wasn't raining. He had no clue what his plan was for the day, but what he did know was he needed a coffee. He recalled how delicious the coffee was at the general store and was also reminded of their homemade blueberry muffins. It was settled. His first activity of the day would be a trip to the general store.

On the drive over, he tried not to get his hopes up. A lot can change in seven years. Maybe they switched coffee brands. Maybe the muffins were no longer homemade. If so, then they were probably tiny store-bought muffins; the kind that don't even have real blueberries.

These first-world problems were the only thing on his mind as he entered the store. It took only three seconds for those thoughts to disappear and for his mind to be blown.

Standing behind the counter was Charlotte. She was in the process of ringing in a customer, so it took her a moment to notice John had entered. As soon as their eyes met, John looked away and quickly walked over to the coffee station. Although tempted, the entire time he fixed his coffee, he never once turned around to steal a glance at her. He was too worried that she might bust him staring. Little did he know, she had already busted him seventeen times the night before.

It was a good thing he didn't look back at her, for her eyes never left him. Even as she rang one customer in after another, she continued staring over at John. The big difference was that Charlotte was calm, cool, and smiling ear to ear, while John was nervous, anxious, and clumsy. So clumsy, in fact, he accidentally dropped his sugar packets into his coffee. And when he tried to fish them out with his fingers, he nearly burned the tips off.

Mother fucker that's hot, his inner voice yelled out.

When he finally had the situation under control, he snapped the lid on, grabbed a homemade blueberry muffin, and headed towards the counter.

"Find everything you were looking for?" Charlotte politely asked.

John's younger self would surely have had a slick, flirty response to her comment. But pathetically, the thirty-nine-year-old version could only muster a slight smile and a nod. Yup, that was it, a smile and a nod— not even a verbal *yes*. John *actually* thought he was playing it cool. And considering the smile never left her face, he assumed he was doing a great job at that.

He wasn't exactly sure what it was, but she certainly had him mesmerized. So much so, she remained on his mind the entire ride home. It wasn't until he pulled into the driveway that his mind turned to something else. *Now what do I do with my day?*

The wind was light, but the temperature was cold and raw. Seeing as it wasn't raining, John decided to bundle up and take a little walk to the cove. He hadn't even made it to the path in the woods, yet his sneakers and jeans were soaked from the wet grass. The path itself was barely visible. It didn't appear that anyone had trampled through it in years.

Just like last time, as he neared the end of the path, the smell of salt air hit his nose. And even before he entered the cove, he could hear the thunderous sounds of the waves against the shore. He was surprised at how large the waves were. He walked this beach many times when he was here before, but he never saw waves this big and rough. The cove was set in enough that it was usually protected from waves like this. A gentle lapping was the most he had ever experienced down here.

He was used to the sound of his feet crunching over the small rocks and seashells, but this time was different. The rocks were much bigger, and the entire beach was covered with piles and piles of seaweed. Not to mention, there were tons of driftwood and broken lobster traps everywhere.

Even though he didn't really expect to see Clarence or his boat, a feeling of disappointment coursed through his body. John recalled the last time he walked the cove. Clarence and his boat had mysteriously disappeared, and there was a peaceful, almost hopeful feeling in the air. But now, seven years later, the cove felt cold and unsettled. Once again, flashes of doubt crept into his mind.

Did I really help an old ghost fix up his boat?

His surroundings were familiar, but his memories were hazier than they'd ever been. Considering it was the middle of summer, John couldn't believe how frigid it was down by the water. It literally chilled him to the bone. It got so cold that he decided to head back, but even when he returned to the house, he couldn't get himself warm. He tried to turn the heat on, but the furnace hadn't been used for years and years. Not to mention, the oil tank was bone dry. At one point, he attempted to get the fireplace going, but unfortunately, he was out of luck finding any dry firewood around the property. He decided to hop back into his truck and explore the island.

His first thought was to drive out to Harbor Cove Park, but a mile past the stop sign he came across a barricade with a ROAD CLOSED sign attached to it. Just as he turned around, the light mist turned into a steadier rain. Any thoughts he had on exploring the island on foot would have to wait for another day. He would have to settle for good tunes in a warm vehicle. On more than one occasion, John found himself shaking his head, wondering why the hell he chose Applewood for his vacation. It was cold and rainy, and for the life of him, he had no idea what he was going to do to pass the time. At least last time he had outdoor projects to keep him occupied.

Throughout his little drive, he passed by the general store several times. And each time he contemplated stopping in. It was too soon to get another coffee, and seeing as he hadn't checked if the refrigerator was still working, he didn't want to do any grocery shopping yet. He knew he couldn't go in for just a candy bar; that would be much too obvious. On his fourth drive-by, it hit him: *cleaning products… oh, and mousetraps!*

This time, he stepped up his game and said actual words to Charlotte. Well, word… singular.

He awkwardly managed a solid, "Hi."

To which she replied, "Looks like someone has a fun day planned."

To which John reverted to a non-verbal half smile and nod. He was a little disappointed with himself on the ride back to William's house but vowed that next time would be different. Little did he know, next time would be much sooner than later. Just as he entered the freezingly cold house, it hit him. "Shit! I should have bought some firewood when I was there."

He placed the bag down on the table and thought to himself, *There's no way I can go back there for a third time in a day. She'd totally assume*

I was checking her out… like in a creepy way. Yup, I definitely can't go back again today.

The next thing he knew, he was once again walking through the front door of the general store. The wood was five dollars a bundle, and John decided that ten bundles should do just nicely. And for the third time that day, he headed up to the counter to pay for his newest excuse to see this cute woman.

"Did you say fifty or fifteen dollars of firewood?" she asked.

"Fifty. I like my fires big. Not like in a pyromaniac-type of way… just trying to take the chill off the house. I can't believe it's this cold in July."

"Welcome to life on the island. Though, it's not usually this cold here in the summer." Charlotte then pointed to the small tray of Bic lighters next to the register and asked, "Lighter?"

"No, that's okay. I don't smoke."

She tried but couldn't hold back her laughter. John quickly caught on.

"Oh, you meant a lighter to get the fire started, didn't you?" Embarrassed, he grabbed a green lighter and placed it on the counter.

"Just trying to save you a trip back here," she said, smirking.

"Thanks," he said, handing her the money.

Without making another comment, John paid for his things and left. He tossed the bundles of wood into his truck and headed back to William's house. It didn't take long for his mind to start to overanalyze Charlotte's comment. By her telling him she was trying to save him a trip back there, was that her way of joking, or was it her way of saying his multiple trips were highly weird and creepy? She was smiling when she said it, so he took it as a good sign that she was just joking with him. But just to be on the safe side, he would avoid any more trips to the store—at least for the day.

Once the fire was lit, it didn't take long for the house to warm up. John did a little bit of cleaning in the living room and kitchen, but the old vacuum he found seemed to shoot out more dust than catch it. He knew he needed more cleaning products than the general store could offer. He assumed there were much bigger store options in the next town over, but the last thing he wanted was to head back out. The wind and rain had picked up, and he was more than content with being lazy by the fire. He found a deck of cards in one of the drawers and spent the rest of the afternoon playing Solitaire and listening to tunes on his phone.

The next thing he knew, it was 6pm and his stomach was letting him know it needed more than the half-empty bag of beef jerky. The wind and rain had all but subsided, and John decided to hit the diner for a home-cooked meal. Before he even entered, he already knew what he was going to order: an open-faced turkey sandwich with mashed potatoes and extra gravy.

The place was a little busier than last time, but not by much. He headed straight for the counter, and before he even sat down, the waitress motioned to the pot of coffee in her hand. John smiled and nodded. He wasn't a big nighttime coffee drinker, but you can't go to a diner and not order coffee. He wasn't sure what it was, but diner coffee always hit the spot.

The waitress placed the piping hot mug in front of him, sliding the bowl of creamers next to it. John thanked her then placed his order. No sooner did she walk away, he heard the bell on the front door ring. Normally, he wouldn't have paid much attention to it, but for whatever reason, he turned around to see who it was. The next thing he knew, he was making direct eye contact with Charlotte for the fourth time that day—fifth time in the past twenty-four hours.

His intentions were to give her a warm, welcoming smile, but it came out as more of an awkward deer-in-the-headlights look. He spun back around and quickly took a sip of coffee. It nearly burned his tongue off, but the embarrassment of whatever type of look he just gave her far outweighed any pain his mouth was feeling.

Charlotte scanned the diner, and when she noticed that her usual booth was occupied, she decided to sit up at the counter. John being there *might* have had something to do with her decision. As soon as she sat down, the waitress approached with a mug and pot of coffee.

"Hey, Charlotte… coffee?"

"You know it. Thanks."

"How was the old general today?"

"Eh, just another day."

"I hear ya," the waitress said, and then lifted the pot in John's direction and asked, "Need a top off?"

"Um… yes, please. Thanks."

As the waitress walked away, Charlotte pulled out a pen and a notebook. While she did that, John was desperately searching his brain for the perfect icebreaker. He needed to say something. After a few minutes of staring at a blank page, Charlotte looked over at John and asked, "So, how's the fifty dollars worth of firewood holding up?"

John answered her question then felt the need to explain and justify his many trips to the store that day. She didn't necessarily buy it, but she didn't want to make John feel any more awkward than he already did.

"I'm the same way," she said, laughing. "I'm always forgetting things… and I even make a list!"

"Yeah, I should probably start doing that myself."

"New to the island, I assume?"

"Just on an extended vacation… kinda."

"And you chose *this* place? No offense, but when you drop fifty bucks on firewood to stay warm in the summer, it might be a sign that you made the wrong decision."

John nodded in agreement.

"I'm just kidding with ya. It's usually pretty nice here in the summer. We've just been in bad weather pattern for a while… for a long while."

"I've never been to Applewood in the summer, but the last time I was here the weather was perfect."

"Oh yeah? When was that?"

"It was in the fall… back in 2004."

"Ah, that's right around the time I got married."

As discreetly as he could, he looked down at her finger. Not a ring in sight. He knew an empty ring finger didn't always mean single, though. He learned that the hard way once upon a time. Not wanting to come right out and ask if she was still married, his brain searched for the right approach.

"Does your husband work at the store with you?"

Charlotte laughed. "Yeah, right. We couldn't even live together, never mind work together. We've been divorced just over two years now."

Verbally, he told her he was sorry, but on the inside, he was victoriously fist-pumping as if he'd just won some big prize. She went on to explain that she was *temporarily* working at her mother's store and *temporarily* living in the apartment upstairs with her mother as well. She made sure to accent the word temporarily.

"What did you do for work before?" John asked.

"Up until my divorce, I worked for the Applewood Weekly… for almost twelve years."

"Like a reporter?"

"Yup. Just a boring reporter."

"What? Being a reporter sounds fun."

Again, she laughed. "Fun? Applewood? The biggest story in the last ten years was the great white shark scare of 2008. There were three of them reported to be in and around the lighthouse area."

"Great whites? This far north? That sounds like a big story, no?"

"Oh, it was. The whole island was in a frenzy. They shut down all the beaches and everything."

"Wow. So, Applewood turned into the real-life Amityville, huh?"

Charlotte giggled. "You mean Amity. Amityville is where *Amityville Horror* took place. Amity is the island from *Jaws*."

"Oh yeah," John said, grinning. "I always get them confused."

"Rookie mistake," she said, taking a sip of coffee.

95

"What ended up happening? Were there any shark attacks?"

"Nope. Turned out to be three sunfish, not great whites. That was the highlight and lowlight of my tenure there. I just got tired of the monotony of small-island news. Mostly, it was reporting on land disputes, or vandalism, or the big ten-thousand-dollar reward Ms. Beasley offered for her missing cat."

Their conversation was briefly interrupted when the waitress came over and placed John's food in front of him.

"Anything else I can get you?" she asked with a pleasant smile.

"Nope, I think I'm good. Thanks."

On her way back to the kitchen, she stopped to chat with Charlotte. The conversation seemed to revolve around the waitress's "loser boyfriend." Her exact words.

John overheard and thought, *Jesus, is every guy on the island a dickhead?* Knowing it wasn't his business or place, he decided to keep his thoughts to himself. Instead, he focused on the heaping portion of turkey, which was loaded with extra gravy. There were hundreds of things he still missed about Kristen; her nightly home-cooked meals being one. John was never much of a cook, and for the most part, he spent the last eight years living on takeout and fast food.

While John dug into his meal, Charlotte was attempting to scribble down some ideas in her notebook. As he hungrily ate, he searched for something to say to restart his conversation with her. The best he could come up with was, "Did anyone ever find the cat and get the reward?"

"Yes and no," she said, smiling and brushing her hair out of her face. "The cat was eventually found safe and sound, but as it turned out, the woman didn't actually have any money to pay the reward."

"Uh oh. What happened?"

"The lady who found the cat was none too pleased and ended up taking her to court."

"Like, Judge Judy?" he asked, grinning.

"Something like that. It actually never got that far. They ended up settling."

"How much did the woman have to pay?"

"Nothing. She gave the cat up as payment."

"Wait... what?"

"Exactly!" Charlotte said, placing the pen down on her notebook. "Those are the type of stories that I was forced to cover. And those are the type of stories that drove me to come work for my mother."

Again, they were interrupted by the waitress. This time, she placed a giant piece of pie in front of Charlotte and offered both her and John a refill on coffee.

"Don't judge my dinner choice," Charlotte said in his direction. He held up his hands and smiled. After that, they both concentrated on their meals, and it would be another fifteen minutes before another word was exchanged between them. Charlotte had also noticed John's ring finger was empty and decided to do some fishing of her own.

"So, are you here on vacation by yourself?"

"Yup. Just trying to recharge my batteries. Work and life have become a bit monotonous lately."

"I hear that. What do you do for work?"

John told her about his woodworking business back in Chicago, and he also mentioned how he was slowly becoming burned out. She voiced that she'd never really been outside of New England, but she had always wanted to visit Chicago.

"Well, you'd definitely have more than just cat rewards and shark sightings to report. And by that, I mean plenty of crime and corruption to write about."

There was just something about Charlotte that John was taken with. The more they talked, the more smitten he became with her. It was a feeling he hadn't felt in quite a while. In his head, he knew he was only going to be in town for a short time and that nothing would come of it. But still, he couldn't take his eyes off her, and he couldn't stop coming up with ways to keep the conversation going. Charlotte was much better at hiding it, but she also felt the same way. There was something about him that piqued her interest—even beyond his obvious good looks.

"So, where are you staying?" she asked, as her own way of continuing the conversation.

"The same place I stayed last time. A friend of mine has a house up on Atlantic Lane."

"Oh yeah? Who's that?"

"William... William Galloway."

"Hmm... any relation to Mary and Clarence Galloway?"

"Yup. Those are his parents. They passed the house onto him and his wife. You knew them?"

"No, not personally, but I've heard their names." She pondered and continued. "Actually, wasn't Mr. Galloway the one who died out to sea?"

John nodded. "He was caught out in a horrible storm... from what I've heard."

"Yeah, I think I remember that. I was young at the time, but I remember hearing about it. Unfortunately, tragedies like that happen all too often around these parts. That's another bad thing about working at the newspaper... covering horrible stories like that."

Her comment caused John to remember the large granite memorial up at Harbor Cove Park, which honored all the fishermen and people who had been lost out at sea.

"Is your friend here with you?" she asked.

"My friend?"

"The guy whose house you're staying at. What did you say his name was... William?"

Without going into detail, John informed her that William had passed on and that his wife was allowing him to use their house. He told her about the repairs he did the last time he was in town and how it looked like the house was ready for some more.

"Unfortunately, even if I wanted to, there's not much I can do with the weather being as it is. It's too wet to even cut the grass, never mind climb a ladder and work on the side of the house. It's kinda funny, back home I had a million things I could be working on or fixing, but I chose to be lazy and veg out the past month or so. But now that I'm technically on vacation, I feel the need to—"

"Keep busy and do something productive?" she said, finishing his sentence.

"Exactly! Weird, I know."

"Nah. I'm totally the same way."

"Now I'm stuck on vacation with no TV, and if this weather doesn't improve, no ability to tinker around outside on the side of the house."

"What about the inside?"

"The inside? There's plenty of remodeling I'd do... if I owned it. But seeing as I don't, I don't want to get carried away. I was thinking about maybe giving some of the rooms a fresh coat of paint, though. The walls are pretty faded and outdated, but..."

"But what?"

"I'm horrible at picking out color schemes."

John didn't say it, but he thought back to his first apartment with Kristen. She laughed at and vetoed every color selection he made. He remembered how insulted he felt, until he saw the final result of Kristen's paint choices. From that point on, he deferred all color schemes to anyone other than himself.

Charlotte turned her attention back to her pie and coffee, and John assumed the conversation would end there. To his pleasant surprise, it didn't. She jotted down a few things in her notebook, made quick work of the pie, then looked over in John's direction and said, "I have the day off tomorrow... and I'm pretty good at picking out color schemes. I could take a look at the place and give you some suggestions... if you want?"

Luckily for John, his mouth was full of food, or else he would have answered *yes* well before she even finished her sentence. When he was done chewing, he composed his excitement and casually accepted her offer. Of course, he said all the typical comments first. Comments like: "I appreciate it, but you really don't have to... I know it's your day off and all... the last thing you want to do is help a complete stranger pick out paint colors."

He only said all of that because it was the cliché and polite thing to do, but secretly, he was crossing his fingers that she would hold true to her offer. She did. She had him write down the address and told him she'd be there first thing in the morning.

9

John knew when she said *first thing* that she probably meant eight or nine, but that didn't stop him from waking with the sunrise and taking an extra-long shower in preparation for her arrival. When she arrived at 8:45, he had already changed outfits three times. He knew how pathetic it was, but at that point, he didn't really care. It had been far too long since he felt that newness feeling, and the last thing he was going to do was question it. Little did he know, Charlotte had also woken up bright and early and was also on her third outfit as well.

Not wanting to seem too eager and excited, John counted to ten Mississippi before answering the door. Well, that was his intention, but he actually only made it to five Mississippi.

"Hey, how are you?" he said, opening the door.

"I'm good, thanks. I hope this isn't too early? I realized after the fact that I should have given you a more specific time, but…"

"No, this is perfect. I just rolled outta bed and got dressed a few minutes ago." He invited her in and said, "Well, this is it. Pretty outdated, huh?"

The first thing that caught her eye was just how bare the place was. Aside from a few pieces of furniture, it lacked all the things that made a house a home. There were no pictures hanging, no knick-knacks—not even a clock. The lack of these things made the faded and filthy walls stand out even more. Dirt and dust were the next things that stood out to her. John had done his best to give the place a quick clean, but as Charlotte pointed out, it was in desperate need of a *deep* cleaning.

"I already have plenty of ideas for paint colors," she said. "But you do realize we need to do a deep and thorough cleaning of this place first, right?"

"We?" John said, fighting back his hopefulness.

Charlotte grinned and confessed that she didn't have anything better to do on her day off. He knew there was no way this could be true, but there was no way he was going to argue against it. When she asked to see what type of cleaning products he had, John's answer caused her to laugh out loud. The vacuum was broken, the broom had only a handful of bristles left, and the mophead had been completely chewed by the mice. And speaking of mice, Charlotte couldn't help commenting on the half dozen traps set throughout the living room and kitchen.

"Do they not have mice in the city?"

"Why do you say that?"

She motioned to the traps by the refrigerator. "Did you really bait them with beefy jerky?"

Slightly embarrassed, he shrugged and said, "It was either that or Chicken in a Biskit. I kept forgetting to pick up some cheese."

"You really are a city boy, aren't you?" She went on to explain that not only was he using the wrong bait, but he needed to attach it to the trap. "Otherwise, the little buggers will just drag it away without ever setting it off. Oh, and it's a giant misconception that mice love cheese."

"It is?"

"Yup. Peanut butter. That's your best weapon of choice."

John wasn't sure if she was putting him on or not, but considering he had yet to catch anything, he thought there might be something to her logic. Charlotte walked around the entire house and continued adding to their list of things to get. After she saw the bare and dusty mattress John had been sleeping on, she recommended that he should get a steam cleaner for the couch, the rugs, and all the mattresses. She told him they rented them at the general and that she'd hook him up for free. She also offered to lend him her vacuum, but John insisted on buying a new one. He said it would be his gift to the Galloways.

With the amount of things on their list, Charlotte thought it best to hit some of the bigger stores off the island. They spent the next two hours shopping over in Gerrish Falls. While they were at one of the home improvement stores, Charlotte picked up a handful of paint swatches to get a better idea of the exact colors she was going to choose.

John wasn't a big fan of shopping, especially for things like vacuums and bed linens. But if he had to be stuck doing it, he couldn't think of a better person than Charlotte to be doing it with. She was easy going, fun, and quite talkative. And she wasn't the annoying kind of talkative either. Her comments were smart and inciteful, but it was her sense of humor that John really took a liking to. It was right up his alley, and he had to bring his A-game just to keep up with her.

After they returned to the house, they wasted no time and jumped right in. They started with the upstairs bedrooms and worked their way down. They talked, laughed, and deep-cleaned the entire afternoon away. By the time they finished, it was just after 5pm. It was the most cleaning John had done in years. He wasn't a lazy or overly messy person, but doing the bare minimum was about as much as he usually did. Kristen, on the other hand, was meticulous with her cleaning. This caused many a tiff back in their younger days. Her stance lightened up over time, especially once Hannah was born. With a toddler *and* John dirtying up the house, Kristen found it nearly impossible to keep up with her high standards. Eventually, she went from needing the house to be *spotless* to *eh, that's good enough.*

When they finished cleaning the walls, Charlotte labeled them with the proper color swatch she had chosen. The house had a musty, unlived-in smell to it. John's solution was to Febreze the hell out of the place. Charlotte chose a much classier route and bought a handful of beautifully-scented candles.

As they stood back admiring their hard work, John found himself feeling a bit depressed. The place looked and smelled great, but he lamented the fact that neither William nor Rachel were here to appreciate it—or Clarence and Mary, for that matter. It saddened him to think about Rachel continuing to hold onto the house yet having no desire to ever return to it.

As if reading his mind, Charlotte looked around the house and said, "I've never met him, but I bet your friend, William would love it. All the Galloways, actually."

"Yeah," John said with a smile. "I think they would. And I'm excited to see what the walls look like with the colors you chose."

"Well, just keep in mind that I'm not a professional interior decorator."

"No, I think the colors are going to be perfect. They're certainly better than what I would have picked. I really do appreciate all your help today. I'm not sure I could have found the motivation to do it on my own."

"Seriously, you don't have to thank me. Besides, it was kind of fun."

John tilted his head, giving her an incredulous look.

Charlotte placed her hand over her face and embarrassingly said, "The fact that I just called cleaning *fun* tells you all you need to know about my social life."

John laughed. "Trust me, my social life isn't much better. I spent over four hours the other day playing cards by myself."

"That's not that bad. Solitaire can be fun and addicting."

"Oh, I didn't just play Solitaire. I was playing actual card games against myself. I played War, Gin Rummy, and a few others."

"Against yourself?" she asked, smirking.

"Yup. Who's the pathetic one now, huh?"

Charlotte didn't say a word, but her look conceded the title to John. She thought about asking if he played strip poker by himself, too, but seeing as they'd only known each other for less than twenty-four hours, she held back her perverted sarcasm. Despite filtering her thoughts, she did find it weird just how comfortable she felt around him. He was feeling the exact same way. So much so, he decided to try and extend their time together that day.

"I don't know about you, but I'm starving," he said, rubbing his stomach.

The only thing they had eaten all day were some snacks they bought at the general when they stopped by to pick up the steam cleaner.

"Yeah, I'm pretty hungry myself."

"If you're not sick of me yet, do you maybe wanna go grab a bite to eat over at the diner?"

"That sounds perfect."

"One condition, though…. my treat. It's the least I can do for your help today."

Charlotte decided to forgo the polite back and forth of telling him he didn't need to pay for her. Instead, she simply grinned and said, "Deal."

They took separate cars so that Charlotte could just head home afterwards. They ended up eating and talking right up until closing time. As a matter of fact, they were the last customers remaining. Neither of them wanted the night to end, but neither wanted to suggest anything further. Charlotte mentioned her mother was venturing out of town for a couple of days and that she'd be stuck at the store from open to close. She also mentioned how bored she was going to be. John wasn't sure if that was her way of hinting that he should come pay her a visit at the store. He certainly didn't need a hint, for he already had every intention of stopping in to see her.

The night ended with him profusely thanking her for helping him throughout the day. He held the door for her as they exited the diner and was tempted to open her car door as well. He was tempted, but he didn't. He figured it would come across as a little too over the top and romantic. In his mind, he thought he had played everything cool up until that point, so he didn't want to ruin it now.

John moved closer to her, and for a brief hopeful second, Charlotte thought he might be leaning in for a goodnight kiss. Instead, he thanked her one last time, and for whatever reason, he reached out and shook her hand. Needless to say, he spent the rest of the night verbally chastising himself for being, as he put it, "a giant fucking idiot!"

He also told himself numerous times that there was no way he could show his face at the store the next day. He went to bed that night convincing himself it would be at least a few days before he'd swing by the store and say hi.

***

It didn't take long for John's embarrassment to fade and for him to visit Charlotte at the store. Ten hours, to be exact. Bright and early the next morning, he showed up for his usual coffee and muffin. Between Charlotte's beaming smile and her easy-going nature, John was put at ease, and he assumed she didn't even remember his awkward handshake from the night before.

"Any luck with the peanut butter?" she asked.

"Oh my God! All six traps had mice in them this morning."

"Nice. See, told ya peanut butter would do the trick."

John almost reached up to give her a victorious high-five but figured that would be about as lame as last night's handshake.

"That's actually why I came in this morning… needed to pick up some more traps. I know I can probably reuse them, but there's no way I'm touching those disgusting little things."

Charlotte knew John was just using the mousetraps as an excuse to visit her, but she wasn't about to make a big deal of it. Even though he was more or less a stranger, she was flattered at the attention. It had been a long time since anyone had shown interest in her—real interest anyway. Plenty of guys had tried to get with her since her divorce but none were seemingly as sweet as John. He seemed genuine and kind, and she also loved that his sense of humor meshed with hers.

One conversation led to another, and the next thing they knew, two hours had passed by. With customers coming in and out, there were plenty of opportunities for John to excuse himself and leave. On multiple occasions he uttered the words, "Well, I should probably get out of your hair. Lots of painting to do today." He said it yet never actually followed through and left.

The same could be said for Charlotte. There were more than enough opportunities for her to say, "Well, I should probably get back to work. Lots to do today without my mom being here." If John was being creepy or annoying, she would have done just that. But he wasn't. Not at all.

It took the small lunchtime rush for John to finally leave. And even then, he stuck around to help her out as much as he could. He made a couple pots of coffee and moved some heavy boxes from the backroom up to the front. He even helped old man Thompson lug a case of water out to his car.

By the time he returned from buying paint over in Gerrish Falls, it was already late afternoon. As he drove back by the general store, he thought about swinging in again but ultimately decided against it. The last thing he wanted was to come across as overanxious. Instead, he waited until dinner time and drove over to the diner in hopes of Charlotte also being there. If the last two nights were any indication, the diner was her go-to spot after work.

Unfortunately, when she got out, she had a bunch of odds and ends to take care of and never made it over to the diner. She knew there was a good chance John would be there, and although she wanted to see him, she decided to play it cool. Besides, she had a strong feeling she'd probably be seeing him first thing in the morning. She wasn't wrong.

John had an inkling that she was into him. Well, maybe not *into him*, but he thought she at least found him interesting and tolerable. At this point in his life, he considered that a win. After all, she was the one who volunteered to help a stranger clean his house for an entire day. But as much as John told himself he needed to play it cool, he wasn't nearly as good at it as Charlotte was. Just as she predicted, as soon as she opened the next morning, John showed up for his coffee and muffin.

"You're here bright and early today," she said, knowing he was absolutely into her.

"Yeah, I wanted to get in a full day of painting today. I spent most of last night taping everything off."

"Ah. I'd volunteer to help you, but I'm stuck here two more days open to close."

"Are you and your mother the only ones that work here?"

"No. We have a couple of part time teenagers, but they're not the most reliable workers. We have another woman who usually works full time, but she's recovering from minor surgery. I think she's supposed to back next week sometime."

"That's good. It'll give you a little time off."

"Eh, not that it really matters," she said, shrugging. "I wasn't lying when I said I don't have much of a social life. I can't remember the last time I went out after work and had some fun."

Her comment wasn't said by accident. She gave John the perfect opening to ask her out. If this were twenty years ago, he would have done just that. Back then, he was brimming with confidence when it came to the opposite sex. But now that he was pushing forty, that confidence seemed like a lifetime ago. In the years since Kristen passed away, Jain was his only relationship. Even more than that, Jain was the only person he had gone on a date with. He knew his confidence was lacking and that his flirting game was rusty at best. Case in point, the awkward handshake two nights earlier.

After a brief moment of silence, John finally said, "Well, I should get going. The walls aren't gonna paint themselves."

As the door shut behind him, Charlotte was left stunned and

confused. *Did I read the signs wrong? Is he not interested in me? Ugh. I've been out of the game too long. I can't even tell if a guy likes me or is just being friendly.* Disappointed and feeling pathetic, Charlotte went back to work.

John also felt disappointed and pathetic, but he added anger to the list as well. The anger was strictly aimed at himself. It lasted beyond just the car ride back to William's. Every so often, he'd throw down the paint brush and start berating himself.

"What the fuck is wrong with you, John? How hard is it to ask a girl out? Especially a nice one!!!" As was customary with his self-conversations, he slowly turned the tables and began justifying his actions. "To be fair, what's really the point? You're only here on vacation. Why start something romantic and shit, only to head back to Chicago in a week or so? Yeah, I didn't really chicken out... I did the smart thing."

Just then, his cell phone rang, interrupting his little back and forth with himself. It was Kevin checking up on him.

"Hey, bro. How's the coast of Maine treating you? You're missing a nasty heatwave here."

John started the conversation off by telling him the weather was quite the opposite there in Applewood.

"I even had to get the fireplace going the other day it was so cold."

"Jesus. It's been like ninety-five here every day since you left. So, what have you been doing with yourself?"

"Just puttering around the house and doing a little interior painting. Nothing major."

There was no way he was going to mention anything about Charlotte. The last thing he needed was for Kevin to confirm how stupid he was for even entertaining the idea of asking this girl out on a date while on vacation. John hated getting advice from his younger brother. Not because it was bad advice—quite the opposite. Kevin always offered level-headed and sensible advice, which is why John always did the opposite. There was no way he could give Kevin satisfaction by agreeing with his smart advice.

Yup, John had no intention of mentioning one word about Charlotte—until he did. And it wasn't just one word either. He rambled for a solid fifteen minutes straight about her, including telling Kevin he was contemplating asking her on a date. Before Kevin could respond, John answered for him. "I know, I know, it's a stupid idea. I'm only here for a little bit… why start something only to leave. Trust me, I know."

At any minute, John expected Kevin to start laughing at him, agreeing how stupid the date idea was. Instead, after a long pause, Kevin shocked the shit out of his brother by saying just the opposite.

"I don't think it's stupid. You're both adults, and she's aware that you're only there on vacation. And it sounds like you guys are getting along well."

"We really are," John chimed in, still surprised. "And we have a lot in common, too."

"Do you want my advice?" Kevin asked.

"Not really," John replied, more out of habit. The truth was, he desperately wanted Kevin to finish his thoughts on the matter. "Go ahead… what's your advice?"

"I say, if you have fun together then keep having fun until it's no longer fun… or until you decide to come home. Either way, jump off that bridge when you get to it. Life is too short to preemptively end something because of what ifs. Anyway, that's my advice to you. As always, take it or leave it, bro."

John was absolutely going to take it. But old habits die hard, and he wasn't about to give Kevin total satisfaction.

"Eh, we'll see, I guess." Before getting off the phone, he made sure to throw in a more heartfelt, "Thanks for the advice, Kev,"

From the moment he got off the phone, his mood completely flipped. He spent the rest of the morning painting the upstairs bedrooms and excitedly planning his next move. He rehearsed at least a half dozen ways to ask Charlotte out. He also tried to come up with some clever date ideas.

Ultimately, he decided on simple and cliché. He would ask her out for dinner, like a nice dinner—not a diner dinner. And maybe he'd suggest a movie afterwards. He'd play it cool and be smooth about it. Maybe something like: "I haven't been to the movies in forever. Maybe we can catch one... if there's anything good playing." *Yup, that's a winning line*, he thought.

Proudly, he placed the paint roller in the tray and stood back to admire the room. So far, Charlotte had nailed it with her color choices for the bedrooms. His next big decision was *when*; when would he ask her out? He knew she was working until close the next two nights, so he assumed she'd be too tired to go out afterwards. Three nights from now would be the logical choice. Like always, though, John's impatience trumped logic. Knowing she'd be closing in a couple hours, he washed the paint off his hands and drove over for the big question. If she said yes for tonight, it would still give him a chance to go back and shower and change into proper date clothes.

By the time he pulled into the parking lot of the general, his lines were well-rehearsed. As he checked his hair in the rearview mirror, he said aloud, "Let's do this." His confidence couldn't have been any higher. Somewhere between the car and the front door of the store, his confidence began to wane. And when Charlotte flashed him her smile and said "Hi," his confidence disappeared altogether.

"How's the painting going?"

"What?" he asked, trying to regain his focus.

"You said you had a big day of painting ahead of you. Did you get anything accomplished? Or did you spend the day playing cards against yourself?"

"Ha ha. For your information, I got all the bedrooms painted... two coats."

"And?? How did I do with the colors?"

He thought about saying something sarcastic but ended up simply speaking the truth. "Perfect. They're absolutely perfect. I can't wait to see how the living room turns out. That's my project for tomorrow.

How was your day?"

Charlotte went on to tell him the highs and lows of her day, and for the time being, his hopes of asking her out were put on the back burner. When she wasn't talking about her day, she was getting interrupted by one customer after another. John couldn't have picked a worse time to visit. It was just after 5pm, so the after-work crowd were picking up a few necessities on their way home. Beer and tobacco products were two of the biggest necessities; a twelve-pack of Natty Light and Marlboros being the most common.

The customers were almost exclusively male, and everyone knew everyone by name. Considering it was a small island, this didn't really surprise John. But what did surprise him was just how many guys attempted to flirt with Charlotte. It wasn't even *real* flirting either. It was just a bunch of sophomoric comments and perverted sexual innuendoes. Seriously, if John had a dollar every time he heard one of them say: *That's what she said* or *That's what he said*, he'd be a millionaire.

He was also shocked at how jealous he was getting. He'd only known this woman for a few days. There was no way he should be feeling this jealous. What made it a much easier pill to swallow was Charlotte didn't play into any of it. For the most part, she simply rolled her eyes at their immaturity. But when she did respond, it was usually a sarcastic quip that put them in their place.

When most of them filtered out and headed home, John shook his head at Charlotte in disbelief and said, "You deal with that every day?"

"With what? Oh, them? Eh, they're harmless. Perverted animals, but harmless."

"You must get hit on constantly working here, huh?"

John wasn't sure why he asked that question.

"Me? Nah. Most of them have girlfriends or wives, and the ones that don't... well, they don't have the balls to ask a woman out. Not properly anyway."

Once again, she left the door wide open for John to swoop in and ask her out. He wanted to. He really did, but right at that moment, he forgot everything he'd been rehearsing. He began to fidget and stumbled over his thoughts, but he did manage to make a comment about how tired she must be.

"Nah, not really. When I work open to close, I'm usually wired when I get out. Not that there's anything around here to do... or anyone to do it with, but yeah, I'm definitely wired when I get out."

As John stood there continuing to fidget, he started to recall some of the lines he'd been rehearsing earlier. He remembered them, but the fear of rejection took hold. Knowing it wasn't going to happen, he decided it best to just head home.

"I should let you get ready to close up shop. Have a good night," he said, hanging his head in defeat as he slowly made his way towards the door.

Charlotte wasn't the most proactive person in the world, but this was ridiculous. Without thinking too heavily on it, she blurted out, "Hey, do you like to play pool?"

"What?" he said, curiously turning back around.

"Do you play pool?"

"Um, yeah. It's been a while, but Kevin and I used to play all the time."

"The Rusty Anchor just put in a pool table... if you're interested?"

John paused before saying a word. It was purely out of shock— not hesitation. But just in case he *was* hesitating, Charlotte quickly pointed out, "And I'm not sure if you've eaten yet, but they have the best burgers around. Super greasy, but that's kinda what make them the best."

Still, John said nothing. It wasn't until she tried to give him an out that he spoke.

"You don't have to if you don't want. You probably have some more painting to—"

"No... I don't have any plans. And a greasy burger and pool sounds perfect."

They planned to meet back up at the general at 7:30. This gave them both an opportunity to shower and change. On the drive home, John's mind was racing. He was excited to hang out with Charlotte but was still quite disappointed in himself. *He* should have been the one to ask *her* out. It wasn't until he hopped in the shower that his mindset began to shift. And as the hot water hit his face, he realized it didn't matter who did the asking.

This proved that it wasn't all in his head; she *did* like him. He wasn't sure how high her *like* ranked on the romantic scale, but he knew without a doubt that it ranked way higher than any of the shlubs that were flirting with her earlier. And for now, that was good enough for him.

Seeing as it wasn't a fancy restaurant, John chose to go casual—but nice casual. He put on his nicest pair of jeans and a semi-ironed blue button-down shirt. After much contemplating, he decided to go baseball hat-free. With a liberal amount of gel in his hair, he grabbed his keys and rushed out the door. His next dilemma came about a mile away from the store when his mind did what it does best. It started to sweat the little details.

Am I supposed to go upstairs to get her… like, knock on her door and shit? Or is that too date-like? Maybe I should just sit in the car and wait until she sees that I'm there… or maybe give a honk or two.

By the time he pulled into the parking lot, the only thing he had ruled out was the honking. That would be something those Natty Light-drinking idiots would do.

"Yeah, definitely no honking, John," he said aloud as he put his truck in park. Luckily for him, his poor brain didn't have to stress too much. He had no way of knowing this, but Charlotte had also been sweating the little details.

Do I wait and make him come up to the door to get me? Or do I watch out the window and head down as soon he pulls in? If I do that, I need to make him wait at least a minute or two. I definitely don't want to seem too eager.

In her head, she said a minute or two, but in reality, it was less than thirty seconds before she exited her apartment. John breathed a sigh of relief as he watched her saunter down the side staircase. This would prove to be the most nervous and anxious moment either of them would feel for the rest of the night. As soon as she climbed in his truck and shut the door, everything felt... comfortable.

The Rusty Anchor was busy, and John recognized a bunch of the guys from the store earlier. He thought it was a bit weird that they all purchased twelve-packs of beer at the store, only to spend the night drinking at a bar. As if reading his mind, Charlotte said, "They spend half the night drinking here, and the other half drinking at home. Kind of pathetic, if ya ask me."

"Yup. I was just thinking the same thing," he said, nodding along.

Most of the tables were taken, but Charlotte motioned to two free stools up at the bar. "Are those okay?"

"Yeah, perfect."

The bartender was a cute redhead, who looked to be in her forties.

"Hey, Charlotte. Long time no see."

"Hey, Shannon. Yeah, I've been working a ton lately."

"Is Karen still out?"

"Yeah, but she's due back to work next week."

"That's good. How's your mom doing?"

"She's okay. She's actually out of town for a few days." She smirked then said, "With her new man friend."

"What? Your mom has a boyfriend? How'd that happen?"

"Apparently, it's the magic of eHarmony."

"Ahhh, been there done that. Though, not much luck for me. Have you met him yet?"

"No, not yet, but she hasn't stopped raving about him. I'm not a big fan of online dating sites, but it's been so long since I've seen her this happy, it's hard to argue with it."

"Aw, good for her. She deserves it. You both do." With that, Shannon focused in on John.

"Oh, this is my friend, John. John, this is Shannon. He's here on

115

vacation from Chicago."

"Chicago? Wow. And you chose Applewood?"

Charlotte chuckled. "That's exactly what I said."

John shook his head, and Shannon followed with, "Just kidding. Applewood has its charm… especially if the weather ever gets back to normal. Worst summer I've ever seen here."

"Yup," agreed Charlotte.

Shannon placed two coasters down. "What are guys drinking?"

"A glass of red wine for me," Charlotte quickly answered.

John also answered without hesitation. "Can I just get a Coke… with extra ice, please?"

"You got it. You guys eating? Need a menu?"

"Definitely," Charlotte said, smiling. As soon as Shannon walked away, Charlotte turned to John. "Not sure if you're a beer drinker or not, but they have a great line of craft beers from a brewery up in Portland."

"Actually, I don't drink."

Although he said it matter-of-factly, Charlotte still felt horrible for choosing a bar for their date.

"Oh my God, I'm so sorry. We don't have to stay here. I can find someplace else to—"

"Relax," he said, laughing. "It's not a big deal. Like, not at all. My brother and his wife own a bar right next door to my shop. I hang out there all the time. I've been sober almost seven years now."

"Wow. Good for you."

After a brief moment of silence, Charlotte excused herself to go to the bathroom.

"Breaking the seal already? You haven't even had a drink yet?"

"Ha. Tell that to the large coffee I had about an hour ago. That's probably also why I'm so wired."

John nodded in agreement then watched as she headed off to the bathroom in the back. It wasn't until Shannon placed the drinks in front of him that it hit him. The last time he was here, he was seeking solace in a glass of Jameson. He entered seeking solace but quickly left on babysitting duties for Sara. It had been a long time since he thought about that memory. He laughed to himself as he remembered their walk on the beach that night. Well, *he* was walking. Sara was stumbling her way down the beach. John laughed even louder when he pictured Sara soaked from head to toe after she attempted to jump the four-foot-wide gully. When Charlotte returned from the bathroom, John was still smiling and staring into his drink.

"You're not laughing at me, I hope?"

"What? Oh, no… not at all. Was just thinking of an old memory, that's all."

Charlotte settled herself on the stool and looked down at their drinks, in particular, his Coke. "Are you sure you don't wanna…"

"Seriously, Charlotte, it's fine. I have no desire to drink. But what I do have a desire for is one of these burgers." He pointed down to the small paper menu in front of him.

She cracked a smile. "They really are amazing… and greasy."

They spent the next two hours eating, drinking, and laughing. Charlotte limited herself to one glass of wine before switching to water for the night. She claimed she wasn't much of a drinker and seeing as she needed to be at work bright and early, one glass of wine was all she wanted. John knew she was just being polite and considerate. Two more things to add to his growing list of things he loved about her. So far, there wasn't a thing he didn't like about her.

Eating greasy burgers and playing pool in a bar full of redneck fishermen was a far cry from John's idea of a fancy dinner and a movie. But as he sat there nursing his Coke, he couldn't help but think of a phrase his wacky therapist used to tell him. She used to say: "Just because things don't work out the way you intended, it doesn't mean they don't work out the way they're supposed to."

He chuckled to himself, knowing that once again his hippy-chick therapist was absolutely right. Little did he know at the time, Hope was less than a half mile away. She was sitting in a chair attempting to read, but her reoccurring migraines were making it nearly impossible to concentrate. It would only be a matter of time before they would come face to face with each other.

When John and Charlotte first arrived at the bar, there were at least a dozen people milling around the pool table awaiting their turn. Fortunately, most of the fishermen started their workday well before the sun came up, so it wasn't long before they filtered out and headed home. Like most activities, John was highly competitive when it came to playing pool. He and Kevin had many contentious games back in the day. That being said, John had every intention of taking it easy on Charlotte. The last thing you want to do with a girl you're interested in is to embarrass her in a silly game of pool. It took less than five minutes, however, for John to change his tune. She not only beat him—she destroyed him.

"Are you kidding me?" John said, picking his jaw up from the floor.

She smiled and said, "I had three competitive older brothers growing up... and we had a pool table in the basement."

"Jesus, you're like a little pool shark."

"Nah, I'm not that good."

"Are you kidding me? You didn't just beat me, you dominated me."

Charlotte smirked and couldn't help herself. "That's what she said."

Again, John's jaw dropped. He thought, *She's smart, good looking, sweet, funny, an amazing pool player, AND has a perverted sense of humor? Did I just hit the jackpot or what?* He also thought, *I can't believe I was going to take it easy on her. Game on!*

He looked down at the lone cue ball sitting on the table and announced, "Rematch!"

Charlotte grinned. "Okay, but I'm not gonna go easy on ya."

John's competitive fire was officially lit. He began chalking up his stick, and Charlotte sarcastically murmured, "Loser racks 'em."

Without a word, he placed the chalk down and began racking the balls. Channeling his inner Cobra Kai, he thought to himself, *NO MERCY!*

They played a total of four games that night with John winning one—barely. Despite the beat-down, he was thoroughly enjoying himself.

"You said you have three older brothers?" John asked.

"Yup. I'm the youngest and the only girl in the family."

"Yikes. That doesn't sound fun at all."

"They definitely tortured the hell out of me when I was little, but as soon as I entered my teen years, they turned into the typical over-protective brothers—like, times three."

"That's kind of endearing, don't ya think?"

"When I was much younger maybe but certainly not now. Even to this day, they've been known to spy on my dates."

Suspiciously, John looked around.

"What are you doing?" she asked.

"Just making sure."

"Why, John, are you saying you consider this a date?"

His face turned red. "What? No. I was... I was just being silly, that's all. I definitely wasn't considering this a date."

"Hmm, that's too bad," she said with a shrug then looked away.

John just sat there, unsure what to say. Finally, he said, "Well... I guess it's kind of a date... sorta."

Before any more words could awkwardly fumble out of his mouth, she looked over at him and let him off the hook with a giggle.

"I'm just busting your chops. It's been so long, I'm not even sure I'd remember what a real date looked like. I've only been on a few since my divorce and not one of them made the cut for a second date."

"Well, hopefully I can change that," he said, more confident than awkward.

She looked over at him and held her deadpan look for as long as she could before cracking up laughing. And just like that, his confidence faded. With more than a hint of humility, he grinned and said, "I'm really bad at this flirting thing, huh?"

"You really are," she said, continuing to laugh. "But it's okay, so am I. And yes, this is my awkward way of saying I'd love to go out with you again."

This time, both their faces turned similar shades of red. For as far back as he could remember, he'd always loved the initial getting to know someone stage—the newness stage—awkward flirting and all. It had been a long time since he felt this type of a connection. He felt it immensely with Kristen, and although not as strong, he felt it with Jain. He'd also felt it with Sara, but he wasn't sure that counted, considering Sara was just a ghost… or a figment of his imagination… or… actually, he still had no idea who or what she was.

Over the years, his original Applewood trip had become like a strange blurry dream. There were many times he questioned if any of it ever happened at all. And now, as his mind thought of Sara, he couldn't help but wonder if the same thing would be true of Charlotte. Was *she* just another ghost—another Applewood mirage?

John paused his over-thinking long enough to gaze into Charlotte's eyes. That was all it took for him to decide to keep living in the moment. It didn't matter if she was real or not, he felt a connection and an overwhelming sense of happiness when he was with her, and for now, that's all that mattered. Little did he know, in less than twenty-four hours, their connection was about to go off the charts—in the strangest, most Applewood way possible.

"I'm sorry again about the whole divorce thing. That must have been hard on you."

"The hard part was finding out he was cheating on me. The easy part was kicking his ass out and filing for divorce."

Although she smiled, John knew it was her way of concealing her true feelings. He regretted bringing it up. Partly, because he knew it was probably a sore subject, but mostly, he didn't want his question to prompt her to ask if he'd ever been married. Even though he'd gained quite a bit of healing and closure since the accident, he was still hesitant to talk about it, especially to someone he just met.

"So, have you lived here in Applewood all your life?" John asked, attempting to move the topic away from marriage.

"Yes, sir. I'm a true islander through and through. Although, I'm the only sibling in my family still living here. Pathetic, I know."

"I wouldn't call it pathetic. Not at all. This place is beautiful."

She shrugged and said, "I used to think this was the most beautiful place on earth, but... but it's changed over the years, especially recently. It's run down... vacant... and totally depressing."

"There are a lot of houses that could use some TLC, and I did notice a ton of For Sale signs, but I'm not sure I'd call this place depressing. It's probably just the stretch of weather you've been having."

"I can't really explain it, but trust me, it goes well beyond just the crummy weather."

From the moment John returned to Applewood, he had also felt this change she spoke of. It was hard to explain it exactly, but it was an eerie and depressing feeling.

"So, where are your brothers living now?" he asked.

"Boston... Vermont... and one is in upstate New York. All married. And all have kids. All except me," she said with a sad smile. "Anyway, enough about me, I wanna hear more about you."

John tensed up. He felt comfortable with Charlotte, but he wasn't ready to go into details about Kristen... or Hannah. Instead, he started talking about his woodworking business.

"That's sounds cool. Do you have any pictures of your work?"

John thought a second then pulled out his phone. "Actually, I do."

He showed her picture after picture of some of his projects over the years.

"Wow. You're very talented. Wait—who's that?" she asked, pointing to his phone.

"Oh, that's my brother, Kevin."

"Older or younger?"

"He's a year younger."

"Nice. Do you have any other siblings?"

"Nope… just Kevin." John started getting nervous that her next question would revolve around whether he'd ever been married before. He certainly didn't want their night to end, but he panicked and blurted out, "Whoa, it's almost midnight. You're gonna be exhausted tomorrow."

She looked down at her watch and sighed. "Yeah. I guess I should probably head home and get some sleep."

John hated that he caused their *date* to end prematurely, but he nodded and said, "I'll go settle up the check, and then we can get out of here."

"It's all set."

"What?"

"I paid it when you went to the bathroom."

"Charlotte, you didn't have to do that."

"It's not a big deal. This was my idea anyway. Besides, it's the least I can do for embarrassing you all night on the pool table."

If Kevin had said that, John might have punched him in the face, but coming from Charlotte, it had a different effect. Quite the opposite effect. He knew he was totally smitten with this woman, but for the first time since they met, he was thinking seriously about kissing her. He wasn't thinking about a tongue-filled passionate kiss. Well, maybe a little. But mostly, he was thinking about a *simple* goodnight kiss. It consumed his mind the entire ride back to the general store, and as it turned out, it was far from simple.

Charlotte had taken the initiative in asking John out, but that's where she drew the line. She desperately wanted him to kiss her, but she was determined to let *him* make the first move. Unfortunately, he didn't. His anxiety got the better of him, and he chickened out.

It wasn't entirely a lost cause. John thanked her for a fun night and suggested they do it again sometime. She responded with,

"Absolutely. I would love to."

It wasn't a goodnight kiss, but it was something. Something he could build on. Normally, he would have spent the rest of the night berating himself for not kissing her, but he decided to turn over a new leaf and look at things in a more positive light. He might not have had the courage to kiss her, but at least he didn't offer a handshake this time. He considered this a small victory. He didn't know it at the time, but a much larger victory was looming ahead. Even more than that, a much larger surprise was in store as well.

10

As usual, the next morning John drove over to the store for his coffee and muffin. And as usual, it was rainy, foggy, and extremely windy. When he arrived at the store, it looked unusually dark. There didn't appear to be any lights on at all.

Oh, shit! I bet Charlotte overslept, he thought, and felt guilty for keeping her out so late. With his hands cupped around his eyes, he peered into the store. It was completely dark. Just for the heck of it, he tried the door. To his surprise, it was unlocked.

"Hello?" he called out.

"Sorry… power is out… we're closed," Charlotte yelled from the back.

"Charlotte?"

"John? Is that you?" she said, returning from the back.

"No power, huh?"

"Nope. It's been out for about an hour now."

"That sucks. Are you waiting around until it comes back on?"

"I was going to, but one of our regulars just told me they heard it would probably be late afternoon before it's restored. If that's the case, I guess there's no sense in me kicking around."

Without hesitation, John surprised himself by asking, "Do you wanna do something today?"

Equally surprised, Charlotte paused. Her pause caused John to nervously say, "Although... you probably want to go back to bed and get some rest, huh?"

"Nah. Once I'm up, I'm up. What do you have in mind?"

He didn't go to the store that morning with the plan of asking her out, and he certainly didn't expect her to say yes if he did. But now that she had agreed, he was at a loss for what to suggest.

"Umm," was all he could muster.

"Want me to help you do some painting?" she asked.

"What? Oh, no, you don't need to spend your day off helping me paint."

"I don't mind," she said matter-of-factly. "I actually enjoy it. Well, interior painting, that is. I wouldn't volunteer if it was exterior. I'm not a fan of ladders."

John smiled and said, "Me neither."

"Okay then, let me tie up a few things here, and then I'll go change into my paint clothes and meet you over at your place."

John was about to reiterate that she really didn't have to help him paint, but his inner voice emphatically told him to shut the hell up and to just go with it. He didn't realize it until he caught himself in the rearview mirror, but he spent the entire drive back to William's with a giant smile on his face.

Ironically, the same thing was happening with Charlotte. As she slipped on a baggy sweatshirt and pair of old ripped jeans, she caught herself smiling in the mirror. They say if you start your day off with a smile, it's a sign that you're going to have a good day. If that's true, then John and Charlotte both knew they were about to have an amazing day. What they didn't know was that there'd be a major bombshell dropped later in the night.

When she arrived at William's, she came bearing gifts. As John opened the door, he curiously gazed down at the large cardboard box in her hands. Inside the box was a small coffee maker and a can of coffee.

"What's this?" he asked, grinning.

"I assumed you didn't have a coffee maker here or else you wouldn't make the drive to our store every morning."

Charlotte didn't say it, but by now she had a sneaking suspicion that John's early morning trips had just as much to do with seeing her as it did getting his coffee.

"And they're not my famous homemade muffins," she said, pointing to an assortment of Hostess pastries, "but I figured these are better than nothing."

John took the box from her and further examined its contents.

"You brought sugar and cream? And coffee cups? Jesus, you thought of everything."

She shrugged. "I figured you didn't have any of this stuff, so…"

"Thank you. It's very sweet of you."

"Eh, not a big deal. Besides, it's just as much for me as you. I haven't had my caffeine yet today."

"Well then, let's go make some coffee."

She followed him into the kitchen and couldn't help but notice him looking at her outfit.

"Ignore the old ratty clothes," she said. "I know I look like crap, but these are the best painting clothes I could find."

John laughed and told her she looked fine, but what he really wanted to say was she looked beyond fine. He especially loved how she pulled her ponytail through the back of her tattered and faded Red Sox hat. The only thing that would have made it better was if it were the Cubs. He made it a point to comment on her hat. In particular, he mentioned how jealous he was that not only had the Red Sox broke their long-standing curse and had won the World Series, but they had done it twice in the last six years.

"If only we could break *our* stupid curse now," he said, wryly.

Charlotte explained that one of her brothers gave her the hat years ago, and she confessed that she wasn't really a big Red Sox fan or big into sports. She was much too cute and sweet for John to even think of holding that against her.

After making them each a cup of coffee, he showed her the rooms he had already painted. She was surprisingly impressed, even though she was the one who picked out the colors. They decided the living room would be first on their list. There wasn't a lot in the way of furniture, but what there was they pushed into the middle of the room. They spread out a tarp along the back wall and began what would be a full morning and early afternoon of painting. By the time 2pm came around, they had painted every room downstairs except for the kitchen. The kitchen walls were covered in wallpaper, and although outdated, John didn't want to overstep his welcome by removing it.

When they were finished, they wandered through the house admiring their handywork. As a proud, accomplished feeling washed over them, Charlotte smiled and said, "Wow. It's amazing how a fresh coat of paint can completely transform a room."

"A room? I think it transformed the entire house. I just hope Rachel doesn't mind what I've done."

In his heart, he had a feeling Rachel *and* William would most definitely approve of the new color schemes.

"I don't know about you, but this girl could use some food right about now," Charlotte said, rubbing her stomach.

"Agreed."

They spent the next ten minutes cleaning up their brushes, rollers, and paint trays. When they were finished, they headed out in search of some food. Unfortunately, the power on the other side of town was still out, so the diner remained closed. Charlotte suggested driving over to Gerrish Falls for lunch.

They found a quaint little café in the downtown area, and when they were done with their meal, John suggested they continue their day by taking a drive further up the coast.

"Although, I totally understand if you're sick of hanging out with me… or if you have other things to get done today."

He had no idea why he always said stupid shit like that. He knew better than to follow up a suggestion by giving her an opportunity to back out. Luckily, he didn't get a chance to be too hard on himself.

"I think a drive up the coast would be perfect," she said, completely ignoring his last comment.

They gassed up and began driving north on Route 1. It didn't take long before the grey skies broke, and the sun appeared. Even the temperature went up by at least twenty degrees. They spent most of the afternoon meandering through one coastal town after another. They drove up through Ogunquit and made it as far as Harpswell before turning around. On their way back, Charlotte took him to L.L. Bean.

"Ya can't visit Maine without stopping by the Bean… or without having a Maine lobster. You have had one of those, haven't you?" His look told her differently. "Seriously? I guess we need to change that."

On their way home, she made it a point to stop in Kennebunkport for John's first-ever Maine lobster dinner. Despite his best objections, Charlotte slipped the waitress her credit card and paid for the entire meal.

"It's not a big deal, John. You paid for lunch."

"That was sandwiches at a café. This was dinner… an *expensive* dinner."

"Seriously, it's fine. I tell ya what, you can get it next time."

He started to respond but didn't quite know what to say. All that was going through his head was, *Next time? She wants there to be a next time!* On the inside, he was smiling and practically jumping for joy, but he made sure his outside remained cool, calm, and collected.

"Fine. I'll get it next time," he said as nonchalantly as he could.

Without even realizing it, both their faces were beaming as they walked out of the restaurant and climbed into John's truck. On the ride home, there wasn't as much conversation as earlier. It wasn't for lack of topics or because of any uncomfortableness with each other. It had been a long day, and with the radio now turned on, they both sat back and just enjoyed the ride. As soon as they crossed over the causeway into Applewood, they were greeted with a light mist, which was followed by a looming layer of fog.

John shook his head and said, "It's like the bad weather is directly hanging over the island and nowhere else."

"Yup. It totally feels like that."

Charlotte's car was still at John's place, and as they passed by the general store, she noticed a couple of lights on.

"Looks like we got power back."

"That's good. What time is your mom coming home?"

"She's not. I wasn't sure when the power would be back on, so I called her and told her she might as well stay another night. She said she'd be back to relieve me sometime tomorrow morning."

It was just after nine when John parked alongside Charlotte's car. He wanted desperately for the date to continue. And yes, in his head he considered this a date. But seeing as they had just hung out for twelve hours straight, he didn't want to push his luck by asking for more.

As his car remained idling, Charlotte asked, "Any big plans the rest of the night?"

"Well, seeing as there's no TV at my place, I'll probably spend another wild and crazy night playing cards against myself."

"Ah. Hopefully you win," she said, smirking. Before John had a chance to come up with a reply, she surprised him by asking, "If you want, you can come up and watch a movie or something." She then threw one of his own lines at him. "Although, I totally understand if you're sick of hanging out with me… or if you have other things to get done tonight."

He wasn't sure if she also considered this a date or not, but at this point, it didn't even matter. He let out a laugh, and without hesitating or overthinking, he answered, "I would love a movie night." And for good measure, he added, "And no, I'm definitely not sick of you yet."

By now, it was dark enough outside and in the car for John not to notice her blushing. He told her he had to take care of a few things and that he'd be over shortly. The first thing he did when he entered the house was rip off his shirt. After being in the car most of the day, he was sticky and sweaty. He thought about taking a quick shower but figured that would seem like he was trying to impress her a little too much. He rushed into the bathroom and grabbed his stick of Old Spice. One by one, he lifted his arms and heavily caked the deodorant to his pits. Seeing as he didn't pack any cologne for his trip, he applied the deodorant to the rest of his body. After tossing on a new shirt, he vigorously began brushing his teeth. He'd been out of the dating game for a long time, but back in his day, when a girl asked you to come over to her place, it usually meant there'd be good chance of kissing being involved—if not more. Maybe times had changed, and maybe she legitimately wanted to just watch a movie, but either way, he wanted to be fully prepared.

When he finished brushing his teeth and buttoning up his shirt, he gave himself a quick pep talk in the mirror then drove straight over to Charlotte's. As she opened the door, John did his best from cracking a smile. Not only was she wearing completely different clothes, but her hair was still wet.

"I was so sticky from being in the car all day, I had to take a quick shower. Sorry, I'm just gonna go finish drying my hair… make yourself at home."

"Yeah, of course. No need to apologize."

Charlotte walked down the small hallway and into the bathroom. John made his way over to the couch and wiped his sweaty palms on his jeans. *Yup, there's definitely gonna be some kissing tonight,* he thought, more nervous than excited.

A few minutes later, she entered the living room. She looked *and* smelled amazing. Both of their hearts were racing.

"Do you want something to drink?" she nervously asked.

"Um, sure."

"I'm not sure what we have," she said, disappearing into the small kitchen. A second later, she called out, "All we have is water, orange juice, and Diet Coke. Oh... we also have cream soda."

"Cream soda would be perfect," he yelled back.

She was tempted to pour herself a tall glass of wine to help calm her nerves, but ultimately decided against it. She entered the living room carrying two bottles of Capt'n Eli's Cream Soda and a box of Chicken in a Biskit. For the moment, John's nervousness disappeared.

"Wow. Cream soda *and* Chicken in a Biskit? You certainly know the way to a man's heart."

"Really? That's all it takes, huh?" She giggled as she handed him his drink.

"That's all it takes with this guy anyway. My brother and I love these things. Our foster mother introduced us to them."

"Oh, I didn't know you grew up in a foster home."

"Three of them, actually."

"Really? I'm sorry," she said, telling herself not to pry any further.

"It's okay. It is what it is." The topic didn't affect him like it used to, but still, he was eager to change the subject. "Cheers," he said, raising his bottle. "To an extremely fun day."

"Cheers," she replied, clinking his bottle. "It was a fun day. I almost forgot what those were like."

"You and me both," he said, taking a swig of cream soda.

Just then, her cellphone rang.

"Oh, I gotta take this. It's my mom."

"Of course."

As she answered the phone, she walked back into the kitchen for privacy. While she was in there, John stood up and began wandering around the living room. The walls were plastered with framed pictures of Charlotte and her brothers. They ranged from newborn pictures all the way up to present day. There were three 8x10 pictures in a row of Charlotte's brothers and their brides taken on each of their wedding days. There appeared to be an 8x10 spot missing, and John assumed it used to contain Charlotte's wedding picture. They hadn't talked much about her ex, but he could only imagine how hard it was to go through a divorce. Just to the right of the wedding pictures was a smaller and much older photo. It was a little girl dressed in a pink tutu and ballet slippers. Her black hair was up in a tight bun, and she appeared to be doing a pirouette. He assumed it was Charlotte, but he leaned in for a closer examination.

"Yeah, yeah, that's me," Charlotte said, reentering the living room.

John turned, and with a big smile said, "A ballerina, huh?"

"Ha. Far from it. I took lessons for a total of three months."

"You didn't like it?"

"Not really. My mother kinda forced me into it. I was horrible at it. I'm the biggest klutz ever."

"I'm sure you weren't that bad."

"I fell three times during our recital."

John shrugged. "So? That's not—"

"Off the stage. I fell off the stage three times."

John did his best to fight back his laughter. "Well, ballet isn't for everyone, I guess." He continued scanning the photos on the wall. "Ohhh, what do we have here?" His eyes fixated on a collage of tiny pictures of Charlotte. It was every school picture from kindergarten through high school.

"Oh God! Do not look at that!"

"How can I not?" he said, giving it a closer look. "That's some sweet hair styles… and some interesting fashion statements, too."

Charlotte shook her head, covering her face with her hands. "My mother calls this her wall of memories, but what it really is, is a wall of shame."

"Nah. You were cute… in a big hair sorta way. Although, I think those shoulder pads are bigger than some football players I know."

"Ok, ok, enough. Let's just pick a movie and pretend none of these exist," she said, motioning to the wall.

"Trust me, this is way more entertaining than any movie could ever be."

John continued walking around the living room, and Charlotte was resigned to sitting on the couch and cringing as he looked at one embarrassing photo after another.

"Almost done yet?" she asked, wishing she would have poured herself a big glass of wine.

Figuring he'd let her off the hook, John began walking back towards the couch, but just before he sat down, a 5x7 framed photo caught his eye on one of the end tables.

"Is that you?"

Somberly, she nodded and said, "I had just turned two."

The photo was of two-year-old Charlotte sitting on the shoulders of a dark-haired man with a classic 70s mustache and beard. Up until that point, Charlotte hadn't mentioned her father, nor had John felt comfortable enough to ask. But looking at the photo, he just couldn't help himself.

"Is that your father?" he hesitantly asked, gauging her reaction.

With her eyes now fixated on the photo, she slowly replied, "Yeah. He died not long after that picture was taken."

John's heart sank, and he felt horrible for even asking.

"Oh, Charlotte, I'm... I'm so sorry."

"It's okay. It was a long time ago. Ironically, as much I make fun of my mother for having all these pictures, they're the only thing I have to remember him by. I was much too young to have any memories of him... any *real* memories that is."

"What do you mean by real memories?"

"I don't have any memories of when he was alive, but..."

"But what?"

"It's stupid. Just forget it."

"No, tell me, Charlotte."

After a long hesitation. She stared down at the photo and said, "When I was little, I used to have the freakiest dreams about him. Well, it was actually the same dream over and over and over."

"What was it about?"

Charlotte wasn't used to opening up, especially regarding that particular dream. Even when she was married, she never once mentioned it to her husband. Until recently, she hadn't had the dream since she was a kid. She, like Kevin, had simply repressed it all these years, so she never saw the point in talking about it to anyone. But now, as she sat there on the couch, she realized John wasn't just anyone. She felt a connection and a sense of comfortability with him. After a deep exhale, she hesitantly told him about the dream.

Instantly, John noticed the resemblances to Kevin's dream were uncanny: the pitch-black ocean, the huge pounding waves, trying to call out but can't. From what John could tell, the only difference between her dream and Kevin's was Charlotte could see her father's face in the dream, and the faces in Kevin's were blurred. The only thing she failed to mention was the phrase her father kept calling out—*Help her to help us.* If she had revealed that, it would have completely floored John. As it was, he was a little freaked out at the similarities of the two dreams.

"Wow. That's super weird," he said.

"I know, right?"

"No, it's weird because my brother used to have a very similar dream. Except, there were *two* drowning people in his, and they were both faceless."

"That sounds creepy."

"Yeah. Kevin gets freaked out by it."

"Does he still have it… the dream?"

"He said it went away when he was younger, but I guess he recently started having it again."

Charlotte didn't respond, and she certainly didn't reveal that she also had started having the dream again. Charlotte and Kevin's dreams were eerily similar, but both John and Charlotte decided to chalk it up as merely a coincidence.

Charlotte lifted the framed photo of her and her father and sadly spoke. "Like I said, I was much too young to have any real memories of him... pictures are all I have to remember him by."

John's mind raced to his own parents. He also had no real memories of them. The only things he had were the photos and brief stories provided to him by Mary. Even though he could totally relate to her, he had no intention of revealing any of that to Charlotte. Once again, he scrambled to switch topics, but it was too late. The bombshell of all bombshells was about to emit from her lips.

"My only real knowledge of him is from what others have told me. Apparently, he was quite the popular guy around here, and it seems everyone has at least one or two stories about him. At first, it was a little depressing and difficult hearing their stories, but now I take comfort in them. I know Applewood is just a small island, but it still amazes me how many people he came in contact with—and how many beautiful impressions he made on them. Some people told me stories about going to school with him... some recalled how much they loved seeing him play at the Rusty Anchor. He was the lead singer in a sixties cover band."

Charlotte paused and laughed.

"I also heard stories about my mother giving angry glares to any groupies who even attempted to flirt with him. And if you knew my mother, you'd know her glares were just as effective as a punch in the face."

Warmly, John smiled and continued listening to Charlotte talk about her father.

"And it seems that almost everyone on the island had flown with him at least once."

"Flown with him?" John curiously asked.

"Yeah, he loved to fly planes. He owned his own company called Island Air Tours. Actually, that photo was taken out in front of the airstrip."

John's jaw dropped and chills shot up his arms—up his whole body. It was his face turning a pale white that caught Charlotte's attention.

"John? Are you okay? You look like—"

"Your father is Kyle Blaisdell?"

Slowly, she nodded and asked, "How do you know his name?"

It had been a while, but John had read and reread the newspaper article regarding his parents and the plane crash. One particular sentence flashed through his mind: *He left behind a wife and four children.* Before Charlotte had a chance to repeat her question, John thought to himself, *Four children… Charlotte and her three brothers.*

"Seriously, John, what's going on? You're starting to freak me out here."

"Your father was the pilot who died in the plane crash, wasn't he?"

She nodded, assuming he heard the story from one of the islanders.

"That's how *my* parents died," he said, sitting down next to her.

Shocked, she looked over at John and asked, "Your parents died in a plane crash, too?" Her shock was about to be multiplied by a hundred.

"Not just any plane… they died on your father's plane… they were his passengers."

This time it was Charlotte's face that turned white. Goosebumps ran up her arms. John wasn't the only one who had read the article over and over. When Charlotte was eight, she discovered a cardboard box buried in the back of her mother's closet. It contained all sorts of memories of her father. The box was filled with old letters, photos, and sentimental trinkets he had given to her mother. It also contained the newspaper article about the crash. Charlotte never told her mother, but she swiped the newspaper and hid it in her room. Over the years, she must have read it a hundred times, if not more. Eventually, when she was a teenager, she did the exact same thing her mother had done. She placed the newspaper in a box and buried it in the back of her closet. Even though it had been over twenty-five years since she'd laid eyes on the article, she still had every word memorized.

A sick feeling entered the pit of her stomach as she recalled one of the lines: *His two passengers, Robert and Caitlin Mathews of Chicago were also killed in the crash.*

"The Mathews were your parents?" she said, more doubting than anything. "This is a joke, right?" Her tone was becoming angrier. "Just a sick and twisted joke! Well, it's not funny! Not at—"

Before she could get up and storm away, John grabbed her hand. "Charlotte, I'm not joking. I swear." He quickly reached into his pocket and pulled out his wallet. After nervously fumbling with it, he showed her his license. "See, John *Mathews.* Robert and Caitlin were my parents."

Her hand was trembling, but she remained standing there, allowing John his attempt at an explanation.

"Apparently, they used to vacation here when we were little. I was only three when it happened." He tightened his grip. "July 20th, 1975."

Between his tight grip and the seriousness in his eyes, she knew he was telling the truth.

"I think I need to sit," she said, becoming lightheaded.

John led her back to the couch and slid closer to her. Neither of them knew what to say, so they both just sat there in silence. Finally, Charlotte spoke. "This has to be the craziest, most insane coincidence ever."

John nodded and once again they sat in silence. Their minds were spinning a mile a minute. After a while, Charlotte stood up and began pacing around the room. She eventually made her way back over to the framed photo of her and her father. Clutching it in her hands, she sadly spoke, "Photographs… that's all I have… that's it."

"Yeah, me too. No memories, just photos. We didn't even find out what really happened to our parents until seven years ago."

Charlotte cocked her head and raised an eyebrow. "What? Really? I don't understand."

Not wanting to go into detail, he gave her the abridged version.

"Like I said before, Kevin and I grew up in foster care. Three homes total. And up until recently, we thought our real parents had just abandoned us."

"Oh my God, John. That's horrible." Charlotte placed the picture back onto the table and then returned to her spot on the couch next to John. "So… how did you find out the truth?"

A slight smile formed as he gazed into her eyes. "I'll be honest with you, Charlotte. I really enjoy hanging out with you, and I would love to go on another date… or whatever this is, but…"

"But what?"

"But I'm afraid if I tell you the truth, there's no way you'd go out with me again. Even worse, you'd probably have me committed."

The thought of John wanting another date caused Charlotte to grin, and for a moment, the seriousness was broken up.

"I promise I won't have you committed. And I'd say as of now, there's a pretty good chance of us going on another date."

John felt a strange yet powerful connection to her; a connection that went beyond just the plane crash. But even though he felt extremely comfortable with her, there was no way he could tell her everything, could he?

"Seriously, John," she said, reaching over and touching his leg. "I promise I won't laugh… or judge… or think you're crazy. Please, tell me how you found out about your parents and the plane crash?"

Any hesitation he might have had, completely fell by the wayside as he looked into Charlotte's eyes. It was at that point that John knew he needed to tell her everything. He needed to tell her every crazy, magical, and unexplainable thing that had happened to him, including

William, Clarence, Mary, Medillia's Lament—everything. He even told her about the reoccurring dreams he used to have of Applewood.

As John told one fantastical story after another, she sat back and listened but didn't say a word. Although she was politely attentive, some of her facial expressions led John to believe she thought he was off his rocker. Even so, he didn't stop there. He spent the rest of the night talking about his past: the foster families, Kristen, Hannah, and the accident. Ironically, the last time he had revealed so much was right here in Applewood. It was with Sara by the campfire. This time it was far less emotional. He'd already found his peace and closure with everything.

There were so many things spoken and so many emotions felt, by the time 2am rolled around, they were both left speechless. It was their first and longest lull of the entire night. Charlotte literally had no idea what to say. Her heart broke for him—for everything he had gone through in his life: being in foster care, the O'Neils, and the tragic accident that took his wife and daughter. As much as she tried, she couldn't find the words to express how sorry she felt for him. She also couldn't find the words to describe how she felt about everything else he told her regarding the strange magic of Applewood. It was hard enough to believe that John had conversations with actual ghosts, never mind everything he told her about meeting the teenage version of William, which eventually caused the course of William's life (and Rachel's) to change drastically.

The lull in conversation lasted a solid ten minutes. John's quietness was partly because he was emotionally exhausted from doing most of the talking throughout the night. He was also still reeling from finding out that her father was the pilot, not to mention the fact that Charlotte's and Kevin's dreams were eerily similar. The entire time he was telling her about all the strange occurrences of Medillia's Lament, Charlotte didn't have much to say. Judging by some of her expressions, John assumed she thought he was making it all up. She never came out and said it, but he figured she was just being polite.

There are comfortable silences, and then there are uncomfortable and awkward ones. After the ten-minute mark, it turned more uncomfortable and awkward than not. Neither of them had a clue what to say next, and the thought of a goodnight kiss was the last thing on either of their minds. It was John who finally broke the silence. He gave an exaggerated yawn then said, "I should probably hit the road. You have to get up in a few hours."

Charlotte looked over at the clock, sighed, and then nodded in agreement. Even as she walked him to the door, she still had no idea what to say. There were no words to express what had been revealed over the last four or five hours. "Thanks for today," was the only comment Charlotte could manage.

John's parting words weren't much better. "Yeah, it was… *interesting*." With that, he opened the door and left.

11

Neither of them got a wink of sleep that night. Their lame parting comments were just one of many things that keep them tossing and turning. At one point, John's thoughts turned to his brother. He needed to tell him that Charlotte's father was the pilot of the plane. Even more than that, he needed to tell Kevin that Charlotte was having the same exact dream as him. But how? How was he going to do it? Should he do it over the phone? Or maybe he should just head back to Chicago and tell him face to face. But if he did the latter, he would probably want to leave Applewood sooner than later. The more he thought about it, the more he knew he wasn't ready to leave—not yet. As strange and uncomfortable as last night was, John still felt an attraction to Charlotte. If anything, their weird, coincidental connection only added to it.

Charlotte didn't even bother climbing into bed, for she knew it was only three short hours until she had to get up and open the store. She spent most of her time pacing around the apartment. Her mind was racing a mile a minute, not the least of which was how she handled John's confessions of what went down the last time he was in Applewood. She barely said a word to him and was sure her facial expressions told John that she didn't believe a thing he was saying. As she paced, she tried to justify her initial reaction.

I mean, why would I believe him? What he was telling me was like a cross between It's a Wonderful Life and Back to the Future. Who in their right mind would believe that? Yup, there's no way I should feel bad about not believing him.

She plopped herself onto the couch, let out a big sigh, and said aloud, "Except... except I do believe him. Who in their right mind who make up something like that?"

Charlotte had met plenty of people (especially guys) who were either full of shit or a bit touched in the brain. Her gut feeling told her John wasn't one of them. *There are too many coincidences for him to be full of shit*, she thought. *His parents being on my dad's plane... his brother having the same dream as me... not to mention, the fact that we just happened to meet and hit it off.*

Again, she let out a sigh and knew she owed John an apology. He opened up about so many personal things to her. He put his heart on his sleeve and his credibility on the line, and all she could muster was, "Thanks for today."

Placing her hands over her face, she loudly mumbled, "Ugh!"

If she didn't have to open the store in less than an hour, she would have driven right over to John's house and apologized. Instead, she crossed her fingers and hoped he would show his face at the store this morning as he usually did. She picked herself up off the couch and made her way into the bathroom for a long, hot shower. As the water hit her face, she promised herself if John showed up at the store, she would most definitely give him a heartfelt apology.

Similar thoughts ran through John's mind as he continued to toss and turn in bed. He was sure Charlotte assumed he was a giant nutjob. *I can't blame her*, he thought. *Who the hell would believe that? I shoulda just kept my stupid mouth shut.* Before his eyes briefly closed, he told himself he needed to give this poor girl some space. There was no way he could show his face at the general store or the diner, for that matter—at least not for a while.

Just as the sun was coming up, John finally dozed off. Unfortunately, his sleep lasted less than two hours. He was awakened by an annoying pounding sound outside—more specifically, a pecking sound. He tried to throw the pillow over his head, but the pecking only got louder and more frequent.

"Jesus Christ!" he yelled, throwing the pillow across the room.

John grabbed a hoodie and made his way downstairs. Not only was the pecking even louder than upstairs, but it seemed to be coming from the backyard. He put on his sneakers and walked out onto the deck. The pecking echoed throughout the yard and seemed to be coming from a large pine tree in the far-left corner by the shed.

John rubbed his tired eyes and did his best to focus on where the pecking was coming from. And there, about twenty-five feet up, he spotted a woodpecker. For whatever reason, his mind flashed back to when he was eleven. He and Kevin had made makeshift slingshots and were shooting at a tree off in the distance. John remembered nailing the tree nine out of ten times. If only he had that slingshot now, he'd certainly shut that annoying woodpecker up.

His mind also flashed back to the last time he was in Applewood and had that rock-throwing contest with Sara's son, Ben. No matter what the weapon of choice was, John knew he was an expert marksman. He didn't need a slingshot to scare this bird off, all he needed was a rock. And yes, all he wanted to do was *scare* the bird off, not harm it. He was exhausted and annoyed, but he could never harm a living creature.

He leaned over the railing, trying to find the perfect rock to use, but the grass was much too thick and high to see a thing on the ground. As if taunting him, the bird let out its longest and loudest peck yet.

John was just about to yell at the woodpecker but paused when he heard a familiar voice behind him.

"Beautiful bird but annoying as hell."

Startled, John spun around. On the opposite side of the deck was Clarence. He stood with his back against the railing, wearing a big smile on his face. He was also wearing the same exact clothes as the last time.

Oh shit… here we go again, John thought to himself.

"Clarence?"

The old fisherman made his way across the deck and reached his hand out towards John. "Nice to see ya again, young fella."

John shook his hand but said nothing. Most people would be questioning how it was possible to have a conversation with a ghost. John was beyond that. He was simply trying to wrap his mind around how it was possible to physically feel and shake a ghost's hand.

"I knew you'd come back to Applewood one day," Clarence said, pulling a cigar and lighter from his pocket. After lighting it, he offered one to John.

"No thanks," he said softly.

"Yeah, probably for the best. It's a nasty habit. I quit years ago but recently picked it back up." He released a puff of smoke into the air and before John could formulate an actual sentence, Clarence looked up at the house and said, "I like what ya did to the place. It looks good. Is that gazebo your handy work, too?"

John nodded and looked up at the house and around the yard. It felt like forever ago, yet it also felt like it was just yesterday he was here doing the repairs. Of course, at the time he didn't realize this place belonged not only to William but to Clarence and Mary as well.

"I didn't really do that much," John finally said.

"I think you underestimate your abilities. You accomplished quite a bit the last time you were here. You understand that, right?"

"To be honest, Clarence, I'm still not sure what the hell happened the last time I was here. Ever since I got back to Chicago and found out that you and Mary were…"

"Dead?" Clarence said matter-of-factly.

John slowly nodded and said, "I've been trying to understand it ever since."

Clarence took another puff then smiled and asked, "Come up with any answers?"

John shrugged then thought for a moment. "Well, I once read that sometimes when people die with so much regret and unfinished business that they can't move on to the next world until everything is forgiven and made right."

"You read correctly."

John looked directly over at Clarence and said, "William wrote those words."

A proud yet sad smile formed on Clarence's face. "I always knew my son was talented with words. I knew it... but I never told him."

"Trust me, Clarence, he knew... he knew."

The old fisherman nodded his appreciation then looked away as John continued to speak.

"I'm not the smartest guy in the world... not by a long shot, actually... but my gut kept telling me that one of the reasons I was here last time was to help you and Mary move on to heaven... or the next world... or wherever you ghosts go."

Clarence grinned. "You're smarter than you give yourself credit for, John. And your gut was right... you *did* help Mary move on. She's in a much better place now, and it's all because of you."

"I don't know about that. I didn't really do much."

"Once again, you underestimate your ability... and your gift."

Uncomfortable with receiving compliments, John lowered his eyes down to the floorboards of the deck. That's when it hit him. "Wait... but what about you? Why are *you* still here? Shouldn't you have moved on, too?"

"That's a bit more complicated, my friend. The short answer is I can't... I can't move on from here."

"What's the long answer then?"

Clarence took another puff and let out a huge billow of smoke. "You're gonna think I'm crazy," he said in John's direction.

"Are you serious? I'm talking to a cigar-smoking ghost. I think I'm the one who should be questioning my own sanity here."

"Good point," Clarence said, letting out a chuckle. "The last time you were here you experienced some of the magic this island has to offer."

"I'd say. I still don't think my brother completely believes me about what I experienced here."

"This island is most definitely magical, but what you might not know is this island also has a dark side to it... an Evil Spirit, if you will."

"An Evil Spirit?"

"It used to reside in the heart of the island, until one day it was banished from here and sent to the depths of the ocean. It's been there ever since, biding its time. Since then, it's been slowly making its way back to the island. But recently, it seems the process has sped up. The island looks and feels differently from the last time you were here, doesn't it?"

John thought for a moment and nodded.

"It's become darker... more depressing. As if the life is being sucked out of the island."

"And you think that's caused by this Evil Spirit?" John asked.

"I do. The Evil Spirit poisons everything it comes in contact with... eventually killing it. And if that's not bad enough, once dead, it prevents the soul from moving on."

"Wait a second," John interrupted. "Are you telling me that anyone who has ever come in contact with this Evil Spirit thingy has not only died, but their soul is trapped here on the island?"

Clarence dipped his head in agreement. "When my boat capsized during that big storm, I was determined to swim for as long and far as I could. Unfortunately, the waves were much too big... the sea much too rough. I didn't get but twenty feet and was already exhausted and out of breath. I could see the lighthouse off in the distance... its red light piercing through the rain and fog. Just when I was about to give it another go, I felt it. It was like a painful jolt was being shot right through me, nearly paralyzing my entire body."

"What happened?" John asked, completely engaged in Clarence's tragic tale.

"With the last bit of energy I had, I shook free and swam towards the light. I was no longer thinking about what had just poisoned me... all I was thinking about was Mary... and the final argument we had.

The next thing I knew, I blacked out. And when I awoke, I was laying in the cove with my busted-up boat next to me."

"Were you… dead?"

"Dead as a doornail. It's hard to explain it, but I knew right away that I was no longer alive. I also knew I was trapped there… in the cove."

"Wow," was all John could muster.

"There are others here that are just like me… many others. They're trapped… just wandering around hoping to one day move on."

"You can see them… the others?"

Clarence glanced around the yard. "No, but I can feel them."

"So, you're all on different planes? Different dimensions?"

Clarence shrugged. "Your guess is as good as mine. I suppose I should probably consider myself lucky, though."

"Why do you say that?"

"I was at least able to make it back to the island. A lot of people didn't, and now they're forever stuck out in the ocean in the area known as the Dark Waters."

"The Dark Waters?"

Clarence laughed. "I told you this would be quite the unbelievable story."

"You weren't lying," John said with a smile.

Clarence's laughter faded, and as he locked eyes with John, he quietly spoke. "I do owe you a huge debt of gratitude, son."

"For what?"

"For your kindness… and for helping Mary move on from this place."

"I still don't know what I did."

"For better or worse, most people don't realize the power of their words… or their actions. Mary was only stuck here because her guilt wouldn't let her move on. She's in a much better place now, and I have *you* to thank for that."

147

Once again, John was uncomfortable with Clarence's compliment, and once again, he lowered head. "I'm sorry I couldn't do the same for you, Clarence," John said with his eyes glued to the ground.

"Are you kidding me? You helped me fix my boat. I might not have been able to move on from here like Mary, but at least now I can sail in and around the cove area. Until you showed up, I couldn't even do that."

Just then, a couple of squirrels darted across the back yard, catching John's attention. They paused for a moment then scurried up a tree. Continuing to stare out at the woods, John said, "There's got to be something someone can do to help you move on."

"Help her to help us," Clarence's voice boomed from behind John.

By the time John spun around, Clarence was gone. The only thing that remained was the lingering smell of cigar smoke. John's thoughts immediately turned to Kevin's dream. He could have sworn Kevin mentioned that the voice in his dream kept saying, *Help her to help us*. Without hesitation, John dug into his pocket and pulled out his phone. He dialed then paced back and forth on the deck.

"Please don't go to voicemail... please don't go to voicemail," he murmured to himself.

"Hello?" Kevin answered, half asleep.

"You still in bed?"

"Uh... kinda," Kevin said, looking down at the couch. "What's up? Let me guess, you want some more of my expert advice on women?"

John wasted no time with small talk. "Tell me about that dream again."

"What?"

"That dream you told me about. You know, the one you've been having since you were little."

Laughing, Kevin said, "Have you started drinking again?"

"Kevin, tell me! Please."

Realizing John was being completely serious, Kevin looked around to see if Julie was within earshot. Lowering his voice, he asked, "Why do want to—"

"Kevin, please! Just tell me about the dream again."

The more Kevin described the dream, the more John realized he was talking about the Dark Waters that Clarence had mentioned.

When Kevin finished, John impatiently asked, "But what about the voice? You said there was a voice."

"Oh, yeah. The voice keeps repeating, *Help her to help us.*"

"Holy shit!" John said, slumping into one of the deck chairs.

"Holy shit, what? Why do you wanna know about the dream so badly?"

"I'll tell you everything when you get here."

"Wait... what?"

"I can't explain it right now, but you just need to trust me, Kev. And you need to get here as soon as possible. There really *is* something strange about this island. I thought it was just me, but... but for whatever reason, I think *you're* connected to it, too."

"Connected how? What do you—"

"Kevin, please! Just get out here. Please. I'm kind of freaking out right now."

By now, Kevin had walked into the kitchen and lowered himself into a chair. A part of him was worried that John had started drinking again. But the seriousness and urgency in his tone told Kevin otherwise.

"What do I tell Julie?"

"I don't know. Shut down the bar and bring her with you. Tell her it's a surprise vacation or something."

Kevin wasn't the most spontaneous person in the world, but he knew he needed to be there for his brother.

"Okay," Kevin finally said. "I'll make up something and see you soon, I guess."

A sense of relief washed over John. "Thanks, Kev. Thanks for not

149

thinking I'm crazy."

"Oh, I totally think you're crazy, but you're my brother... and I trust you."

"Thanks. I'll see you soon," John said then hung up.

If John thought he was freaking out now, it was nothing compared to what the next twenty-four hours had in store—or the next week.

When Kevin exited the kitchen, Julie was in the living room getting ready to head out to the gym. She didn't ask, but he informed her that was John on the phone.

Only half paying attention, she responded with, "Oh yeah? How's he doing?"

"Good. He says he's doing good. Apparently, he met someone there that he's been hanging out with. Seems like he's pretty into her."

"Ah... meeting someone on vacation... I'm sure that'll last," Julie said, zipping up her gym bag.

Due to her snarky response, Kevin wasn't sure if this was the right moment to run the idea by her.

"See ya," she said, opening the door to leave.

He hesitated but knew it was now or never. "Hey, what are your thoughts on you and I taking a little trip to Maine?"

She started to close the door behind her but stopped. "What?"

"John said there's plenty of room at William's house for us to stay there with him."

"You want *us* to drive out to Maine... to Applewood?"

Kevin shrugged. "I mean, you've always wanted to visit there, so... yeah, why not?"

Julie reentered the house. "And what do we do about the bar?"

"Um... I say we just close it for a week or so."

Curiously, Julie took a step forward and gave Kevin a sniff. "Have you been drinking?"

"No, Julie. I haven't been drinking. Let's face it, the last month or so hasn't been so easy around here. And yes, I know it mostly has to do with me. I've just been out of sorts lately and have been feeling a bit stressed and overwhelmed. And believe it or not, I really am sorry for taking it out on you. I think stepping away from the Wild Irish Rose for a little bit would do me some good… both of us some good."

A smile crept over Julie's face. "A little vacation would be kind of nice. And I have always wanted to go to Maine, especially Applewood. Wait, you're not just suggesting this because of the guilt trip I've been giving you about us never taking a vacation, are you? Because I—"

"No. Like I said, I think we both need to get away from here for a while. And besides, didn't William always tell us that Applewood was the perfect place to clear your head? God knows I could use that."

For the first time in a long time, she felt something other than irritation and annoyance for Kevin. Slowly, she reached out and grabbed her husband's hand. "Do you really think we should close the bar altogether while we're gone? I could ask Devon and Cat if they could—"

"Nah. Do we really want the added stress of worrying about the bar while we're on vacation?"

Julie's smile was her answer. "When do you want to go?" she asked.

Without thinking too heavily on it, Kevin responded, "How about as soon as we get packed?"

Julie continued smiling as she dropped her gym bag and gave Kevin a big hug. Less than two hours later, they were on the road heading towards Maine. On their way out of town, they stopped by the Wild Irish Rose, and Julie put a sign on the door—a sign she'd wanted to put for a while now:

CLOSED FOR 2 WEEKS
GONE ON VACATION!

Between the loss of income for those two weeks and the looming rent increase, Kevin knew what little savings they had would soon be gone. He knew this, but he told himself not to get too stressed out about it. After all, he had more important things to worry about.

Things like: *What the hell is going on with John in Applewood? And why did he sound so weird on the phone? And what was so urgent that he needed me to be there ASAP?*

Kevin also knew he needed to take this opportunity to work on mending his marriage. Unfortunately, he still wasn't ready to tell Julie about what had been going through his head lately: his pending midlife crisis, his lack of desire to remain at the Wild Irish Rose, and of course, the dream.

12

Despite vowing hours earlier that he would give Charlotte some space, John found himself sitting in the parking lot of the general store. After last night, he assumed Charlotte probably thought he was a raving lunatic. He knew this, but he had to talk to her. Clarence's visit changed everything. There was no way Charlotte and Kevin's dreams were coincidental. He wasn't exactly sure how or why, but he knew the Dark Waters Clarence spoke of had something to do with their dreams.

As soon as John entered the store, he could sense the awkwardness between him and Charlotte. Neither of them said a word about the previous night. The most they could muster was generic small talk and even that only lasted about five minutes. John paid for his coffee then headed back out to his truck. He sat there for the longest time just staring at the front door to the store. When he couldn't stand it any longer, he jumped out and reentered.

"I'm so sorry for last night, Charlotte. I didn't mean to overwhelm you or freak you out with all the shit I told you."

"No, John... I'm the one who needs to apologize. I guess you just caught me off guard with everything, and I didn't know how to respond to it. You opened up to me, and I feel like a horrible person for not saying more."

"Trust me, you don't need to apologize. If someone told me what I told you, I wouldn't know what to say either. I know some of the things I told you were probably the most outlandish shit you've ever heard, but I swear I was telling the truth. But... I totally understand if you—"

"John, stop," she said, reaching across the counter and placing her hand on his. "I'm not sure what's crazier... some of the things you told me or... or the fact that I think I actually believe you."

Just then, a few customers entered the store causing Charlotte to remove her hand from his. She politely greeted them, then John lowered his voice and said, "You do? You believe me?"

After a long pause, Charlotte smiled and softly replied, "I... I think I do."

He returned her smile. "Good, because something else happened this morning that I think you need to hear."

Curiously, she cocked her head, but before she could reply, a customer approached the counter with their coffee.

"What time do you get out?" he asked.

"My mother said she'd be here by noon at the latest."

"Meet me at the diner for lunch?"

"Okay."

John left the store in a much better headspace than when he arrived. There were still a million thoughts and questions swirling around his head, but at least Charlotte was on his side. He had no idea what was going on, but he hoped that between Charlotte and Kevin, they could somehow all figure it out. The first thing he did when he got back to the house was walk out onto the deck. He knew it was a longshot, but he hoped Clarence would once again be there to answer some of his many questions. He wasn't. He thought about heading down to the cove, but he had a feeling Clarence would only appear on his own terms.

Still exhausted from the night before, John decided to take a quick nap before meeting up with Charlotte over at the diner. Even though his mind was racing a mile a minute, it didn't take long for his eyes to shut and for sleep to take hold. Luckily, he set the alarm on his phone, or else he would have overslept. Before hopping in the shower, he sent a quick text to Kevin asking if everything was all set. It wasn't until John parked out in front the diner that Kevin replied. He breathed a sigh of relief when he read Kevin's text:

We're leaving Chicago soon! See you sometime tomorrow.

Charlotte arrived at the diner first and snagged the most private booth possible. She wasn't sure what John needed to tell her, but the last thing she wanted was for any of the locals to hear what was about to be said. Rumors were bad enough on a small island; she couldn't imagine if anyone had overheard what John told her the night before. The locals would have a field day with that.

Before he even sat down, he blurted out, "I just want to thank you again for not thinking I'm bat-shit crazy."

"Don't thank me yet," she said, grinning. "I haven't heard the newest thing you're gonna tell me."

"Oh, it's a doozy," he said, sliding into the booth.

By now, John could barely contain himself, but he waited long enough for the waitress to take their order before rambling on about Clarence's newest appearance. He told her everything that Clarence had said to him, especially the part about the Dark Waters.

"Have you ever heard of that?" he asked.

"The Dark Waters?" Slowly, she nodded and said, "It's another old legend of the island. I remember hearing bits and pieces of it growing up. I knew the Dark Waters were supposedly where the Evil Spirit lived, but I never heard the other part of it... the part about the Evil Spirit preventing its victims from moving on to the next life."

"Don't you get it?" he asked.

"Get what?"

"Your dream... Kevin's dream. Your father's plane must have crashed into the Dark Waters, and the Evil Spirit is preventing them from moving on."

"That might be the craziest thing you've said yet... and that's saying a lot." Charlotte cracked a smile, but it was only to hide the fact that she was completely freaking out.

What if he's right? she thought. *What if my father is stuck out there... out in the Dark Waters?*

She continued to smile and asked, "Did you run your theory by Clarence?"

"No. He disappeared before I could ask." John could tell Charlotte was teetering on the fence of whether to believe him or not. "I know you think I'm crazy, but Clarence's final words were a direct quote from Kevin's dream."

"What do you mean?"

"Kevin told me that right before his dream ended, a voice would call out, *Help her...*"

"*To help us,*" Charlotte finished. Her jaw gaped open, and her face turned pale.

"How did you know that?"

"The same exact words are said at the end of my dream, too. Holy shit," she said, leaning against the back of the booth. "Have you told your brother this yet?"

"No, but he's gonna be here in the next day or so."

At that point, they officially hit a lull in their conversation. They were literally speechless regarding this whole crazy situation. John decided to switch gears into something more lighthearted.

"What do you have going on the rest of the day?" he asked.

"I'm heading down to Boston for the night. My brother and his wife are going out and asked if I would babysit my nieces. I should be back in the morning... swing by and see me, if ya want."

"Sounds good," he said, smiling.

***

Not long after the sun went down, John closed his eyes and was out cold for the night. He briefly woke up around 7am and thought about driving over to the general for a coffee, but seeing as he knew Charlotte wasn't there, he decided to remain in bed. It was just before noon when he finally got up. At that point, he decided to head over to see if Charlotte was back from her brother's house.

He knocked on her door several times, and when no one answered, he decided to see if she was down in the store. There were a handful of customers milling about, but the only worker he noticed was an older woman. Due to the uncanny resemblance, he assumed she was Charlotte's mother. John waited in line behind two younger kids, who appeared to be on a major candy run. On the left side of the counter, they dumped a ton of penny candy, and each of them placed a pack of baseball cards down. They then pulled out handfuls of pocket change, dumping it onto the right side of the counter. Normally, John would have been impatiently cursing under his breath, but he couldn't help being reminded of him and Kevin when they were kids. They paid for many a candy bar and many a pack of baseball cards with pocket change.

Charlotte's mother was even more patient than John as she carefully counted the coins one by one. "You need another two dollars and seventy-five cents," she said, smiling down at the boys.

Frantically, the boys dug their little hands back into their pockets. John smirked and sympathetically watched as only lint fell out. Embarrassed and panicked, the young boys looked over at one another. "We have to put some of it back," one boy whispered to the other.

Before each of them could decide on what to return, John placed a five-dollar bill down in front of them. "Don't worry boys, I got ya."

"Really?" they both asked in unison.

"Really," John said, winking.

"Thanks, Mister."

"Yeah, thanks, Mister," the other boy echoed.

Charlotte's mother smiled, and she took the five and placed it into the register. She then slid two dollars and twenty-five cents onto the counter. The boys stepped aside, allowing John to grab his change.

"You boys can keep the change."

It was as if they'd won the lottery. Their eyes nearly bulged out of their heads, and they were grinning ear to ear.

"Thanks again, Mister!"

"Yeah, thanks again, Mister!"

They each reached down and grabbed one of the dollar bills, and that's when the real dilemma began—how to split the quarter? For an eight-year-old, this was most certainly classified as a dilemma. Neither of them wanted the other one to end up with more money. John reached into his pocket to see if he had another quarter, but before he could pull it out, the boys surprised him. They whispered to one another, nodded, and then they placed the quarter in the charity jar labeled:

THE JIMMY FUND - HELP FIGHT CANCER

John and Charlotte's mother both smiled and watched the boys as they clutched their candy bags and rushed outside.

"Maybe there's hope for our youth yet," she said to John.

He took a step forward. "I was just thinking the same thing."

"That was a very nice gesture on your part."

John shrugged. "Eh, we've all been there. Young, poor, and in desperate need of candy," he said with a chuckle.

She nodded in agreement and pleasantly asked, "How can I help you today?"

"I was just wondering if Charlotte was here. I know she was at her brother's last night, but she said she'd probably be home sometime this morning."

"I'm sorry, she's not. She called earlier and said she was going to do some shopping with her sister-in-law for a while today."

"Oh, okay… no biggie."

"Would you like me to leave her a message?"

"No… that's okay. I was just stopping in to say hi." He started to walk away but turned back around. "Actually, can I leave her my cellphone number?"

"Of course," she said, handing him a pen and small piece of paper.

He wrote down his name and number and handed it back to her.

Charlotte's mother looked up at his Cubs hat and smiled. "Let me guess, you're the mystery man from Chicago my daughter has been hanging out with?"

John felt his face flush red. "I don't know about *mystery man*, but yes, we've hung out a few times."

"I only say mystery man because she never told me your name. She might be nearly forty, but she's still as vague as ever when it comes to her dating life."

"Oh, we're not dating," he pointed out, feeling his face redden even more. "Just enjoying each other's company, that's all."

"Right, that's what I meant," she said with a mischievous smile. "Well, I'll definitely tell her you stopped by."

Throughout their brief conversation, the bell on the front door rang out multiple times. Being a Saturday, the store was busier than John had seen it all week. He looked around at all the customers and then back to Charlotte's mother. "Are you the only one working today?"

"We have a couple of high schoolers who work weekends, but my day-shift girl called out this morning. If I'm lucky, my next worker will be in at three."

"I'm sorry," John said. "I'd offer to help, but considering I have no idea what I'm doing, I'd probably just get in your way."

"Thanks, but I think this old lady can handle it. I appreciate the offer though. I'll be sure to let Charlotte know you stopped by."

Politely, John nodded and began to walk towards the front door. Just as his hand grasp the knob, Charlotte's mother called out, "Actually… I could really use a huge favor."

"Of course," he said, turning back around. "What do you need?"

She explained to him that she needed some groceries delivered to a customer.

"Sure. I didn't know you guys deliver."

"We usually don't, but there are a few regulars that we do it for. Most of them are up there in age and have a hard time getting around. It's only a couple of bags, and she lives right up the road. It's the Great Blue Heron Inn. It's not in business anymore, but Janice has always been one of our best and sweetest customers. It should only take five minutes or so. Are you sure you don't mind?"

"No, not at all. Whatever you need."

She smiled graciously and said, "My daughter said you were sweet and funny, but I guess you can add helpful to that list now, too. Just give me a quick second, and I'll put together the order for you."

As soon as she walked off, John's mind focused on two of the words she just used—*sweet* and *funny*. Both were positive words, and any normal person would love to be referred to as sweet and funny. Unfortunately, John was far from normal. He was hoping for something more like *super-cool* and *hot*. *Sparkling personality* and *easy on the eyes* would have also been acceptable. By the time Charlotte's mom returned with the groceries, John's twisted brain deduced that maybe Charlotte *did* use those better words, and maybe her mom was just trying to not embarrass him too much. *Yeah, that's probably it,* he thought, as she approached carrying two brown bags.

She handed him the bags, wrote down the address, and after thanking him two more times, she sent him on his way. A few minutes later, John pulled into the long driveway of the inn. If it weren't for his phone buzzing, he probably would have noticed the Illinois plates on the Subaru. He pulled out his cell and saw it was a text from an unknown number. He began to smile as he read the text.

Hey, it's Charlotte. My mom told me u stopped by to see if I wanted to do something today. I'll be back in town in a couple of hours. I can meet u at your house if u want. And hopefully she didn't embarrass me too much:)

His smile grew bigger. Charlotte's mother must have called her right after he left the store. He continued grinning and laughing to himself as he texted her back. It took him three tries to settle on the right thing to type.

"No! That's much too long and wordy," he grumbled, then tried again.

"Ugh. That one is much too stupid… and way too many emojis." Finally, he settled on short and emoji-free.

Sounds good. See you then.

As soon as he hit enter, a notification appeared:

Message not sent. No service.

Before he could get too upset, he thought better of it. It was probably for the best. He didn't want to text back too quickly or seem too anxious. He slid the phone back into his pocket, grabbed the two bags, and headed up the walkway towards the front porch. He placed one of the bags on the small table next to the door then knocked.

Moments later, he heard a woman's voice calling out. It was too faint for him to completely understand, but he was pretty sure she was telling him to come in. Hesitantly, he opened the door. He poked his head in and called out, "Hello?"

"Yes, yes. Come in," Janice said, slowly making her way down the hall from the other side of the house.

"Sorry," John said with a grin. "I wasn't sure if you were saying *coming* or *come in*. I'm here with your groceries, ma'am."

"First of all, it's Janice, *not* ma'am." A kind smile filled her face. "And secondly, come on in, and I'll show where to put them."

John grabbed the other bag and followed her down the hall.

"I haven't seen you before. Are you new to the store?"

"Me? No, no, no. I don't work there. They were short of help today, so I was just doing them a favor."

"Ah, I see. Good help is hard to find nowadays, that's for sure."

She led him into the kitchen and motioned to the large granite countertop. As he carefully placed the bags down, he couldn't help but notice her eyes curiously staring at him.

"You're new to Applewood, aren't you? I've lived here more years than I care to count, and I know every face on the island... and you, my friend, you are a new face."

"Um, yeah. I'm just in town for a little mini vacation, that's all."

"I see. Where are you from?" she asked, then quickly followed with, "I'm sorry. I'm a nosy old lady, aren't I?"

"It's okay," he said, smiling. "Chicago. I'm here from Chicago."

"Get out!" Janice exclaimed. "The woman staying with me is from Chicago, too. Maybe you know each other?"

"Maybe," John said, laughing to himself. He knew that Chicago had a population of over two million and the chances were slim to none that he knew this other person.

"Here, follow me. She's in the living room reading."

Janice motioned for John to follow her down the hallway. Hope was lounging on the couch, but she wasn't reading. She had a book in front of her, but her mind wasn't allowing her to concentrate properly. She had read the same page at least a dozen times.

As they neared the living room, Janice called out, "Hope, I have a fellow Chicagoan here." Janice turned back to John and asked, "That's what you call yourselves, right?"

"Yes ma'am—I mean... Janice."

Hope sat straight up and closed the book as soon as she heard her name called.

"Apparently our new delivery driver is from Chicago, too," Janice said entering the room.

John followed directly behind her with a smile on his face, but as soon as he saw Hope, his smile turned to a look of shock.

"Doc?"

"John?"

At the same time, they both asked, "What are you doing here?"

Janice giggled. "I was actually joking when I said you two might know each other. What are the chances?"

Neither of them said a word, and they both stood there dumbfounded.

"How do you two know each other?" Janice asked.

Hope wasn't sure what to say. "Umm… John was my…"

John cleared the air with a more matter-of-fact answer. "She's my shrink. Well, she was." John's initial shock wore off and the smile crept back onto his face. "I thought you were taking a road trip around the country. How did you end up here?"

Hope looked to Janice and then back to John. It was obvious she was still surprised and at a loss as to what to say. "Have a seat," Janice said, motioning to the reclining chair. "Let me get you something to drink. I'm thinking you two have a lot to catch up on."

John sat across from Hope and continued shaking his head and grinning over at her.

"Seriously, what are the chances? How'd you even hear about this island, Doc?"

Hope had no intention of going into details with John about her past on the island with her father, so she did what she had been accustomed to lately, she lied.

"I… I guess I randomly came across it on my travels and thought it seemed like a nice place to hunker down for a bit."

It didn't take long for Hope to realize that one lie wasn't going to be enough. John's questions came hard and fast.

"Wait, you're staying *here*? I thought this inn was closed?"

Hope panicked and gave John some made-up story.

"So, you thought this place was open? And when Janice told you it was closed, she *still* offered you to stay here?"

Hope figured saying less was better, so she simply shrugged and nodded yes.

"I mean, she seems sweet enough… but it sounds kind of shady, doesn't it, Doc? Do you want me to do a background check on her?"

For the first time in a long time, a smile appeared on Hope's face. "No, I don't think that'll be necessary. I'm pretty sure there's nothing to worry about. I don't think this sweet little 92-year-old woman is a serial killer or anything."

"I don't know, I've been watching an awful lot of crime shows lately, and it's always the person you least expect."

John's little comment was just what Hope needed to lighten her mood.

"What are *you* doing here in Applewood?" she asked.

"Just taking a little vacation to try to clear my head. Unfortunately, the weather has been horrible since I've been here."

"Yeah, I haven't seen the sun once," Hope said. "What made you choose this place?"

"An old friend of mine owns a house here. This is where I came seven years ago, remember?"

Hope thought for a moment, and then it started to come back to her. During their session following his return from Applewood seven years ago, John mentioned he had just got back from Maine. "You came here to help a friend fix up his house, right?"

"Yup. He's since passed away, but his wife is letting me use the house again."

"I am so sorry to hear about your friend."

"Thanks. I appreciate it."

Hope still couldn't believe out of all the places in Maine, *this* was where he had come seven years ago. Just then, Janice returned with two tall glasses of lemonade. Shakily, she handed them to John and Hope. They both felt a little guilty for making this elderly woman wait on them.

"Thank you," John said. "But you really didn't have to go through all that trouble."

"Yeah," Hope said. "You really don't have to wait on me."

Janice brushed them off with her hand. "Old habits die hard, I guess. It might take me a little longer, but I can still take care of my guests." She gave them each a wink and then excused herself to let them continue talking.

John waited until she was completely down the hall and said, "Maybe she's not a serial killer after all."

Hope rolled her eyes. "It really is good to see you, John."

She took a sip from her drink and leaned back onto the couch. As she placed the glass next to her on the end table, John couldn't help but notice her hand was just as shaky as Janice's. It was then he took notice of the rest of her. She looked thinner than he remembered.

"Hey, Doc, you feeling okay? You're looking a little weary and pale."

She shook off his comment by saying, "I'm fine. Just fighting something off, I guess. This dreary weather isn't helping any either. I probably just need some good old-fashioned vitamin D."

Hope felt embarrassed. She knew she had been lethargic and depressed lately, but she didn't realize it was so noticeable on her physical appearance. She assumed Janice hadn't said anything out of politeness. But Hope could always count on John to say what needed to be said. Before he could delve any further into Hope's health or her Applewood trip, his phone notification went off.

"Sorry," he said, pulling out his phone and checking it. It was a return text from Charlotte. John couldn't hide his excitement as he read it: *Leaving Boston now! See you soon!*

"Everything okay?" Hope asked.

"Yeah, everything is definitely okay."

"Would you like to stay for lunch?" Janice called out from the doorway.

Nearly spilling his lemonade, John jumped up and exclaimed, "Jesus! You scared the crap outta me."

"Sorry about that" Janice said.

John grinned. "It's okay. And thanks for the lunch offer, but I really should get going. I've got plans in a little bit."

"Very well then. But now that you know Hope is staying here, feel free to stop in anytime."

"Thanks. I will. Actually," John said in Hope's direction, "Kevin is coming into town tomorrow. We should all hook up and do something while he's here." He turned to Janice to specify. "Kevin is my baby brother. And he's also one of Doc's patients. Technically, I'm her favorite, but Kevin is probably a close second... or so. Isn't that right, Doc?"

Hope smiled back at him, but her mind was elsewhere. As much as she adored John and Kevin, the last thing she wanted was for them to be hanging out at the inn with her. Not only was she still depressed and feeling antisocial, but she was nervous that Janice might reveal that she had been to Applewood before with her father. If that happened, she was sure the boys would have many questions for her. Questions she didn't want to get into.

13

John was never good at having patience, so he knew it would be a long day or so waiting for his brother to arrive. Luckily, he had Charlotte there to take his mind off things. As soon as she came back from Boston, they sat and talked. He told her that Kevin and Julie were on their way, and he also informed her that Julie had no clue what was going on.

"Julie doesn't even know all the stuff that happened to me when I was in Applewood last time. As a matter of fact, besides my brother, you're the only person I've ever told. I've never even mentioned it to my shrink." John paused, then laughed and said, "Oh, and speaking of my shrink, I just found out today that she is staying here in Applewood right now! Can you believe that?"

"Your therapist... is here in Applewood?"

"Yup. I ran into her when I was doing a delivery for your mother earlier today."

"At Janice's house?" Charlotte asked.

"Yeah. Apparently, she's staying there for a little bit."

All at once, it hit Charlotte. "Wait... are you talking about Hope?"

"Yeah. How do *you* know her?"

"I don't... not really. I only met her once and that was about a week ago when I did a delivery there. She seemed like a nice woman."

"Yeah, she is. Quirky and unorthodox, but she has the patience of a saint."

Charlotte smirked. "If she's your shrink then she must."

"Ha ha, very funny. But, well… you're not wrong. I used to be quite a handful for her, especially when I was drinking."

"Well, I'm glad I met this version of you. I'm not a big fan of drunken idiots."

"Yeah, I'm glad you met this version of me, too."

They talked a little more about everything that had been revealed over the past couple of days, but ultimately, they both agreed to take a little break from trying to analyze all the unexplainable events that had presented themselves.

"How about this, until your brother gets here, let's try to do as many things as possible to take our mind off this?"

"Sounds good," John said. "Any suggestions?"

Charlotte smirked. "I would suggest we go shoot some pool tonight… but that would probably just put you in a bad mood."

"Cute, real cute, Charlotte."

Just before John could accept her challenge, she switched it up. "How about bowling? They do that in the city, don't they?"

Bowling was even more in John's wheelhouse than pool. He and Kevin spent most of their twenties in a Tuesday night bowling league. He started to brag about his mad bowling skills but decided to play coy.

"Bowling huh? It's been a while, but I've probably been two or three times." Deviously, John chuckled to himself, knowing it would only be a matter of time before he got his revenge.

A couple hours later, they drove to Gerrish Falls, ate dinner, and then hit the bowling alley—a *candlepin* bowling alley. Upon entering, John's cocky smile disappeared when he saw the size of the balls.

"What the hell is this?" he asked.

"What are you talking about? It's a bowling alley. Probably not as fancy as your big city—"

"This most certainly is *not* a real bowling alley. Why are the balls so small?"

Charlotte couldn't resist. "That's what *she* said."

As soon as he asked the question, John knew he had set himself up. Of course, he laughed at her immature comment, but just as quickly, he turned the focus back to the bowling alley.

"Seriously, this isn't bowling. And why do the pins look so funny?"

Charlotte looked at him like he was crazy. "You're kidding me, right? Are you serious? You've never been candlepin bowling?"

"I've never even heard of it. I'm used to *real* bowling... you know, ten-pin bowling... with the big balls—don't even say it."

As Charlotte giggled, John pulled out his phone and did a quick Google search. "No wonder why I've never heard of it. It says here it's pretty much just a New England and Canadian thing."

"Really?" she said, looking down at John's phone. "Well, this is the only bowling alley we have in town. We don't have to stay. We can go do something else if you want?"

John was discouraged, but before he said a word, something caught his eye. *Someone* caught his eye. It was a little girl no more than eight-years-old. She was standing and preparing to bowl. Her tiny hand gripped the ball, and John watched as she carefully rolled it down the lane. It struck just off-center, knocking over all but two pins. It was at that point, he noticed multiple kids bowling, many of which knocked over almost every pin.

Hmm, he thought, *if these little shits can do this well, I'll probably get a strike every frickin time!*

"Ya know what, we can stay," he said, smiling. "Bowling is bowling. This is probably just like the JV version of the real thing."

He continued smiling right up until they slipped their bowling shoes on. Little did he know that would be his last smile, at least in the next ninety minutes. They played three strings, and Charlotte won each and every one. By the time the third game was underway, John had gotten the hang of it and had vastly improved his technique. Even so, Charlotte still beat him by nearly twenty pins.

It was obvious just how frustrated and angry John was; not from what he said, but from what he *didn't* say. Not one word was spoken as he took off his shoes and returned them. She knew he hated losing, but she tried her best to be supportive, even if she was laughing and jumping for joy on the inside.

"For someone who's never been before, you were really getting the hang of it towards the end."

John shot her a glare, which caused her even more joy on the inside. The ride back to Applewood was quiet. Although, there were a few times she could have sworn she heard John angrily mumbling under his breath. Things like: "stupid game... stupid little balls... it shouldn't even be called bowling... stupid."

Charlotte knew the chances were slim, and due to his bad mood, she assumed there would definitely not be any attempt at a goodnight kiss. She was correct. It wasn't for lack of desire on John's part, not at all. Even though he was pissed at losing, the goodnight kiss was firmly on his mind the entire ride home. But like always, he didn't feel the moment was right, and he ultimately chickened out.

14

The long drive from Chicago to Maine started off promising. Neither of them ever said it, but they both knew this trip was a much-needed time to reconnect and to work on their marriage. They both started the trip off in good moods and were happy to take time away from the Wild Irish Rose. And because of that, neither of them brought up any of the tension from the previous month. Most of their conversations were small talk, revolving around the trip itself.

Unfortunately, it didn't take long for the tension to rear its ugly head. It wasn't anything major, but it was enough to make the final leg of the trip uncomfortable. Seeing as this was their first big road trip as a married couple, Julie was hoping to take their time and do some sightseeing along the way. Normally, Kevin would have been all for this, but he made a promise to John to get to Applewood as soon as possible.

Julie had a list of at least a half dozen attractions and scenic overlooks that she wanted to stop at along the way. This included her longtime dream of seeing the bright lights of Times Square in New York City. Unlike the previous month, Kevin wasn't mean, sarcastic, or short with her. He did his best to be the mediator and to quell any arguments.

"Honey, I want to stop at all these places as well, but I just think we should head to Maine first and then on our way back home we can totally take our time and see everything we want. I promise. To be honest, I'm just really excited to see this island that I've heard so much about from William… and from John."

Julie was still a little unhappy that she wasn't getting her way, but she, too, was excited to see the coast of Maine and to see where William once called home.

"Okay, fine," she said, cracking a smile. "But I just don't want to get to Maine and have it be all about you and John hanging out together. You know I love your brother, but this is *our* vacation. I want to do as much sightseeing as possible."

"I couldn't agree more. We should be in Maine sometime tomorrow afternoon. We'll settle in, get a good night's sleep, then I promise the next day will be one hundred percent sightseeing… just you and me. I promise."

***

Despite hitting massive amounts of standstill traffic in parts of New York and Massachusetts, they made it into Maine by four o'clock the following day. As soon as Julie saw the iconic Welcome to Maine sign, she made Kevin stop and take a picture of her next to it. She was even more eager and excited to stop and get her picture taken next to the Welcome to Applewood sign.

"Look, look! It says Maine's Magical Island! Just like William said."

Kevin smiled and glanced up the road. "Looks more like Maine's fog-covered island."

"Wow, you ain't lying," she said, gazing up ahead. They quickly went from warm and clear skies to rainy and cold. Despite the weather's rude greeting, Julie was on the edge of her seat with a huge grin on her face the entire drive through the small island town.

"Look! It's a classic old general store! We totally have to stop in while we're here. I bet William used to go there when he was a kid. Oh, and look! A classic old diner."

Kevin smiled along but wasn't quite as excited as Julie was. He was still extremely anxious as to why his brother so frantically summoned him to the island. *And why was John so suddenly curious about my dream? Why did he want to know what the voices were saying?* Kevin also knew he needed to tell his brother about the new twist in the dream.

No sooner did they pull into William's driveway, John rushed out of the house and greeted and helped them with their luggage. Julie took one step into the house and stopped. She moved her gaze from the right to the left and then back again.

"This looks exactly like I pictured it would," she said, smiling. "And it smells nice in here, too."

"Yeah, I picked up some scented candles the other day," John said.

"And it also smells like fresh paint," Kevin commented.

"Yep, that's been my big project so far. Can't do much on the outside of house… not with this weather."

"Has it been like this the whole time you've been here?"

"Yep. Every day. It's like this weather pattern has been stuck right over the island. It's not bad if you go inland."

Julie looked over at Kevin. "Well, if it's like this tomorrow, we should do our sightseeing inland. I'm sure there's still plenty to see."

"Whatever you want, hun."

John watched as they both smiled lovingly at one another. It was something he hadn't seen between them in a long time. After they got settled into their room, John took them out to eat down at the diner. This pleased Julie greatly. She loved classic old places with history and character.

About halfway through dinner, Julie blurted out, "So, when do we get to meet this new woman of yours?"

John shot a hot glare his brother's way, causing Kevin to smirk and shrug. "She's not my new woman. We just have fun together and like hanging out, that's all."

"Have you kissed her yet?" Julie asked, grinning.

"What's with all the questions? My personal life isn't any of your business."

Julie continued grinning and whispered to Kevin, "That would be a no on the kissing."

Kevin laughed and shook his head in agreement.

"You guys are idiots. I can't believe I actually invited you here."

"Oh, relax," Julie said, reaching out for his hand. "We're glad you met someone to have fun with."

"It's nothing serious," John quickly pointed out.

"It's okay," Julie said. "It doesn't have to be. I just like seeing you happy. And I am very glad that you invited us here."

As soon as dinner was over, they all headed back to the house, and for the next few hours, they sat around talking and playing cards. And when they weren't playing cards, Julie was on her phone trying to come up with a perfect sightseeing itinerary for the next day. She wanted to drive up to Kennebunkport to see President Bush's summer house. And then they would make their way up to Portland and hang out down at the Old Port. John suggested that while they were up there, they should go to Freeport and stop in at L.L. Bean.

Still exhausted from their long drive, by the time nine o'clock hit, Kevin and Julie could barely keep their eyes open. Julie let out a big yawn and then reached her hand towards Kevin. "Are you coming up to bed with me, hun?" It was a question she had stopped asking weeks ago.

"Actually, I think I might stay up a little later and hang out with John a bit."

"Oh... okay," she said, releasing his hand. Kevin could see the disappointment in her eyes. He knew it had been a rough month, and he also knew he had a lot to make up for. He wanted to go upstairs with her, but his curiosity was growing by the minute. He desperately needed to talk to John in private and find out exactly what was going on.

"I promise I'll be up in a little bit," Kevin said as sincerely as possible.

She placated him with a nod, said goodnight to John, then headed up the stairs.

John could also sense the disappointment in Julie's response, and as soon as he heard the bedroom door close, he turned to his brother and said, "You should really go up to bed with her. We can talk tomorrow."

"No," Kevin sternly whispered. "You *have* to tell me what the hell is going on. Why did you tell me to come here? And why were you so concerned about my dream?"

John let out a big sigh then leaned back on the couch and tried his best to explain everything to his brother. About five minutes in, Kevin's mouth dropped open and remained that way for the rest of the conversation. He couldn't believe Charlotte's father was the pilot of the plane that killed their parents. And Kevin certainly couldn't believe that Charlotte had been having almost the exact same dream as him all these years.

He absorbed as much as he could and finally said, "I… I have no idea what to say."

"I know, pretty crazy stuff, huh? Now we just need to figure out what *Help her to help us* means."

Kevin turned to John and figured this was as good a time as any to tell him about the new development in his own dream. But before he could utter a word, John's phone rang. Curiously, Kevin listened as John had a brief conversation then hung up.

"Who was that?"

"It was Charlotte. She says that she might know someone who can help us analyze your dreams… someone who might have the answers."

"Who?"

"I don't know, but she said for us to meet her at the general store tomorrow morning around nine." John glanced at the clock on his phone and then over to his brother and said, "You should head up and get some sleep. We'll talk more tomorrow."

"But—"

"Seriously, Kev, go upstairs and be with Julie. We'll talk in the morning."

Kevin knew there was no way he was going to get any sleep that night, but he went upstairs like his brother asked. The next morning didn't start off any better for him and Julie. She was not happy about Kevin blowing off their sightseeing plans to go hang out with his brother. John made up some excuse about having to go help Charlotte move some heavy furniture around.

"We'll probably be gone an hour at the most," John said. He had no clue if this was true or not, but he said it anyway.

Kevin went along with it and said, "See, we'll still have the rest of the day to go sightseeing."

Julie wasn't buying any of it. "I knew this was going to happen. I knew it! This whole trip was just about you guys hanging out and doing brotherly things."

"Aw, Jules, come on," John said, laughing. "Do you really think I want to do brotherly things with *this* guy? Trust me, he's just helping me help a friend, that's all."

Julie was having none of it. "Whatever," she said, then turned and stormed back upstairs.

Kevin hated seeing his wife hurting, especially knowing that he was the reason behind it. John sensed his apprehension and placed a hand on his brother's shoulder. "It'll be okay, bro. You'll have plenty of time to make this up to her."

15

The brothers arrived at the store at nine o'clock on the dot. John introduced Kevin to Charlotte, and despite meeting under strange circumstances, they seemed to hit it off. It wasn't raining, but there was a thick fog looming about. John and Kevin were on edge and were more than a little curious as to where Charlotte was taking them. There wasn't a lot of conversation on the ride, and it wasn't until they turned onto Hawkeye Road that John finally spoke. The sign on the side of the road read:

WELCOME TO THE ABENAKI STABLES
THE OLDEST & MOST SCENIC IN MAINE

"Please tell me you're not taking us horseback riding?"

"The stables are our destination, but no, we're not going horseback riding." She then smirked and murmured, "But I would give anything to see you two city boys on a horse."

Both brothers scoffed at Charlotte.

"You obviously underestimate us city folk," John said, as Charlotte pulled into the stables.

"Oh, so you two have ridden before?"

John looked over at Kevin, who reluctantly shook his head no. Knowing he had never been on a horse either, John switched the subject. "So what are we doing here then?"

She shut the car off and replied, "If anyone is going to know about the inner workings of Applewood, it's Daniel. His Native American roots run deep here. He actually comes from a long line of shamans."

"Ya mean like a witch doctor?" John asked.

"No, I mean like a shaman. You might want to let me do the talking," Charlotte said, shaking her head.

Kevin also shook his head and glared at his brother.

"What? I'm just trying to lighten the mood. This whole situation is… well, it's fucking crazy, don't ya think?"

As all three nodded in agreement, they watched a woman walk out of the stables and head towards them. They exited the car, and Charlotte smiled and said, "Hey, Brooke. How are you?"

"I'm good, thanks," Brooke said, giving Charlotte a hug.

"Brooke graduated a few years ahead of me, but we used to run in the same circles."

"Of course, that was back when I had a social life," Brooke said. "Now our hangouts are relegated to my shopping trips to the general store."

Charlotte nodded. "We really need a girls' night out."

"We really do," Brooke said, grinning.

As Charlotte introduced Brooke to John and Kevin, the fog began to thicken around them.

"This weather lately can't be good for business, huh?" Charlotte asked.

"Nope. Although, it's been bad for a while now. The island ain't what it used to be, that's for sure." Just then, one of the horses let out a loud neigh. "Looks like Lightning needs some attention. Wanna say hi before I take you to my grandfather?"

"Absolutely," Charlotte said with a big smile.

"You do know you can come riding any time you want? Any of you," she said, looking over at John and Kevin.

Charlotte continued to smile and said, "You'd have to give them your fastest horses. They're quite the experienced riders."

Unamused, both guys shot Charlotte a glare. After hanging out with the horses for a bit, Brooke led them into the house and settled them into the living room.

"Do any of you want something to drink?" Brooke asked.

All three shook their heads no.

"Well, I've gotta head back out to the stables, but Grampa will be in soon. Make sure you come say goodbye before you leave."

"We will," Charlotte said. "Thanks again, Brooke."

After she left, the boys gazed around the room. From artwork to hand-carved wooden sculptures, the room was filled with Native American culture. As they waited for Daniel's arrival, the brothers sat next to each other on one of the couches. Their palms were sweating, and their legs were nervously twitching a mile a minute. It was as if they were back in school waiting for the principal to come scold them. Or even worse, it was like they were getting ready to sit in front of Hope for their first therapy session ever.

Grinning, Charlotte shook her head at them and said, "Both of you, relax! You're gonna pull a muscle twitching that much."

"How the hell are we supposed to relax!" John said. "I don't even know up from down anymore, and now we're sitting in some strange house waiting for some crazy witch doctor to come give us some answers."

Before Charlotte had a chance to respond, the door on the other side of the living room opened. A second later, Daniel rolled through the threshold in a wheelchair.

"There he is!" Charlotte announced. She then stood up, and with a big smile, she approached and gave him a hug.

"Ahh, Charlotte Blaisdell. It's great to see your face again. I was pleasantly surprised when Brooke told me you were coming to see me. It's been a while. As you can see, it's hard for me to get around these days."

"Luckily, you have an amazing granddaughter like Brooke to run your errands for you. Though I must admit, Mom and I miss seeing you around the store."

"Well, you tell your mother I said hello and that my shopping days are far from over. You haven't seen the last of me yet," he said, giving Charlotte a wink.

"We'll look forward to it."

"So, who did you bring with you today?" Daniel asked, turning his attention to John and Kevin.

"These are my friends from Chicago, John and Kevin Mathews."

Daniel rolled his chair into the living room and extended his hand towards the boys. Both brothers stood up and shook his hand.

"Nice to meet you, sir," Kevin said.

John followed with, "Yes, nice to meet you, Mister..."

"You can just call me Daniel. Or Mister Witch Doctor, if you prefer?"

Daniel's expression was completely serious, which caused both brothers, especially John, to squirm in embarrassment.

"Sorry, sir," John said, not making eye contact. "I didn't mean any disrespect."

"Yeah, my brother has a problem with inappropriate humor," Kevin said.

Daniel held his deadpan stare for as long as he could before he and Charlotte burst out laughing.

"I'm just playin' with ya," Daniel said, trying to compose himself.

Great, a witch doctor and a fucking comedian, John thought but didn't say.

"City folk are always so uptight, aren't they?" Daniel said in Charlotte's direction. She nodded and continued laughing. Daniel looked over at the boys and said, "Please, no *sir*... no *Mister*... just call me Daniel."

Kevin took the lead. "It's nice to meet you, Daniel. Thanks for having us in your home. This is a really cool room."

John followed with, "Did you do all those carvings yourself?"

"I did," Daniel proudly said. "It's been a while, though. When you get to be my age, your hands don't work as well as they used to."

"They're amazing. Especially the fine details," John said, continuing to admire.

"Why, thank you, son."

"My brother actually owns a woodworking shop back in Chicago."

"Ahh, I could sense you were a craftsman," Daniel said to John.

John moved his look from Kevin back to Daniel. "I certainly don't do anything like this," John finally said.

"We all have our own talents, and we all follow our own paths. I'm sure whatever type of work you do is equally as amazing."

"Thanks," John quietly said and looked away. John was never good with compliments.

"So, what can I do for you three?"

Not knowing where to begin, Charlotte looked over at John and Kevin for some help. Under his breath, John mumbled to her, "You're the one who told us to let *you* do most of the talking."

She returned her gaze back to Daniel, took a deep breath, then said, "I remember way back in high school you came in and gave a speech about Native American culture and its importance to this island."

"I'm impressed you remember that. It was a long time ago."

"You also talked about the importance of dreams and visions. I think you said something like: 'When we learn how to properly analyze our dreams, it is then we'll discover their true significance and meaning.'"

Daniel grinned. "Sounds like something I'd say. Again, I'm impressed it stuck with you all these years. So, is that what brings you here, Charlotte? Your dreams?"

"Kinda," she said with a shrug. "Rumor has it, you're an expert at analyzing them."

Daniel laughed. "I'm not sure about that. The truth is, only the person having the dream can be the true expert." Daniel watched as disappointment washed over Charlotte's face. "That being said, I have been known to help people find meaning in their dreams."

When John saw Charlotte not saying anything, he gave her a nudge and motioned her to tell Daniel. Hesitantly, Charlotte turned back to Daniel and once again took a deep breath. She then started to describe her dream in its entirety. She also mentioned the dream had stopped sometime around her teenage years, but it had very recently started back up.

Even though John had already told Kevin that Charlotte's dream was very similar to his, hearing her describe it in person caused the hairs on Kevin's arms to stand up. With the exception of the people involved, their dreams were exactly the same: the same-colored sky, the same dark ocean, the same rough waves, the same exact phrase being called out, and ultimately, the same empty and helpless feeling.

When she finished, Daniel's face softened, and he leaned back in his chair. "It's hard to believe that accident was over thirty-five years ago. I remember it like it was yesterday. Your father was a good man. I actually flew with him a few times." Daniel paused. "If I remember correctly, you were quite young when it happened, weren't you?"

"I was only two. I don't remember anything about the accident… or anything about my father, for that matter. My only memories of him are from photographs and stories that others have told me."

"I'm very sorry about what happened to your father, and I'm sorry you've been having these nightmares of him. But I must tell you, Charlotte, it's not uncommon to…"

"To dream of loved ones that we've lost?" Charlotte interrupted. "That's what every therapist I've ever seen has said to me. But this is different, Daniel. The dream is so real… like, real!"

Sympathetically, Daniel gazed over at Charlotte, thinking of what to say next.

"And before you say anything else," Charlotte said, "you need to know there's more."

"More to your dream?" he asked.

"Sorta," she replied. "The whole thing has kind of a weird twist from here." She turned to Kevin and gave him a look, telling him it was his turn to speak.

Kevin wiped his sweaty hands on his jeans, and without making eye contact with anyone, he began to speak. "For as far back as I can remember, I've had the same dream as Charlotte. Exactly the same. Except, instead of her father, it's... it's our parents," he said, looking over at his brother.

Confused, John looked over at Kevin and said, "What? I thought you said the people in your dream were faceless?"

Kevin nodded. "They were. They've been faceless for as far back as I can remember. But recently... ever since the dream has returned, their faces became more familiar."

"Jesus, Kevin. Why didn't you tell me?"

Kevin had no response and just shrugged.

Charlotte interrupted. "Maybe it's because you never knew what they looked like when you used to have the dream as a kid."

The brothers looked at one another, thinking.

"Ya know what," Kevin said, looking at John, "I think Charlotte might be right. I never knew what they looked like until you showed me a picture of them when you returned from this place."

Slowly, John nodded in agreement. "Yeah, that's the first time I saw what they looked like as well."

Kevin looked back over at Daniel and said, "So, other than the people being different, our dreams are exactly the same... right down to the voice saying, *Help her to help us.*"

Slightly taken aback, Daniel took a moment to gather his thoughts. He started to speak but found himself unsure what to say.

"I told you there was a weird twist to it," Charlotte said with a hint of a smile.

Daniel looked back and forth from Charlotte to Kevin then asked, "How long have you two known each other?"

Kevin paused and said, "We met about twenty minutes ago. This is my first time in Applewood."

Still puzzled, Daniel looked over at John. "And you?"

"Um, I've been here once before, but I just met Charlotte for the first time last week."

"Let me get this straight," Daniel said. "Two complete strangers... with no apparent connection... from halfway across the country... are having two very similar dreams? I'll tell ya what, this old man has heard and seen a lot in my life, but this is new one."

"Actually..." Kevin began, "we do have one big connection between us."

Kevin tried to explain, but the words failed to fall from his mouth. Seeing this, Charlotte stepped in. "There were two other people on my father's plane when it went down."

The wheels slowly turned in Daniel's head, and after a brief second, it hit him. His eyes widened, and he looked directly at Kevin and John. "That was *your* parents who were on the plane with Kyle?"

Perfectly synchronized, the brothers nodded their heads. Daniel grasped the wheels of his chair and began rocking himself back and forth. When he finally came to a halt, he offered his condolences to Kevin and John. His eyes then moved back over to Charlotte.

"I'm sorry for *all* your losses. You were all so young, and I can't imagine how this affected you." He took a long pause, carefully forming his next thoughts. "I think your dreams are starting to make more sense to me. It's like I said earlier, after losing someone close to you, it's very common to have these types of dreams about them... especially dreams that seem so real." Daniel noticed the look Kevin was giving to John. "Oh, boy... let me guess, there's more?"

At this point, Charlotte leaned in and said, "I think we all agree that it's common to have dreams about people who have passed on, but..."

"But in our case," Kevin interrupted, "John and I didn't learn about the plane crash until recently. As a matter of fact, we always just assumed our parents were still alive. And if that was the case, then how come I was having this dream when I was a kid?"

The old, weathered lines on Daniel's forehead crinkled together, and a confused look formed on his face. To his best ability, Kevin went on to explain the entire situation regarding their youth. He told Daniel about being put in the foster care system and how they always just assumed their parents had abandoned them. Kevin didn't go into detail about how or when they found out the truth—that would come a little later. The entire time Kevin spoke, Daniel sat perfectly still in his chair with his hands resting on his lap.

"So, you see, Daniel, I was having these dreams about my parents before I even knew they had died... before I even knew what they looked like. I think that's why they were faceless figures when I was younger. Because now that I've seen photos of them, and now that the dream has returned, the faces in the water are definitely them."

Up until now, John had remained quiet and let Charlotte and Kevin do all the talking. He was never good at holding back his thoughts, so during the next lull in conversation, he decided to cut right to the chase.

"This all has to do with the Evil Spirit and the Dark Waters, doesn't it? Our parents and Charlotte's father are trapped, and they can't move on to where they're supposed to go until it's defeated, right? Right?"

John's voice boomed through the living room. He didn't intend on being so shrill or abrupt, but he'd been so quiet for so long and he just couldn't help himself. Kevin and Charlotte were taken aback by his loud and over-eager comments. Kevin shot his brother a look as if telling him to chill out and take it down a notch. Daniel seemed unaffected. If anything, he was a little amused by John's outburst.

"I see you've read some of the old legends of our island. Although, I must admit, there aren't many versions that mention the soul not being able to move on once it's infected by the Evil Spirit."

"So, you don't think that's the case?" Charlotte asked, much softer than John.

"Oh, I didn't say that... I didn't say that at all. I think that's exactly what's going on here," Daniel said, slowly nodding his head.

"Do you think that's what caused my father's plane to crash... the Evil Spirit?"

Daniel clasped his hands together and replied, "That I can't tell you, my dear. But it definitely sounds like when the plane went down, the Dark Waters took hold. And it's obvious that your parents have been trying to speak to both of you through your dreams."

"So... you don't think we're crazy?" Charlotte asked.

Daniel grinned. "I never said you were."

Once again, John couldn't control himself. He wasn't as over-eager as he was impatient. "How do we fix it? How do we get rid of this Evil Spirit?"

Even as he spoke the words, John realized how crazy he sounded. There was a time not too long ago he would have laughed at the thought of believing in legends, and ghosts and spirits, evil or otherwise. He remembered laughing and making fun of William's tale of Medillia's Lament. He certainly wasn't laughing now. He'd seen and experienced too much here in Applewood—much more than his brother had so far.

Hearing John's question, Charlotte and Kevin inched towards the edge of their seats in anticipation of Daniel's response. Unfortunately, it wasn't exactly what they wanted to hear. Even worse, Daniel's response left them more confused than ever.

"I'm afraid it's not as simple as anyone being able to *fix* it. Supposedly, the only thing that can end the curse and defeat the Evil Spirit is an event known as Medillia's Lament. That's another one of our island's old folklores. Perhaps its most famous."

Daniel watched as confusion set in on his three guests. They looked at one another, but it was John who finally spoke. "With all due respect, sir, I don't think that's the case."

Daniel didn't share the same seriousness as the three of them. Instead, he smiled at John and said, "You don't think *what's* the case? You don't believe in the story of Medillia's Lament?"

"No... I mean, yes... I do believe in it, but... but if the story is true then the Evil Spirit and its Dark Waters would have been defeated seven years ago."

Daniel was still amused but was also a bit curious by John's comment. "Seven years ago, huh? And why is that?"

Without hesitation, John blurted out, "Because that's when Medillia's Lament occurred."

Assuming they were all just putting him on, Daniel started to laugh, but the seriousness on each of their faces caused him to hold back. It was then that Daniel's amusement turned into a full-on curiosity. "And you personally witnessed this amazing event?"

John paused. "Um, not exactly. I... I..."

Like always, Kevin jumped in to save his brother. "It's true. Our friend William saw it... kinda. It came to him in a dream, but he swore it was really occurring."

Daniel settled himself deep into his wheelchair and gathered his thoughts. No one said a word, causing an air of uncomfortable silence to float about the room. After a few moments, Charlotte gave John a nudge and whispered, "You should just tell him... everything."

John started to shake his head no, but before he could verbally deny her request, Daniel spoke up and said, "Please do, son... tell me *everything.*"

Besides telling Kevin, John had made it seven years without telling anyone what had happened in Applewood in those two weeks he was there. And now, in the span of a few days, he was about to tell two complete strangers about his unbelievable experience. And that's exactly what it was—unbelievable. If Clarence's ghost hadn't made an appearance earlier in the week, John would have chalked up what happened seven years ago as just a weird, crazy, and unplausible dream.

"Yeah, John, tell him everything," encouraged Kevin.

With all eyes on him, John felt like he was back in junior high getting peer pressured by his classmates to smoke a cigarette or something. And just like back in school, John caved in, and over the next hour, he poured his heart out and told Daniel everything—absolutely everything.

Even though Kevin and Charlotte had already heard the story, they both sat on the edge of their seats in awe of all the magical twists and turns John was revealing. Daniel also listened intently, but his face remained expressionless, making it hard for John to tell whether he was buying any of this. By the time he finished his story, he was emotionally exhausted. As he slumped against the back of the couch, his eyes, along with Kevin and Charlotte's, looked directly over at Daniel.

It wasn't until a smile appeared on Daniel's face that John blurted out, "You think I'm crazy, don't you? You think I'm making all of this up?"

Daniel continued to smile as he spoke. "I don't think you're crazy, son. I don't think any of you are crazy. And I certainly don't think any of you are making this up."

Then why are you fucking smiling so much, John thought to himself.

"The magical powers of this island are what attracted my ancestors to settle here. It was these same magical powers that kept them here despite the appearance of the Evil Spirit. I've lived a long life here on the island, and I, too, have seen and experienced things that most people wouldn't believe. Certainly not to the extent that you've just described," he said and grinned. "But that doesn't make what you say any less true."

"So, you *do* believe that Mcdillia's Lament has already occurred?" John asked.

"Although I've never been able to actually see the Dark Waters, I have been able to sense its evilness… its pure black evilness. And although I haven't had specific dreams like you two, I have felt the pain and hopelessness of all who are stuck here and unable to pass on to their next life. For as far back as I can remember, I've felt their despair—*all* of them… and there are many. And as I sit here today, the presence of the Evil Spirit is stronger than ever… closer than ever. And that is how I know Medillia's Lament has yet to occur."

Confused, Kevin and Charlotte looked over at John, who was slowly shaking his head no. He was more adamant than confused.

"No, that can't be right," John said, standing up. "I'm telling you, everything stated in the legend came true." John surprised himself by remembering and reciting every word of the final part of the legend. "During that brief moment in time, Applewood was turned into a magical place; a place where old wounds are healed, and a place where regrets find second chances. During this occurrence, time becomes irrelevant. The past, present, and future all get blurred together somehow, and within those nineteen sunrises, anything is possible… anything. And I swear to you, Daniel, every one of those things happened to me!"

John crossed his arms and sat back down. He had the look of a lawyer, who had confidently just given his closing arguments. It was now Daniel's turn, and by the wide grin on his face, John could tell he had something up his sleeve to poke holes in John's story. Over the next few minutes, that's exactly what Daniel did.

"John, as I told you earlier, I don't doubt anything you've told me… not at all. But the legend you just recited isn't the real legend… not exactly anyway."

More subdued than John, Charlotte inched forward and said, "But that's the same legend I grew up hearing, too… pretty much word for word."

Daniel continued smiling as he addressed Charlotte and the boys. "Have any of you ever played the telephone game?" As they looked over at one another, their faces became even more confused. "Oh, come on. You must have played it when you were younger. Everyone sits in a giant circle, and someone whispers a phrase into the first person's ear… only once, no repeating. And then they pass it on to the next person and so on and so forth."

Charlotte was the first to let a smile break free. "We used to play that in Girl Scouts."

Kevin looked over at John and smirked. "We used to play that at recess back in elementary school, remember?"

John gave his brother a slight nod, but his face was far from smiling. He turned his attention back to Daniel and asked, "What does this have to do with anything?"

Daniel replied, "Inevitably, what happened when the last person reiterated what they had heard?"

The question was directed more at John, but it was Kevin who answered. "It sounded nothing like the original phrase."

Grinning, Daniel nodded and said, "Precisely! Sometimes legends are no different. To be honest, this is exactly what happens to most legends and old stories. Over generations they become exaggerated, enhanced, and most definitely altered from their original versions."

John wouldn't let it go. "So what you're basically saying is the legend all three of us were told is complete garbage?"

"No, not at all, son. *Most* of what you heard is true."

"What's not true then?" Charlotte asked.

"Like I said, I'm only going by the story I was raised on. In the version you've been told, I believe Medillia plunges from the sky because she has lost all faith… all hope. Is that right?"

All three nodded in agreement.

"In the version I was told, Medillia didn't jump because she was sad or depressed… and she certainly hadn't lost all faith. Quite the contrary. Medillia plunged from the sky so that the people of Applewood would never have to feel any of those things."

"By defeating the Dark Waters?" Kevin asked.

"Exactly."

Charlotte thought for a moment then said, "So technically, if Medillia's Lament hasn't happened yet, I guess that makes it more of a prophecy than a legend?"

Daniel rubbed his chin and responded, "I suppose in a way it is. But still, things need to fall precisely into place for everything to happen the way it's supposed to."

John still wasn't buying it. "But what about William? Are you saying he never saw Medillia's Lament in his dream? Are you saying he was full of shit?"

"I'm not saying that at all. I'm sure he *did* have that dream. Sometimes, people believe so hard in something... that they see what they want to see. All I'm saying is the true legend states that when Medillia's Lament occurs, it cleanses the island of the Evil Spirit once and for all. And *if* that's the case, Medillia's Lament has yet to occur, because like I said earlier, the Evil Spirit is most definitely still here."

Considering that Kevin and Charlotte were still having their nightmares of their parents in the Dark Waters, they tended to agree with Daniel. And considering John's conversation with Clarence days earlier, he also knew that not only was the Evil Spirit still here, but it was only growing stronger. Still, John was confused by a few things.

"If Medillia's Lament has yet to occur then how do you explain what happened to me the last time I was here? Clarence... Mary... Sara... the whole crazy William-Bill-Rachel thing? It follows the legend exactly. The past, present, and future get blurred together... a magical place where old wounds are healed and where regrets find second chances..."

"He's right," Charlotte interrupted. "John must have been here during those nineteen sunrises."

Daniel burst out laughing then quickly apologized. "I'm sorry, dear. I'm honestly not trying to make fun, but... but I must tell you, the nineteen-sunrise thing is completely made up. I'm not sure when or how it came about, but I assure you, it was not part of the original story. Other than that, everything else you experienced is completely plausible. But I don't believe it was because of Medillia's Lament. You see, Applewood has always had those magical capabilities... long before my ancestors ever set foot on it. Of course, not everyone experiences what you did... not at all."

"Then why me?" asked John.

With a shrug and a smile, Daniel addressed his guests. "I'm afraid I can't answer that. But the fact that you experienced what you did... and the fact that you two are having dreams of the Dark Waters... it makes me think that all three of you are deeply connected to the magic of the island."

John continued to push. "But what about the phrase they keep hearing in their dreams... Help her to help us? Who the hell is *her*?"

"Once again, son, I can't answer that. But what I do know, is when the time is right, the answers will find us, and it's usually when we stop looking so hard."

In typical John style, he thought to himself, *Are you fucking kidding me? Then what the fuck did we come here for?* John was tempted to ask if there was a fortune teller on the island. *We'd have a better chance getting answers from a fucking Zoltar machine than this old witch doctor dude.*

Kevin and Charlotte didn't share the same colorful thoughts as John, but they did share in his disappointment. They came seeking answers, but the only thing they were leaving with was the knowledge of the true legend of Medillia's Lament, which, in their minds, did them no good.

As they were saying their goodbyes, Daniel mentioned to John that he had grown up with Clarence and Mary on the island. "If you ever see him again, tell him Daniel says hi."

At first, John thought he was mocking him, but between the honest and sincere look on Daniel's face and his tight-gripped handshake, John knew otherwise. The old man really did believe every word John had told him. Unfortunately, that would be the only slice of satisfaction John would leave with.

It didn't take long for them to voice their disappointment. Before they had even gone a mile, Kevin said what everyone was thinking. "Well, that was kind of a dead end."

"Ya think?" John blurted out from the passenger seat.

"I'm sorry, guys. I thought Daniel would have been more help."

John softened his tone and looked at Charlotte and said, "It's okay. At this point, anything was worth a shot."

"What do we do now?" asked Kevin.

Simultaneously, John and Charlotte shrugged but said nothing. Despite everything he'd experienced in Applewood, his pessimism was about to rear its head.

"What if this is all just bullshit?" John said.

Kevin poked his head forward. "What if *what* is bullshit?"

"All of this! What if it's just a coincidence you two are having similar dreams? And what if I'm just a giant nutjob who can talk to ghosts?"

"You don't believe that," Kevin said.

"I don't know what the fuck to believe in anymore! For a while, I actually started to believe the whole Medillia's Lament thing was real… and that I had experienced it. But now… now I'm told it never even happened. And are we really gonna believe there's a such thing as an Evil Spirit? This is real life… not some fucking Harry Potter movie." He used his best (worst) English accent when he said Harry Potter. John was reverting to his pessimistic self, which included using sarcasm as a defense mechanism.

"Relax, bro. You don't have to get all worked up."

Charlotte remained quiet, allowing the brothers their back and forth.

"Relax?" John huffed. Again, his sarcasm kicked in, and he changed his voice to that of a horror movie narrator. "But how can I relax knowing that the Evil Spirit is out in the ocean… and its Dark Waters are slowly making its way to the island? And once it does, we are all dooooomed! Dun dun dun!"

Annoyed with his wise-ass brother, Kevin leaned back against the seat. He knew it was useless to engage with John when he was like this. Charlotte seemed more amused than annoyed. Kevin shook his head at her as if to tell her not to encourage him.

She smiled and put her hand on John's leg. "I know this all seems crazy and confusing, but I think Daniel is right. All three of us are connected somehow. Maybe it's just the plane crash... or maybe it's something deeper. I don't really know. But what I do know is our parents are still out there in the Dark Waters, and we need to figure out how to help them."

From the backseat, Kevin nodded in agreement. John was about to once again use his sarcasm to deal with the situation, but as he looked into Charlotte's big brown eyes, he relented.

"Oh, shit!" Kevin exclaimed, looking down at his phone.

"What?"

"We've been gone almost two and a half hours. I have two missed calls and three angry texts from Julie." Kevin tossed his phone down and let out a huge sigh.

"What's going on?" Charlotte asked in John's direction.

John briefed her on the situation between Kevin and Julie. Charlotte sympathized with Kevin, and she pressed down on the gas, trying to get him back home as soon as possible. As they pulled into the driveway, John tried to reassure his brother.

"Relax, bro. I'm sure she's not that pissed."

Just then, they spotted Julie exiting the house. The look on her face said it all.

"I take that back. She looks *really* pissed. You should get going," John said, watching Julie march up the walkway.

"Aren't you coming?" Kevin asked, in a pleading sort of way.

"Me? No way. Besides, I gotta go back to the store to get my truck."

Halfway to the car, Julie paused and impatiently placed her hands on her hips. Reluctantly, Kevin unbuckled and exited.

Normally, John would have taken extreme pleasure in his brother getting in trouble with Julie. And if this were any other circumstance, he would have rolled down the window and yelled out, *Dead man walking*. Maybe John was softening up in his older age, or maybe the gravity of the situation had gotten to him; either way, he decided against any sort of sarcasm and ended up doing the opposite. He knew how much Kevin hated keeping things from Julie, and he also knew how impossible something like this would be to tell her... or anyone, for that matter.

John did roll down the window, but it wasn't to give his brother shit. It was to bail him out. "Sorry, Jules. It was totally my fault," John called out. "It took way longer than we expected. And not to mention, we had no cell service until just a little bit ago."

"Actually," Charlotte yelled out her window, "the whole thing is my fault. My mom and I were desperate to get everything lugged up to the second floor before the rain came. These guys were our saviors. We could never have done it on our own. Again, I'm so sorry it took so long."

Kevin gave Julie an apologetic kiss on her cheek and said, "I promise I'll make it up to you. I'm all yours for the rest of the day... I promise."

He gave her his best puppy-dog eyes, which never quite lived up to its name. It was more goofy than anything, but nonetheless, it served its purpose. Julie pushed away her irritation and cracked a tiny smile.

At that point, Charlotte got out of the car and reached into her purse and said, "Let me treat you guys to a nice dinner later tonight... it's the least I can do for you helping me today."

Kevin waved her off. "No, you don't have to do that, Charlotte."

Julie responded with, "Yeah, we appreciate it, but it's okay. I was just going stir crazy in the house, that's all. I'm glad the guys could be of help."

Kevin took his wife by the hand and started to head back inside. He paused, and looked back at John and Charlotte and mouthed,

Thank you. Kevin was glad he was off the hook with Julie, but his guilt was far from dissipated. So much so, that throughout their day of sightseeing, he broke down and ended up telling Julie *certain truths.*

As soon as Charlotte climbed back into the car, John reached out his hand. "I'll gladly take payment for today. A nice dinner tonight would be perfect."

She smirked and said, "Somehow I knew you were gonna say that."

He grinned and shrugged.

She looked down at her watch. "I'll tell ya what... how about lunch at the diner? My treat."

"Deal!" he said, knowing full well he wouldn't really allow her to pay.

About a mile down the road, John turned to her and said, "That was really cool what you did... covering for my brother back there."

"Eh, I was just following your lead," she said and winked. "You're a good brother to him."

"Aw, thanks. That's sweet of you. I mean, you're still paying for lunch, though." They both smiled as John lightly tapped her arm and said, "Just kidding. I do appreciate the compliment, though."

"You're welcome," she said, smiling and almost blushing.

John's eyes danced with admiration as he soaked her in from head to toe. He focused on her face and watched as she pushed a strand of hair behind her ear.

Without thinking, he blurted out, "You have beautiful features. Your *face*... your *face* has beautiful features, I mean. I wasn't referring to your body. Not that your body doesn't have beautiful features. I... ummm... are we almost at the diner or what?" He quickly looked away, placing his hand over his face.

By now, Charlotte was full-on blushing with the widest of smiles. Luckily for John, it was only another minute or two before they reached the diner. At one point during lunch, Charlotte's mother called her. Charlotte informed John that she had to head to work later that afternoon.

From the moment the waitress delivered their food, there were no more comments about the Dark Waters, the Evil Spirit, or the unexplained dreams Charlotte and Kevin were having. Seeing as Daniel provided no answers, and seeing as they had none of their own, they both came to a mutual agreement. They decided to push the heaviness of their situation aside and focus on more lighthearted subjects. The next thing they knew, they found themselves talking about music. It stemmed from an obscure 80s song, which was blaring throughout the diner. Within seconds, Charlotte proudly identified the name of the song.

"Yeah, I know," John replied, almost defensively.

Charlotte giggled. "Suuuure you did."

Her smile—her giggle—everything about her was adorable. Of course, this didn't stop John from doing what he always did; turning something innocent into a competition.

"First person to identify the title of the next song gets a point… and the first person to five points wins."

Charlotte started to laugh but realized John was serious—deadly serious. Smirking, she said, "Okay, you're on. What's the bet?"

"Loser pays for lunch… and dessert."

"Deal!" Charlotte reached out her hand to make it official.

Their little name-that-tune game went on for nearly an hour. It certainly lasted longer than their lunch did. After each point, they spent the rest of the song reminiscing about certain memories they had from that song. The closer each of them got to five points, however, the banter during the songs lessened quite a bit. By the time the score was four to four, not one word was spoken. They each sat on the edge of their seat with their ears perked up. It was as if they thought the closer their ears were to the speaker, the better chance they had of hearing the song first.

After being down four to two, John tied it up with two songs that were right up his alley—Night Ranger's "Sister Christian" and Queen's "Under Pressure." Technically, Charlotte was first to respond to the Queen song, but she made the rookie mistake of blurting out "Ice Ice Baby."

"Ha!" laughed John. "Wrong! It's Queen! The huge comeback continues! Four to four… next point wins!"

It had been forever since John was this excited from a competition, silly or not. With renewed confidence, he pumped his fist in the air and spent most of the song trash-talking Charlotte.

"Johnny Boy is on a roll! It was only a matter of time. You're actually pretty lucky to have gotten four points against me. I usually dominate this game with Kevin." And by dominate, John meant he usually won 51% of the time against his brother. "Pffft, Vanilla Ice. What were you thinking?"

A smile remained on Charlotte's face, but make no doubt about it, she was just as competitive as John—maybe more. *He's right*, she thought to herself. *What was I thinking blurting out Ice Ice Baby? I know better than that.*

As the song neared the end, the trash talking ceased, and they both put on their best game faces and tilted their ears toward the back speaker. At one point, the young boy busing the table next to them was apparently being too loud with his handling of the plates and dishes. Both John and Charlotte shot the poor kid a venomous glare. As Bowie and Mercury's finger snaps started to fade out, the boy scurried into the kitchen just in time. By now, John was standing and anxiously awaiting the deciding song. He crossed his fingers and prayed for something in his wheelhouse: Led Zeppelin, a little Pink Floyd, or maybe some AC/DC. If that was the case, he would surely win in less than two seconds.

Not to be outdone, Charlotte also stood. The rest of the diner was oblivious to their little game, but they wouldn't be for long. The anticipation of the next song seemed to last forever, but once it started to play, it only took 1.5 seconds for the game to end.

"Madonna—'Material Girl!'" Charlotte yelled and raised her hands above her head.

The entire diner stopped what they were doing and looked over at the two contestants. Charlotte was doing some sort of victory dance while John had slumped into his chair and was mumbling, "I can't believe I lost... to a fucking Madonna song." He then raised his head and voice up to Charlotte. "That might be the lamest song in the world."

"Do you know what else is lame?" Charlotte asked, grinning. "Losing!" The bill had been sitting on the edge of the table for a while, and Charlotte reached down and slid it in front of John and said, "Winner, winner, free diner dinner!"

If this was Kevin (or anyone else), it would have put John in a bad mood for the rest of the day. But it wasn't Kevin. It was a fun, funny, vivacious, and utterly attractive woman; a woman he was crushing on more and more as the minutes passed by. John snatched the bill and reached for his wallet. Even before the contest, he had every intention of paying for lunch, but the fact that he now *had* to pay because he lost, left a sour taste in his mouth—and on his face.

"Aww, is Johnny Boy a sore loser?" she asked, smiling and with a devilish twinkle in her eye. She was tempted to point to his Cubs hat and tell him he should be used to losing, but even she knew that was a low blow.

John placed some money on the table, and as they headed out of the diner, "Kashmir" by Led Zeppelin began to play. It stopped him in his tracks, causing him to shake his head up at the speaker and then up to the heavens above. "Are you fucking kidding me?" John mumbled. *Maybe God is a woman*, he thought. *Why else would the deciding song be a stupid Madonna song?*

They exited the diner, and by the time they reached Charlotte's car, the contest was all but forgotten. As soon as she looked at the clock in her car, she grunted. "Ugh. I gotta go to work soon. I'll drop you off and then head in."

Overeagerly, John suggested, "If you want, I can hang out with you at the store."

Charlotte loved the idea but chose a more subtle approach. "You don't have to do that. You'd probably be bored to death."

"Nah. No way I'd be bored with you. Besides, you said it's only for a few hours, right?"

"Yeah."

"Okay then, it's settled."

John leaned back against the seat, feeling quite content with himself. In his mind, he was being totally smooth and unrevealing of his feelings for her. Like most guys, John was easy to read. Charlotte knew without a doubt he was into her. Despite what he thought, his flirting was more awkward and obvious than smooth and subtle. Not only that, but on numerous occasions Charlotte caught him checking her out. It wasn't in a creepy or overly sexual way, and if truth be told, she liked how he admired her. It had been a long time since she felt that.

Charlotte was just as excited to hang out with John, for she had also developed feelings for him. But she, like most women, had a much better poker face when it came to stuff like this. She said and did just enough to make him think she *might* be into him, but she also did just enough to make him wonder and question himself. And make no doubt about it, she was attracted to him, and she also found herself checking him out. She was just much better at concealing it. It was like she was playing chess and he was playing checkers.

John spent the entire afternoon at the store hanging out with Charlotte. He didn't even mind when she put him to work. It was delivery day, and not only did John help unload it from the truck, but he helped put price tags on everything and restock the shelves. At one point, Charlotte had John running the register. After the store was closed, they went upstairs and watched two movies. They were practically cuddling on the couch, and there were multiple opportunities for a kiss, but John was still way too nervous. She even walked him out to his car, hoping he would finally make a move. He didn't.

John's drive from Charlotte's house back to William's was becoming pathetically similar each time, for he spent the whole drive yelling profanities at himself for chickening out yet again. With each step he took up the walkway, the same thoughts replayed in his head: *I should have kissed her. Why didn't I kiss her? Idiot, idiot, idiot!* It wasn't until his hand grasped the doorknob that his thoughts turned to his brother and Julie. He hoped their day was as half as good as his was. He also hoped that he wasn't about to walk into the middle of another one of their arguments. If that was the case, he'd rather sleep in his car. Either way, he had no idea what to expect as he opened the door.

What he wasn't expecting was the greeting he was about to get from Julie. Before the door had even shut behind him, Julie stood up from the couch and looked directly at him. For a second, he feared she was going to rehash her anger from earlier in the day. But to his surprise, Julie tilted her head and gave him what he thought was a warm and sympathetic gaze. His thoughts were confirmed as she walked towards him and gave him a long, heartfelt embrace.

In his ear, she whispered, "I'm so sorry about your parents, John."

Hesitantly, he pulled away. "What?"

"It's okay, Kevin told me everything."

John's jaw dropped open. "Everything?"

Just then, Kevin exited the bathroom and realized he was about ten seconds too late. "Hey, you. Did you get my messages?"

"Um, no," John said, still processing Julie's statement. "I left my charger here... my battery died earlier today."

Julie led John over to the couch. "Do want something to drink? I can make some tea if you want?"

"No thanks. I'm okay."

John's eyes continued looking over at his brother, wondering exactly what he had told Julie.

"I still can't believe your parents died in a plane crash... right here in Applewood. And the fact that Charlotte's father was the pilot... the whole thing is crazy. I guess the only good thing about this is at least you know they never abandoned you like you thought."

John nodded, but his eyes remained fixated on his brother. Kevin knew exactly what John must be wondering, so he stepped in and offered him some clarity. Apparently, after a long and very fun day of sightseeing together, Kevin couldn't take it anymore. There was no way Julie would believe everything that had been going on, but he needed to let her in on some of it, so he chose to tell her about his parents and the plane crash. And even then, he altered some of the facts.

"I told Julie that we had hired a private investigator a few months ago to track down our biological parents."

John knew his brother was slightly twisting the facts, but he nodded along with everything he was saying.

"And I told her how shocked we were when we read his findings."

"Disbelief is more like it," John added.

"Yeah, I told Julie we were both pretty skeptical... and a little freaked out, too."

"I can't imagine how you two must have been feeling," Julie said. "Finding out that your parents never abandoned you and had died in a plane crash is one thing... but to find out it happened in Applewood of all places... well, that would have blown my mind. I mean, what are the chances?"

"Astronomical," John replied.

"And what are the chances out of everyone here on the island, it was Charlotte that you start hanging out with? And not to mention, you wouldn't even have known about this island if it wasn't for..."

"William," John solemnly answered.

With a sad smile, Julie looked from John back to Kevin. "I don't know about you guys, but I have chills right now."

And to think, you don't even know half of it, John thought and laughed to himself.

"I told Julie that we only kept this from her because we wanted to find out for ourselves and see firsthand if this was all true. Which is why you came out here last week... to do some digging of your own."

Again, John nodded along with his brother's story and said, "Yeah, I'm sorry, Jules for keeping this from you."

"You don't need to apologize, John. Neither of you do. Yes, I would have loved to have known what was going on, but I get it. You wanted to be totally certain about everything. At least now I know why both of you have been so stressed out this past month or so."

Over the next few minutes, not much was spoken—by any of them. Julie let out a big yawn and then looked at her watch. "Well, I'm sure you boys have a lot to talk about. I'm going up to bed to do some reading. Goodnight." She leaned down and gave them a kiss on their foreheads. "Love you both," she said, smiling.

"Love you, too," replied Kevin.

"Night, Jules."

She stopped at the foot of the staircase and turned back and said, "I'm glad we're all here together. I really like this place."

As soon as she disappeared up the stairs, John looked over at Kevin. "You're pretty damn lucky, ya know? She's definitely one of the good ones. Don't fuck it up."

"I know," Kevin said, nodding. "That's kinda why I had to tell her what I did. I tried to call you to prepare you but..."

"It's okay, Kev. You did the right thing."

"I was tempted to tell her everything, but... but I had no idea where to even start. Not to mention, whenever it gets said out loud, it..."

"It sounds even crazier than when it was in your head?"

"Yeah... exactly." Kevin looked up at the staircase then turned back to John and lowered his voice even more. "There really *is* something weird about this island, huh? You were telling the truth about everything that happened to you the last time you were here, weren't you?"

"Well, yeah. You thought I was lying?"

Kevin shrugged. "Obviously I believed you about our parents. I mean, you had actual photos and a newspaper article, but... but how you found out about them is a bit... far-fetched."

"Are you shitting me? Do you really think I made up the whole Clarence and Mary thing? And how do you explain how William went from being single to being married to his high school sweetheart? Huh?"

Again, Kevin shrugged. "But to be fair, you're still the only one who has met this so-called wife of William's."

Although Kevin said it with a smirk, John took offense. He leaned even closer to his brother and raised his voice to a loud, defensive whisper. "You think I'm lying? As soon as we get back to Chicago, I'll fucking take you over to meet her! We'll see who's smirking then!"

"Calm down," Kevin said, now laughing. "I'm just trying to lighten the mood a bit."

"Well don't do it by questioning what I've experienced! You don't see me questioning or laughing at your fucking dream, do you?"

Kevin cocked his head and pondered. "Actually..."

"Okay, fine! I may have laughed the first time you told me. But come on, faceless drowning figures is kinda funny... not so much now, though."

"I guess what I'm trying to say is when you first told me, I was more focused on our parents rather than all the other stuff. We never really talked much about it after that, so I..."

"So, you thought I was crazy and made most of it up?"

Kevin smirked and said, "To be fair, I thought you were crazy way before you told me all that ghost stuff."

John shook his head in disgust, but before he could say a word, Kevin continued talking. "Relax, bro... I believe you... everything you've told me."

John was skeptical. "Really? You do?"

Kevin nodded and chuckled. "I should probably be seeing a whole team of psychiatrists, but yes, I really believe you."

Kevin's comment was intended to be a joke, but he didn't expect John to laugh as hard as he did.

"Oh my God," John said, slapping Kevin's leg. "Speaking of which, I totally forgot to tell you this. Guess who is on the island right now as we speak?"

Kevin shrugged. "You mean like a living person or one of your ghost friends?"

Completely ignoring Kevin's sarcasm, John stated, "Our hippy-chick shrink!"

"What?"

"Yup. She's staying over at the Great Blue Heron Inn. Well, it's not actually open anymore, but that's a whole other story."

John went on to tell his brother about the chance encounter he had with Hope the other day.

"I told her you were coming to town and that we would stop in to see her sometime."

"Wow. How did she even know about this place? I thought you said you never told her about... you know, everything that happened here."

"I didn't. Not a word. I think the only thing I ever told her was I went to Maine to help a friend fix up his house. I don't even think I mentioned the name Applewood."

"So... she just randomly picked this place to visit?"

"I guess so."

Kevin shook his head. "This island is creepy as shit. I mean, was it like this the last time you were here?"

"What do you mean?"

"All gloomy... and eerie... and foggy... and spooky."

"The stuff that happened was eerie and freaky, but as far as the weather was concerned, it wasn't anything like this at all."

"Isn't Stephen King from Maine?" Kevin asked.

"Yeah, he is. Further north, I think."

"Are you sure he isn't from here? Because I feel Applewood is the exact type of place he would be from."

John nodded in agreement then reached his hand into the box of Chicken in a Biskit on the table in front of him. He offered some to Kevin, and both brothers sat there in silence eating one cracker after another. When the box was empty, Kevin looked over at John and said, "I think I'm gonna hit the sack, too." About halfway up the staircase, he stopped and looked down at John. "Oh, by the way, how's the flirting going with Charlotte? Ya kiss her yet?"

"What? What are you talking about?"

"Oh, come on, bro. I might have a lot going on in my head, but I can certainly tell when you're gaga over someone."

"Gaga?"

"Yup, gaga. You get all goofy and shit around her. You think you're being smooth and sneaky, but I got news for ya, bro… you're the most obvious flirter in the history of flirters."

"Whatever," John huffed, with a hint of a smile.

Kevin continued up the stairs, but he knew there was no way that John would let him make it to the top without needing to have the last word. It took two steps to be exact.

"And if it seems like I'm flirting with her, it's only because we have a weird connection… you know, our parents and all."

Kevin grinned and nodded. "Uh huh."

"And even if I did have a little tiny crush on her, so what. I'm allowed."

"Never said you weren't. She seems like a very nice girl."

"She is," John mumbled under his breath. "And there's really no point in trying to pursue anything or to kiss her. I'll probably be heading back to Chicago sooner than later."

Kevin tried to wipe away his grin and act serious. "Well, good for you then… for showing restraint. You're a better man than most would be."

"Thank you," John said, assuming Kevin was being sincere. Kevin then disappeared up the rest of the staircase, but knew John had one more comment left in him. And just like clockwork, John's voice echoed upstairs, "I'm not *that* bad at flirting."

Kevin chuckled and mumbled to himself, "You're not that good at it either."

16

Seeing as the previous few days had been spent in the car, Kevin and Julie decided to sleep in and take some time to relax. John would have also loved to sleep in but that would have cut into his Charlotte time. He had no idea when he was going back to Chicago, so he wanted to make the most of every minute with her.

After hanging out with her for most of the morning, he headed back to the house to see if Kevin was awake yet. He figured it would be a good day to go visit their therapist. They invited Julie to come along, but she wanted to give them some brotherly time alone, so she passed and ran some errands instead. Her errands consisted of a trip to the old general store. She'd been wanting to go ever since they drove by it a few days ago.

It wasn't until she went to pay for her items that she noticed who was working behind the counter. "Hi," Julie said, barely making eye contact. She still felt embarrassed about her behavior yesterday morning, especially after learning the *truth* from Kevin.

"Hi," Charlotte pleasantly replied, and with more eye contact. "It's Julie, right?" Julie nodded and Charlotte reached her hand across the counter. "I'm Charlotte. It's nice to officially meet you."

Julie shook her hand. "It's nice to meet you, too," she said, managing a little more eye contact. "And I think I owe you an apology for yesterday. I didn't mean to come across as…"

"No apology necessary. I'm the one who should apologize to you... for keeping them out for so long."

Julie looked over her shoulder to see if anyone was within earshot. There were no other customers around, but still, Julie lowered her voice and whispered across the counter, "Kevin told me what's been going on... the real reason John invited us out here to Maine. I'm so sorry about your father."

Luckily, John had got a hold of Charlotte earlier that morning and told her exactly what Kevin had told Julie.

"Thank you. I appreciate it. I swear we weren't trying to keep you in the dark..."

"No, I get it. Kevin just wanted to gather all the facts first. I have to admit, the whole thing is such a strange coincidence. I mean, how strange is it that their parents used to vacation here... and Kevin and John never even knew it. And the fact that John just happened to run into you... and then read the article about the plane crash... And then start to put two and two together... It really is a small world, isn't it?"

"Yeah, the whole thing is pretty mind blowing. I still can't believe they went their whole lives thinking their parents abandoned them."

Julie nodded. "They've never really talked about it, especially John, but I could tell the thought of being abandoned weighed heavy on them over the years."

There was a moment of silence, but it was quickly interrupted by the jingling of the bell on the door. Julie turned and watched as a little old lady entered the store.

"Afternoon, Ms. Michaud. How are you today?"

The woman slowly made her way over to the counter. Julie slid her things off to the side to give the woman some room.

"How are you doing today, Ms. Michaud?" Charlotte repeated.

Ms. Michaud spent the next five minutes listing every ailment she was suffering from. She started off talking about her bad back and the arthritis in her hands, but then she quickly moved into the TMI category. It took Charlotte and Julie a second, but they eventually figured out that *pesky bumps in the back alley* was referring to hemorrhoids. It was all they could do to hold back their laughter.

"Enjoy your youthful bodies, ladies," Ms. Michaud announced. "Because one day you'll be old and broken down like me." She then slung her giant purse onto the counter.

It's no wonder she has back problems, thought Julie. *Her purse is just as big as she is.*

"The usual?" Charlotte asked.

"What was that, dear?"

"Do you want the usual?" Charlotte repeated slightly louder.

"Yes, yes, the same as I always get. I have the list here somewhere," she said, digging through her purse.

"It's okay, I think I remember them," Charlotte replied, moving over to the scratch tickets. "Hmm, I think you usually get two number fives, two number eights, five number elevens, and one lucky number seven."

By now, Ms. Michaud had her list and was carefully comparing it to what Charlotte had just recited.

"Am I right?" Charlotte asked, grinning knowingly.

The little old lady's eyes and mouth gaped open. "Wow! You're exactly right! I used to have a good memory like you. They say the key to strengthening your memory is doing crossword puzzles."

"Yeah, I think I've heard that," Charlotte said, ringing her in. "Do you do them… crosswords?"

"Nooo. They make those goddamn things so hard! I'm lucky if I can get three answers right."

"I can't do those either," Julie said. "Way too frustrating."

Ms. Michaud handed Charlotte some money and said, "Yup, no goddamn crossword puzzles for me. I'll stick to reading *People Magazine*… especially their Sexiest Man Alive issue. That George Clooney fella would be perfect for husband number five!"

Charlotte and Julie both burst out laughing.

"Am I right?" she asked in Julie's direction.

"Oh, I totally agree, ma'am. Clooney is a looker. But I might have to make Bradley Cooper husband number two for me."

The old lady's eyes twinkled and as she smiled, she placed her hand on Julie's and said, "Ooooo, I like the way you think. He's a tall drink of water as well."

When the girls finished laughing, Charlotte introduced Ms. Michaud to Julie.

"She's visiting here from Chicago."

"Chicago, huh? I've been there before. Too loud and busy for me. My second hubby took me there… or was it my third? Anyway, nice to meet you, dear."

"Nice to meet you as well."

Ms. Michaud's visit proved to be the perfect interruption for the girls. As soon as she left, Charlotte switched gears from John and Kevin's parents to a different topic.

"So, have you and Kevin done anything fun since you've been here?"

That simple question was all it took to move on from their previous abandonment and plane crash talk. Julie told her about their limited sightseeing adventures on and off the island so far.

"Sorry about the weather," Charlotte apologized. "It's not usually this gloomy for this long. Hopefully it'll clear soon."

The store was in a lull, which allowed the girls to continue their conversation uninterrupted. The more they talked, the more they realized how much they got along. So much so, Charlotte suggested they all go out to dinner. She suggested a quaint little Italian restaurant over in Gerrish Falls.

***

John and Kevin's afternoon wasn't as fun as Julie's. It wasn't that their visit with Hope was bad, not by any means. Kevin was very happy to see his old therapist. They both were. They agreed beforehand not to bring up anything that had been going on with them and Charlotte. And even though they kept the conversation simple, it was comforting to be in her presence.

Their visit lasted less than an hour. As usual, Hope was sweet and kind to them, but there was just something *off* about her. The boys did most of the talking, but even when she spoke, she seemed despondent. No sooner did they get into the car, Kevin said what they both were thinking. "Is it me or did she seem different?"

"Yeah, I was thinking the same thing. She seemed... sad."

"And I think she's lost some weight since we saw her at the bar last. And did you see how pale she was?"

"Yeah, I asked her about that the other day when I saw her. She said she was just fighting something off."

Kevin thought for a moment. "You don't think she has some sort of life-threatening illness, do you? Maybe that's why she retired so early. And maybe she chose some random and isolated place far away from Chicago where she could live out the rest of her days."

Her sad demeanor along with her pale and fragile appearance caused John to think of William. He looked and acted just like that towards the end. John was certainly not the most optimistic person in the world, but he knew he needed to force these depressing thoughts out of his head.

"No... no way. We're totally jumping to conclusions."

"I hope you're right," Kevin said. "I hope you're right."

On the ride back to the house, the brothers agreed that the whole island thing had them all on edge. They also agreed that maybe they should start focusing on something other than the unexplained mysteries of the island.

When Julie arrived back at William's house, she excitedly filled Kevin in on her afternoon over at the general store. "Charlotte and I ended up talking for like an hour or two. She's super cool. I like her."

Moments later, John entered from upstairs, and Julie informed both boys about their double date later that night.

"Sounds good," Kevin said, placing a kiss on his wife's cheek.

John's reaction was slightly different. "Wait… what?"

"I said, we're all going out to dinner tonight. It's an Italian place over in Gerrish Falls. I think you and I walked by it yesterday," she said in Kevin's direction.

Kevin thought a second and said, "Is it the one with the little courtyard and white lights everywhere?"

Julie started to respond but was interrupted by John.

"Did Charlotte use the words *double date* or was that you?"

"What?"

"How exactly did she word it? Did she say, *Hey, we should all go out for dinner tonight*… or did she say the words *double date*?"

By now, Kevin was shaking his head and grinning his way into the kitchen. Julie looked over at John, who was still anxiously awaiting an answer from her. As she watched him wipe his sweaty palms on his pants, she widely smiled and said, "Oh my God… you're totally gaga over her, aren't you?"

A loud, booming laugh came from the kitchen. John's face flushed red. Partly from embarrassment. Partly from anger.

"Ya know what, screw you both!" John huffed then started to march towards the stairs. It was like he was a little kid storming up to his bedroom.

"Relax, John. We're just joking with you. There's nothing wrong with you showing interest in someone. Besides, like I was telling Kevin, I like Charlotte… I like her a lot."

Julie's words caused his anger to subside, and as he paused on the stairs, he looked over and gave her an appreciative nod. Julie's next sentence caused his anger to completely disappear.

"By the way, Charlotte was the one who used the words *double date*, not me."

John tried his best to maintain his poker face, but like always, a smile broke free. Julie gave him a wink and sweetly said, "Love ya, John. And don't worry, we won't embarrass you tonight."

"Speak for yourself," yelled Kevin from the kitchen.

Julie quickly quelled John's nervousness. "Don't worry," she whispered. "I'll keep him on a short leash tonight."

Julie would hold true to her word and keep Kevin in check throughout the evening. Kevin, however, got most of his jabs out of the way long before they left for dinner. Most of his comments stemmed from John hogging the bathroom for well over an hour.

"What the hell are you doing in there? Manscaping?"

"Dude, shut the fuck up!" John yelled from behind the door.

Even when he finally exited the bathroom, his preparation was far from over. The next thirty minutes were spent trying on one shirt after another. The question, "Hey, Jules, what about this one?" was spoken at least five times. John chastised himself for not packing more clothes—especially nicer ones.

He looked at the clock and let out a groan. If he had more time, he would have gone out shopping for the perfect outfit and maybe even a fresh haircut. That exact feeling reminded him of the last time he was in Applewood. He remembered Sara inviting him to the big school dance and how he anxiously ran around trying to find something decent to wear. Not to mention, rushing into town for a cut and shave. The memory caused John to pause and think: *Is this the same as last time? Is Charlotte just a figment of my imagination? Is she just another ghost I can talk to… another strange product of the so-called magic of Applewood?* Just as quickly as the thoughts entered his mind, they left. *No, this is different,* he thought. *Charlotte is most definitely real.*

***

The extreme anxiousness John felt throughout the day quickly dissipated once their double date started. It went even better than he anticipated. There were no uncomfortable silences, no embarrassing moments, and even his awkward flirting was kept to a bare minimum. For Julie, it was nice not being outnumbered by the boys. Overall, the dinner date was a huge success. There were lots of laughs, lots of conversation, and lots of drinking. The drinking was solely relegated to Charlotte and Julie. What started off as one glass of wine each, turned into a bottle or two by the end of the night. The two girls got along so well that it felt like they were old sorority sisters who hadn't seen each other in forever.

By the time the waiter delivered the check, both women were drunk as a skunk. John dropped Kevin and Julie off at home and then proceeded to bring Charlotte back to her house. There were more than enough opportunities for John to finally kiss her, but due to her alcoholic condition, he decided to be a proper gentleman.

17

The countless red wines from the night before had taken a toll on Julie, which is why she barely stirred when Kevin's phone rang just after 9am. Kevin was still in bed but had been awake for a while. He answered the phone on the first ring, but the noise was enough to cause Julie to emit an annoyed groan.

As quietly as he could, Kevin whispered into the phone, "Hey, what's up?"

Apparently, it wasn't quiet enough. Julie let out another groan and shoved a pillow over her head.

"Hold on a sec," he said, climbing out of bed and heading downstairs.

"Are you still sleeping?" John asked.

"No, I'm up, but Jules is still asleep. Those wines did her in."

"I bet," John said, laughing. "Actually, that works out perfectly. Get dressed and come meet me down at the diner. I'm there now."

"Okay, sounds good. See you in a bit."

As quiet as he could, Kevin crept back into the bedroom to grab some clothes. On his way out, Julie's muffled voice emanated from beneath the pillow. "Who the hell was that?"

Kevin approached the bed, grinning. The only times Julie swore were when she was drinking, hungover, or if she was furious with Kevin… or all the above.

"It was John. He wants me to meet him out for coffee."

When she didn't respond right away, he just assumed she'd passed back out. As he took a step towards the door, Julie removed the pillow and asked, "Did he come home last night?"

"Nope. He certainly did not."

Her head was pounding, but she managed to smile and say, "They totally slept together! I bet he wants to meet you for coffee so he can give you all the juicy details."

Kevin grinned and shrugged. "Maybe."

"Take good notes and report back to me. I want the full scoop," she said, sitting up way too quickly. This caused the room to start spinning and her head to start pounding again.

"You just concentrate on getting some rest," he said, pointing to her nightstand, where he had placed a tall glass of water and a bottle of Advil.

"Aw, you're a lifesaver," she said. After she washed down a few Advil, she plopped her head back onto the pillow. With her eyes closed, she murmured, "Remember, details!"

"Yes, dear. Love you."

He assumed she returned the sentiment, but her mumbling was more incoherent than anything. The more he thought about it, the more he knew Julie was right; John wanted to spill the details to him over coffee. Many, many years ago, when they were both single, they'd meet out for coffee and fill each other in on the previous night's events. Kevin was happily married and certainly wouldn't change a thing, but sometimes he did miss those early morning coffee sessions with John, comparing their stories—the good, bad, and hilarious. With that in mind, Kevin rushed out of the house and eagerly awaited John's story.

Upon entering the diner, Kevin's excitement switched to confusion and a little disappointment. John wasn't alone. Charlotte was sitting next to him in the corner booth. *Looks like the details will have to wait*, Kevin thought to himself as he walked across the diner floor.

They both sat there drinking coffee, but it was obvious one of them looked a bit more disheveled than the other. "Rough morning?" Kevin asked Charlotte as he slid across from them.

"Do I look that bad?" she asked, attempting to fix her messy hair.

"Nah. I'm just kidding. At least you're up and about. Julie will probably still be in bed for another five hours or so."

"I bet," John said. "That's the most I've seen her drink in a long time. I think she was trying to keep up with her new sorority sister over here."

Kevin laughed and nodded in agreement.

"Would you rather we didn't get along? Besides, we weren't that bad last night, were we?"

"More entertaining than bad," Kevin replied.

"Entertaining and loud," John chimed in. "Very loud."

Charlotte leaned back and covered her face. "Ugh. I'm never drinking again." Both brothers gave her an incredulous look. "Well, at least not as much as last night anyway. And believe it or not, I hardly ever drink."

"Sure, we believe you," John said with a smirk.

Charlotte let out a frustrated groan and stood up.

"Where are you going?"

"To the bathroom… to fix my hair… and *this*," she said, motioning to her face and body.

"Good luck with that," John said, continuing to smirk.

When she was out of earshot, Kevin repeated John's statement back to him. "Good luck with that? You don't tell a woman that."

John brushed him off. "Oh, she knows I'm only joking."

Kevin smiled. "Well, the fact that you feel comfortable enough to joke like that tells me you guys are getting pretty close." Kevin lowered his voice and said, "Close enough to… *do it* last night?" Kevin followed with a sinister laugh.

"*Do it?* Who are you… Beavis and Butthead?"

John put the rest of his comments on hold as the waitress approached their table asking Kevin what he was drinking. As soon as she walked off to get his coffee, John leaned forward and in a hushed tone replied, "First of all, I don't kiss and tell."

"Ha! Since when? You used to be kissing and telling anyone who'd listen."

John started to retort but realized his brother was speaking the truth. "That was the old John. This version ain't kissing and telling you shit! Besides, you'd just go run and tell everything to Jules."

Kevin started to deny it, but he realized John also spoke the truth. He also knew there'd only be one reason John wouldn't be kissing and telling.

"Nothing happened, huh?"

"Nope. Nada. I still haven't even kissed her yet."

"Wow."

"I mean, she was more than a little drunk and flirty on the drive back to her place, so I'm sure I probably coulda got some, but that wouldn't have been very gentlemanly of me."

If Kevin didn't know his brother so well, he would have been impressed. But seeing as he knew him like the back of his hand, he grinned and said, "She passed out on you, huh?"

John tried to act offended, but even he couldn't pull it off. "Out cold before we even walked through her door. I put her into bed and crashed on the couch."

They both started laughing and were still laughing when Charlotte returned to the booth.

"Come on, guys," she said, fixing her hair again. "I did the best I could in there."

"Relax, Charlotte. We're not laughing at you."

"And you look fine," added Kevin.

John took it one step further. "You actually looked fine before you even went in there. Not sure you could ever look bad," he mumbled, but loud enough for her to hear.

She blushed but pretended not to have heard. "What was that?" she asked.

"Huh? Oh, nothing," he said.

John knew full well she heard him, but he pretended to fall for her pretending. The waitress placed the mug in front of Kevin, and as he added cream and sugar, he shook his head at the flirting games that were being comically played out in front of him.

After the waitress took their order and headed back into the kitchen, John turned his attention over to Kevin and said, "I know you and I talked a little about this yesterday, but Charlotte and I have been discussing it even further this morning. Until Clarence decides to pay me another visit with some new details… or until your dreams reveal something more specific regarding *Help her to help us*, I think we should just chill out and start enjoying ourselves a little. After all, we are on vacation here."

"Speak for yourself," Charlotte interrupted, grinning. "Some of us still have to work around here."

Usually, Kevin was never one to avoid facing any sort of issues in his life. He was always great at analyzing, dissecting, and facing problems head on. He was much better at it than John ever was. But ultimately, Kevin knew his brother was right. The heaviness of this whole situation was wearing on him, and seeing as the answers weren't coming easily, he knew that having some fun and relaxing was just what he needed.

"And on that note, I scored us two free rounds of golf at a premier course a little farther up Maine."

Loudly, Charlotte cleared her throat.

"Well, Charlotte was actually the one who scored them for us."

"Technically, it was my brother," she said. "He's a big-time Boston attorney and has connections everywhere."

"We'll have to rent clubs, but you can't beat two free rounds of golf. So what do ya say, bro, are you down?"

Kevin would have loved nothing more than an afternoon of golf, free or otherwise, but he hesitated.

John sensed his apprehension and said, "I know what you're thinking, but I already checked the weather up there. And believe it or not, it looks warm and sunny... nothing like here."

"No, it's not that," Kevin said.

"Are you worried about Julie?" John asked.

"Well... yeah. This is supposed to be our vacation. I can't leave her home alone while we go golfing for the—"

"Don't worry, I'll take care of her," Charlotte interrupted. "My brother has golf connections, but *I* have spa connections! I'm thinking a little day spa action is just what us girls need."

Slowly, a smile crept over Kevin's face. "Julie does love the spa... and it has been a while."

"It's settled," John said, raising his mug for a toast, "Golf day tomorrow!"

"Sorry, it can't be tomorrow. I have to work until three. Told ya, not all of us are on vacation here. I have the day after off, so we can do it then."

The guys were disappointed, but they figured two days from now was better than nothing.

"What about today?" John asked. "What should we all do today?"

Charlotte yawned and stretched her back out. "I don't know about you guys, but I'm going back to bed. Last night did me in. I am definitely not twenty-one anymore."

"You're not even thirty-one anymore," John sarcastically mumbled loud enough for her to hear.

"Ignore that idiot," Kevin said to Charlotte. "Besides, I do believe *he's* the oldest one at this table."

As John's smirk turned into a playful snarl, he slowly raised his middle finger at Kevin.

"Is he always this mature?" Charlotte asked.

"Yup," Kevin said, smacking John's hand.

Before they left, Charlotte mentioned that Janice was scheduled for another small grocery delivery and asked if the boys wanted to bring it to her. The brothers agreed and figured it would be a good chance for them to find out what was going on with Hope. Unfortunately, they never got the opportunity to talk to her, never mind see her. After they handed the bag of groceries to Janice, they asked if Hope was kicking around.

"I'm sorry, boys, but she's upstairs laying down. She said she wasn't feeling well."

John and Kevin started to leave but stopped. In unison, they turned and asked, "Is she okay?"

They looked at one another, and if this weren't such a serious matter, they would have called out, *Jinx, you owe me a Coke.*

Kevin clarified their question. "We're both concerned with her health."

John cut right to the chase. "Is she dying? Does she have some sort of cancer?"

Sympathetically, Janice smiled and placed her hand on John's shoulder. "No, no, no... it's nothing like that."

"What is it then?" Kevin asked. "We've known her for a long time, and she doesn't seem like herself... or look like herself."

Janice motioned to the chairs on the porch. "Here, have a seat."

After the three of them were seated, she did her best to explain her theory on Hope's condition. Janice claimed it was more emotional than physical.

"Keep in mind, I'm not a doctor or even a therapist, but I think Hope is suffering from post-retirement depression. I went through the same thing when I retired from the inn years ago. As much as I was exhausted and burned out, and as much as I was looking forward to some long-overdue *me* time, there was certainly an adjustment period. The first couple of weeks were amazing. I didn't worry about cleaning, or washing sheets, or cooking meals... I simply kicked back and did lots of reading and relaxing."

"Sounds pretty good if ya ask me," John interrupted.

"Oh, it was. But somewhere around week three I started getting antsy… bored even. When something ends that you've been doing most of your life, there's a certain emptiness that goes along with it. And it wasn't long before I found myself in a deep, dark depression."

"Really? You did?" Kevin asked.

"Of course. Nobody is above depression. It can get to the best of us."

John said nothing, but he knew she was one hundred percent right. Janice continued drawing a parallel to what she went through and what Hope was probably going through now.

"It might even be worse for Hope than it was for me. I was well beyond the typical retirement age when I called it quits… Eighty-two, to be exact. Hope is still quite young. I think it's normal for her to start questioning where her life is going from here… maybe even start questioning her life in general."

"What do you mean by questioning her life in general?"

"We all reach a point where we start questioning things. Things like: did I do everything I wanted to… do I have more regrets than accomplishments… what's my purpose here?"

"Like, questioning the meaning of life?" John asked.

Janice thought for a moment then said, "More specifically, I think she's questioning the meaning of *her* life. We all go through it. It might hit us at different ages, but at some point, we'll all ask ourselves that same question."

"Wow, we didn't realize she was this depressed about things," Kevin said. "I wish we could do something to help her."

"You can," Janice said, smiling. "Keep coming by to visit her. I saw the way she looked when you two were here last. She lit up like a Christmas tree."

John laughed. "I don't know about that."

"Oh, it's true. My eyesight might not be what it once was, but I certainly saw her expression. She adores you two."

John nodded, conceding Janice's comment. "Well... we kinda were her favorite patients... especially me."

Kevin rolled his eyes as if to apologize to Janice for his arrogant and idiotic brother.

Janice laughed and addressed John. "I'm not sure about *you* specifically, but you're not far off with regards to you two being her favorites. When you guys left the other day, she went on and on about you two. How she had known you since you were teenagers... how she always enjoyed her sessions with you... and most of all, how proud she was at the amazing men you've become."

Even John couldn't muster up a sarcastic response to this. They both sat there in silence as they pondered what needed to be done. They weren't sure how long they'd be in Applewood, but they knew they needed to visit and cheer up Hope as much as possible while they were here.

On the ride back, Kevin suggested they try to get Hope out of the house and take her to do some of the things that she loves.

"Yeah, that's a good idea," John said. "But... what exactly does she love to do?"

Kevin was equally as stumped as John. Hope had been their therapist on and off for nearly twenty-five years, yet they realized they didn't really know a lot about her life outside of the office.

"Hmm, she likes lava lamps," Kevin said.

"And Chinese stuff," John added.

"And Japanese, too."

They went back and forth reciting all the eclectic items found in her office over the years.

"Oh, and she loves crystals. And—"

"I got it!" John yelled out. "Ohhh, this is so perfect."

John explained his idea to his brother and told him it came from a flyer he had seen at the general store a few days earlier. Kevin loved it and even added another idea as well. When their plan was complete, they gave each other a high five and agreed to present their idea to the girls later that night.

Not long after they returned home, Kevin noticed one of the packing boxes at William's was labeled: *Games*. He opened it and was pleasantly surprised to find tons of classic old board games. As soon as he showed John, they both agreed that tonight would officially be game night at William's.

By the time their game night commenced, Julie and Charlotte were well-rested and feeling much better from their wine hangovers. Of course, that didn't stop the brothers from making one joke after another at their expense. The girls would have the last laugh, however. Julie knew all too well that the best way to shut the Mathews men up was to beat them at anything—especially board games.

It was either Julie or Charlotte who won every single game that night. The more they won, the quieter and more pissed off the guys were getting—especially John. Everything they had played so far were individual games with Julie winning six times and Charlotte four. As soon as Julie crushed everyone with her nearly perfect Yahtzee score, the boys knew they needed a new strategy. They knew they needed to combine their powers to defeat the girls.

"I think it's time for some team games," John said, tossing the dice aside.

"What do you have in mind?" Julie asked.

Kevin was already on it. Out of the packing box, he dug out Pictionary.

"What are the teams gonna be?" Charlotte asked, already knowing the answer.

"Guys against girls!" John and Kevin yelled out.

Long story short, both brothers went to bed that night feeling defeated, frustrated, and highly pissed off.

18

Charlotte had to work until three, but late in the morning, John, Kevin, and Julie all headed over to the Great Blue Heron Inn to pay Hope a surprise visit. A light rain was falling when the three of them exited the car. They spotted Janice sitting on the porch bundled in a blanket. She pointed to each of them as they walked up the stairs.

"I know you. I know you. But I don't know this one yet," she said pointing directly at Julie.

Kevin gave proper introductions and then Janice motioned for them to have a seat.

"Hope will be right out. She is making us some tea."

Right on cue, Hope exited the house and paused when she saw everyone sitting and looking up at her.

"Look who's here, Hope. Your fan club from Chicago came to pay you a visit."

"Here, let me help you with that," Kevin said, grabbing one of the mugs. He carefully handed it to Janice and watched as Hope took a seat next to her. "You remember my wife, Julie, right?"

"Yes, of course," Hope said. "Nice to see you again."

"You too. I have to tell you, the guys were beside themselves when they found out that you had randomly picked this place to retire to."

Hope politely smiled but lowered her eyes to the floorboards. Janice quickly stepped in with, "People have come from near and far to visit this magical island. Believe it or not, at least one person from every single United States has stayed in this inn before. Not to mention, people from over twenty different countries have stayed here as well."

"Wow," Julie said. "I was just commenting how beautiful this place was as we drove up the driveway."

"You should see the inside," Kevin said. "It's a living museum; it's like taking a step back in time. And don't even get me started on the architecture."

"Yeah, please don't get him started," John said, laughing. "These two are total nerds when it comes to old buildings or anything to do with history."

"Well, if that's the case," Janice said, "then I'm the queen of the nerds. Would you two like a tour?"

Eagerly, Kevin and Julie nodded their heads yes. Kevin helped Janice to her feet and aided her as they walked towards the front door.

"Are you coming?" Julie asked John.

"Nah, I think I'll just sit here and hang with Doc. As soon as the three of them entered the house, John turned to Hope and asked, "How's everything going, Doc?"

"Okay," she said, not very convincingly. "I'm sorry I missed you and Kevin yesterday. Janice told me you stopped by. I wasn't feeling very well, so I took a little nap."

"Well, I hope you're feeling better today. And I *really* hope you're feeling better by the time tonight rolls around."

"Why is that?"

"Because we're all taking you out tonight."

Hope started to laugh until she realized he was being serious. "What are you talking about?"

"Me, Kevin, Julie, and Charlotte are all taking you out for a nice dinner... and then a big surprise after."

"I appreciate the offer but—"

"Sorry, Doc, but I'm not taking no for an answer. And if you remember correctly, I can be quite stubborn."

That was the problem. She *did* remember how stubborn he was. And she knew there was no way he was going to let her come up with an excuse not to go.

"Just because the weather has been crummy, it doesn't mean you can't still enjoy yourself. And besides, I promise you this, you will absolutely love what we have in store."

While John continued softening Hope up and getting her excited for the mystery night, Kevin and Julie were in the middle of a detailed tour led by a master storyteller. Janice told them all about the history of the inn, and she had at least one story for every room they walked through. She might have been in her 90s, but she remembered details from fifty or sixty years ago just like they were yesterday. And for every story she told, Kevin and Julie had question after question for her.

"And this last room down here is another one of my favorites. I've said that about every room so far, haven't I? What can I say," Janice said, shrugging. "I love everything about this old place. Anyway, this last room is our living room slash library." Janice watched as Kevin and Julie stared around at all of the floor to ceiling bookshelves.

"Whoa. I love this room," Julie said, clutching Kevin's arm. "It has such a lived-in and comforting feeling to it… all the rooms, actually."

"Oh, this place has certainly been lived in, that's for sure."

"I love the old furniture," Kevin said. "It gives the place such character and a warmth."

"Thank you dear. But do you want to hear a confession? Everything in this room has been in the same location now for probably over thirty years."

Kevin laughed. "It's a good thing you don't live with us then. Julie rearranges our living room on a monthly basis."

"Not monthly," Julie said, giving him a playful slap on the arm.

Janice looked around the room and said, "I know this place isn't in business anymore…and I really have no one but myself to please, but I've been thinking a lot lately about doing some rearranging."

"You should," Julie said.

Again, Kevin laughed. "I bet Julie's wheels are already turning with what she would do with this room."

Janice tapped her finger on her lips as she gazed around. "How would you rearrange it?" she asked Julie.

"Oh, I think it looks fine the way it is."

Both Kevin and Janice gave her an incredulous look.

"Come on, dear. Even I can see your wheels turning."

"Well… maybe I would do a few different things in here."

Julie quickly went on to explain her ideas on the new arrangement for the living room. When she was finished, Janice remained quiet and continued looking around. Julie took it as a sign that maybe she had overstepped.

"Keep in mind that I'm not a professional interior designer, that's for sure. I mean, at the end of the day you should probably just go with what you—"

"I love it!" Janice exclaimed. "And I love your idea about buying some indoor plants for that corner over there. I really should have more indoor plants, especially now that I don't have my beautiful gardens outside. You're hired!"

Assuming she was joking, Julie laughed.

"I'm serious. You should stop over this week and help me do some rearranging. I'll gladly pay you. It's money I have, but energy, creativity, and strength I lack," she said, attempting to flex her bicep.

Proudly, Kevin looked over at his wife.

Julie smiled and said, "I… I would love to! But there's no way I'm going to accept any money."

"How about this… you help me do a little interior decorating, and I will cook you and your husband a special home-cooked meal."

"Deal!" Kevin yelled out.

When the agreement was settled, Janice peered out the window and happily said, "Looks like the rain has stopped for now. Let's go out back and I'll show you the courtyard."

Kevin and Julie helped her out the back door and onto the patio. It had been a while since Janice had been out in the courtyard, and her initial reaction was one of sadness. She sighed deeply as she slowly gazed around.

"I know it's been neglected for years… and it's not much to look at now… but just try to picture this with flower gardens as far as the eye can see and white lights all about the trellises."

"I can absolutely picture it," Julie said with the widest of smiles.

Kevin pointed up ahead. "Wow. I love this old fountain."

"Ah, yes. She's the centerpiece of my courtyard. Believe it or not, this was one of my first purchases here."

As they moved closer to the fountain, they could see it was overrun with rainwater, leaves, and debris.

"Unfortunately, it, too, is neglected. It needs to be cleaned out, and the water pump needs a good fixin'. Sadly, this whole place is getting neglected. Everything is old and broken down, including me," she said with wink. "Yup, this place used to be quite impressive. Let's go back inside, and I'll show you some pictures of what this courtyard looked like in its heyday."

While Janice was showing them one photo album after another, John was baring his soul to his old therapist.

"I know you're retired and the last thing you want to do is listen to my problems, but this is really bothering me, Doc."

Expressionless, Hope stared at John for the longest time then said, "Let me get this straight, you're extremely bothered by the fact that the girls beat you guys at game night?"

"Well, yeah," he said, matter-of-factly. "Every. Single. Game. It's frickin' embarrassing, Doc."

Hope cracked a smile. "You do realize that you might be the most overly competitive person I've ever met, right?"

"Aw, thanks, Doc. It's what keeps me young."

"Maybe I should try that myself," Hope said, joking.

"Doc, you're barely ten years older than me. You just need to regroup and get ready for the second half of your life. And it should be even more fun, considering you don't have to listen to people's problems anymore. Anyway, consider tonight your first venture into post-retirement fun."

"You're not going to give me any clues as to what we're doing?" she asked.

"Nope. Just be ready to go by five o'clock. Okay, maybe one little clue. All I can say is you *might* want to wear one of your tie-dye outfits. I'll leave it at that."

Hope was still beaten down and feeling depressed, but she had to admit, her curiosity was piqued.

***

True to their word, they all arrived back at the inn at 5pm on the dot. And just as instructed, Hope wore one of her favorite tie dye shirts. Of course, due to the continued rain, she had a lined jean jacket on over it. And to top off her outfit, she wore one of her classic free-flowing full length hippy skirts. Charlotte was driving, and John gave the front seat to Hope.

"You look great," Charlotte said, as Hope got into the car.

"Yeah, and I love that skirt you're wearing," Julie said from the back seat.

Hope tried to hide it, but her face was blushing as she quietly thanked them. Charlotte and Julie looked over at the boys as if waiting for them to give Charlotte a compliment as well.

"Don't look at us," John said. "We're shocked she's actually wearing shoes and not going barefoot." He started to say something about her wearing a bra, but he smartly held his comment. Either way, the mood was lightened, and John's comment produced a smile on

Hope's face. It would remain there until she climbed into bed and went to sleep later that night.

They started off by browsing a few stores in downtown Gerrish Falls. One of them was a new-age store full of crystals, rocks, and all the kinds of trinkets Hope loved. They also went to a Native American shop, where Hope was mesmerized with the display of hand-made dreamcatchers. For dinner, they went to a funky little Asian restaurant, which offered a fusion of Chinese and Japanese food.

Proudly, Kevin pointed out, "See, Chinese *and* Japanese. We knew you like both cultures."

"Yup, China and Japan," John interrupted. "Just like yin and yang."

"No, not like that at all," Julie chimed in, causing everyone to laugh.

On more than one occasion throughout the night, Hope found herself staring over at Charlotte. She still couldn't shake the familiarity she sensed. The feelings weren't as strong, but there were a couple of times Charlotte also looked over and felt the same thing. It would still be another few days until the truth would come to light.

When the bill was paid, Kevin looked at his watch and said, "We should get going. The show starts in twenty minutes."

"It's okay," Charlotte said. "It's only a two-minute walk from here."

"What kind of show are we going to?" Hope asked.

"You'll see, Doc," John said. "Prepare to be wowed."

As all five of them walked towards their final destination, they passed by the giant fountain in the main square. Hope slowed her pace and came to a stop. Her heart was racing, and her hands began to shake. It was the exact same place her father had taken her to play her guitar.

When the others noticed that Hope had stopped, they turned and headed back over to her. They assumed she was watching the guitar player, who was busking next to the fountain. She was, but it wasn't the guitar player's face she was seeing. It was a twenty-year-old version of herself.

Charlotte interrupted Hope's thoughts. "This area is known for its street performers, especially guitar players."

Hope looked over at Charlotte and smiled. She then reached into her purse and grabbed a twenty-dollar bill and placed it in the man's guitar case. He gave her an appreciative nod and mouthed the words, *thank you.*

The entire next block, Hope's heart pounded, and her thoughts remained on that fateful day thirty years ago. She hadn't thought about her busking performance in a long, long time, and she hadn't picked up her guitar in even longer. At one point, she was breathing so fast that she thought she was going to hyperventilate.

Charlotte and John were leading the way, and without even thinking about it, they began holding hands. As soon as they turned left at the next block, John paused and motioned for Hope to look up. They had arrived at the Gerrish Falls Music Hall. Hope looked up at the well-lit marquee, which read:

THE SUGAR MAGNOLIAS – THE ULTIMATE GRATEFUL DEAD TRIBUTE BAND

And just like that, her heart and breathing returned to normal, and a smile slowly crept over face. The next two hours were spent singing and dancing and getting completely lost in the music. By the time they returned Hope to the inn, she had thanked them at least twenty times.

"Again, thank you all so much for tonight. It was the most fun I've had in years."

Kevin leaned forward. "I know it wasn't the real deal, but—"

"Are you kidding?" Hope said. "They were amazing." She then looked directly at John and Kevin and said, "Thank you. I know they're not really your cup of tea, so I really appreciate you putting up with it just for me."

"It actually wasn't that bad," Kevin said, grinning.

Julie added, "I've never been a big Grateful Dead fan, but I loved it!"

"Agreed," Charlotte said.

They all looked to John for his response.

"Eh, they were okay. I mean, I'm probably gonna smell like patchouli and dead hippy for a month, but other than that…"

"John!" Charlotte said, smacking his arm.

"Oh, it's okay," Hope said, still smiling. "I am well-versed in John's sarcasm. It's endearing," she said, giving him a wink.

19

Bright and early the next morning, John and Kevin headed out to play golf. On their way out of town, John made sure to stop by the general store for a coffee and muffin. He claimed he wouldn't be able to function without some caffeine, but Kevin knew the real reason for the stop. John tried to act surprised that Charlotte was working, but Kevin knew differently and was quite amused listening to John play it off as a giant coincidence. Charlotte was only working a few hours and then was planning on picking up Julie at 9:30am and hitting the spa.

The golf course was only thirty minutes from Applewood, but the weather couldn't have been more opposite. It was eighty degrees without a cloud in the sky. In the past seven years, they had only managed a few rounds here and there. They used to go all the time in their early twenties, but life and work slowly put a crimp on their golf excursions.

In between games, they relaxed for an extended lunch at the club's restaurant. They sat out on the deck overlooking the course. Fresh air and some good old-fashioned competition were just what they needed. At times, it felt like they were twenty again. Kevin listened as John went on and on about how amazing Charlotte was. John even listed all the things he liked about her—personality and physical-wise. John wasn't the only one in a sharing mood. Kevin admitted that ever since they arrived in Applewood, he and Julie had found a renewed spark in their marriage.

"The sex has always been good, but ever since we got here, it's been off the charts!"

In the past, John loved hearing Kevin's juicy details, but this time it hit him a bit differently. It was all fine when Kevin and Julie were simply dating, but now that they were married, Julie was technically family. John didn't want to hear kinky details about his sister-in-law. And to make matters creepier, all this crazy sex was happening in William's house—William's parents' house—more specifically, in Clarence and Mary's bedroom.

"Ew!" John said, cringing. "You guys can't be doing that shit in there."

Kevin was quick with a retort. "You and Kristen used to have sex in her parents' bedroom up at their lake house. What's the difference?"

"Kristen's parents were still alive. Clarence and Mary are dead. That's not right, man. That's not right at all."

"I'll tell ya what, if Clarence's ghost pays you another visit and voices his displeasure, we'll stop. But until then, no way!"

John shook his head and grinned. "Just don't be doing it when I'm home. I left my headphones back in Chicago, and I don't need to be listening to your wild animal sex."

They leaned back in their chairs then both cracked up laughing. That moment was pretty much a snapshot of their entire day together: relaxing, joking, laughing, talking, and overall, just enjoying each other's company. Over the years, Julie and the Wild Irish Rose had taken up most of Kevin's attention. It wasn't a bad thing, but between the wedding, the marriage, and the bar, Kevin had little to no free time. It was the same with John and his woodworking business. Even when he and Jain broke up, he simply put all his extra time into the business. The brothers still caught the occasional Cubs game and tried to hit the batting cages as much as possible, but most of the time their schedules didn't line up. Either that, or they were just too exhausted to go out and have fun.

Their excursion to Maine was just what they needed. Due to the strange circumstances surrounding the trip, they were hesitant to call it a mini vacation, but that's just what it was. They didn't have the stress of running a business; there were no annoying customers, and certainly not a greedy landlord to deal with.

***

The girls stayed at the spa for a couple of hours and then went out for lunch and drinks. Due to some issues at the store, Charlotte had to go back in for the remainder of the day. Julie decided it would be a perfect time to take Janice up on her offer. For the rest of the afternoon, she helped Janice rearrange three different rooms. She even convinced Janice to take a ride with her and pick out a bunch of indoor plants. Julie didn't feel like she did much, but Janice was extremely happy with the new look of her downstairs rooms.

Janice gazed around the living room. "It's like a breath of fresh air." She placed her arm around Julie and sweetly said, "And you, my dear... you're like a breath of fresh air as well."

"Thanks, but I didn't do much. Do you really like it?"

Janice smiled and said, "The one thing you can always count on with me is I say what I mean, and I don't mince words. You have an exceptionally good eye for this sort of stuff. Not to mention, a sparkling personality as well. The hospitality business... that's where your calling is."

Julie laughed. "Technically, that's what I do. Kevin and I own a small bar back in Chicago."

"Ah, very nice. But I was talking about something more on the lines of... something like... like this place." Janice gave her a wink and then called Hope downstairs to admire the new, rearranged rooms.

Janice made some afternoon tea, and the three of them sat and talked for the better part of an hour. As soon as the clock struck five,

Janice stood up and said, "Five o'clock already? I better get going on that dinner for you and your hubby."

"Oh, you really don't have to do—"

"Nonsense! A deal is a deal."

"At least let me help you with it."

"Yeah, I'll help, too," Hope added.

"This wasn't part of the deal, but… it might be nice to have an extra hand or two in the kitchen."

Kevin and John were nearly halfway home when Julie called him about their dinner plans.

"Sounds good," Kevin said. "We'll be back on the island in about twenty minutes. I'm gonna take a shower and then I'll head over."

It was exactly 5:30pm when they crossed back over the causeway into Applewood. As they drove by the general store, John noticed Charlotte's car was there. She texted him earlier to let him know that she'd been called in to work for the afternoon. He thought about stopping in but decided to drop Kevin off at home before returning to visit. He didn't need Kevin making fun of him any further about his obvious crush on Charlotte.

"I had fun today," Kevin said, getting out of the truck.

"Me too," John said with a sly smirk. "It's always nice whipping your ass not once, but twice!"

"Yeah, yeah, yeah. I almost beat you."

"Ha! Horseshoes and hand grenades, my friend, Horseshoes and hand grenades."

"I definitely want a rematch."

"I'm free tomorrow morning."

"I'll see what Julie has going on for us tomorrow. Actually, we should see if Julie and Charlotte wanna come play a round with us." Kevin regretted his words as soon as he said it.

When John was dating Jain, they all did a foursome at one of the local courses. To say it didn't go well would be an understatement. Neither of the girls had ever played, and it showed. It took Julie nine swings and misses before she finally made contact with the ball, and although it traveled a total of twenty feet, Julie and Jain excitedly danced around as if she had just got a hole in one. John and Kevin weren't as excited, and neither was the growing line of impatient golfers behind them. Sometime around the fifth hole, the girls asked where the bathroom was because they both needed a "potty break." If that wasn't bad enough, they kept asking when halftime was. The final straw came during one of Jain's tee offs. Her hands slipped off the club during her backswing, causing it to fly into Kevin's family jewels. Needless to say, that would be the final hole of the day.

"Ya know what, just forget I even suggested that," Kevin said, as John stared blankly at him.

"Trust me, I will," John said, grinning. "What are you and Jules planning on doing after your dinner at Janice's?" Before Kevin could answer, John interrupted. "Actually... I don't wanna know. I don't wanna know at all. Whatever it is, just get it over with before I get home tonight."

Kevin smiled, almost blushing. "See ya later, bro. Say hi to Charlotte."

During the short ride back over to the general, John found himself laughing at all the random topics he and Kevin had talked about throughout the day. He was still smiling as he entered the store.

"Looks like someone had a fun day today," Charlotte called out from behind the counter.

"Actually, it was. Really fun. I mean, does it get any better than whipping your brother's ass twice in one day?"

Charlotte rolled her eyes. "Is that how you judge if something is fun or not—whether you won or lost?"

John gave her a child-like shrug then began to describe some of the highlights from his victories on the golf course. In particular, his amazing chip-in from the bunker on seventeen. The more he talked about certain shots and club selection, the more he realized she had no clue what he was talking about.

"You have no idea what I'm talking about, do you?" he asked.

"Sorry. I'm not really into golf... at least not real golf. Mini golf is a different story. I kick ass at that! Except, sometimes I whack it way too hard with that putter-stick-thingy."

Yup, he thought to himself, *inviting her and Julie to go golfing with them would be an abject disaster.* Still, he could definitely picture himself going on a mini golf date with her. It had been years since he had done that. He and Kristen used to go all the time when they first started dating. John remembered being so smitten with Kristen that he let her win most of the time—on the early dates anyway.

Not so long ago, remembering things like this would have spiraled John into a sad and dark place. He would have felt guilty for even entertaining the thought of going mini golfing with someone other than Kristen. It was guilty feelings like this which haunted him throughout his time with Jain and was partially to blame for the downfall of their relationship.

Strangely, as John envisioned mini golfing with Charlotte, he didn't feel that familiar twinge of guilt—not at all. Of course, being an overthinker, John wondered if *not* feeling guilty should make him feel extra guilty. Before he started to overanalyze his twisted thoughts, he decided to switch topics.

"I'm sorry you had to come back to work today."

"Eh, it is what it is. Good help is hard to find. On the bright side, as long as everyone shows up when they're supposed to, the rest of the week is pretty light for me. I just have to work here and there."

"That's good."

"Yes, it is. So, any big plans tonight?" she asked.

John assumed her question was her way of hinting that she wanted to do something with him.

"No, not at all. Why, did you want to go out to dinner or something?"

"I'm sorry, I can't. I already have plans."

Embarrassed for his assumption, John did his best to play it off. "No biggie… no biggie at all."

For whatever reason, he just assumed her plans were with another guy, but before his glass-half-empty pessimism kicked in, Charlotte clarified her comment. "My mom wants to have a little mother daughter dinner and a movie night over in Gerrish Falls. I know, I know, between working and living together, you'd think we be sick of each other."

"I think it's cool you guys are so close," John said, breathing a sigh of relief that her plans didn't involve another dude. "I'm probably just gonna go back to the house and crash early. It's exhausting kicking your brother's ass in golf. I did mention I beat him twice today, didn't I?"

She placed her hand over her face and shook her head. "You have some serious issues, don't you?"

"Oh, you have no idea," he said, laughing. "Just ask my shrink, she'll tell ya."

***

With a little help from her friends, Janice prepared her famous pot roast for dinner. She also baked a blueberry pie for dessert. Janice spent most of the dinner raving to Kevin about how wonderful his wife was. He wholeheartedly agreed. Throughout dinner, Janice asked what they had done so far on their vacation.

"Due to the weather, not a lot here in Applewood," Kevin answered.

"We did spend some time up in the Ogunquit and Kennebunk area. And we drove up the coast as far as L.L. Bean."

"Ah, ya can't come to Maine without stopping at the Bean," Janice said. "I haven't been up there in years."

"Are there any mountains around here?" Julie asked.

"There certainly are. The White Mountains up in New Hampshire are beautiful, and they're only a couple of hours from here. And if you go, definitely drive the Kancamagus Highway. The views will take your breath away."

Long after Janice went to bed, Julie and Kevin remained at the inn playing board games with Hope. And just like the previous night, Hope went to bed in a much better mood than she'd been in a long time.

20

First thing the next morning, Kevin and Julie took Janice's suggestion and headed up to the White Mountains for a couple of days. As soon as they left the house, John got up and drove over to see Charlotte at the store.

"You don't have to work the entire day, do you?" John asked.

"Nope. My mother and I have reinforcements coming in at noon. We're going down to see my brother and nieces for the day."

"Nice. That'll be fun."

That's what he said, but what he was really thinking was, *Now what am I supposed to do today? No Kevin… no Julie… and now no Charlotte. Shit.*

"How about you? What are you guys up to today?" she asked.

"Kevin and Julie went up to the White Mountains for a couple of days, so I'm not sure what I'll do. Maybe I'll go see what Doc is up to."

"I think it's sweet that you and Kevin are spending so much time with her… trying to pull her out of whatever she's going through."

"It's the least we can do. Despite being a tree-hugging hippy, she's always been there for us… even when I didn't want her to be. Don't tell her I said this, but she's one of the kindest and most non-judgmental people I've ever met. Uniquely cool, too… for a wacky hippy-chick shrink, that is."

Charlotte giggled as a handful of people entered the store. "Don't worry, your secret is safe with me," she said, and then waved hello to the new customers.

"I will say this, out of all the crazy coincidences that have gone on here, I still think one of the biggest is Doc ending up here with all of us. Out of all the places she could have traveled to, she chose Applewood, Maine. How random is that? Like, seriously, how'd she even hear of this place?"

Charlotte shrugged. "It's not *that* random… I mean, she has been here before."

"What are you talking about? No, she hasn't."

"Um, yes, she has. When Janice originally introduced us, she told me that Hope was an old friend and that she had stayed at the inn with her father like thirty years ago or something."

"Really? I'm almost positive she said otherwise."

"You probably misunderstood her, that's all."

Before he could say another word, he noticed a few customers making their way over to the register. The store was busier than normal, so John thought it best to get out of her hair. Before he had a chance to tell her he'd stop in and see her tomorrow, she beat him to it.

"I'll let you know if we get back early enough tonight and maybe we can hang out. If not, hopefully I'll see ya tomorrow," she said, pushing the strand of hair from in front of her face to behind her ear.

It'd been a while since he'd been in the game, but as he walked out the door, he was sure that the hair-flip thing was something that girls do when they're into you. He was pretty sure anyway. He made a mental note to run that theory by his brother, or better yet, run it by Julie.

During the drive home, his thoughts were scattered. They started off by thinking of Charlotte and her hair flip, but they quickly turned to thoughts of Hope.

"I didn't misunderstand shit," he said aloud. "I remember exactly what Doc said."

John recalled their conversation from a week earlier.

"How'd you even hear about this island, Doc?"

244

"I guess I randomly came across it on my travels and thought it seemed like a nice, quaint place to hunker down for a bit."

It didn't take long for more of Hope's lies to catch up with her. She definitely made it seem like her and Janice had never met up until recently.

I knew something was suspicious about that whole situation, he thought.

It wasn't until he pulled into William's driveway that his thoughts went all the way back to a conversation that he had with Hope seven years earlier. It was their first session right after he returned from Applewood. It took him a minute, but as he sat in the car, the exact conversation came back to him:

"Where did you go?"

"I actually went out to Maine… to help a friend fix up his house."

"Aw, that's where I'm from."

"You're kidding, right?"

"Well, I've actually never been there, but that's where my ancestors are from."

John slapped the steering wheel and exclaimed, "Son of a bitch! Doc was even lying to me back then!"

People told lies all the time: big ones, little ones, white ones. In most cases, John could care less, but this was different. This lie was told by Hope. He always considered her to be strange and wacky, but in his mind, she was as honest as they come.

Why the hell would Doc lie about this? What the hell went on thirty years ago with her and her father that would cause her to lie to my face… twice?

Seeing as Kevin and Julie were gone, and seeing as Charlotte was working, John planned on spending the day tackling another little project. He wanted to repaint the kitchen cabinets, but for whatever reason, his thoughts kept going back to Hope; more specifically, to her lies. Eventually, this bothered him so much that he cut his painting short and got back into his truck and headed straight to the inn to confront Hope. Technically, he was more curious than bothered. No matter what went on thirty years ago, the fact that they all shared some sort of history with Applewood caused John to think maybe this was more than a coincidence.

***

John knocked three solid times and waited. About thirty seconds later, the door slowly opened, revealing Janice's smiling face.

"Good afternoon, John. How are you?"

"Good afternoon, Mrs…"

"Janice. Just Janice," she said, giving him her signature wink.

"Good afternoon, Janice. Is Hope kicking around?"

Janice giggled. "I should have known you were here to see her. She's a popular one lately. She's had more visitors this week than I've had in a year."

John wasn't sure how to take that, so he found himself apologizing.

"Oh, goodness. No need to apologize. I think it's wonderful you all are spending so much time together." She looked around then whispered to John, "Between you and me, I think you're pulling her out of whatever funk she was in."

John thought about asking Janice if Hope had indeed visited Applewood before. He was tempted but decided to wait and take it up with Hope directly. Janice gave a yell up the staircase, informing Hope someone was here to see her. The floorboards creaked with every step Hope took down the hall. Finally, she peered her head around the corner and looked down the stairs.

"John? If you're here for game night, you're a day late," she said, giggling as she made her way down the stairs.

"Yeah, I heard about that," he said. "I also heard you and Julie won every game."

"I don't know about *every*… just lucky, I guess."

"You do realize if I woulda been here, I woulda dominated. I'm kinda like the king of board games."

Again, she giggled and said, "Your brother predicted you'd say exactly that. So, to what do I owe the pleasure?"

"Actually, I kind of have a bone to pick with you."

Janice tugged on Hope's sleeve and joked, "Uh oh, Hope, looks like you're in trouble."

"I guess so," Hope said, pretending to be scared. "No matter what Kevin told you, I promise I never told him he was my favorite."

This caused John to laugh out loud. "We'd really have a problem if that were the case." He continued smiling and said, "Not really a bone to pick with ya... just have something I wanna talk to you about."

He gave Janice a look which insinuated a talk in private. She caught on right away and suggested they go into the living room and that she'd make them some tea. Hope settled herself on the couch, while John chose the well-worn leather recliner. He was used to sitting across from her, but in the past, it was almost always Hope who spoke first. She would try her best to coax John's true feelings out, only to have him use sarcasm to deflect her every step of the way. This time was different. This time the roles were reversed. It was John who spoke first, and it was John who asked direct questions. Hope didn't use sarcasm to deflect. Her method was lowering her head and remaining quiet.

Not wanting to beat around the bush, John went right to the heart of the matter. "Hey, Doc... why did you lie to me?"

Hope grinned, assuming John would follow this up with some sort of punchline or wisecrack. His next comment wiped the grin completely off her face, leaving her speechless.

"You told me that you'd never been to Maine before... but you were here with your father, weren't you? Right here in Applewood. Right here in this very inn."

Hope gave him a deer-in-the-headlights look then lowered her head, avoiding any sort of eye contact. As she began squirming on the couch, John realized how uncomfortable his question had made her. He quickly attempted to lighten the mood.

"I was only joking about having a bone to pick with you. I'm not mad or anything. Just curious why you lied to me last week, that's all."

He said it with a goofy smile, as if to convince her it really wasn't that big of a deal. Her head was still lowered, and she didn't even see his expression. Hope was horrible at lying, but she was even worse at lying about lying.

"And technically, you lied to me seven years ago, too."

Hope had completely forgotten about that conversation, so she did her best to play it off. "I... I didn't really lie. I guess the subject never came up."

"Never came up?" he asked with a sly smile. He spent the next few minutes refreshing her memory of that session seven years ago in her office. Half the time, John was in his own little world during their sessions, and she just assumed he never heard a word she said, never mind remember them years later. So, when he recited word for word their exact conversation, she was more than a little surprised.

Hope knew she was busted. Even worse, she knew that John knew she knew she was busted. She was so uncomfortable that she began to fidget and pick at the afghan on the arm of the couch. She didn't notice a smirk creeping onto John's face. *My, my, my, how the tables have changed,* he happily thought to himself. It wasn't long ago that he was the one fidgeting after one of her pointed questions.

Finally, she took a deep breath and confessed. "You're right. I did lie to you. And I apologize. I'm sorry, John."

"Seriously, Doc, it's not that big of a deal. But... but why did feel the need to lie?"

Hope shrugged and said, "I've never really talked about my past... with anyone."

"Even with your best friends... or your boyfriends?"

She thought a second then shook her head. "No, not even with them. Sometimes it's easier to keep the past in the past, you know?"

Never in a million years would he think that Hope was just as jaded and guarded as he was. It was like he was having a conversation

248

with himself. So much so, her comment caused him to have a quick flashback and then burst out laughing.

"What's so funny?" she asked.

"Easier to keep the past in the past? I remember telling you that exact same thing during one of our sessions. To which you told me I needed to start facing the issues that I had buried over the years. I think your exact words were, 'I know it seems easier not to face this, but you need to start finding closure and to start coming to terms with things from your past.' That's when I said, 'Why, it's not gonna change things, is it?' And then I think you did your answering a question with a question thing… which I frickin' hate, by the way. But ultimately, you told me, 'No, John, facing your demons won't change the past… but it's a great starting point for the healing process to begin.' Yup, that's exactly what you said! So, unless you're the type of therapist who doesn't take her own advice, then I suggest you start the healing process and spill your demons to me."

Proudly, John crossed his arms and leaned back against the soft, cushy chair. "And you have it easier than I did," he said, pointing to the couch. "You have a comfortable couch to emit your feelings from. I had a futon… a frickin' futon."

She smiled and said, "It was a little uncomfortable, wasn't it?"

"Ya think?"

With her legs and bare feet tucked beneath her, Hope sunk deeper into the couch, allowing its soft cushions to envelop her entire body. "In hindsight, maybe I should have kept that old leather couch from when I first started out."

"Yes, yes you should have," John said, joining her in smiling. "In all seriousness, Doc, I think it'd do you some good to talk about your past."

"You do, huh?"

"I do. I'm not the smartest guy in the world, but it's pretty obvious what you're suffering from."

"Oh, really? And what is that?"

"Elastic overload."

She cracked a curious smile and said, "Elastic overload? What's that?"

"You don't remember?" John refreshed her memory by telling her about the time when she shoved elastic bands into a fishless fish tank. "You released a handful of elastic bands at the bottom of the tank and said, 'You can bury your feelings as deep as you want, but eventually they always come back to the surface. So, the sooner you deal with this, the sooner you'll avoid, as I like to put it, elastic overload.' You really don't remember that, Doc?"

"It's all coming back to me now," she said, giggling and covering her blushing face. "Sounds like something I'd do. I can't believe that *you* remember it… I can't believe you actually remember word for word the things I said. To be honest, I just assumed most of the time you had tuned me out."

"It might have seemed like that, but… but I heard every word. Whether I wanted to or not. You were a great shrink… and friend. I owe you more than I'll ever be able to repay."

"Oh, man," she said, covering her face once again. "You really are going to make me blush tonight, aren't you?"

"Consider it payback for making me sit on that damn futon."

They were both still laughing when Janice entered the room with their tea.

"Something must have been a hoot. I could hear you two laughing all the way in the kitchen."

"Sorry," John apologized. "I've been known to have a loud laugh."

Janice placed the tray of tea down and said, "I wasn't saying it was a bad thing. This house has been so quiet for so long… it's nice that you kids have brought some life back into it… maybe even back into each other." The final phrase was said with a wink and a smile. Neither of them said a word, but they knew Janice spoke the truth, especially Hope.

Janice looked in John's direction. "I was planning on starting an early dinner soon. Shall I set an extra place for you?"

Ordinarily, John would have politely declined, but as he looked over at Hope curled up on the couch, he knew he needed to stay and listen to her story.

"If it's no trouble."

"No trouble at all. Is shepherd's pie okay?"

"Perfect," he said, giving her a double thumbs up.

As soon as Janice left the room, John stirred some sugar into his cup and added a splash of milk. He gazed over at Hope and said, "I haven't had shepherd's pie in forever. Kristen used to make it, but no one could compete with Mrs. O'Neil's recipe."

"That's a name I haven't heard in a while. Have you ever had any contact with her... or *him*, for that matter?"

John started to comment, but before the words flowed from his lips, he thought twice. *She doesn't want to know about the O'Neils... not really anyway.* John realized this was her way of taking the spotlight off herself and placing it on him. He knew all about the old bait and switch. He perfected it.

"This session isn't about me," he said in his best therapist voice. "I want to hear about you... about you and your father's visit to Applewood."

"It's a long, strange story. You don't wanna hear about that."

John continued his imitation of Hope even further by slipping off his shoes and socks and sitting crisscross on the recliner. "Why do you think I don't want to hear about it?" he softly asked, trying his best not to smirk.

When she finally caught on, she cracked a smile and said, "Well played Mr. Mathews... well played."

"Come on, Doc. Out of all the things I've told you over the years, surely you can spill it regarding your earlier vacation to Applewood."

"The difference is, you told me those things because I was your therapist."

251

John took a sip of tea. "If it makes you feel more comfortable, Doc, I can charge you by the hour?"

She continued to smile, but there was a sadness to it. "I appreciate the offer, I really do. But I was serious about it being a long story... a long, complicated, and depressing story."

"Now you're speaking my language, Doc. Those are the best kind!"

John reclined the chair all the way back, placing his bare feet on the footrest. A second later, the stench hit his nose. "I'm just gonna put these back on," he said, grabbing his socks and sneakers. Not wanting to offend Hope, he stopped himself from making a wisecrack about hippies and smelly feet. Besides, in all their barefooted sessions, not once did her feet ever smell. If they did, the incense and patchouli masked it well.

When his shoes were back on, he once again reclined in the chair and gave Hope a look, letting her know he was ready for her to begin.

"You really want to hear this?" she asked.

"Yup, I really do, Doc."

Before beginning her story, she took a long sip of tea and an even longer inhale and exhale. She quickly realized that she couldn't fully tell the story of her and her father's week in Applewood without telling John everything, well, pretty much everything. She started by telling him about her mother dying during childbirth and how her father bolted town soon after. She didn't go into details, but she did mention that her father suffered from many things, including mental illness and alcoholism. She chose to omit that her mother also had a history of mental illness. She briefly talked about being raised by her grandparents and told him about the mysterious phone call every year on her birthday.

For the most part, John sat back and listened, but every so often he interjected with a question or a sympathetic comment regarding her situation. "What about caller ID? Couldn't you have figured out who it was all those years?"

Hope laughed. "Caller ID wasn't a thing back then. Besides, I didn't really need it to know it was him… I just knew."

She told John about the call on her twentieth birthday; how it was a collect call and how its location was revealed.

"So, you just up and left Chicago? You drove to Maine based on a gut feeling?"

Embarrassed, Hope dropped her head into her hands and groaned.

"I wasn't insinuating that it was a bad thing, Doc. Not at all." John lowered the footrest and sat up straight. "I think it's pretty badass! I'm seeing you in a whole new light, Doc."

"Ha. Thanks, but you might want to hold that thought until I finish telling you how I embarrassed myself that week."

She filled John in on everything that happened that week: her father planning the perfect anniversary, him showing her all the places where he romanced her mother, and ultimately, the final day she and her father spent together. The embarrassing moment she was referring to was when her father once again up and disappeared on her.

"I can't believe I was stupid enough to think he'd come back to Chicago with me and let me help him… and for us to start again."

"That's bullshit! Total bullshit!" John said, springing to his feet.

Hope gave a slight smile and asked, "Which part?"

"The part about him ditching you. I can't believe he'd do that… again." He watched as Hope cradled her teacup and shrugged. "And it's bullshit that you feel embarrassed. I think it's admirable as fuck that you wanted to reconnect and to help him."

For maybe the first time ever, John wanted to walk over and give his hippy-chick shrink a giant hug. He was seeing her in a completely different light. Instead, he paced around the room shaking his head back and forth. Between the abandonment of her father and the fact that she never met her mother, John realized just how much they had in common.

For a moment, he thought about telling Hope the real story about his own parents. Even after he returned from Applewood the first time, he never revealed any of the magical weirdness that went on, especially the part about how his parents died in a plane crash on the island years earlier. The moment was fleeting, and John thought better of it. Again, this conversation wasn't about him, it was about Hope.

He stayed the course and hesitantly asked another question. "Did you ever see him again… your father?" Hope dropped her gaze down to the floor, and he quickly followed with, "I'm sorry, I don't mean to be so nosy."

She gathered her thoughts, raised her eyes back up, and told John the rest of the story. She told him that her uncle had informed her about her father's death, and how she later found out the truth about Applewood.

"Wait," John interrupted. "So, your parents never met here?"

Slowly, she shook her head. "As far as I know, they've never even been to Maine before. My father must have randomly picked this place then sneakily tricked me into coming. Like I said, he wasn't well in the head… or well, period. To be honest, there's always been a part of me that wishes it never happened."

"Wished *what* never happened?"

"The whole week with him. I mean, what was the point? Up until then, I'd made it my whole life without seeing him. Seriously, what was the point of him being in my life for one measly week?"

Once again, John thought about his own situation. He remembered thinking how random it was for William to send him halfway across the country to this tiny, insignificant island. As it turned out, there was nothing random or insignificant about it. He also thought about something Hope had said to him when he was helping her pack up her office.

"Just because someone doesn't *stay* in your life, it doesn't mean they were never meant to enter it."

She started to speak, but instead, she leaned back, soaking his words in. "Wow. Those are some pretty wise words, Mr. Mathews."

"They should be. You're the one who said them. Also, Doc, maybe it wasn't so random... your father choosing this place. A friend of mine once told me, 'Everything happens for a reason, even if we don't see it at the time.' Actually, I think you said something similar to me as well. Something about how there's no such thing as coincidences and that everything happens for a reason... or something like that."

"Jeez Louise," she said, cracking a smile. "You're really using my own words against me tonight, aren't you?"

"What, don't you believe in what you say? You give good advice, Doc. And you say some pretty wise things, too. Don't get me wrong, you say and do some wacky and nutty off-the-wall shit, too."

Her smile grew and she nodded along in agreement.

"I guess what I'm saying, Doc, is... is you should listen and follow your own advice. I mean, be honest, didn't it feel a little good to get all that off your chest just now? When was the last time you told anyone that story?"

"About me and my father here in Applewood?" she asked.

He nodded. "About all of it."

She hesitated, and as her face reddened, she admitted that besides her uncle, John was the only person she'd ever told.

"Are you shitting me?"

"I told you earlier that I hadn't told anyone."

"Yeah, but I thought you were bullshitting me. So, not even Kevin?"

"No, John, not even Kevin."

Proudly, he leaned back and fully reclined the chair. A victorious smile swept across his face.

"Oh, Janice knows most of it, too. She was partially involved, so I felt like I needed to tell her."

In all honesty, as long as John knew before Kevin, it wouldn't have mattered if Hope told the whole world. Knowing this wasn't about him, John cut his celebration short and turned his attention back to Hope. He thanked her for trusting him enough to reveal her past.

"So, I guess that's why I technically lied to you back then. I buried my past so deep… I guess I just wasn't ready to talk about it. Not to mention, it was *your* session, not mine. But at the very least, I should have told you the truth last week when we ran into each other here. I apologize."

"No need to apologize, Doc. I get it. I really do."

A bolt of guilt shot through him as he thought about all the times he secretly made fun of her quirky ways; not to mention, all the times he referred to her as his wacky hippy-chick shrink. But despite her appearance and her unconventional ways, John always assumed she had her shit together. Never in a million years would he have guessed she had that dark of a past. His sympathy grew even more, knowing she had devoted her entire adult life to listening to other people's problems.

"I'm so, so sorry you had to go through all that. I wish—"

John's comment was interrupted by Janice calling out that dinner was ready. Dinner proved to be a welcomed reprieve from the heaviness of their conversation. It was almost as if Janice could sense this heaviness, for she turned the dinner table into one hilarious story after another about some of her more outlandish guests. Hope chimed in and told John about the lovey-dovey couple, the Hendersons.

"That's one thing Kristen and I never did, use pet names. It used to drive us nuts listening to other couples who did that. Thank God Kevin and Julie don't do that crap. I might have to disown them."

John's comment caused Janice to ask a simple question; a simple question to most, but Hope knew full well it would trigger John and cause him to shut down.

"Who's Kristen?"

Watching John out of the corner of her eye, Hope held her breath.

"Oh, she was my wife," John said, more quickly and smoothly than Hope anticipated. "She and our daughter died in a car accident a while ago."

"You poor soul," Janice said, clutching her heart. "I'm so very, very sorry."

John thanked Janice for her sympathy. He then continued talking about Kristen and Hannah with surprising candor and ease. The entire time Hope listened, she wore a warm, beaming smile on her face. It was nothing compared to what she was about to feel.

"I'm glad you can hold onto the good memories of them," Janice said. "I think most people would have sunk into a deep, dark hole of depression. I'm sure I would have."

"Oh, I did. I spiraled out of control and sunk into the deepest hole imaginable." John looked over at Hope. "Luckily for me, Doc threw me a rope and helped pull me out. I'd still be in that dark hole if it weren't for her."

John knew that Kevin and William had also played a big part in his recovery, but at that very moment, he knew Hope needed to hear how integral she was in his life—he just didn't realize how much.

Hope chose her profession to make a difference in people's lives, and for the longest time, she believed she did. Unfortunately, over the years she'd become more and more jaded. For the most part, being a therapist is a tough and thankless job. You see and hear the worst possible things with your patients, and even if you're responsible for a breakthrough, they rarely return to voice their gratitude. Hope didn't choose to be a therapist for thanks or gratitude, but like all living beings, it's a beautiful thing when it's shown. And because of that, John's comment hit her like a ton of bricks. So much so, her eyes welled up, and she was forced to wipe them with her napkin.

Usually, whenever John made someone cry, he immediately felt like shit, but this time was different—different in a much better way. He knew she needed to hear those words, and he also knew she probably hadn't heard them enough over the years. He wanted her to realize how big of a role she played in his life, but he also didn't want to overly embarrass her.

"This shepherd's pie is out of this world," he said, looking over at Janice. "It tastes very similar to what they serve over at the diner."

"I should hope so. I'm the one who gave them my recipe."

By now, Hope composed herself enough to chime in. "It really is delicious, Janice. You should taste her pot roast, too. Best I've ever had."

John made a wisecrack about Hope eating meat. He assumed all hippies were vegetarians. Hope shook her head, telling him not to believe all the stereotypes.

"Are you telling me you're not a pot-smoking, tree-hugging, granola-eating, run-naked-around-the-woods, singing Kumbaya kind of hippy?"

For a couple of reasons, John's question made Hope giggle. For one, it sounded just like something her father would have said. Actually, she recalled him saying something very similar. Hope also giggled because she knew she never fit into the typical hippy stereotype. Even Janice seemed eager to hear Hope's response. They both looked over and awaited her answer.

After a long pause, Hope decided to go the mysterious route. "Let's just say, out of all the things you listed, I *might* have done one of them."

John and Janice looked over at one another. His mind raced with funny comebacks, but before he could let one fly, Janice beat him to it.

"I've never seen her eat granola or actually hug a tree, have you?"

John burst out laughing, knowing that was exactly what he was going to say.

"No, no I haven't. I guess that only leaves a couple things left."

"I plead the fifth," she said, covering her blushing face.

Luckily for Hope, John's referral of running around naked reminded Janice of another hilarious story of one of her more unique guests, who preferred to walk the halls sans clothes.

"Please tell me that wasn't my father," Hope said, giggling.

"No, no, no. Believe it or not, your father was normal compared to some of my guests."

John polished off his final bite and said, "You should tell all your stories to Charlotte. She's an amazing writer. Maybe she can write a book about it. You can call it *The Diaries of the Great Blue Heron Inn.*"

"That's a wonderful idea," Hope added.

Janice laughed. "It would certainly be quite the book, I'll give you that. And you're right, Charlotte is a very talented writer, but... but I think she's destined for much bigger projects," Janice said, more in Hope's direction.

With her words still hanging in the air, Janice stood up and began clearing the plates.

Hope and John also stood and helped bring everything into the kitchen, and despite Janice's resistance, they both began to wash and dry the dishes.

"It's the least I can do," John said. "One of the best meals I've had in a while."

"Why, thank you, dear. Hopefully you're sticking around for dessert. I was going to whip up some chocolate and butterscotch pudding."

John was stuffed beyond belief but was reminded of something Hannah used to say after a big meal. She would clutch her stomach and groan, "I'm soooo stuffed!" John would make a comment about her being too full for dessert. "There's always room for dessert, Daddy," she said, perking up and giggling.

Hannah's right, he thought. *There's always room for dessert... especially pudding.* "Whipped cream, too?" he asked in Janice's direction.

"Is there any other way to eat it?" she asked, smiling.

Janice then ordered them out of the kitchen and told them to settle themselves back into the living room and that she'd bring them some more tea.

"You two drink a shit-ton of tea, huh?"

Hope nodded. "It's my favorite. No matter what time of year or what time of day, it always comforts me."

"Yeah, Kristen used to be the same way. Don't even get me started about a hot tea, a warm bath, and…"

"And a good book," Hope interrupted.

"Yup. How'd ya guess?"

"She sounds like my kinda gal."

"Yeah, she was pretty special."

Hope loved that John wore a smile as he said it. She commented how refreshing it was for him to talk so fondly and freely about Kristen and Hannah. She also mentioned that Hannah sounded like a firecracker. This made him laugh. He could have talked for hours about the crazy antics of his daughter, but he wanted to keep tonight's focus on Hope. He knew a lot of this was hard for her to talk about, but he also knew that was kind of the point. She needed to let it out, and he was more than happy to be on the receiving end.

"Can I ask you a personal question?" he said, out of the blue.

Hope laughed. "I think that line was crossed hours ago, don't you?"

"Good point," he said, and then let it fly. "Have you ever been married? To a guy… or girl. No judging here."

Normally, the marriage question caused Hope immense anxiety, but the way John worded it, she couldn't help but laugh.

"You really are caught up in your stereotypes, aren't you? Despite what you might think, not all hippies are lesbians, and before you say it, not all lesbians drive Subarus."

They both laughed at her comment.

"Not that it matters, like, not at *all*… but I'm very much straight."

"Good for you," he said, not knowing what else to say. "I mean, it would be fine either way, but... yeah, good for you. So, is that a no to marriage?"

"Yes, John, that's a no to marriage." She took a long pause and said, "Tulsa... Tulsa, Oklahoma."

"Huh?" John asked, confused.

"You told me that the beginning of the end with you and Jain was the suggested move to Houston, right?"

"It was kind of going downhill before that, but yeah, that was the final straw, so to speak."

"Mine was Tulsa."

Hope got as comfortable as she could, and then filled John in on her own failed relationship. The relationship lasted three years, and it was the closest she had ever come to marriage. Her boyfriend was also offered an amazing job, which would have required her to move to Oklahoma.

"I came close, I really did. We even spent a week down there looking at houses and potential spots for my new office, but..."

"But you didn't want to leave Chicago, did you?"

She thought for a moment and said, "I think it's just like you described it before, John. I wasn't opposed to leaving Chicago... just not Tulsa. At least that's what I told myself. But the truth is... it could have been any city and I just wasn't feeling it, ya know?"

John nodded and continued listening.

"For better or worse, I've always trusted my gut feeling, and at the time, it was telling me I needed to stay in Chicago. We briefly talked about trying a long-distance relationship, but I knew in my heart that if I stayed in Chicago, it would be over."

"I'm sorry," John said, looking into Hope's eyes. "That must have been hard for you. How long ago was that?"

"It was back in 2003."

John had his own memories from that year. That's when he was at the peak of his happiness. A beautiful wife... a sweet little daughter... on the verge of owning a bar with his brother. That was also the year all of it was taken away from him. Just as quickly as those thoughts entered his mind, John pushed them away. This was the most personal Hope had ever been with him, so he knew he needed to give her his full attention.

"Have you seen or talked to him since?" he asked. Hope took a long pause. Long enough to make John think he was overstepping. "I'm sorry. It's really none of business, Doc."

"It's okay. Yes, I did reach out a few years ago. He was... happily married... with a kid on the way."

John was the king of using sarcasm and jokes to lighten the mood, but this didn't seem like the time or place for any of that. Before he could offer his sincere apologies, Hope spoke up. "Do you want to know what the craziest thing is? If I had to do it all over again, I think I'd still make the same decision. I'm not exactly sure what that says about me, but..."

"It says that deep down you knew he wasn't the one. And that probably goes for me and Jain as well. I guess she just wasn't the one."

"Despite your sarcasm, you're a pretty smart man, Mr. Mathews."

"Ha, thanks. I have my moments. But I do apologize for bringing up a sore subject."

"It's okay. I just haven't talked about him in a long time, which is music to my therapist's ears. I used to talk about him nonstop to her."

"Wait... you see a shrink? No way."

Hope laughed. "Most every therapist I know has their own therapist. I'm no different than you."

"You always acted and dressed a little weird, but I just assumed you had your shit together."

This caused Hope to laugh even louder. "My *shit* is nowhere near together. You of all people should know that. You used to make fun of all the different philosophies and cultures I followed."

John thought about all the eclectic décor she had throughout her office: new-age crystals, Buddhism, Hinduism, Grateful Deadism, and of course, a strong Native American presence.

She really was all over the map when it came to this stuff, he thought.

"I believe you once asked me if I got my degree at the University of Jerry Garcia. Remember?"

"Vaguely," he said, smirking. "Sounds like something I'd say, though."

John was about to list the many wacky items she had throughout her office but held off when he heard her comments.

"You also told me something like, 'How am I supposed to take you serious when you can't even settle on a stupid philosophy or culture.'"

John's smirk was replaced by a remorseful look. He said a lot of mean and regretful things when he was drinking. At the time, he thought he was being hilarious, but hearing his words repeated back to him caused a wave of guilt to crash down over him. Hope saw the remorse in his eyes and was quick to point out the sad truth.

"You were right. You were absolutely right. I've been pathetically searching for some sort of spiritual meaning and guidance my entire life. And look at me now… I'm no closer to finding it than when I was as a kid. Yup, pathetic."

Her revelation caused John to feel even more guilty for his sarcastic comments. He couldn't help but think that he'd gone through life with his head up his ass, thinking his problems were bigger than most. As they both sat in silence, John began to focus on the two dreamcatchers hanging on either side of the fireplace.

"Hey, Doc, didn't you also tell me that your ancestors were from Maine? Something about you being related to a Native American chief?"

Slowly and sadly, Hope nodded. "Another one of my twisted truths. Do you remember that seashell necklace I used to wear? It was given to me by my father. I later found out that its origins were somewhere here in New England. Supposedly, those type of seashell necklaces were worn by the wife of a great chief. I never actually had proof it came from my own family, but… but I loved the idea of it so much that I convinced myself it was the truth. I told you, pathetic."

"Nah, not pathetic at all, Doc. Besides, you don't know for sure that it's not true, right?"

"No, but… what are the chances?"

"Trust me, Doc, weirder shit has happened on this island."

He certainly could have gone into much more detail about this, but he figured this was a good place to end their chat for the night. Hope profusely thanked him for his kindness and for listening to her.

"No need to thank me. I told you, Doc, I owe you more than you'll ever know."

Hope ended her night by doing some writing in her journal. She'd been doing that quite a bit since being back in Applewood.

21

The past few days had put Hope in a much better frame of mind. So much so, that when she awoke the next morning, she decided to take a nice drive around the island revisiting all the places and memories from thirty years ago. Once again, the general store was as far as she made it before she started second-guessing her plan. She sat in her car for twenty minutes then decided to go inside the store. Surely, a hot herbal tea would calm her nerves.

Charlotte was working, and as soon as she spotted Hope, she felt a little guilty. After all, she was the one who blabbed to John that Hope had been to the island before. Charlotte wasted no time apologizing. As soon as Hope approached the register with her tea, Charlotte said, "I'm so sorry I told John that you had been here before. I just assumed…"

"Oh, there's no need to apologize, Charlotte. You did nothing wrong. In my head, I guess I didn't think I was purposely keeping it from him… it's not really a subject I talk much about to anyone. Let's just say it was a long, long time ago, and it was a strange and dark period of my life—especially that week here with my father. Anyway, I'm sure John filled you in on all of it."

Charlotte shook her head. "No, not really. The only thing he mentioned was that your father brought you here to show all the different places where he originally romanced your mother. He said that's all he could tell me. Something about doctor/patient confidentiality."

Hope laughed. "Aw, that's kinda sweet he still considers me his therapist."

Charlotte giggled and said, "Actually, I think he was referring to *himself* as the therapist and *you* as the patient."

Hope continued laughing. "That works, too. That's actually why I'm here this morning. I'm trying to find the courage to finally drive around the island and revisit some of the places my father took me to that week. I've been trying to do it since I've been here, but your parking lot is usually as far as I ever make it." Hope paid for her tea then said, "And for the record, I wouldn't have cared if John told you what we talked about. Like I said, I'm not trying to hide my past. Besides, it's not that exciting... and to be honest, neither am I."

Hope grabbed her tea and started for the door but was halted by Charlotte's voice calling out. "I don't believe that. I don't believe that at all. I bet your life is a lot more exciting than mine, that's for sure."

Hope offered a sad smile then turned and headed back to her car, which is where she remained for the next thirty minutes. She tried to play one of her Grateful Dead CDs, but even that wasn't helping her gain the courage to put the car in gear. She sat, sipped her tea, and did a little writing in her journal.

Charlotte found herself peering out the window every five minutes to see if Hope was still there. When the store was down to just a couple of customers, Charlotte walked outside and gently tapped on her window. Hope jumped up, nearly spilling the hot tea all over herself.

"Sorry to scare you," Charlotte said, as Hope rolled down her window.

"It's okay. I was just sitting here drinking my tea... and doing a little writing... but mostly procrastinating." Hope lowered her head.

"That's kinda why I came out here. I have a proposition for ya. As long as my help shows up, I'm out at eleven this morning. How about I chauffeur you around the island, and you can show and tell me the whole story of how your parents met?"

Hope was hesitant, but Charlotte's tone was genuine, and her eyes were kind.

"Feel free to tell me if I'm overstepping. I sometimes have the tendency to do that."

Deep down, Hope knew it was time; time to revisit the island and all its memories. Tentatively, she smiled and said, "I… I think I'd like that."

"Excellent!" Charlotte peered at her watch and said, "I should be out in an hour, so I can either pick you up at Janice's, or if you're still here, I'll come out and get you."

"Okay. I'll probably stay here and do some more writing."

"Sounds good. I'll see you in a bit."

***

At exactly 11:07am, Charlotte exited the store and pulled her car next to Hope's Subaru. Hope gathered her things, locked her car, and then got into Charlotte's Jetta. She couldn't help laughing to herself when she locked her car. Her father's snarky comments replayed in her head: *What the hell are you doing locking your car? We're in Maine for Christ's sake!*

"Okay, let's hear this big romantic story of how your parents met," Charlotte said, grinning over at Hope.

Hope was anxiously excited, but she felt like she needed to be completely honest with Charlotte. Before they even pulled out of the parking lot, Hope revealed that her father was mentally ill, and the whole story she was about to tell was something he had made up in his head.

"The truth is… neither one of my parents have ever been to Applewood before… or Maine."

Charlotte shrugged and quickly replied, "That doesn't make it any less true… at least not in his eyes, right?"

Charlotte's comment immediately triggered something in Hope. She recalled a line from one of her father's old notebooks. She allowed it to spin around her mind until she remembered the exact quote. With a sad smile, she looked over at Charlotte and said, "My father once wrote, *'Truth, like beauty, is in the eye of the beholder.'* I found it in one of his old notebooks."

"Exactly," Charlotte said, smiling.

Hope thought for a moment and said, "His story was kind of sweet and funny, though."

"Sounds like my kind of story then. Where to first?"

Hope's mind raced, and for whatever reason, she blurted out the first thing that came to her. "Um, how about the Willows?"

Charlotte laughed. "I haven't heard it called that in a long time. They changed the name back when I was a teenager. It's called Algonquin Park now."

"Oh."

"Algonquin Park it is!" Charlotte said, turning onto the main road.

They drove by the Great Blue Heron Inn, and as they approached the marina, Hope smiled and pointed over at the Rusty Anchor.

"Actually, that's where my father first met my mother... supposedly."

"The Rusty Anchor? Really?"

Charlotte slowed and turned into the dirt parking lot. It wasn't open yet, but she parked out front and listened as Hope filled her in on the details. She told her it was supposedly where her father first laid eyes on her mother. They both laughed when Hope mentioned the part about her mother dumping a beer over her father's head. Charlotte began reminiscing about the countless guys she had also dumped beers on.

"I've never been much of a bar person," Hope confessed. "So, I have no idea how that feels."

"Exhilarating and completely satisfying!" Charlotte said, giggling.

"I've never dumped a drink on anyone, but I did slap a guy in the face once… hard."

Impressed, Charlotte looked over at Hope and asked, "What did he do?"

"Grabbed my butt… with both hands."

"That's just creepy," Charlotte said then smirked. "I mean, if it was a one-handed grab, that might be permissible."

Hope also smirked and uncharacteristically said, "Yeah… especially if he was actually good looking."

They both giggled like teenagers and Charlotte said, "We're just as bad as guys, aren't we?"

Hope nodded. "We're better at being discreet about it, though."

"Very true," Charlotte said, starting to drive off.

As they passed through the marina, Hope mentioned how they had taken a lighthouse and whale watching tour from there.

"Yeah, they stopped doing that a while ago. Like I said, the island's tourism is all but dead."

On their way over to Algonquin Park, Hope thought it was best if she filled Charlotte in on the entire backstory of her and her father. And just like the night before, she revealed everything: her mother dying at childbirth, her father's disappearance from her life, and subsequently, his reappearance via the birthday phone call. By the time they got out of the car at Algonquin Park, Charlotte's heart was breaking for Hope. Considering she'd lost her father at age two, Charlotte had always thought of her own life as sad and tragic but hearing what Hope had gone through caused her to rethink her self-pity.

With the exception of some added benches, the park was the same as she remembered it. The rain was only a light drizzle, but the wind was cold and stiff, and it wildly blew the branches of the willows.

"Supposedly, my mother used to love to read under those trees," she said, pointing to the willows.

"Looks like the perfect spot," Charlotte said. "Not on a day like today, but…"

Hope then turned her attention to the riverbank. She smiled as she thought of another one of her father's stories. She smiled even more when she spotted a Great Blue Heron perched on a giant branch in the river. She told Charlotte about her father serenading her mother from high up in one of trees along the banks. And she told how the branch broke and how he crashed into the river, guitar and all. Both women cracked up laughing, and Hope thought to herself how refreshing it felt to laugh like that again. It was long overdue.

There were a few more walking paths than last time, and as they meandered through the park, Hope stopped and pointed up ahead and asked, "What's that?"

"What's what? Oh, the statue?"

"Yeah. That wasn't here the last time."

Charlotte thought for a moment. "I think they put it in the same time they changed the name of the park. I believe it's one of the original chiefs of the island."

As soon as Hope got up close and saw the giant copper chief pointing up to the sky, her eyes widened. The plaque underneath read:

*May all lost souls find the peace they search for
and the path that leads back home.*

"I've… I've seen this somewhere before." And just as quick, it all came back to her. "Oh my goodness. John gave me a framed photo of this very statue from the last time he was here in Applewood."

"Aw, that was nice of him. Are you into Native American culture? Is that why he gave it to you?"

Hope chuckled and said, "I've been known to be into a lot of different cultures… but yes, Native Americans are one of them."

It was difficult for her to read the inscription on the photo John had given her, but now that she was face to face with it, she couldn't take her eyes off of it.

"That's a beautiful quote," she said, smiling over at Charlotte.

"Yeah, I've always thought so, too."

Hope didn't have her nice camera with her, so she took out her phone and snapped two pictures: one of the statue, and one close-up of the plaque.

"Okay, where to next?" Charlotte asked.

Hope shrugged. It had been so long since she had thought about that week with her father and even longer since it had actually happened.

"I'm sorry. It feels like a lifetime ago since I was here with him. I'm having a hard time recalling places and details."

Charlotte sensed Hope was getting a little anxious and stressed, and she decided to offer a suggestion. "How about I just drive around the island, and whenever something looks familiar or a new story pops into your head, let me know?"

"That sounds like a plan," Hope said.

They headed back towards town, and as Charlotte approached the general store, she turned to Hope. "We probably should have done this when we were here earlier, but how about we stop and get some supplies?"

"Sure."

Luckily, it wasn't very busy, or else Charlotte would have felt guilty for not sticking around and helping out. Hope grabbed a large bottle of Poland Spring water and a bag of trail mix.

"My father used to love stopping here for his *staples*. Of course, his staples consisted of Marlboros and vodka... oh, and a bag of pork rinds."

"Oh, I love those. The pork rinds, not the cigarettes and vodka. You'd actually be surprised how many people consider alcohol and cigarettes staples. Sadly, we sell more of them than we do coffee and homemade muffins... especially lately. I think this gloomy, depressing weather causes people to drink more." Charlotte threw the items in a bag and said, "Ready?"

Hope nodded and asked, "Are you sure I can't give you some

money for those?"

"I'm sure," Charlotte said, grabbing a bag of pork rinds off the shelf. "In honor of your father," she said in Hope's direction.

Hope smiled as she held the door open for her. After they got into her car and buckled up, Charlotte handed Hope her water and trail mix. "You coulda got something more, ya know?"

"This is perfect, thank you."

Just then, an old green pickup truck loudly rumbled into the spot next to them. In faded white lettering, the side door read: Island Landscaping. Hope focused on the back of the truck, which contained gas cans, a lawnmower, and other various equipment. "I feel bad for these companies," Hope said. "With all this rainy weather, their business must be taking a beating."

"Yup. But I certainly don't feel sorry for that little shit," Charlotte said, focusing on the man climbing out of the truck. "Speaking of dumping drinks on dudes… once upon a time, I wasted a good Sam Adams on that asshole! Worth every penny, to be honest."

He slammed his door shut, and before heading in, he turned and gave a quick look at the girls. Charlotte threw an icy stare his way and proceeded to raise her middle finger at him. He paused and took off his backwards baseball hat. He ran his fingers through his greasy greying hair, placed his hat back on, and then strutted into the store. The whole time, he wore a cocky look of arrogance.

"Oh my God," Hope said, lowering and covering her face.

"Eh, don't worry. He's not gonna start anything. He knows better than to mess with me."

The whole time Charlotte was talking, Hope's mind was flashing back thirty years. She remembered that blue-eyed, blonde hunk she fell for… that she kissed… and that she almost went to a party with. Although there were certain similarities, the person she just watched walk inside looked quite a bit different than the boy she remembered. His face for example, looked as though he had lived a long, rough life, causing him to age beyond his years. And judging by his giant gut, it was apparent that his long, rough life included an awful lot of beers.

"What's his name?" Hope whispered.

"Adam… Adam Briggs."

Holy cow, Hope thought. *It's him.*

"What? You don't know him, do you?" Charlotte asked.

Hope was too embarrassed to go into details, so she played it off as a vague recollection. "I think he used to mow Janice's yard at the Blue Heron."

"Yup, that's him. He's probably on his fifth company since then, but yeah, he's still doing the same ole same ole. At the very least, you'd think he'd own his own landscaping company by now. He's too much of a dumbass, though."

Hope couldn't help herself. "Is he… is he married? Kids?"

Charlotte laughed. "I think he just recently got divorced… for the third time. Hard to believe there are that many dumb girls around here but obviously there are. Thankfully, he's never procreated. The last thing this island needs is a bunch of Adam juniors running amuck."

Not wanting to be too obvious, Hope decided to keep any other questions or comments to herself. Of course, Charlotte's next comment caused Hope to reconsider.

"Actually, lobsterboy can't ever have kids."

"Lobsterboy?"

Charlotte giggled. "It's probably just one of those urban legends, but supposedly, when Adam was younger, he had a little run in with an angry lobster… or I should say, his man parts had the run in. Talk about karma," she said, continuing to laugh.

Hope's face turned bright red, and as she recalled that fateful night, she couldn't help but feel guilty. Her father's little prank caused this poor boy to never be able to reproduce. Her guilt would be short-lived, however.

With a tin of Skoal in one hand, and a six-pack of Natty Light in the other, Adam exited the store. He tossed them into the truck through the passenger side, and as soon as he shut the door, he turned around looking directly at Charlotte. Hope did her best to cover her face, but she was still able to see Adam give Charlotte double birds. He then leaned down and gave her window a disgusting kiss—tongue and all. Amused with his immaturity, Adam strutted back to the driver's side, climbed in, and then sped off. And to add to his immaturity level, he burned rubber on his way out.

That was pretty much all it took for Hope's guilt to disappear and for her to reveal the entire story to Charlotte—lobster incident and all. The whole time Hope spoke, Charlotte listened intently with her mouth gaped open. By the time Hope finished, Charlotte was smiling and shaking her head in disbelief.

"I swear, I always assumed that lobster story was just an urban legend. I can't believe it's really true, and I certainly can't believe *you* of all people were the perpetrator."

"Technically, it was my father's idea."

"Then you're both my heroes!"

Charlotte pulled out of the parking lot and drove until she came to the four-way stop sign. Hope looked down to the right and asked, "Is the road still closed that takes you out to the lighthouse?"

"Yeah, I'm afraid so. It's probably going to be closed for a while. Apparently, there was a giant sinkhole. A huge chunk of the road just caved in. It's been out for about a month now. Was that one of the places your father took you to?"

Sadly, Hope nodded. "Supposedly, it was a very special place for my parents... and for me and my father as well."

Charlotte drove straight ahead, and it wasn't long before Hope spotted another familiar sight. It was the small wooden bridge where Hope had done her bridge jumping from. As Charlotte rumbled over it, Hope smiled and said, "I actually jumped off this bridge."

Charlotte immediately slowed the car to a stop. "You what?"

"That little bridge we just crossed over... I went bridge jumping from it."

Charlotte pulled over to the side of the road, and then they both walked back onto the bridge. As they leaned against the old wooden railing, Hope told her the entire story. When she was finished, Charlotte looked down at the river and then back over at Hope and said, "You're a badass! Like, seriously."

"I don't know about that," Hope said, blushing.

"Are you kidding me? First, I find out you're the one responsible for the lobster maiming Adam's pecker. And now you tell me that you actually jumped from this bridge?"

Hope blushed then smirked and said, "I... I also threw two buoys at Adam, too. They were decorative ones from Janice's front yard."

Hope continued to blush as she looked down at the river below. "Maybe I am a badass," she said with a smile.

"Damn right you are!" Charlotte said, patting her on the back.

The more they drove around, the more things started coming back to Hope. The next place that caught her attention was the Applewood Country Club.

"Is it still open?" Hope asked.

"It is, but obviously nobody has been golfing this summer because of this weather. I actually had my wedding reception here."

Hope could sense the divorce was still a sore subject, so she switched the focus back to she and her father. She told Charlotte about how her father crashed a wedding just so he could play her mother a song on his guitar.

"And after the real band came back on stage, they dedicated a song to my parents. And that's when they had their first dance together."

During the first part of the day, whenever Hope told Charlotte one of her father's stories, she would always preface it by saying, *supposedly*. And she would always end a story by saying, *of course, he just made it up, it didn't really happen*. But as the day wore on, she started leaving out those comments, and she started enjoying them for what they were: sweet, funny, and romantic stories.

They made their way up to the Cliffside restaurant, which was where Hope and her father had dinner on their final night in town. Hope was saddened to see it was covered with graffiti, and there was a huge FOR SALE sign out in front. Charlotte told her it had been closed for a while now.

"Do you mind if we get out and take a closer look?" Hope asked.

"Of course I don't mind. Do what you gotta do. Today's all about you, Hope."

Charlotte left her car running, and they walked up to one of the huge windows out in front. They cupped their hands around their eyes and peered in.

"Believe it or not, I've only been here two or three times."

Hope barely heard Charlotte's words. Her mind had transported her back thirty years, and she was watching her father strut through the restaurant in his extremely wrinkled and way-too-small suit.

"What's so funny?" Charlotte turned and asked.

Hope didn't even realize she was laughing out loud. She went on to tell her all about their dinner experience.

"He borrowed the suit from Janice's *dead husband*?"

"Yup. Those were his exact words. He looked ridiculous, but… but it was kind of endearing. The entire day was."

While they were standing in front of the restaurant, the rain became steadier and the wind, colder. "Where to now?" Charlotte asked, after they got back into her car. "We could head up to Mount M. Did you father take you up that way?"

Hope thought for a second and said, "No, but…"

"But what?"

Quietly, Hope murmured, "Adam did."

"Oh, God. Lemme guess, he took you up to the Devil's Lair?"

Hope grinned. "He tried to. But the road was closed, so we had to turn around."

"That fucker is so cliché. Sorry for the harsh language, but it's true. The Devil's Lair was one of the main party spots back in high school. Although, my guess is he's still trying to take girls up there.

Okay, so definitely no Mount M today. Hmm, where to, where to?"

Charlotte drove a little further then turned to Hope and asked, "Have you been to the house that John's staying at? It's right around the corner from here."

"No, I haven't. Is this the house he did some work on the last time he was here?"

"Yes. The first time he came, he did a lot of exterior projects, but since the weather has been so crappy, this time he's been doing a lot of inside stuff. I've been helping him paint most of the rooms... I picked out the colors," Charlotte said, feeling the need to point that out.

"So, who's this friend of his again? John never really went into details with me."

"William. William Galloway."

"And how did he meet him?"

"I guess he met him at their bar back in Chicago."

"Ah, the Wild Irish Rose."

"Yeah, that's it. Have you ever been there?" Charlotte asked.

"Just once."

A few moments later, Charlotte turned onto William's road.

"Let's do a quick drive-by, and I'll show you the house."

"Sounds groovy."

As soon as they turned and Hope saw the sign reading: Dead End Road, her memory was triggered.

"Hmm," she said, scanning her surroundings.

"Hmm what?"

"This road seems familiar. I think..." and then it hit her. "Um..."

"Um what?" Charlotte asked, looking over at Hope.

"As much as I hate to keep talking about him... Adam took me on a road that looked just like this one. We parked on the side and cut through someone's backyard to a path that led out to a beautiful cove."

Charlotte busted out laughing. "The path that you speak of is located behind that house right there," she said pointing up ahead.

"Which, ironically enough is the house that John is staying at."

"You're kidding, right?"

"Nope. I guess it really is a small world."

Charlotte turned into John's driveway, and when she saw that his truck wasn't there, she couldn't help feeling disappointed. "It looks like he's out for the day."

Charlotte was about to suggest they park and walk down to the cove, but just then, the sky opened up and the rain began to pour down.

"I'd say let's wait it out, but it looks like this heavy rain is here to stay."

"Yeah," Hope said, looking up at the dark sky. "Maybe we should call it a day."

Charlotte nodded. "I'm sorry, Hope."

"Oh gosh. No need to be sorry… not at all! I had an amazing time today. Thank you so much for driving me around and reminding me of everything my father had told me. I don't know if I could have done it on my own. If it weren't for you, I'd probably still be sitting in my car in your parking lot."

"You're very welcome, Hope. It sounds like the week you had with your father was pretty special."

"Yeah, I guess you're right. It was special. And I'm glad we got to have that time together."

Slowly, Charlotte backed out of the driveway, and with her windshield wipers on full blast, she made her way back to Hope's car at the store. They never made it to the west side of the island, so she never got a chance to tell Charlotte about their horseback riding adventure at the Abenaki Stables. Before getting out of the car, Hope made sure to give Charlotte one last heartfelt thank you.

"I truly appreciate you driving me around today. It meant more than you'll ever know."

"You're very welcome."

Before Hope got out of the car, she found herself curiously

looking over at Charlotte. There were many occasions throughout the day that they found themselves looking over at one another, trying to figure out why they each seemed so familiar.

Originally, Hope was worried that she might not be able to remember anything from that week with her father. She'd buried those memories so deep and hadn't thought about them in so long that she just assumed they were gone forever. Even worse, over the years she had gradually convinced herself none of it ever happened at all.

By the time she returned to the inn, Hope knew without a shadow of a doubt that the week she spent with her father really *did* happen. For the rest of the night, Hope floated around the inn, and for the fourth night in a row, her head hit the pillow with nothing but happy thoughts. Her new-found energy and overall happiness didn't go unnoticed by Janice, and it didn't really come as a surprise to her either. Janice assumed it would only be a matter of time before the island's magic would pull Hope out of her funk. But Janice also knew that the island's magic was slowly weakening. When Hope returned home that night wearing a huge smile and an even bigger appetite, Janice knew things were working out as they were supposed to.

As soon as she finished dinner, Hope rushed into the living room and began writing in her journal. For years and years, she had done her best to convince her patients that the simple act of talking out loud about their feelings or even writing them down would help greatly with the healing process. Ironically, this week it was her former patients who taught her that same lesson. The attention John, Kevin, Charlotte, and Julie had given her caused Hope's spirit to be lifted. As hard as it was at first, she was glad that she had opened up to each of them.

John nailed it when he said that she was probably the type of person who didn't take her own advice. Even when she saw her own therapist, she never truly talked about her past. Mostly, Hope and her therapist talked about the stress of the job, or occasionally, they talked about Hope's relationships—or lack thereof. She never talked about her mother dying during childbirth or her father splitting town. There was no mention of their mental illnesses, and never once did she talk about the week she spent with her father in Applewood.

Hope was a brilliant therapist, and deep down she knew her lack of communication stemmed from her grandparents. She loved them dearly, and she knew they did the best they could, but they were horrible about discussing feelings. Her mother's name was hardly ever mentioned growing up; at least not in the ways Hope would have wished for. Sadly, she learned more about her mother from that week with her father than she had in the previous twenty years. And even then, she was unsure how much of what he told her was true.

22

It was just after sunset when Kevin and Julie made their way back to Applewood. They had such an amazing time up at the White Mountains that they were already planning their next excursion. The following day they planned on driving all the way up to Bar Harbor for a few days. John couldn't believe how lovey-dovey they had become with one another since arriving on the island a week earlier. There were many times he was tempted to make fun, but after seeing them so unhappy and at odds the past couple months, he wasn't about to mock it with his sarcasm.

Charlotte was already at the house when Kevin and Julie returned from the White Mountains. She told them about her day with Hope. "I think she was really disappointed that we couldn't get up to Harbor Cove Park. It sounds like it was a very special place for she and her father."

"The road is still closed, huh?" John asked.

"Yeah, but…"

"But what?"

"There is another way up there. It's a little bit of a hike, but I think we should take her."

"I'm dying to see it," Julie said. "I've only ever seen it in pictures."

"You'd love it, Jules," John said. "It's breathtaking up there. I've been wanting to go back up there myself. And to think, all this time you knew of another way up there," he said in Charlotte's direction.

"Sorry. It just kind of came to me that there was another way."

"When were you thinking of going?" Kevin asked.

"Dunno. What time were you two planning on driving up to Bar Harbor tomorrow?"

"Late morning probably."

Charlotte looked over at the three of them and asked, "How about around 9am?"

Excitedly, they all nodded and smiled.

***

First thing the next morning, they all drove over and surprised Hope with their proposition.

"I'm going to warn you," Charlotte said. "It's a little bit of a hike, and I'm not sure how good the trail is. It's been years since I've been out that way."

Hope was embarrassed that she was getting so much attention from the four of them, but the excitement of visiting the park far outweighed any embarrassment she felt. Hope grabbed a jacket, her camera, and on the way out, Janice offered up her binoculars. It was the exact same pair Hope had borrowed thirty years ago.

Charlotte drove them down the road leading to the park, and just before the concrete roadblock, she pulled off to the shoulder and parked. They all got out of the car and followed her up the road until they came to a hidden path on the edge of the woods.

"It used to be maintained better when I was a kid. It's overgrown and uneven, but it'll get us there."

Before they even started, Hope offered her gratitude. "Thanks again for doing this. I really appreciate it."

It wasn't that strenuous of a hike, but it didn't take long for Hope's breath to shorten and her chest to tighten. She knew she'd been tired and unmotivated for a while now, and she knew she had just turned the big 5-0, but she didn't think she was this out of shape. By the time they made it off the path and up the steps to the park, Hope was out of breath with sharp pains shooting throughout her body.

"Ya doing okay?" asked Charlotte. "Told ya it was a hike."

"Yeah, I'm fine. Just a little out of shape, that's all. That's what happens when you get to be my age."

"Eh, age is just a number. You're only as old as you feel."

Hope smiled but thought to herself, *Gosh, I hope not... because I feel closer to seventy than fifty.*

"I don't want to jinx it, but it looks like we picked a good morning to come up here," Charlotte said.

The sky was grey and there was a light mist, but there was no fog to speak of. By the time they reached the first park bench, Hope's exhaustion was noticeable, especially to Charlotte.

"Wow, that path was longer than I remembered it," Charlotte said, sitting on the bench. "Why don't you guys go ahead. I'm just gonna catch my breath for a second. Wanna join me, Hope?"

Hope saw right through Charlotte's fake exhaustion, but appreciatively took a seat next to her anyway. After the other three walked away, Hope softly said, "Thanks."

"I have no idea what you're talking about," Charlotte said, grinning.

The park was nothing like Hope remembered. The once gravel paths were now paved. Normally, this would have been an improvement, but there were hundreds of cracks with weeds growing up through them. The paved paths weren't the only thing neglected; the well-manicured gardens were now reduced to dirt beds and were also overtaken with weeds. And then there was the grass. Hope remembered it being the brightest green she'd ever seen. *This must be what it's like in Ireland*, she remembered thinking. But now, it was more brown than green. Actually, it was completely brown.

"You would think with all the rain we've gotten lately that the grass would be thriving, but... but not so much."

Hope gazed around. "It looks so different from the last time I was here."

"Yeah, me too," Charlotte said, getting a sick feeling in the pit of her stomach. She honestly couldn't remember the last time she had stepped foot in the park.

Hope also had a sick feeling in her stomach. But unlike Charlotte's, which was more emotional, Hope's feeling was more physical. There were sharp pains in her stomach and sides—her entire body ached. Despite this, she was determined to see the lighthouse she'd fallen in love with years ago.

They watched as John, Kevin, and Julie walked up one of the paths and stopped at the granite memorial dedicated to those lost out to sea. With their arms around one another, Kevin and Julie gazed out at the Atlantic Ocean and eventually focused on the lighthouse. Excitedly, Julie took picture after picture. Eventually, they meandered towards the other side of the park.

"Sorry again for being so out of shape."

"Seriously, Hope, there's no need to apologize. Why don't you tell me about this place and your father. I mean… if you want to."

Hope leaned back on the bench and told her about their final night up at the lighthouse. She told how her father finally opened up to her and how he broke down reminiscing about her mother. Hope squinted then pointed up past the memorial and said, "I think that's where we sat and looked at the stars and talked most of the night."

"Do you wanna walk up there?" Charlotte asked.

Hope paused then smiled and said, "I do."

By now, the other three had disappeared to the other side of the park. As Charlotte and Hope walked up the path, Charlotte's phone began to ring.

"Oh… sorry," she said, reaching in her pocket for the phone. "I didn't realize the volume was on." As soon as she saw who it was, a smile flashed across her face. "Do you mind if I take it?"

"Of course not. Go ahead."

"Thanks. I'll meet you up at the top, okay?"

Hope nodded and started back up the path. Charlotte wandered onto the grass and quietly answered the phone. "What, did ya miss me already?"

"Ha. I was just checking on you girls," John said. "Everything okay?"

"We're fine. We're almost up at the top of the park. Where are you guys?"

"I have no idea. At the far end of the park, I guess. I'm just following their lead. I don't think I've ever been out to this part before."

"That's the most remote part of the park. There are a couple of really pretty scenic overlooks on that side."

"Oh, I know. Apparently, I'm the official photographer for the happy couple. Can't they just take selfies like the rest of the idiots?"

"Aww, you're just being a good brother," she said, laughing.

By now, Hope was nearly at the top of the path. Charlotte watched as Hope paused and dug into her bag, pulling out the binoculars Janice had given her before they left. She placed them around her neck and carefully made her way to the edge of the cliff.

Charlotte was just about to turn her attention back to the conversation with John, but she stopped cold when she saw Hope's reaction. As the entire ocean and lighthouse came into view, Hope's breath was taken away, and her legs nearly buckled. Curiously, Charlotte watched Hope cover her mouth in apparent shock. It wasn't until Hope lifted the binoculars to her eyes that it all came flooding back to Charlotte.

The next thing Charlotte knew, her mind was carried back thirty years. She was eight years old and wandering around Harbor Cove Park. She remembered spotting a young hippy-dressed girl looking out at the ocean with giant binoculars. The memory was hazy, for it had been buried deep within Charlotte's subconscious for many years. As the memory became clearer, Charlotte remembered approaching the woman and asking to look through the binoculars. She also recalled the exact conversation that ensued:

"Hey, do you know why that little section of the ocean looks so much darker than the rest?" the young woman asked.

"What did you say?" Charlotte asked.

"I was just wondering why that area out past the lighthouse looks so different than the rest of the ocean. The waves look bigger and rougher, and the water looks way—"

"You can see it, can't you?" Charlotte interrupted.

"See what?" the woman asked.

"The Dark Waters," Charlotte remembered saying, wide-eyed.

At that point in the flashback, the young woman's face came into perfect focus. It was Hope—thirty years younger.

Into the phone, Charlotte uttered, "Oh my God... I knew she looked familiar."

"What? What are you talking about?" asked John. "You knew *who* looked familiar?"

"I gotta go," she said, then abruptly hung up.

As Charlotte headed towards Hope, she thought, *She can still see it. She can still see the Dark Waters.*

By the time Charlotte made up to the edge, Hope's face was as white as a ghost, and her hands were trembling. Charlotte didn't quite know what to say, and all she could muster was, "Everything okay?" When she didn't respond, Charlotte repeated, "Hope... are you okay?"

Very slowly, Hope peeled her eyes away from the ocean and looked over at Charlotte. "Um, yeah... just not feeling so good all of a sudden. Not at all."

Charlotte wanted to tell Hope that she recognized her, and she desperately wanted to ask about the Dark Waters, but for whatever reason, she didn't. Instead, she helped Hope over to one of the benches. Thoughts swirled through her mind as she sat down beside her.

"I'm sorry," Hope apologized. "I'm sorry I'm not very good company today."

"No need to apologize, Hope. It's totally fine. Take as long as you need." She placed her hand on Hope's shoulder.

It was the same exact bench they sat on thirty years ago. She remembered sitting there crying, and how Hope sat next to her and tried to console her. She also remembered telling Hope about her father… and the dream. Come to think of it, Hope might have been one of the last people Charlotte talked to about the dream.

As they continued sitting on the bench, Charlotte wasn't the only one putting the pieces together. Hope looked over at her, and all at once, the memory came flooding back. She remembered consoling that little girl… she remembered her talking about the Dark Waters… she remembered everything. Just like Charlotte, Hope decided not to mention anything about recognizing her. Less than five minutes later, John, Kevin, and Julie made their way up to the bench. By now, the wind had picked up, and as the fog rolled in, rain began to fall.

"Looks like you totally jinxed us," Kevin said in Charlotte's direction.

"Yeah. Looks like I did. We should probably head back before it gets worse."

They all did their best to rush back down the path towards the car. At one point, John whispered to Charlotte, "Everything okay? What's going on?"

"I'll tell you later. Let's just say, this one's a doozy."

Just as they got back into the car, the sky opened up, and the rain poured down.

"Jesus, it's coming down hard," Kevin exclaimed from the backseat.

"Looks like we got out just in time," added Julie. "Thanks again, Charlotte, for taking us up there. It was beautiful. I can't imagine what it looks like on a clear, sunny day."

As the wipers quickly sloshed back and forth, Charlotte forced a polite smile and said, "You're welcome."

Her quiet demeanor didn't go unnoticed by John. Neither did Hope's. Something definitely went on between the two of them up at the lighthouse, and John was more than curious to find out what. Luckily, it wasn't that far of a drive back to the inn, and Kevin and Julie carried on most of the conversation.

"I hope it's not like this up in Bar Harbor," Julie said.

"It's a four-hour drive," Kevin replied. "I'm sure it'll improve as we go."

The excitement of their upcoming trip caused them to be oblivious to the uncomfortable silence of the other three passengers. Still feeling a little weak, John and Kevin aided Hope into the inn. Before getting out of the car, Hope thanked everyone for taking her out. She then shared a brief and awkward look with Charlotte. John was the only one who noticed it.

"Too bad you have to work," Julie announced from the back. "Or else you and John could join us."

John could see that Charlotte's mind was a million miles away and that she didn't even hear Julie's comment. Covering for her, he replied, "Eh, you don't need us imposing on your romantic getaway."

"Yeah, that's exactly what I was thinking," Kevin said, placing his hand on Julie's leg.

While the two reinvigorated lovebirds gave each other loving looks, John continued staring over at Charlotte. *Whatever happened with them must have been huge*, he thought. He shifted back and forth in his seat, anxiously fidgeting with his hands. Dropping Kevin and Julie off couldn't come fast enough. When they arrived at William's, John didn't even bother going inside. He told them he was going to head back to the store with Charlotte and that they were probably going to hang out the rest of the day. He said his goodbyes and told them to have a safe trip. By now, Charlotte had snapped out of her deep thought and offered her best wishes on their trip.

"Have fun and take plenty of pictures," Charlotte said, gazing into the backseat.

"Thanks, we will," Julie said, excitedly clutching Kevin's hand. "You guys have fun, too." With that, they exited the car and rushed into the house.

After a mile of complete silence, John finally said, "So? Are you gonna fill me in or what?"

Softly, she answered, "Just wait until we get back to my place, okay?"

Charlotte's mother was working, so they had the entire apartment to themselves. As soon as they entered, Charlotte poured herself a red wine and settled herself on the couch next to John.

"Sorry, but this is much needed," she said, taking a giant sip. "Oh, do you want anything?"

John shook his head no and answered, "Just for you to spill the beans already. What the hell happened up there?"

For good measure, she took another sip before telling John everything. When she was finished with her story (and with the wine), she looked over to gauge John's reaction. His jaw was dropped open, and his eyes were filled with disbelief.

"Are you really suggesting that my shrink can see the Dark Waters?"

Slowly nodding yes, Charlotte replied, "And I think it even goes beyond that."

"Beyond *that*? What does *that* mean?"

"What if Hope is *her*?"

"Her?"

"Help *her* to help us. What if Hope is *her*? What if she's the key to helping our parents?"

Still confused, John pondered and said, "Then that would mean she's the key to helping Clarence… and everyone else."

Charlotte lifted up her empty glass. "I think this calls for a refill." She stood up and made her way back into the kitchen.

John called out, "This might be the craziest thing that's happened on this island yet. And that's saying a lot. I can't believe my wacky hippy-chick shrink is somehow connected to all this... connected to me. This has to be the biggest coincidence in the world."

Charlotte returned with a full glass of wine, and when she was once again settled in on the couch, she said, "What if it's not a coincidence? What if she was meant to be your therapist? What if you and I were meant to meet?"

Her words resonated, and despite his initial skepticism, John knew she was probably right. "Just like William was meant to come into our bar. I was meant to see and talk to Clarence and Mary, wasn't I?"

"I think so," she said, nodding. "Just like I was meant to randomly meet Hope all those years ago."

For the first time in a long time, John was tempted to join Charlotte in her alcohol consumption. A glass of Jameson would totally hit the spot right about now. Thankfully, the desire was fleeting. John knew whatever was going on needed to be faced with a clear mind.

"And you're absolutely positive she can see the Dark Waters?" he asked.

"It took a while for it to come back to me, but now I remember it like it was yesterday. I approached her... I asked her what she was looking at... and she asked if I knew what that dark area was out past the lighthouse. And I swear to God, John, the entire ocean was pure blue. I didn't see anything resembling a dark area. And I even borrowed her binoculars. That's when I knew... she could see it."

John rubbed his fingers on his stubble and pondered. Finally, he asked, "And how do you know she saw it today? Did she tell you?"

"No... but I could just tell by her expression. As soon as her eyes looked out at the ocean, it was like her breath was taken away... and not in a good way. I'm telling you, whatever she saw, scared the shit out of her."

While John sat back thinking, Charlotte continued to work on her glass of wine. When she had completely polished it off, she set the glass on the table, then turned to John and asked, "So what do we do now?"

"I think it's obvious. We need to find out exactly what she saw."

"You mean go ask her face to face?"

"Yup."

"As in, right now?"

"No. I need to eat first. I'm starving. Besides, you could probably use some food in you, too." He glanced down at her empty glass and smirked. "We don't want you all loopy when we get to the bottom of this."

"I'm fine," she said, springing to her feet. After a quick light-headed moment, she confessed, "Well, maybe a little food would be good."

"Come on, let's hit the diner."

"Wait... what about Kevin? Should we let him know what's going on?"

"No. Not until we know more ourselves. No need to interrupt their trip... not yet anyway."

23

What started off as a late-afternoon lunch, turned into hours of contemplating, planning, and trying to figure out exactly what they were going to say to Hope. Charlotte thought they should ease into it slowly, while John thought it was best to just rip the Band Aid off and get right to the point. They left the diner just after six, and by the time they reached the inn, Charlotte convinced him to let her do most of the talking—at least to start with.

"Let me guess, you're here to see Hope?" Janice asked, laughing. "Come on in. She's been up in her room most of the day. She didn't even want any dinner... said she wasn't feeling well."

"Can you tell her that we're here?" John hastily asked.

"You got it," Janice said with a wink. Instantly, Charlotte and John felt guilty as they watched this old woman clutch the railing and slowly start to climb the stairs.

"I can go up and get her," Charlotte called out.

"Yeah, let Charlotte go get her," John said, reaching out to give her a hand. "You don't need to be climbing up those stairs."

Without turning around, Janice announced, "The day I'm too old to climb these stairs is the day they put me six feet under. It might take me a little longer than you spring chickens, but I can do it."

At that point, they had no choice but to let her do it on her own. Her stubbornness and determination were all too familiar to John. He'd spent a lifetime perfecting those traits. As soon as she made it to the top, she turned and motioned with her hands as if to say, *See, easy peasy!*

She then disappeared down the hall towards Hope's door. A few minutes later, Janice reappeared at the top of the stairs. John and Charlotte assumed she was about to give them bad news; either Hope was still sleeping, or she wasn't feeling up to having visitors. They were pleasantly surprised when she called out, "She'll be down in a few."

They both breathed a sigh of relief, only to hold their breath once again as they watched Janice struggle with the stairs. John sprinted up and offered his hand. "Okay, young lady, you proved you can climb them on your own, now let me help you down. And I'm not taking no for an answer."

Realizing she was more tired than she thought, Janice graciously took his hand, allowing him to escort her down the stairs. As Charlotte stood there watching, she found herself warmly smiling at John. There were so many strange and crazy things going on lately, that their new-found attraction almost got lost in the shuffle. It was at that moment she realized just how much she was falling for him. As John guided Janice down the last few steps, he returned Charlotte's smile, and he, too, knew he was falling deeper by the day.

When both her feet were firmly back on the first floor, Janice thanked John and told them to make themselves comfortable in the living room. She also told them she was heading into her bedroom to relax and watch some TV.

"If you're hungry or thirsty, help yourself to anything in the kitchen," she added, and then made her way to her bedroom at the opposite end of the house.

Anxiously, John and Charlotte paced around the living room awaiting Hope to come down. A few minutes later, Hope poked her head into the doorway and curiously said, "Hey, guys. I didn't expect to see you again so soon. Is everything okay? Nothing happened to Kevin and—"

"No, no. Nothing like that," John interrupted. "They're fine. We just… um… we just…" After drawing a blank, he turned to Charlotte.

"We were just hoping to talk to you about a few things."

"Um, okay," Hope replied, more hesitant than enthusiastic.

John and Charlotte sat next to each other on the couch, and Hope took to the recliner. When they were all settled, John looked over at Charlotte. She shifted her weight back and forth, took a breath, and then began.

"When I first met you a couple of weeks ago, I thought there was something very familiar about you. I just couldn't put my finger on it."

At that point, Hope knew for sure Charlotte recognized and remembered her. She also knew this little meeting had everything to do with what happened at the lighthouse today… and what happened thirty years ago.

But why is John here with her? Hope thought. *He had nothing to do with this. They barely know each other… there's no way she would have revealed anything that personal to him, would she?*

Charlotte paused, but John impatiently motioned for her to continue.

"Anyway… when we were up at the lighthouse today, it all came back to me. I remember you from the last time you were here… thirty years ago. We met up at Harbor Cove Park… twice. Do you remember that?"

Hope couldn't bring herself to lie, not anymore. Hesitantly, she said, "Not until today, but yes, I remember you."

Now that the ice was somewhat broken, the two women lightly reminisced about it. They talked in generalities, basically dancing around the heart of the matter. John did his best to curb his impatience, but after five minutes went by and there was no mention of the Dark Waters, he knew he had to butt in.

"You can see the Dark Waters, can't you? Can't you, Doc?"

So much for easing into it, Charlotte thought, giving John a glare. Charlotte sensed Hope's anxiousness, and she gave John a look that said, *Pump the brakes… I'll keep taking it from here.*

Charlotte smiled at Hope and calmly said, "After all these years, you're still the only one I've ever met who can see it. I reached a point a long time ago where I stopped believing in all these silly legends of the island… and to be honest with you, I think I reached a point where I stopped believing in fairy tales and happy endings as well."

Charlotte's comment hit home for Hope. Her own belief in magic and happy endings died a long time ago as well. Hope had no idea what to say, so she gave a slight shrug and tried to play it off.

"It was thirty years ago. I… I don't really know what I saw. I'm sure it was just my eyes playing tricks on me."

"But you saw it again today, didn't you?" Charlotte asked.

Hope's heart raced, and her head began to spin. John couldn't hold his tongue any longer. Softening his original tone, he leaned forward and said, "It's okay, Doc. We're all a part of this, too. Me… Charlotte… Kevin… you."

Confused, Hope looked from John to Charlotte and then back to John and said, "I… I don't understand."

Charlotte stepped in. "Remember I told you about my father? And how he died in a plane crash when I was two?"

Slowly, Hope nodded and looked over at John. "But… but what does this have to do with…"

"There were two other people who died on his plane that day," Charlotte interrupted.

"My parents," John quietly said. "My parents were on that plane."

Even more confused than earlier, Hope inched forward in the chair. "One of your foster families?"

John shook his head and stood up. He then began aimlessly pacing around the room. This time, Charlotte didn't interrupt. She allowed John to gather his thoughts and reveal the truth to Hope. After about thirty seconds of pacing, he stopped and said, "Our *real* parents. It was our real parents."

"What? But I thought you and Kevin were…"

"Abandoned by them? Yeah, that's what we thought, too. It's what we were constantly told by Mr. O'Neil."

Still to this day, John cringed when he said his name.

"Hold on, hold on," Hope said, covering her face with her hands.

She thought back to her first session with the teenage boys. For whatever reason, she remembered their records were incomplete. All she ever knew was that the boys had been in multiple foster homes since a very young age. Neither of them said much during those first three sessions. It wasn't until years later, when Kevin returned, that he mentioned they had been abandoned by their real parents. As a matter of fact, when John sought her out after the accident, she remembered how much the abandonment still bothered and haunted him.

"So let me get this straight, your real parents were on," she looked over at Charlotte, "*your* father's plane?"

They both nodded yes, and then Charlotte reached into her purse. She pulled out the old newspaper article telling of the accident and handed it to Hope.

"You brought that with you?" John asked.

"I figured she'd have an easier time believing us if we had proof."

Carefully, Hope read the article, and they could tell by her expression that she knew they were telling the truth. When she was finished, she handed it back to Charlotte and said, "I… I just don't understand. How… how did this happen?"

John knew he needed to fill Hope in on as much as he could. He returned to the couch and began to speak. At first, he tried to dance around some of the details of how he found out—namely, all the weird and magical stuff that occurred the first time he visited Applewood. He started his story by telling her how William mysteriously appeared at the Wild Irish Rose, and how they unexpectedly began to forge a friendship over the following weeks. Eventually, he told her about the night he attempted to end it all: the pills, the smashed mirror, and how he passed out and cracked his head. He didn't realize it until halfway through his story, but this was the first time he'd ever told Hope about that night.

"Oh my God, John, I never knew."

"It's okay, Doc. You tried your best with me, but I was determined to head down a self-destructive path."

He told her how Kevin had found him and rushed him to the hospital. And he told her about William's visit—and his subsequent offer to go to Maine to do some work on his house. At this point, it was becoming harder and harder for John to dance around what happened to him in Applewood. He told Hope that he'd randomly met an old woman who told him the truth about his parents. This is where his story began to fall apart.

"Wait," Hope interrupted. "I don't get it. You met an old woman? And she recognized you from when you were three? No offense, but that sounds…"

"Highly unlikely? Not plausible? A bunch of bullshit? Yeah, that's what I thought, too." Nervously, he wiped his sweaty palms on his pants and began to squirm in his seat. It was like he was back in Hope's office in the middle of a therapy session.

In a calming manner, Charlotte placed her hand on his knee and said, "John, I think you need to tell her… *everything.*"

Curiously, Hope looked from Charlotte back to John and said, "Yes, please do. I really have no idea what's going on here."

He placed his fingers to his temples and stood up. If he was going to tell her everything, it needed to be done on his feet. He did his best babbling while pacing.

"You're gonna think I'm crazy, Doc," he said, pacing by her chair. "Like, certifiably insane."

She reached out and grabbed his hand. "Relax. Take a deep breath and relax, John. I've never judged you… and I never will. Okay?"

He hesitated a second but followed her instructions. He took a couple of deep breaths before lowering himself back onto the couch. This time, it was Charlotte who clutched his hand, and she held it the entire time he told his story about each magical twist that happened to him. Hope sat perfectly still and listened intently as John filled her in. On more than one occasion, she couldn't believe her ears. Over the twenty-five plus years of being a therapist, she'd heard a lot of crazy stories, but this was by far the most outlandish and unbelievable thing she'd ever heard. Even so, she kept a straight face, and holding true to her word, she never once laughed or judged John. He ended by telling her how he and Charlotte met and how he found out who her father was. When he was finished, it was Hope who stood up and began slowly pacing around the room.

"See, I told ya, Doc… you think I'm crazy, don't ya?"

It wasn't that she thought he was crazy, not exactly anyway. Truth be told, she had no idea what to think about any of this.

"Um, no… no, John, I don't."

Although she said it in the politest way possible, John and Charlotte both sensed how skeptical she was. Deep down, Hope had always sensed there was something mystical about the island but certainly not to the extent of what John had just told her.

"I just don't understand what all of this has to do with me. You said earlier that we were *all* a part of this together."

John looked to Charlotte for some help, and over the next few minutes, she took over the storytelling.

"Do you remember when we first met thirty years ago, and I told you about that dream I was having?" Hope thought for a second then nodded yes. "About how I was watching my father drowning in these dark and giant waves? I could see him, but I don't think he could ever see me, but right before the dream ended, he would always call out, *Help her to help us.*"

"Yes… I remember you telling me about it. Do you still have that dream?" Hope asked, sympathetically.

"I stopped having it when I was probably around ten or eleven. It seemed the older I got, the more faded the memory of it became. Eventually, it got to the point where I didn't think about it at all, and if I did, I just assumed the dream was something I had made up in my head and that it never really happened. I... I just recently started having it again."

It was John's turn to reach over and clutch Charlotte's hand.

"Sometimes dreams can feel so real and unnerving. I'm so sorry, Charlotte." Hope paused then said, "But I still don't understand how—"

"Kevin is having the same dream," John blurted out.

"What?" Hope asked, confused.

"Well, pretty much the same dream anyway."

He went on to explain the eerie similarities of the two dreams. He told her that Kevin also stopped having the dream around ten or eleven, but it had recently started up again.

"And the voices in Kev's dream say the same thing as Charlotte's... *Help her to help us.*"

Charlotte leaned forward and softly spoke. "We think it's the Dark Waters... our parents are stuck in the Dark Waters, and—"

"It's just like Clarence said," interrupted John. "They can't move on until... until the Dark Waters are defeated for good."

Charlotte stood from the couch and knelt beside Hope's chair. She placed her hand on Hope's leg and knowingly asked, "Thirty years ago you were able to see the Dark Waters... and you saw it again today, didn't you?"

Hope's heart raced and her breath quickened. She had no idea what to say as she looked back and forth from Charlotte to John. Well, she knew what to say, but she just couldn't bring herself to say it—to admit it. Without a doubt, she absolutely saw the Dark Waters earlier that day, but it was nothing like it was thirty years ago. It was much bigger and so much closer than before. What Hope saw earlier literally scared the hell out of her.

"It's okay, Hope," Charlotte coaxed. "You can tell us."

All at once, Hope became overwhelmed with emotion, and her hands began to shake uncontrollably.

John got on one knee next to her and gently placed his hand on hers. "We think it's *you*... we think the voices in the dreams are referring to *you*, Doc... *Help her to help us.*"

Hope did her best to fight back her tears, but it was too late. They freely flowed down her cheeks. She shook her hand free from John's, and as she unsuccessfully swiped at her tears, she stood from her chair. John had never seen her this frazzled before—or this upset.

Shaking her head back and forth, she wandered around the room mumbling, "No, no, no... none of this is real. It can't be. I have no idea what's going on, but... but I think I need to go to bed now... I'm not feeling very well... I need some sleep."

Sympathetically, Charlotte started to make her way towards Hope, but Hope wanted nothing to do with it. As if in protest, Hope raised her hands to Charlotte and uttered, "Please, stop. I'm not trying to be rude, but I think you guys should go. I'm exhausted and I just need a good night's sleep. I'm sorry... I'm sorry," she repeated as she rushed out of the room.

"What do we do now?" Charlotte asked, turning towards John.

He shrugged and answered, "I have no idea."

"I feel horrible. I can't imagine how overwhelmed and confused she must feel. But I know she saw it! She saw the Dark Waters back then, and she saw it again today. I just know it."

"I think you're right," John said. "I could tell she was hiding something big."

"What now?"

"Maybe just give her some space. We can come by and check on her tomorrow. It'll give her a chance to process everything."

Hope sprinted up the stairs and threw herself onto her bed. She was shaking and crying, and although she did her best to calm herself down, nothing seemed to work. So many emotions were racing through her head. Mostly, she felt overwhelmed and confused—very, very confused. From that point on, Hope completely shut down. Over the next few days, she rarely left her room and barely ate a thing.

John and Charlotte tried to stop by twice the next day, but Janice regretfully told them that Hope wasn't feeling very well. After getting turned away for the second time, they headed over to the diner and tried to regroup. This consisted of John blaming himself.

"What the hell was I thinking telling her all that shit?" he loudly whispered. "Of course she freaked out. We basically anointed her the Savoir of our parents... hell, the Savoir for everyone who has ever been poisoned by the Dark Waters. I really need to learn to keep my big mouth shut!" John looked at all the people in the diner and said, "I don't need the whole world thinking I'm crazy."

"I don't think you're crazy. Not at all."

"Ha! But you did. You totally thought I was off my rocker that first night I told you everything."

"That's not true," she said, and then watched as John shot her a dubious look. "Well, maybe I thought you were a little crazy."

"And I'm sure Kevin thought I was nuts the first time I told him, too. I think the only one who didn't flinch was your friend, Daniel. I felt like he totally believed me."

"He should. He knows these legends inside and out. Not to mention, he completely believes in them himself. Also, he has a very soothing and non-judgmental way of talking and listening to people. He can pretty much put anyone at ease." Charlotte paused, then half-laughed and said, "We should have had *him* tell everything to Hope... maybe it would have resonated better."

As John pondered her last comment, the waitress stopped by refilling their coffee. When she was out of earshot, John leaned forward and said, "That's it! We should take her to see him. As long as I've known her, she's been into Native American culture... a bunch of other cultures, too... but definitely Native American. I bet Daniel could explain everything in a more believable way. And once he finds out that she can see the Dark Waters, maybe he can figure out what her connection is to this whole thing."

Charlotte ripped open a pack of sugar and dumped it into her cup. As she gave it a stir, she contemplated John's idea. "There's only one problem," she said, placing the spoon back onto the table. "How are we supposed to get her to go? She won't even see us right now."

John took a sip of his coffee and said, "Don't worry... I'll find a way."

After they finished and paid for their meals, John and Charlotte drove out to see Daniel. John didn't go into too many details, but he did tell Daniel that they met someone who *might* be connected to this whole Dark Waters thing. Neither of them revealed that Hope had the gift to see it. They simply asked Daniel if Hope could stop by and talk with him. The old man was more than receptive to John and Charlotte's request.

"I'm not sure I can be of any help," Daniel said. "But you can tell your friend that she can stop by anytime. I'm always here."

They both thanked Daniel then left. When they exited the house, they noticed the intensity of the rain had picked up. They made a mad dash for the car, and once inside, Charlotte asked, "What next?"

"Back to the inn."

Not a lot was spoken on the ride over. At one point, John's phone buzzed, alerting him of a message. He pulled it from his pocket and quickly read the text.

"Is everything okay?" Charlotte asked.

"Yeah, it's just Kevin. They're having a blast up in Bar Harbor and will be back sometime tomorrow evening."

John closed the screen and placed the phone on his lap. There were two more sentences to Kevin's text, but there was no way John was about to read it aloud.

Have you made your move yet? Hopefully you've at least gotten a kiss.

For good measure, John promptly deleted the entire text. Little did Kevin know; kissing was the last thing John was thinking about—at least for the past twenty-four hours. Of course, after reading the text, the thought of kissing Charlotte once again floated to the forefront of John's mind. And just like that, he found himself staring at her as she drove. More specifically, he focused on her soft skin, her full lips, and that little strand of black hair, which fell across the right side of her face. He remembered Kristen used to have a similar strand, albeit blonde, which hung over her right cheekbone. He used to affectionately refer to it as her sex-strand. Without even realizing it, he continued staring at Charlotte with a giant smile on his face.

"What are you smiling at?" she said, noticing.

"Huh? Oh, nothing. Just thinking of what I'm going to say to Hope when we get there."

"Come up with anything?"

"Nah. I'll just wing it."

"Oh boy," she murmured to herself.

A few minutes later, Charlotte pulled into the inn and parked next to Hope's Subaru. Before she could exit the car with John, he held out his hand and instructed, "No sense in both of us getting wet... wait here. I got this."

"Really?"

"Yeah, totally."

Hesitantly, she sat back in her seat and once again mumbled, "Oh boy."

He exuded confidence, but in all actuality, he had no clue what he was going to say to Hope. John slammed the door and sprinted up the walkway. As soon as he made it to the porch, he noticed Janice sitting in her favorite cushioned wicker chair. She had a light blanket draped over her lap and a cup of hot tea in her hand.

"Another banner day on the island," she called out to John.

"This is miserable," he said, wiping the rain from his face and hair. "My brother just texted me from Bar Harbor and said the weather has been perfect there. Crazy."

"Doesn't surprise me," she said, and then took a tiny sip from her mug. "If you're here to see Hope, I'm afraid she's still not feeling well. She never even came down for dinner last night... or breakfast this morning."

"Do you mind if I just run up and say hi? I just want her to know that we're here if she needs anything."

"Of course you can, dear."

John entered the house and slowly made his way up the creaky, old staircase. He crept down the hallway until he found himself face to face with Hope's door. He assumed there'd be no response but knocked anyway. When there wasn't so much as a stir, he decided to move on to plan B.

"Hey, Doc. It's John... John Mathews. I know that Janice said you weren't feeling well, but I can't help but think this has to do with the other night. If so, I just want to apologize. I never should have told you all that stuff. I know you're much too polite to ever tell me that I've completely lost my marbles, and trust me, I've been questioning my sanity for a while now. I know I've been a sarcastic pain in the ass over the years... and sometimes I tend to lie or exaggerate, but you need to know... everything I told you was the truth. I swear. I know you have a lot going on in your head... and that's probably why you came out here—to try and figure some things out. But maybe you shouldn't have to do it alone... maybe you should talk to someone. And no, I'm not talking about me. I think we both know I'd be the worst shrink ever."

He paused and placed his ear to the door. Not a peep from the other side.

"Look, I'm not sure what's going on in your head, Doc... and I'm not sure if you really have the ability to see the Dark Waters or not, but... there's this man here on the island that might be able to help you figure things out. From what Charlotte tells me, he's kinda like the wise man of the island. Oh, and he's Native American, too, which is right up your alley. Ya know, with all those dreamcatcher thingies you have. Not to mention, all that incense and sage shit you like to burn."

Again, John paused, and it was almost as if he could feel Hope smiling through the door.

"See, I'd be the worst shrink ever," he said, laughing to himself. "We already talked to this guy, and he said you are more than welcome to stop by anytime. And no, I didn't tell him any details about… about your gift. I just told him I had a close friend who might need some guidance. But just so you know, he does know everything that's been going on with me, Kevin, and Charlotte. I told him everything that I told you the other night. I guess we were looking for our own guidance. Again, I'm sorry for overwhelming you and freaking you out the other night. The last thing I want is for you to avoid me… or to be mad at me. I know I'm not the best at communicating my true feelings—not at all, actually. But you need to know, you're one of the most important people in my life, Hope."

Reaching into his pocket, he pulled out a piece of paper.

"Anyway, I guess I'll stop babbling to ya. Here's his name and address." John slipped it under the door. "I hope you get everything figured out, Doc."

With that, John turned and left. He headed downstairs and onto the porch, where Janice remained sitting under her blanket.

"Did you get a chance to see her, dear?" she asked.

"Um, no. I think she must have been asleep."

"I'll let her know you stopped by. I think it's very sweet how you check in on her."

I'm sure she doesn't think so, John thought to himself.

As if reading his mind, Janice kindly said, "And I'm sure Hope appreciates it as well. Actually… I guarantee she does."

It was still raining hard, but rather than sprint, John methodically walked back to the car. He could have cared less about staying dry. He was more concerned with the fact that he failed at his mission. At some point during his little speech, he honestly expected Hope to open the door and talk to him face to face. The fact that she didn't, led him to believe this was more serious than he thought.

Swinging open the car door, he plopped himself into the passenger seat. "Oh, John, you're drenched," Charlotte said.

"Yeah," was all he responded with.

"So? How'd it go? Did you talk to her?"

Slowly, he nodded and ran his fingers through his soaked hair.

"Was she receptive? Is she gonna go talk with Daniel?"

He shrugged and mumbled, "I guess time will tell."

"Where to now?" she asked.

Again, all he could manage was a shrug.

"Well, let's go get you into some dry clothes."

At the same time, Hope sat upstairs on her bed. It was the same position she'd been in the entire time John was talking to her. She heard every word he said, but her mind focused on one particular sentence: *But you need to know, you're one of the most important people in my life, Hope.* The sentiment was beautiful, but what caught her attention even more was the fact he called her Hope. For as far back as she could remember, John had always referred to her as Doc. This was the first time he'd ever called her by her name.

The guilt she felt was palpable. She should have answered the door. She should have responded to him. She hated the fact that John thought she was mad at him. Confused, yes, but definitely not mad. It was ironic how over the years she'd spent so much energy trying to convince John not to be ashamed or scared to reveal his true feelings. No matter what he was thinking or feeling, she always encouraged him to say it out loud. It must have taken a lot for him to open up to her the other night. Yes, what he told her was crazy and far-fetched, but her reaction was highly unprofessional, not to mention rude. Even worse, there was a part of her that believed everything they had told her.

As she quietly sat there on the bed, the question wasn't whether she believed in all the unexplainable things John had gone through. The real question going through her mind was what was *her* part in all of this? It was inconceivable to her that she played a role in this, and even more inconceivable to suggest she had some sort of special gift. She was just a simple therapist—an ex one at that. A boring middle-aged woman, who had never found her true love—or her true purpose. Not to mention, she still couldn't get over the terrifying feeling she had looking out at the ocean the other day.

What if it does exist? What if there really are people poisoned and trapped in limbo? What if I really can see it?

With question after question swirling through her head, her eyes focused on the folded piece of paper on the floor by the door. Finally, her curiosity got the better of her, and she slid down off the high bed. As her bare feet hit the wooden floor, she took a deep breath and slowly walked over and picked up the paper and unfolded it.

Daniel – Abenaki Stables (off Hawkeye Rd.)

An almost familiar feeling washed over her as she read and reread it. By the time she returned to her bed, it was all coming back to her. That was the very same place where her father took her horseback riding. *What was the name of owner of the stables?* she thought. *I could have sworn it was Daniel.*

Placing the paper next to her, she pressed her fingers against her temples and closed her eyes. It was as if she was hoping it would help her remember more clearly. Over the years, she had buried this memory so deep inside that she was having a hard time remembering the actual horse ride, never mind the man's name. Frustrated, she jumped down from the bed and began pacing around the room. "Focus, Hope. Focus," she said aloud.

She couldn't remember his name or his face, but she did remember his eyes—his kind eyes. They were the type of eyes that could look right through you. And they were the type that made you feel safe and at ease. Her pacing came to an abrupt stop, and she exclaimed, "Oh my God." She remembered being so at ease with this man; so much so that she even brought up the topic of the Dark Waters with him.

As hard as she tried, she could barely recall a thing he had told her. The only thing she remembered was the Dark Waters had to do with an Evil Spirit; one that was poised to take over the island by poisoning it.

Hope dedicated her entire life to helping people figure out their problems, yet when it came to her own, she was much better at avoiding them. She knew she couldn't stay secluded in her room forever, so a couple of hours after John and Charlotte left, Hope made her way downstairs. Janice offered a warm hello and asked if she would like some dinner. Hope was thankful that Janice didn't pry. It wasn't that she didn't feel comfortable talking to her; she simply had no clue how to explain what was going on. As promised, Janice told her that John and Charlotte had stopped by multiple times to check in on her.

"I told them you were under the weather and that you'd be back to normal sooner than later."

Hope poked at her food then looked up at Janice and said, "I'm sorry I've been keeping to myself lately… and I'm sorry I've been such a downer since I arrived here."

Janice lowered her glasses to the brim of her nose and sternly said, "Hope, there's absolutely no need to apologize. You're not here for my entertainment. You do what you need to do to find your answers."

Hope placed her elbow on the table with her head perched in her hand. "I'm not even sure I know what the questions are anymore, never mind the answers."

Laughing, Janice shook her head and asked, "Do you want to hear my two cents on the matter?"

Hope nodded.

"I'm not going to pretend to know what you're going through, but this is what I do know… There is so much light and beauty inside of you, Hope… but the sad thing is… you don't even realize it. I also know there's a reason why your father brought you here… just like there's a reason why you decided to return. Only you can figure out what those reasons are, but I have all the confidence in the world that you will. For me, the easiest part about life is realizing that it's all about signs. The hardest part is knowing where to look and how to interpret them. But trust me, dear, there's not a doubt in my mind that you'll find the answers you seek."

Janice gave her a wink, and then they both finished their meals in complete silence. This gave Hope time to think about her next move, and although she tried to ignore it, she had a feeling it would involve a trip out to the Abenaki Stables. When they finished their dinner, Hope helped clear the table. As discretely as she could, she attempted to get some clarity regarding this man named Daniel.

"Hey, Janice… I know this is kind of random, but do you remember when my dad took me horseback riding?"

A smile beamed from Janice's face. "I sure do. And I remember how excited you were telling me all about it."

"Is that place still in business?"

"The Abenaki Stables? Yes, I believe so."

Hope paused a second before continuing her not-so-inconspicuous recon. "Does that same man still own it?"

"No, his granddaughter took it over a while ago. He's had a lot of issues with his lower extremities and is pretty much relegated to a wheelchair now."

With bated breath, Hope asked, "What was his name again?"

"Daniel."

Hope's heartbeat quickened, and a shiver ran up her body. It *was* the same person she had talked to thirty years ago.

"What's with all the questions about the stables?"

"I was just curious, that's all."

"Ah, I see. I'm sure they haven't done much business this summer… not with the weather being like it is."

Hope finished helping Janice with the dishes then went back to her room. She had barely slept a wink in the past forty-eight hours, and tonight would be no different. Between tossing and turning in the bed and pacing the floor, sleep would not come easy. She thought about everything John and Charlotte had told her, and she also thought a lot about that week she spent with her father. Maybe Janice was right. Maybe it wasn't arbitrary that he chose Applewood. And if that was the case, maybe it was no accident that she met Daniel on their horseback riding excursion.

24

It was well after 3am when Hope's eyes finally gave way and closed for the night, but it wasn't before she made the decision to go speak with Daniel the next day. Her intention was to go first thing in the morning when she awoke, but her body was so exhausted that she ended up sleeping until early afternoon. She gave Janice as few details as possible, simply telling her she was going to take a drive to clear her head.

The weather hadn't changed a bit from the day before. Her windshield wipers were on high, and they seemed to be in sync with her quickly beating heart. She was nervous, anxious, and hadn't a clue what she was going to say to him. She did surprise herself by finding her way there without the use of GPS. It wasn't until she saw the sign reading: ABENAKI STABLES – 1 MILE AHEAD, that the nervousness and doubt really began to take hold.

During that final one-mile stretch, she found herself talking out loud. "This is crazy. What are you doing, Hope? What are you doing? You don't even know what you're going to say."

Even when Hope was parked in front of the stables, she continued to repeat herself. For five full minutes, she sat there with the car running, just staring at the front door to the house. After what seemed like forever, she lowered her head and let out a defeated sigh. Knowing that she couldn't go through with it, her hand clutched the gearshift. But before she could put it in reverse, something from the stables caught her eye. It was Daniel's granddaughter, Brooke. She was wearing a light blue raincoat, and as she exited the stables, she threw on her hood and curiously approached the car. The rain poured down on her as she rushed over to Hope's door. Hope was caught off guard, and it took her a second of fumbling to find the proper button.

When the window was finally rolled down, Brooke asked, "Hi, can I help you?" She assumed by the Illinois plates that this woman was probably lost. When Hope didn't say a word, Brooke held her palm out to the rain and joked, "I'm guessing you're not here for horseback riding?"

"Um, no," Hope replied. Nervously, she bit down on her lip and asked, "Is... is Daniel here?"

This was not the answer Brooke expected. "Grampa? Um, yeah, he's here. Is he expecting you?"

Not knowing how to reply, Hope hesitated. "Kind of?" she said, more as a question than a response.

Brooke smiled and said, "Come on in. I'll take you to him."

There was no backing out now. Hope rolled up the window, shut off her car, and followed the woman into the house.

"This weather is nasty, huh?" Brooke said, as they entered through the kitchen door. She then slipped off her hood and raincoat, which for the most part had protected her from the rain. Hope wasn't so lucky. In her haste, she'd left the house wearing nothing but a long sleeve tie dye shirt and her favorite bell-bottom jeans. It was only a short distance, but by the time Hope made it from the car to the house, she was soaked from head to toe.

"Aw, you're drenched. Wait here, let me go grab you a towel."

When Brooke returned, she had a towel in one hand and a thick grey sweatshirt in the other.

"Here. It's not much... but it'll warm you up. It's clean, I promise," she said with a grin.

"Thank you," Hope replied, drying herself off with the towel.

After she pulled the sweatshirt on over her head, Brooke outstretched her hand and said, "I'm Brooke, by the way."

"I'm Hope."

"Nice to meet you," Brooke said, shaking her hand.

Sheepishly, Hope smiled and said, "Actually, I think we met about thirty years ago."

"Really?"

"My father brought me here. Your grandfather took us on a beautiful ride. You went with us as well."

"I did? I must have been super young."

Hope nodded. "You were probably nine or ten at the time. You were young, but you certainly knew what you were doing."

"Ha, I should. I've been around horses my entire life. I'm sorry I don't remember you."

"Oh, no need to be sorry. Like I said, it was thirty years ago."

Although curious, Brooke chose not to ask what Hope was doing in town. She also didn't feel the need to pry regarding Hope's meeting with her grandfather.

"Well, follow me," Brooke said, leading Hope towards the living room.

"Is it just you two that live here?" Hope asked.

"No. My husband and daughter live here, too. They're on a father daughter movie date right now. It's about the only thing to do in this weather. My grandmother passed away a while ago, and even though my grandfather is pretty self-sufficient, I thought it was best for us to move in and help him out."

"That's nice of you. And you're the owner of the stables now?"

Proudly, Brooke smiled. "I am. He gave it to me about fifteen years ago. Unfortunately, our business relies mostly on tourists, but that's been on a steady decline over the years." Brooke motioned to the couch. "Make yourself at home. Do you want anything to drink?"

"I'm good, thank you."

"Okay then, let me go get Grampa for you."

As soon as Brooke left the room, Hope made her way over and sat on the couch. No sooner did she sit down, she started fidgeting with her hands. At first, she began twirling her hair, and then her fingers started to anxiously pull at a couple of loose threads on her jeans.

"There she is."

Startled, Hope looked up and saw Daniel sitting in his wheelchair in the doorway. Upon his entrance, she courteously stood.

"Long time no see," he said.

At first, she was surprised he remembered her, but the more she thought about it, she realized what must have happened. Her lips curled into a grin. "Your granddaughter told you that I've been here before, didn't she?"

"Nope," he replied, wheeling into the room. "She just told me there was a woman here to see me."

"Really? But it was like thirty years ago. You must have given hundreds of tours between then and now. You really remember me?"

"First of all," he said, laughing, "I think you're selling me short. It's more like thousands of people that I've taken on the trails. And secondly, yes, of course I remember you."

Jokingly, she said, "Let me guess, you never forget a face?"

Daniel laughed as he navigated his way around one of the end tables. He finally came to a stop about four feet in front of Hope.

"I've forgotten plenty of faces over the years, but I never forget an aura... especially one as bright as yours." With his left hand, he motioned downward. "Please, sit."

At that moment, the only aura she felt was red—bright red from embarrassment. She lowered back onto the couch and watched as Daniel tapped his wheels.

"As you can see, my horse-riding days have long since been over."

"I'm sorry," she said.

"Oh, don't be sorry, dear. We all get older. That's why you need to enjoy your youth."

"It's nice that you passed the business on to your granddaughter."

Daniel smiled. "Brooke was destined to take it over. She's a natural, that's for sure."

"I can't believe how old she is now. I didn't even recognize her."

Proudly, Daniel nodded and said, "She's grown into a beautiful and amazing woman. As have you."

Again, she felt her cheeks flush red.

"I'm sure your parents are extremely proud of you."

Sadly, she lowered her head and once again began picking at the loose thread on her jeans.

"Even back then I could tell how proud your father was of you."

Normally, Hope would have been uncomfortable talking about her past, especially about her father. But for whatever reason, Daniel's presence put her at ease. So much so, she slowly raised her head and confessed, "My father passed away a few months after we left here. He'd been fighting a sickness for a while, I guess."

"I know," Daniel said, sympathetically nodding. "I sensed it when I shook his hand."

"You did?"

"Yes. There was a black poison within him."

Assuming he was referring to her father's kidney condition, she revealed that he had passed from acute renal failure.

"I'm very sorry for your loss."

"Thanks," Hope said, trying to think of a way to switch subjects. Daniel sensed this and decided to do it for her.

"Your friends talk very highly of you... especially John."

Even at age fifty, Hope was still uncomfortable with any sort of compliment. Without even realizing it, she began fidgeting and tugging on the strings of Brooke's sweatshirt.

"He mentioned that you're his therapist back in Chicago."

"Well, I used to be. I'm kind of retired now... sorta. I don't really know what I am, to be honest with you."

Warmly, Daniel smiled and said, "You're a healer through and through... we don't ever retire from that."

Hope laughed. "I'm not sure I'd call myself a healer. I'll leave that up to the real doctors. I just listen to people's problems, that's all."

"I think now *you're* the one selling yourself short. Healing the mind and spirit are just as important as healing the body. I can't speak for all your patients over the years, but it's obvious how much you've helped John... and his brother."

"They told you that?"

"They didn't need to. I could sense it. Just like I sensed you were destined for big things the first time I ever met you."

Blushing, Hope softly thanked him. She then cracked a smile and said, "I still can't believe you remember me."

"Oh, I most definitely remember you. I remember it was your first time ever riding a horse."

Hope nodded and grinned. "Unfortunately, it was my only time. I always told myself I wanted to go again, but..."

"I remember how innocent and starry-eyed you were... and how you soaked in everything around you: nature, the different landscapes, the horses... and your father. It's a beautiful and rare thing when I see people noticing and appreciating the little things around them. That was you, my friend. That was you." Before Hope had a chance to get too embarrassed, Daniel brought up another memory. "I also remember how inquisitive you were. You were very curious about the many old legends of our island... in particular, the Dark Waters."

Normally, her initial reaction would have been to avoid eye contact and anxiously find something to fidget with—soon followed by the biting down on her lip. Although tempted, she did none of these things. For whatever reason, she felt at ease with Daniel. She felt it thirty years ago and again when he entered the room minutes earlier.

"Actually," she said, looking him straight in the eyes, "that's kind of why I'm here... the Dark Waters."

"Ah," Daniel said, laughing. "Seems like a popular topic amongst you kids lately."

"John mentioned that they told you everything. The strange and unbelievable occurrences he experienced... the coincidental plane crash... and the even-more coincidental dream that Charlotte and Kevin are having..."

Daniel tapped his fingers on his wheels and said, "Is that what *you* think? That the occurrences John spoke of were *unbelievable*? That the plane crash and dreams are merely coincidental?"

The irony of Daniel answering her question with a question was not lost on her.

"I... I don't know what I think. My brain has been racing a mile a minute... even before I left Chicago. I can't seem to focus or to find any of the answers I'm looking for."

"Is that why you're here? You're hoping that I'll give you the answers you seek?"

Hope shrugged and thought, *Dang, he's good. He'd make the perfect therapist.*

"Well, the bad news is... I don't have the answers you seek. But the good news is... *you* do. You should know this more than anyone, Hope... we all have the answers inside us. Most of the time, they're hiding in plain sight. We just need to look hard enough. You need to eliminate all the white noise and outside distractions. Then, and only then, will the answers be revealed."

Hope chuckled to herself, knowing this was similar advice she'd given to most of her patients over the years. "I've tried. I really have, but... but I just can't focus."

Daniel deliberated for a moment. "Hmm, maybe I can help you with that," he said, rubbing his fingers on his chin. "Help you to find your focus. Wait right here. I'll be back."

In one swift motion, the old man spun his chair around and wheeled out of the room. It would be a solid ten minutes before he returned. During that time, Hope found herself wandering around the room looking at all the old photos and ancient Native American artifacts. In particular, she was taken with the many hand-carved wooden statues, which adorned tables and shelves throughout the room. On either side of the fireplace were two beautifully intricate dreamcatchers. John was right, the entire vibe was right up her alley.

Most of the wooden carvings were miniature, but in the far corner of the room stood a large Great Blue Heron. It was almost identical to the one at Janice's house. Curiously, Hope moved closer to examine it. Just then, Daniel reentered the room, slower and more carefully than when he left. Balancing on his lap was a tray with two large steaming mugs.

"Sorry it took so long," he said, returning to his spot in the center of the room.

"It's okay. Can I give you a hand with that?" she asked, motioning to the tray.

"This one is yours," he said, carefully handing her the forest green mug. He placed his mug on the table next to him and then leaned the tray against its legs.

"Thank you," Hope said. She cradled the mug with both hands and stuck her nose closer to take in its aroma. "What is this?"

"A little bit of this and a little bit of that," he said, winking. "It's an old Abenaki mixture. It relaxes the mind and allows you to focus… and ultimately, it'll give you the clarity to find that which you seek."

Daniel reached over and grabbed his mug and took a satisfying sip.

"Do you have the same thing?" Hope asked.

"Me? Nooo. Black coffee. Caffeine is what *I* seek," he said, laughing at himself.

If she wasn't at ease already, Daniel's smile and laugh certainly helped put her there.

"By the way, I love the décor and vibe of this room. It's all so groovy." She immediately cringed at her dated adjective. "Sorry. Once a hippie, always a hippie, I guess."

"Ha. No need to apologize, my friend. You're right, it *is* pretty groovy in here."

"And no TV either," she said, looking around. "You don't see that too often these days."

"Oh, we do. The TV is in the family room down the hall. That's where most of the entertaining and socializing happen. But not this room… this room is my peaceful little sanctuary in the house."

"I can see why," she said, taking a sip of her drink. "And I love all of the carvings."

"Thank you. I've been doing that since I was a young boy."

"*You* did those? Wow. I could never have the talent or patience to do that."

"It's actually quite calming. Unfortunately, I haven't been able to do one in the longest time. These old shaky hands aren't what they used to be. Especially now that arthritis has got the better of me over the years."

"Did you do that one, too?" she asked, pointing to the heron. Daniel nodded, and Hope followed with, "It looks exactly like the one Janice has at the inn."

Daniel smiled. "That's because I carved it for her. I'm not sure if you know this or not, but the Great Blue Heron is very important to this island. Legends tell us the Great Blue Heron represents self-reliance… self-determination. Not to mention, the fishermen have always believed it brought them good luck. The Great Blue Heron is known as the watcher of the island."

"For a little island, it sure has a lot of legends."

"Yes, yes it does. And speaking of which, how much do you know about them?"

"The legends?" Hope hesitated and shrugged. "Just bits and pieces from what people have told me… and I did do a little reading about them online."

"Ha," Daniel laughed. "That's what I was afraid of. Well, no offense to Wikipedia, but how about I tell you the *real* versions?"

She grinned and nodded yes. "I would like that."

Hope curled up in the corner of the couch, and after they both took a sip from their drinks, Daniel wheeled over to the fireplace and lit what Hope recognized to be a stick of white sage. He also tossed in some other items which were all unfamiliar to Hope. It didn't take long for the smoke to filter throughout the room. He slightly opened the damper so as not to overpower the room with smoke. When he was satisfied, he turned to Hope and said, "My granddaughter hates me burning this in here, but I tell her as long as my name is on the mortgage, then it's still my house. My house, my rules."

Daniel returned to his spot in front of her, took one more sip of coffee, and then began his storytelling. Thirty years earlier, he'd given her the abridged version of the Dark Waters: how the island's mysterious and magical elements attracted its original settlers—how they accidentally discovered and unleashed the Evil Spirit—and how they summoned a mighty shaman to banish it out to sea. This time, Daniel went into much more detail and revealed a legend Hope had never heard before—The Legend of Lover's Leap. Not only did it tie into the Dark Waters, but it would eventually tie into Medillia's Lament as well.

The entire time Daniel spoke, he methodically wheeled around the smoke-filled room. As Hope intently listened from the couch, she continued sipping from the special drink Daniel had made for her. She was completely invested in his stories, yet she found her eyes uncontrollably getting heavier and heavier. But even when they were fully closed, Daniel's voice remained in her subconscious.

***

The next thing she remembered, her eyes popped open, and she sat straight up on the couch. It took her a moment to catch her breath from the strange dream she was having. Whatever had been burning in the fireplace was totally out, and the smoke in the room had all but dissipated. In her hands, she was still clutching the mug, which was

320

now empty. She spun around to see if Daniel was behind her, but there was no trace of him at all. She had no idea how long she'd been out, nor did she remember falling asleep in the first place.

"What? That can't be," she said, looking down at her watch. Over three hours had gone by since she arrived at the house.

Placing her mug on the table, she walked over to the doorway and poked her head out into the hall.

"Hello? Daniel?" She waited a second then called out, "Brooke?"

The house was dead silent, and the only sounds she heard were the wind and rain whipping outside. The wind was so strong it caused the windows to rattle. Unsure what to do, Hope made her way down the hall and back into the kitchen. She pushed aside the curtains and peered outside into the driveway. Brooke must have left because Hope's car was the only one there. But if that was the case, then where was Daniel?

As Hope paced back and forth, she shook her head in disgust at herself. She surmised that Daniel was probably offended and left the room after she had fallen asleep during his story. Once again, she called out Daniel's name down the hall. When there was no reply, she bit down on her lip and pressed on her temples with her fingers. Her head was still groggy from her unplanned nap, and she had no idea what to do next.

Hope wandered back into the living room, and when there was still no sign of him, she decided to just leave. There was a small pad of paper attached to the refrigerator by a magnet. She thought about leaving a note but couldn't for the life of her find the right words. *I'm sorry I fell asleep while you were trying to help me*, just didn't cut it. There were a few patients over the years who had dozed off while she was walking around the room talking and trying to help them. She remembered being slightly offended and could only imagine that Daniel felt the same way.

After much deliberation, she decided to skip the note and promised herself to return and give Daniel a proper face-to-face apology. Before she rushed out the door, she slipped off Brooke's sweatshirt and hung it over one of the kitchen chairs. As was the case earlier, the short distance from the house to the car was enough to get her soaked from head to toe. Technically, sunset wasn't for another few hours, but the dark storm clouds made it seem like nighttime had already arrived. As carefully as she could, Hope navigated her way back to the inn.

Upon entering the front door, she sprinted upstairs without so much as a hello to Janice. By the time she reached her room, she was completely out of breath and couldn't stop shivering. The first thing she did was slip out of her wet clothes and put on something warm and dry. She then crawled into bed and pulled the covers over her head. She definitely wasn't tired; not after sleeping so long and soundly at Daniel's, but she just needed it to be dark and quiet as she tried to process her thoughts. It didn't take long for her breathing to slow and for her shivering to stop.

25

Just as Hope was pulling the covers over her head, Kevin and Julie were pulling into William's driveway. Their mini trip to Bar Harbor was a big success. It was three of the best days they had spent together in a long time. They talked, they laughed, and they thoroughly enjoyed each other's company. Their entire trip to Maine couldn't have been more perfect, especially for Julie. For Kevin, the only thing preventing it from being perfect was the return of his dream. Each night at the hotel, he abruptly awoke in a cold sweat. Like always, he didn't go into details with Julie. He played it off as just a *tiny bad dream*. But the truth was the dream was far from tiny. As a matter of fact, it had become more upsetting... more dire.

Kevin wasn't the only one experiencing this. Charlotte's dream of her father drowning in the Dark Waters had also returned. Like Kevin, Charlotte decided to keep it to herself. Ever since John found out that his life-long therapist was somehow involved in all of this, he'd become overly anxious and on edge. Charlotte figured the last thing he needed to hear was that her dream had once again returned. And like Kevin, she also sensed the situation had escalated and become more desperate. Thankfully, she worked open to close at the store, which allowed for plenty of distractions.

As Hope remained curled under her covers, she continued trying to relax her mind. She was attempting to remember the strange dream she had earlier at Daniel's. Bit by bit and piece by piece, it all started to come back to her. Not only did she feel like she was watching a movie, but the entire thing was being narrated by Daniel. Eventually, it hit her. It wasn't a dream at all. She never fell asleep earlier. Her mind must have been so relaxed and so in tune that it allowed her eyes to close without actually sleeping. Subconsciously, she heard every word Daniel had spoken to her. As his story and words replayed in her head, the puzzle pieces began to fall into place. Hope recalled something Daniel had said to her earlier:

You should know this more than anyone, Hope, we all have the answers inside us. Most of the time, they're hiding in plain sight. We just have to look hard enough. You need to eliminate all the white noise and outside distractions. Then, and only then, will the answers be revealed.

"Oh my God," she said, throwing the covers back.

She jumped out of bed and headed straight for her mother's chest. Hastily, she rummaged through its contents until she came across her father's old notebooks. She determined a long time ago that the only notebook worth anything was the one which contained her father's unsent letters to her. The others were filled with random sketches, incoherent rambling, and words and phrases that made absolutely no sense to her.

To her, those notebooks were a sad reminder of just how sick, twisted, and deteriorated her father's mind had become throughout his lifetime. It hurt so much that she hadn't even opened those particular notebooks in almost twenty-five years. But now, as she flipped through page after page, she was seeing everything in a different light. What she once considered gibberish, was now making complete sense. It was just like Janice had told her; her puzzle pieces were slowly coming together.

By the time she read the last page, she was as calm as she'd ever been. She took a moment to absorb everything, and then she placed the notebooks back into the chest. To the left of her father's notebooks were her mother's old diaries, and to the right were her own diaries. Before closing the lid, she reached inside and pulled out her father's leather jacket and the seashell necklace he had left for her. Just then, she heard the faint sound of the grandfather clock in the living room striking midnight. Gently, she closed the lid. She knew it was time for her to go.

***

Charlotte had long since fallen asleep across John's lap, which forced him to finally sit still and refrain from the anxious pacing he had been doing all night. At one point, as he watched Charlotte peacefully sleeping, he was reminded of Kristen. There were so many times Kristen had dozed off on his lap. He loved watching her sleep, but regretfully, he felt as though he never appreciated it as much as he should have at the time. As he sat there watching Charlotte's slow breaths, he vowed to never make that mistake again.

Right around midnight, her breathing changed drastically. It went from slow and peaceful to fast and erratic. He watched as she tossed and turned, but it wasn't until she began to mumble and cry out that he knew she was having *the dream*. Before he had a chance to wake her up, her eyes popped open, and she gasped for air.

"Hey... it's okay," he reassured. "It was just a dream."

Charlotte sat up and looked John dead in the eyes and said, "It's getting worse... it's getting closer."

Knowing exactly what she was talking about, John reached over and pushed the hair out of her face and gently stroked her cheek. Without saying a word, they knew what they needed to do. It didn't matter how late it was; they needed to go see Hope. They still had no idea how or why, but they knew she was the key to all of this.

In preparation for the nasty weather, John threw on his sweatshirt, and Charlotte grabbed her raincoat. When both hoods were pulled over their heads, they sprinted down the outside staircase towards John's truck. Just as he grabbed the door handle, a car drove past the store. They both did a double take and looked over at one another.

"Was that… was that Hope?" Charlotte finally said.

It took John a second to process it, but once he did, he yelled out, "Let's go!"

They jumped into his truck and sped off in hot pursuit of a Subaru Outback. The rain wasn't the only thing impairing their vision. A heavy fog had rolled in, making it nearly impossible to see anything up ahead of them. At the four-way stop sign, John came to a screeching halt.

"Shit! Where'd she go?" he said, looking straight and then to his left.

"There!" Charlotte said, pointing to her right. "I just saw taillights there."

John cranked his wheel and sped off to his right.

Despite the weather condition being as bad as it was, Hope was calm, cool, and composed as she navigated her way down the darkened road. Just then, a large tree branch, which was hanging over the road, snapped and fell straight down. Hope watched it happen, but rather than slamming on her brakes, she pressed harder on the gas pedal. Although the branch clipped the back of her car, the damage could have been much worse. It crashed onto the road, splintering into multiple pieces.

John could barely see Hope's taillights as he tried to keep pace. "Where is she going?" Charlotte asked, but she, as well as John, already knew the answer. Harbor Cove Park. "John, watch out!" Charlotte yelled and pointed ahead.

John swerved left and then right, but it was too late. He struck the large branch, causing him to lose control of his truck. The next thing he knew, he veered into a ditch. As far as ditches go, it was shallow, but it was deep and muddy enough to cause two of his wheels to spin in place.

John slammed his fists onto the steering wheel and started to yell out, "Mother F——"

"Come on," she interrupted. "The road is still closed up around the bend. She's gonna have to use the path we all took the other day. Do you have a flashlight?"

John nodded and reached under his seat and pulled out a red flashlight. "I think I have another one in there," he said, pointing to the glove box.

With flashlights in hand, they got out of the truck and bolted down the road. Sure enough, just as they came around the bend, Hope's car was parked on the side of the road and at the foot of the path. The rain had slowed, but it still didn't take long for them to be soaked from head to toe. By the time they wound their way through the path and into the park, their shoes and pantlegs were covered in mud.

"Hope!" Charlotte yelled out. "Where are you?"

John repeated even louder, but neither of their yells were any match for the wind. It gusted and screeched, nearly drowning their voices out completely. To make matters worse, their flashlights did little to cut through the thick fog looming over the park.

"This is useless," he yelled over to Charlotte. "She could be anywhere. I have a bad feeling about this."

Charlotte heard him but didn't reply. She was too busy shining her light from her right to her left and back again. She knew how big the park was, and she knew the weather would not make it easy to find Hope. Just then, John yelled out, "Jesus Christ!"

Charlotte turned and followed his beam of light. It was directed up ahead and over to the left about fifteen feet. There, on the edge of the cliff, was Hope. She had her back to them and was barefoot and bundled in her father's leather jacket. She was standing on a large flat rock, which extended out beyond the cliff. It was the same exact rock she had stood on thirty years earlier with her father. It was where he honored his wife's memory by tossing a rose into the ocean far below. And it was also where he broke down crying and began apologizing and rambling incoherent thoughts.

When Charlotte saw how close Hope was to the edge, she tightly clutched John's arm and exclaimed, "Oh my God, John! We need to do something."

John knew she was right, but he didn't have a clue what to do or say. He couldn't believe the situation had gotten this dire. Was this because of the conversation they all had days earlier? Before he had a chance to overanalyze the situation, a giant gust of wind swooped in, nearly knocking Hope off balance.

Without thinking, John yelled out, "Hope!"

Slowly, she turned around and looked over at them. They assumed she'd be inconsolable and that her eyes would be filled with tears. What they didn't expect to see was a contented smile on her face. Water droplets tracked down her cheeks, but it was from the rain, not tears.

"What are you doing out here?" John called out.

"Come away from the edge!" Charlotte warned. "It's not safe out there."

Hope's smile grew bigger as she called back, "It's okay. It's all going to be okay. I finally have all the pieces to my puzzle."

John and Charlotte had no idea what she was talking about but assumed her mental state was fragile at best.

John inched closer and yelled, "Why don't you come away from the ledge and tell us more about your puzzle."

"Yeah, let's all go back to the inn and get warm and dry," Charlotte called out. "And then you can explain it all over a hot cup of tea."

Calmly, Hope spoke. "I'm glad you two are here. If it weren't for you guys and Kevin, I wouldn't have broken out of my depression. And if it weren't for you, I never would have gone and talked to Daniel… and I never would have learned the truth."

"The truth? What truth?" John asked, taking another step forward.

"My purpose… my destiny. I've spent my entire life questioning things… questioning my existence." Hope turned her attention to

Charlotte. "You should be proud of the smart and beautiful woman you've grown into. And I'm so glad you two found one another. See, things really do happen for a reason."

Hope continued to smile widely as she focused on John. "And you, my friend... it feels like just yesterday I was having my first session with you and Kevin. I remember how lost, and lonely you both looked... especially you. From the moment I met you, I knew there was something different about you two... something special. It was no accident that we were brought together... that we were ALL brought together. I am so blessed to have known each and every one of you. I only wish Kevin was here right now so I could say goodbye to him, too."

As soon as Hope said the word *goodbye*, Charlotte tightened her grip and dug her nails into John's arm and whispered, "Oh my God, John... do something!"

Like always, John resorted to humor to deal with a tense situation. "Lucky for you, Kevin just got back into town. I say we go wake his ass up and all play some late-night board games. I might even let someone else win besides me."

"That sounds like a great idea," Charlotte chimed in.

Although they both were smiling, Hope read right through it and saw the worry in their eyes.

"Seriously, guys, everything's going to be okay. I promise."

Another strong gust of wind blew in from the ocean. It knocked her back from the edge and down to one knee. If it had come from any other direction, it would have surely sent her over the cliff. John started to move forward and reach out to Hope, but she firmly put up her hand, halting him in his steps.

"Don't come any further," she politely urged. "This is no longer your fight... no longer your burden."

"Hope, please let us help you... please." There was desperation in Charlotte's voice as she pleaded with her.

With the wind still at her back, Hope shakily stood up and said, "Oh, honey, you've already helped me so much… all of you have."

Again, the wind whipped in from the ocean, but this time Hope stood firm. For a brief second, her eyes focused on the giant rock she was standing on. She then smiled and looked up and said, "This whole place was so special to my parents… especially this rock." With the warmest and kindest of smiles, Hope spoke, "It's time."

Slowly, Hope turned and faced the ocean. She closed her eyes and immediately heard her father's voice in her head:

Trust me, the exhilaration you'll feel afterwards will far outweigh the fear you're feeling now. Be brave. Don't let the fear take over. It'll all be worth it… I promise you that. You're stronger than you think. You always have been.

It was from thirty years earlier when they were standing on the bridge.

John knew it was now or never. He needed to spring forward and grab her before she did the unthinkable. Unfortunately, the wind and rain had picked up in intensity. It was so strong and so forceful that John could barely catch his breath, never mind take a step forward. The wind blew directly off the ocean as if trying to prevent Hope from moving any closer to the edge. Her legs wavered, but she was determined to do what needed to be done. Once again, her father's voice popped into her head. This time it was from the last letter he had written to her:

I don't know a lot of things, but I do know that your mother is smiling down right now at the amazing woman you've become. I even think she's smiling down at me too for introducing you to this place. I know being here this week might not make any sense to you right now, but it will. One day, when the time is right, it will… and you will shine like you were always meant to. You were right, Hope, everything does happen for a reason… this week included. But just not the reasons you think. I promise, though, it'll all make sense one day. I promise.

Despite the wind and rain doing their best to keep her in her place, she forced one foot in front of the other until she was an inch from the edge. As she reached up clutching her seashell necklace, a woman's voice echoed in her head:

Shine on, baby girl... shine on.

Hope had never actually heard her mother's voice before, but she knew it was her. With the warmest of feelings shooting through her body, she took a deep breath, closed her eyes, and walked off the ledge. As Hope's body disappeared into the abyss, Charlotte released John's arm and fell to the ground. She tried to scream but nothing came out. John's mouth dropped open, and his body stood frozen. He couldn't believe what he just witnessed.

Tears burst from Charlotte's eyes, and she hung her head and placed her hands over her face. But before any of her tears had a chance to hit the ground—it happened. The sky was filled with a brilliant light. It took John a moment to understand exactly what he was seeing, but when he realized what it was, he tapped Charlotte on the shoulder. She removed her hands from her face and saw that the sky was filled with stardust. It was the brightest and most beautiful sight either of them had ever seen. Without taking his eyes off the sky, John reached down and helped Charlotte to her feet. As if naturally, their fingers interlocked, and they stood there tightly holding hands and gazing up at the night sky. They watched as the stardust scattered over the ocean and onto the land as well. They were so awestruck that they didn't even notice the rain had ceased and that the wind had lightened to a gentle, warm breeze. Even the fog had dissipated.

***

A few minutes earlier, on the other side of the island, Kevin and Julie had fallen into a deep sleep. They were exhausted from their long day of travel, but like always, Kevin's sleep would be short-lived. Not only did the dream return, but the ending was unlike anything he had ever dreamt of before. In the beginning, it was the same as it had always been. The ocean was pitch black; giant waves relentlessly pounded and pushed his parents underwater. But this time, the waves were darker and much bigger than they'd ever been. Kevin felt helpless as he watched the Dark Waters ruthlessly drowning his parents. It was so bad that they couldn't even scream out. As the dream unfolded, Kevin's entire being felt their pain.

Off in the distance, he saw the largest and most ominous wave he'd ever seen. The closer it got to his parents, the bigger and angrier it became. To no avail, Kevin attempted to warn them. He opened his mouth and tried to yell as loud as he could, but like always, no sound came out. By now, the Evil Spirit was looming high above them. Kevin couldn't bear to watch, but just before he turned away, it happened. The entire sky lit up—then nothing. The giant waves were gone, and the water was as flat and as calm as could be. The ocean returned to its blue-green color, and there were no signs of any black or darkened areas anywhere.

Just before he awoke, he saw them—his parents. It was only for the briefest of moments, but what he saw would stay with him for the rest of his life. His parents were no longer struggling—no longer drowning—no longer in pain—no longer in limbo. They were free. For the first time ever, their faces were as clear as they'd ever been, and they were looking directly at him. Before slowly fading away, they gave their son the biggest, most loving smile he'd ever seen.

Just then, Kevin's eyes popped open, and he shot straight up in bed. This, combined with a loud gasp caused Julie to also awaken.

"Are you okay?" she sleepily asked. When he didn't offer a reply, she turned on the lamp. "Oh, honey, you're shivering." She began rubbing his arms. "Did you have a bad dream?"

It was a simple question, but for Kevin, it was much more complicated than that. Even though it was far from a nightmare, Kevin couldn't contain his emotions any longer, nor did he want to. As he continued shivering and trying to catch his breath, tears uncontrollably poured from his eyes.

Completely caught off guard, Julie had no idea what to do or say. Without a word, she tightly placed her arms around her husband and remained that way until every last tear had fallen. When he had finally regained his composure, Julie looked him in the eyes and sweetly asked, "Do you want to talk about it?"

Kevin knew he couldn't keep her in the dark any longer. He took a deep breath, slowly nodded his head yes, and then he proceeded to tell his wife everything. She held his hand and sat perfectly still as he told her the entire story. On more than one occasion, he found himself saying, "I know you're gonna think I'm crazy but…"

So much had happened, and he was sure he'd forgotten some of the details, but when he was finished rambling, he ended by saying, "John and Charlotte can corroborate everything, I swear!"

It took Julie a few minutes to get her thoughts together, but for Kevin, he already felt a huge weight had been lifted by revealing the many secrets he'd been keeping all this time. That being said, he was pleasantly surprised by her reaction. Understandably, she didn't come right out and say she believed every word he had told her, but she did tell him she didn't think he was crazy. Not at all. And for Kevin, that's all he needed to hear.

As she continued clutching his hand, she softly said, "Why do you think you had that dream tonight? What changed to make it end so differently?"

Kevin shrugged. "I have no idea, but… but I think I need to call my brother."

***

John and Charlotte stood side by side and remained mesmerized by the stardust falling all around them. They remained silent as they each tried to process what they had just seen. Tears continued to fall, but the longer they gazed up to the sky, the more mixed their emotions became. They were still devastated after watching Hope jump, but they found it impossible to stay sad knowing they had just experienced the most magnificent and awe-inspiring event of their entire lives.

When his heart rate returned to normal, and when his breathing had slowed, John thoughts turned to his brother. "I gotta call Kevin."

No sooner did he utter those words, he felt the vibration of his phone go off. He pulled it out of his pocket and curiously looked at who it was.

"Kevin? I was actually just going to call you."

Unsure what to say, Kevin remained quiet.

"Kev? Are you there?"

"Um, yeah... I'm here. Um... there's been a new development. You're not gonna believe the dream I just had."

"And you're not gonna believe what I just witnessed... what *we* just witnessed," he said glancing over at Charlotte.

"Where are you?"

After John told him where they were, Kevin responded with, "We'll meet you up there in a few." Before getting off the phone, John quickly mentioned, "And yes, that's my truck in the ditch."

"What?"

"Never mind. We'll see you in a while."

No sooner did Kevin hang up, Julie asked, "What's going on? Where are they?"

"I'm not sure what's going on. But they're up at Harbor Cove Park. He wants us to meet them up there."

As quickly as they could, they jumped out of bed and got dressed. Before rushing out of the house, Julie grabbed him by the hand and said, "Thank you... for telling me."

Kevin smiled back at her. "No. Thank *you*... for not thinking I'm totally and completely nuts."

Less than five minutes later, they were turning onto the road leading to the park. Kevin instructed Julie to grab the flashlight out of the glove compartment. They fully expected the road would still be closed and that they'd have to hike to the park through the long path

Charlotte had taken them down earlier that week. But before they even got that far, Julie pointed to the ditch off to the right. "Hey, isn't that John's truck?"

"Yup. He mentioned we might see that. Do you remember where the entrance to the path was?"

"Just keep your eye out for those concrete barricades. The path was directly in front of them and off to the right, remember?"

They kept their eyes peeled, but they never did see the barricades. The next thing they knew, they were turning into the gravel parking lot of the park.

"Guess the road is no longer out," he said hopping out of the car.

Hand in hand, they climbed the wooden steps, which were built into the hill. Julie had grabbed the flashlight, but she quickly realized it wouldn't be needed. Now that the fog and clouds had disappeared, it allowed the nearly full moon to illuminate the entire park. As soon as they reached the top of the stairs, Julie looked around and exclaimed, "Whoa! This place is beautiful at night."

Kevin nodded. "It looks so—"

"Peaceful," she said, squeezing his hand tighter. She continued gazing around and pointed up to the top of the park. "Is that them?"

Kevin followed her finger and saw two figures up by the cliff. "I assume so," he said, as they continued forward and up the paved path.

Just then, John turned around and spotted his brother and Julie. "What the hell are they doing here already?"

John and Charlotte headed down the paved path and met them halfway.

"How did you guys get here so fast? There's no way you hiked the path in that short of time."

"That's because we didn't," Kevin said.

"Yeah, the road was open," Julie added.

John and Charlotte exchanged a look then said in unison, "It was?"

With the moonlight being as bright as it was, Kevin noticed their eyes looked red as if they'd both been crying.

"What went on up here?" Kevin hesitantly asked.

Knowing the brothers needed to talk in private, Charlotte attempted to get Julie to take a walk with her. At that point, Kevin held up his hand and said, "It's okay, guys. I already filled Julie in on everything."

"On *everything*?"

"Yes, John… on everything."

Julie smiled, then reached over and grabbed her husband's hand.

"And you don't think we're all crazy? John asked.

Julie grinned. "No more than you normally are." She then gazed around the entire park and said, "It's so beautiful up here at night." As her eyes started to look up towards the sky, she paused and squinted. "Are those fireflies?" she said, pointing upwards.

"No," Charlotte said, shaking her head. "It's… it's stardust."

"No way! Like from a shooting star?"

"Yeah… something like that."

"That must have been amazing. Did you guys see it?"

Once again, Charlotte and John exchanged a look. "Yes," Charlotte answered.

"And yes, it was amazing," John added.

Kevin's curiosity had reached its limit. Seriously, John, what went on up here?"

John gave them the abridged version of what had transpired while they were up in Bar Harbor. He told him about Hope's ability to see the Dark Waters and how she was the key to everything. He also told him that they had referred Hope to Daniel.

"What did he say to her?" Kevin asked.

"I have no idea, but it must have been some crazy shit."

"Why? What happened?"

John looked up at the remnants of stardust continuing to fall from the sky. "You're totally not gonna believe me… like, at all. But just so you know, Charlotte will absolutely corroborate everything." John took a deep breath then filled them in on the unexplainable and unbelievable events of the past two hours.

Kevin and Julie were completely floored and left speechless when they heard what Hope had ultimately done. It took a while, but when Kevin finally spoke, he said, "It all makes sense now."

"What does?"

Kevin looked over at Julie, and then he told them about the dream he had earlier and how it differed from its usual ending. "I… I think it's over."

"What are you saying?" John asked. "That our parents are…"

"At peace now," Kevin said, nodding. "They're where they supposed to be."

John didn't have a dream, but he shared the same gut feeling as his brother. As a matter of fact, as soon as the stardust began to fall, John had a brief vision of Clarence. Technically, it was more of a feeling than a vision, but it told John that Clarence had finally moved on and would soon enough be reunited with Mary. Charlotte also admitted to having the same feeling about her father, and she sensed he was free and finally at peace.

The four of them made their way back up the path, and as they stood on the ledge, Julie pointed out to the lighthouse and said, "Whoa. Isn't that the coolest thing you've ever seen?"

It wasn't as prominent as before, but there was still plenty of stardust floating down from the sky onto the ocean. As fast as she could, she snapped a few pictures of the lighthouse. It wasn't until she examined the pictures that it hit her. "Oh my God! Does that look familiar or what?" Before anyone could respond, Julie answered her own question. "It looks just like that postcard William gave me… you know, of Medillia's Lament."

Kevin looked from John to Charlotte and then back to his wife. "It does… it sure does," he said, putting his arm around her.

The four of them remained at the park the rest of the night. At one point, Kevin ran back to the car and grabbed a blanket. He placed it on the ledge, and they sat there watching what they all agreed was: *The most beautiful and magical sight they'd ever seen.* They were so mesmerized and entranced, they remained there until the sun came up. The sunrise that morning was also something to behold. An array of bright colors filled the sky and reminded John of the sunrises he saw the last time he was in Applewood. And even though Charlotte had lived there all her life, she was also awestruck by the sky's beauty.

Julie took a deep breath of salt air and softly spoke, "William was right, this island really is the most beautiful and magical place in the world."

The other three didn't say a word, but they all nodded in agreement. When the sun had made its way well above the lighthouse, John blurted out, "I don't know about you guys, but I'm starving." Again, they all nodded in agreement.

Charlotte looked down at her watch and exclaimed, "Shit. I was supposed to open today."

"Oh no. Should we get going?" Julie asked.

Charlotte thought for a moment, smiled, and said, "Nah. The town can live without coffee and tobacco for a morning. I'll open up later. I say we all hit the diner."

On their way out of the park, John paused at the granite memorial and slowly ran his fingers over the inscription, which read:

> ...... O HEAR US WHEN WE CRY TO THEE
> FOR THOSE IN PERIL ON THE SEA ......

John wasn't sure how many people lost at sea were due to the Dark Waters, but if so, they were in a better place now. Because of the horrible weather all summer, the garden beds throughout the park were all empty and neglected. John made a mental note to return and place flowers around the memorial. Just then, he heard what assumed to be a squeaky wheel from off in the distance. His ears perked up and chills ran up his arms. He turned his head and expected to see Mary pushing her old shopping cart up the path. But the only thing he saw was a lone seagull circling the park in the distance. Although disappointed, he looked at it as sign.

All four of them climbed into the car, and as they left the parking lot, Kevin asked, "Should we try to get your truck out now?"

"Nah. We can come back and get it later. I'm starving."

"You got it," Kevin said and continued up the road. As he drove past the entrance to the path, both John and Charlotte curiously looked at each other. Hope's Subaru was no longer there. It was like it had just up and vanished into thin air. They didn't spend too much time being puzzled, for this was just the latest strange and unexplainable event they'd experienced on the island.

26

When they arrived at the diner, it was much busier than normal. The entire restaurant was abuzz with an energy that hadn't been seen or felt in a very long time. Surely, the re-emergence of warm temperatures and bright blue skies had a lot to do with this. But John, Kevin, and Charlotte knew it went deeper than that. Now that the Evil Spirit and its Dark Waters were finally defeated, it felt like a giant weight had been lifted from the island and its people. There was only one big question that remained.

Charlotte took a sip of her coffee then hesitantly said, "Hey... have you guys thought about what we're going to tell Janice? I mean, she's gonna start to wonder where Hope went."

"Oh, shit," Kevin said, leaning in closer. "I didn't even think about that."

John pondered but said nothing.

"Maybe you should just tell her the truth," suggested Julie.

"I've known Janice for a long time," Charlotte said. "She's one of the kindest and most non-judgmental people I've ever met, but... but there's no way she would believe it if we told her the truth."

"But we have to tell her something," Julie said.

Finally, John added his two cents. "Look, let's not stress about that now. I think we should all just get some food in us and decompress for a while.

Charlotte nodded. "Maybe John's right. It's been quite the night. And as a matter of fact, I think I just decided to close the store for the day and relax."

"Your mother won't care?" Julie asked.

"Nah. She trusts my judgement. Not so much when it comes to men, but she trusts my judgement on everything else."

Julie and Kevin smirked over at John.

"Ha ha," John said, rolling his eyes. "Her mother wasn't referring to me." He paused and then looked at Charlotte. "She wasn't, was she?"

Charlotte let him sweat for a moment and then said, "Relax. She wasn't talking about you. She actually likes you. Well, she doesn't not like you, I should say."

Before John had a chance to reply, Charlotte's phone *dinged*. Her grin grew bigger as she read through the text.

"Who's that?" John asked, with a hint of jealousy.

Kevin wasted no time joking at John's expense. "Probably a guy her mother likes better than you."

Both girls joined Kevin in laughing. John thought about tossing his water at his brother but chose the more mature route—his middle finger.

"If you must know, it was my oldest brother. So, technically, I guess you were right. My mother does like him better."

When everyone was done razzing John, Charlotte said, "One of the perks of having a brother who's a fancy Boston lawyer is he's constantly getting free tickets to anything and everything. I messaged him the other day to see if he could score us some tickets. I thought it would be cool if we all went to Boston for a night or two."

"Yes, yes, and yes!" Julie exclaimed. "Boston is one of my must-visit places!"

John and Kevin happily nodded in agreement.

"I remember you mentioning that you really like musicals. And I'm sure you've probably already seen this one, but I got us tickets to see *West Side Story*."

"Shut up!" Julie squealed, grabbing both of Charlotte's hands. "That's my all-time favorite!"

Kevin and John were much less enthused.

"We're going to Boston to see a play?" Kevin asked.

John added, "A musical play?"

Charlotte smirked then surprised them with, "I assumed you two clowns weren't the theater type. That's why I had my brother hook you up with Red Sox tickets. Red Sox versus White Sox, to be precise."

This time it was John and Kevin's turn to squeal in joy.

"I know the Cubs are your team but at least it's Chicago, right?"

"We don't care who they're playing," Kevin said. "It's been a lifelong dream of ours to see a game in Fenway Park."

"Did you really get us Red Sox tickets?" John asked.

"I really did."

John placed his arm around her and sweetly said, "You're the best."

He then gave her a kiss. It was only on the cheek, but it was the first time he'd ever kissed her—in public or otherwise. Julie had a big smile on her face as she watched Charlotte's face turn red. Kevin was also smiling, and he gave John an approving wink. The only thing Kevin loved more than giving John shit was seeing his brother happy.

When they were finished with breakfast, they drove back over and helped John get his truck out from the ditch. After that, they all agreed to take a long nap before heading into Boston for the night. On their way back over to Charlotte's, John drove right past the store.

"Where are you going?" she asked.

He sighed and said, "I know what I said earlier, but I really think we need to go talk to Janice."

"What are you going to tell her?"

"I don't know yet, but we have to say something."

"But what?" she asked.

He shrugged. "Something will come to me," he said, unconvincingly.

With the inn only a mile away, they didn't have much time to prepare. They had even less time once they parked in the driveway. As soon as they exited the truck, Janice greeted them from the porch.

"Good morning, you two. Are you here to help celebrate?"

"Celebrate?" Charlotte asked as they walked up the steps.

"Well, yeah. In case you haven't noticed, summer has finally arrived on the old island. The bluest of skies... temperatures in the eighties... birds singing... and not a rain cloud in sight. I would say that constitutes a celebration."

"It's definitely a gorgeous day," Charlotte said, smiling.

"Come, sit," Janice said, motioning to the two chairs next to her. Janice held up her glass of tea. "It's so warm out this morning that I switched from hot tea to iced tea. Can I get you two anything?"

"No thanks," John said. "We just came from the diner."

Just as they sat down, Janice hit them with the $64,000 question. "So, what do I owe the pleasure?"

They knew it would come up sooner rather than later, but still, they were left speechless. At first, John looked over to Charlotte as if he was expecting her to start. She began to squirm in her chair and gave John a glare which said, *this was your idea... YOU say something.*

Neither of them got the chance, however.

"This has to do with Hope, doesn't it?" Janice asked.

Surprised, John looked from Charlotte then back to Janice. "Um... yes, ma'am. She... um... she..."

Janice watched and listened as John struggled to find the words. Finally, she let him off the hook.

"It's okay, dear... I already know," she said with a sad smile.

"You do?" John and Charlotte responded at the same time.

"I saw this coming for a while now."

Again, they answered together. "You did?"

Janice polished off the rest of her iced tea and said, "It seems most people come to this island for one of two reasons. They're either running from something… or trying to find the answers to some sort of big life problem… sometimes both. From the moment Hope arrived, I could tell she was searching for something. I tried my best to be there for her, but at the end of the day, we all have to find our own path. But it did break my heart watching her slowly slip into such a dark place."

Janice paused and swirled the ice cubes around in her glass. Eventually, her lips curled into a smile as she focused over at John and Charlotte.

"Whether you realize it or not, you two, along with your brother, helped lift Hope's spirit, which ultimately allowed her to find what she was looking for. As much as I loved having her around the house with me, I always knew once she found her answers that she'd want to return home."

Janice gripped the arms of the chair, gathered as much strength as she could, then slowly lifted herself to her feet.

"Of course, it would have been nice if she said goodbye," Janice said, chuckling. She picked up her empty glass and looked in their direction. "I need a refill. Are you sure I can't get you two anything?"

Still a bit shocked, they shook their heads no. As soon as the screen door shut behind her, John turned to Charlotte and whispered, "She thinks Hope just up and went back to Chicago, doesn't she?"

"I think so," Charlotte whispered back. "For a second, I thought she might have known…"

"Yeah, me too. We should probably get going before she starts asking too many questions."

Charlotte nodded, and they both stood from their chairs. Just then, the front door creaked open, and Janice stepped onto the porch.

"You're not leaving already, are you?"

"I'm afraid so," Charlotte said. "The four of us are going down to Boston for the night, so we should probably head home and get ready."

"Oh, I love Boston," Janice said, slowly returning to her chair. "I'm glad you all are having such a wonderful time together. It should only get better now that the summer weather has finally decided to show its face. I know Hope is no longer here, but each one of you are always welcome here. I could always use the company."

"Does that include one of your famous home-cooked meals?" John asked with a grin.

"That's a given," Janice said, winking.

They started to head towards the stairs, but before they could take a step down, Janice called out, "Aren't you forgetting something?"

Curiously, they turned back around.

"Forget something?" John asked.

"Hope might have been in too much of a hurry to say goodbye to me, but she never would have been in too much of a hurry to forget her chest." Seeing the puzzled looks on their faces, Janice clarified. "The antique chest Hope's mother passed on to her. I do believe it was Hope's pride and joy, and I'm sure she wanted you to have it."

When Janice said the word *you*, her eyes were firmly planted on Charlotte.

"Me?" Charlotte asked, pointing to herself.

"Well, yeah. From what I understand, there's a lot of interesting things in that old chest… things that might inspire a talented writer to pen the next Great American novel." Once again, Janice winked then took a long, satisfying sip from her iced tea.

***

While John retrieved and lugged the chest into his truck, Kevin and Julie were curled up in bed trying to get some rest. Julie placed her head on Kevin's chest and smiled. "You certainly outdid yourself, Mr. Mathews."

"What does that mean?"

"For years I've been bugging you about us stepping away from work and taking a real vacation. And when you finally decided to do it, you certainly pulled out all the stops and made it one of the best weeks of my life. Or I should say, the most magical week of my life."

Kevin smiled then shrugged and said, "Go big or go home, right?"

"Ha! Exactly."

Gently, he began running his fingers through her hair. Speaking of which… we kind of need to start thinking about heading back to Chicago. We have to make a decision on the lease by the end of the month."

Kevin felt his chest vibrating from Julie's laughter. "What's so funny," he asked.

"It's not like you don't already know what you want to do."

"What are you talking about?"

Julie sat up and grinned. "Come on, Kev. Do you really think I don't know what's been going on… why we're *really* here?"

"Huh? I… I told you why we're here. I wanted to see for myself about our parents."

"I know, I know, and I'm honestly glad you two have found closure with everything. I really am. But come on Kevin, you have to admit, you had an ulterior motive."

"Seriously, Julie… what are you talking about?" He joined her in sitting straight up.

She rolled her eyes and continued smiling. "Does the Great Blue Heron Inn ring a bell?"

"Huh? What about it?"

"Do you really expect me to believe when Janice gave us that detailed tour of the place that it was spur of the moment? And how random was it for her to ask me to help her do a little rearranging and redecorating of some of the rooms? And don't you think it was a tad bit strange that she mentioned to me multiple times how she really wanted to sell the place, but she needed to find the perfect couple to buy it? And how coincidental was it that she kept telling me that I had the perfect personality to be in the hospitality business?"

Hesitantly, Kevin shrugged, still not having a clue what Julie was talking about.

"And not to mention, you laid it on pretty thick gushing about how much you loved the architecture of the inn."

"I wouldn't exactly say I was gushing," Kevin said. "Besides, you know how much I love old houses. I've said that to you many times."

"Yup, you have," she said, grinning wider. "Look, I know how much the Wild Irish Rose means to you, but I also know that your heart just hasn't been in it lately. And I also know about the huge rent increase."

"Fucking John."

"Nope. It wasn't John. I had a little visit from our landlord a few weeks back. He wanted to know if we had signed the new contract yet. I pretended to know what he was talking about, and after he left, I raided the office until I found it."

Ashamed, Kevin lowered his head. "I'm sorry."

"Honey, you don't have to apologize. I totally get it. I've been feeling the same way about the bar."

"You have? Why didn't you say anything?"

Julie grimaced at the hypocrisy. "Probably the same reason you never said anything to me. I guess we both could improve our communication skills. At first, I thought you were just stressed over the new lease offer, but then I realized your heart just wasn't in it anymore."

"I don't think my heart has been in it for a while now, to be honest with you."

"I know," she said, placing her hand on his. "And that's why I think we're both due for a big change."

"As in… moving *here*? To Maine?"

She thought for a moment then smiled and said, "Sure, why not? I mean, besides a few close friends, it's not like we have a lot of ties to Chicago. Neither one of us has family there."

"Well, except for my brother."

His comment caused Julie to burst out laughing. "Are you kidding me? Have you seen the way John looks at Charlotte? And the way she looks at him? He's probably going to move here before we do!"

"I don't know about that," Kevin said, laughing. "But for now, let's keep this to ourselves. This is a huge decision we'd be making. We need to put some serious thought into it."

***

Maybe it was the emotion from the events of the night before. Or maybe it was a culmination of the last two weeks. Or maybe, just maybe, it was as simple as John finally feeling comfortable enough to let go and to truly move on. No matter what the reasons were, one thing was for certain: As they all headed down to Boston for the night, Hope's words began to echo through John's head: *You'll know when you know.*

John knew. Without a doubt, he knew.

While the girls were having a blast at the theater, the brothers were in heaven watching the Red Sox play at Fenway Park. When all was said and done, and after each couple went back to their respective hotel rooms, John did what he'd been thinking about ever since he laid eyes on Charlotte. He kissed her, and maybe even a bit more. John didn't need to kiss and tell a thing to his brother the next day. His beaming smile said it all.

John knew that his relationship with Charlotte went well beyond just a little vacation fling. It also went beyond their connection to the recent events on the island. And because of those crazy and unpredictable events, he never had a chance to truly analyze these feelings he had for her. But now that the dust had settled, so to speak, his feelings for her had taken center stage in his mind.

At first, he tossed around the idea of asking Charlotte if she would consider moving to Chicago. After all, she mentioned a few times how much she always wanted to go there. Of course, there's a big difference between wanting to visit a place and actually moving there. Not to mention, Charlotte's entire family lived out here on the east coast. The more he thought about it, the more he realized how unfair it would be to ask her to move for him.

There were a few times John was tempted to go to his brother for advice, but he didn't. He pretty much had his mind made up that he wanted to move to Applewood, he just wasn't sure how Charlotte would take it.

Am I moving too fast? We've only known each other a couple weeks... is this gonna scare her off?

Like always, John overanalyzed the situation to death. And like always, he spent hours and hours rehearsing the perfect speech to give to her. And yes, like always, it never actually came out as he rehearsed it. The night after they returned from Boston, they decided to watch a movie over at Charlotte's place. Neither of them said it out loud, but they were each hoping to pick up where they left off the night before. But there was way too much on John's mind, and the next thing he knew he blurted out, "What are your thoughts on me moving here?"

Charlotte was taken aback and had no idea what to say. Nervously, she started laughing and said, "Yeah, right."

"I'm serious. I've been thinking about it for a while now."

Her laughing subsided, and in a more serious tone she said, "That's a pretty big decision."

"Yeah, I know. But I want to know *your* thoughts on it."

"Wow... well... um... I'm not gonna lie, I would love for you to move here, but... but I just don't want you to regret it. I know Chicago is your home."

John nodded in agreement, paused a moment, and said, "Chicago is my home because that's all I ever knew. But as soon as I stepped foot on this island seven years ago, I felt a connection here. Maybe it's because of my parents... maybe it's because of you... I don't really know. But this is what I do know: I feel like this is the place I'm supposed to be... I feel it with all my heart." His speech wasn't as smooth or as eloquent as he'd rehearsed but judging by the look on Charlotte's face, John knew he did just fine.

***

When he got home that night, he wasted no time in telling Kevin and Julie his big news. Before he told them, he prepared himself for their inevitable pushback. Surely, they would come at him with: *What are you thinking? You barely know this girl. What about your business?*

What John didn't prepare himself for was their overwhelming excitement. It started with Julie smacking Kevin's arm. "Ha! Told you! Did I call that or what?" she said, bouncing up and down.

"You certainly did," Kevin replied.

Julie gave John a big hug. "I'm so happy for you... for both of you."

This was certainly not the reaction he expected. For a second, he thought they were putting him on. When it became apparent that they were actually happy for him, John hesitantly asked, "Are you guys being serious? You approve of this? You're not gonna give me a long list of reasons why this is a bad idea?"

Nearly bursting at the seams, Kevin and Julie looked over at one another.

Curiously, John asked, "What's going on here?"

"Do you want to tell him, or do you want me to tell him?" Although Julie gave Kevin the option, before he could say a word, she blurted out, "We're moving here, too!"

27

A week after their fun-filled trip to Boston, Kevin and Julie packed up and made their way back to Chicago, but not before meeting up with Janice and making her an offer on the inn. To their complete and utter surprise, Janice countered with a number well below what they originally offered.

Not long after Kevin and Julie left the island, John also headed back to Chicago. All three of them had made big decisions, and now it was time to tie up loose ends for their life-changing move. There's an old adage which states: *One should never make a life changing decision while on vacation.* And even though all three of them knew they were doing the right thing; it was much easier making their decisions in Applewood rather than following through with them once they were back in Chicago.

Julie had it the easiest of the three, for she didn't have any real ties to Chicago at all. It wasn't even her hometown. Her father was in the military, so by the time she was eighteen, they had already moved a half dozen times throughout the country. She'd only been in Chicago for two years before she started working at the Wild Irish Rose. And as much as she loved owning it with Kevin, she loved the idea of owning their very own inn even more, especially one in Maine.

Kevin's decision was a little more difficult. Chicago was the only hometown he'd ever known. Most of his adult life he had dreamed about owning his own bar, in particular, the Wild Irish Rose. He'd put his blood, sweat, and tears into the place and putting it up for sale proved harder than he thought. Fortunately, the excitement of what was waiting for them in Maine far outweighed any bittersweet feelings he might have had. The more they packed up their belongings in their tiny apartment across town, the more excited they were for their new adventure together.

John, on the other hand, had a much harder time with the move—but for different reasons. None of which had to do with his woodworking business. He planned on bringing all his tools and equipment out to Maine with him, and he knew he could start up his business again whenever he wanted. Kevin and Julie had no problem leaving an apartment that they never really liked in the first place, but for John, he was forced to sell the house he had once purchased with the love of his life.

That being said, throughout the whole process, John never once second-guessed himself or even wavered. In his heart, he knew it was time to finally get closure and move on with his life. And he knew the only way to truly do that was to officially sell the house and start afresh. Over the years, John's mother-in-law had slowly taken care of most of Kristen and Hannah's personal belongings. Of the remaining items, it was the photos taken by Kristen over the years that he truly couldn't part with. He left all the furniture, which almost exclusively had been picked out by Kristen.

***

About a month before John's house was officially sold, Kevin and Julie had already tied up their loose ends and were all packed up and ready to head east. For old times' sake, the brothers went to their favorite batting cages one last time before saying their goodbyes.

"We're all really doing this, huh… leaving Chicago and moving to Maine?"

"Yeah, but it's a good thing, John. And not to be too cheesy, but I think it's what we're supposed to do… all of us."

John swung and connected solidly with the ball. "Yeah, I know. Just never pictured us leaving Chicago."

Kevin watched John swing and miss. "I know it was hard for you to put the house on the market. Are you okay?"

"Yeah, I'll be fine. It was probably something I should have done a long time ago."

"When do you think you'll be joining us out in Maine?"

"Just waiting on a date for the closing. Maybe another few weeks or so." John crushed the ball deep into the netting and then slowly gazed around. "We've hit a lot of balls in these cages, haven't we? A lot of memories here."

Kevin knew John was referring to more than just the batting cages but did his best to put a positive spin on it. "Yeah, but once we're in Maine I guess we'll just have to make new memories… all four of us."

John smiled over at his brother. He liked that Kevin had included Charlotte when referring to their future. As they made their way from the batting cages to the parking lot, Kevin quietly said, "I know it's been a couple of months now, but I still can't believe everything that happened on that island. Especially with Hope."

Sadly, John nodded. "Me neither. I know the island is in a better place now… and I know our parents and everyone else who was affected are also in a better place now, but… but I'm not sure if I'll ever get that image of her stepping off that cliff out of my head."

Kevin placed his hand on his brother's shoulder, tightly squeezing it. "I think we just have to focus on the aftermath. You said yourself, it was one of the most beautiful things you'd ever seen."

John smiled. "It was. I don't think I'll ever be able to put it to words what happened that night… or what I witnessed that night."

"You don't have, John. You don't have to."

The brothers placed their bats in the back of John's truck, and after they got in and closed their doors, Kevin shook his head and said,

"I still think it's crazy that out of all the people in the world you and I had a small part to play in this."

"Yeah, I agree," John said, starting his truck. "Although, I probably had a little bit bigger part than you did."

"Seriously dude? You're going to turn this into a competition, too?"

"I'm just saying… while you were out driving around Bar Harbor, I was making magic happen."

Kevin started to respond, but instead, he simply shook his head and smiled at his brother.

***

During John's last two weeks in Chicago, Charlotte flew out to give him a hand and to also do some sightseeing of the Windy City. She knew how hard this was for him, so she graciously stayed at a hotel throughout her stay there. As hard as it was for John to say his official goodbye to his house, it was nothing compared to his final stop before leaving for Maine. He knew it was time to say goodbye to his girls. Charlotte accompanied him to the cemetery, but she stopped well short of their headstones.

"I'll wait for you over here," she said, motioning to a stone bench.

With a huge bouquet of flowers in each hand, John walked the rest of the way alone. Between their two headstones was a flowerpot full of white lilies. John assumed it was left by Julie and Kevin on their way out of town.

"How are my two favorite girls doing?" he said, kneeling and placing the two bouquets at the foot of their headstones. "I've missed you. I'm sorry I haven't stopped by sooner, but I've had a lot of crazy stuff going on… and a lot of hard decisions to make. That's kind of why I'm here right now."

Just like always, he found himself tracing their engraved names with his fingertip. This was usually the point where his tears worked their way from his eyes. Although this time, the tears were already falling well before he even made his way over to their headstones.

"I've... I've decided to move to Maine. Kevin and Julie are moving there as well. Actually, they're already out there. They sold the Wild Irish Rose, and believe it or not, they bought a classic old New England inn. You girls would love it there on the island."

John paused and did his best to wipe away the tears. "I know this is sudden... the whole thing is a long and crazy story, and I promise I will tell it to you girls sometime, but... but in order for me to move there, I had to... I had to sell our house."

There was no hiding or escaping his tears. They flowed freely, falling onto the ground. "I'm so sorry. I'm so sorry I sold our house, but I had to. I think it was the one thing holding me back from moving on. A while back, I met and started dating this woman... Jain. She was a great person, and I thought I was ready... I honestly thought I was ready but... apparently, I wasn't. I never mentioned her to you before because I didn't want to upset you or offend you or whatever. I don't know. I suppose I always knew you would never be upset or mad. In my heart, I know you just want me to be happy again. That's what you've always wanted for me. I guess it took all this time for me to actually want it for myself."

Slowly, John turned and looked down at Charlotte sitting on the bench.

"I met this woman while I was out in Maine. Her name is Charlotte. I know that no one of us really knows what the future holds, but for right now she makes me happy, and I think... I think I'm gonna give it a go. A wise person once told me: *You'll know when you know.* And it seems all the signs are pointing me in her direction." John smiled and said, "I know you're big on the whole sign thing, Kristen. I think you'd really like her, though. Both of you. She's kind... funny... and she definitely doesn't have a problem calling me on any of my shit. I know in my heart I'm doing the right thing, but... I'm just so scared."

Again, tears poured from his eyes, falling on the flowers below.

355

"I'm so scared you girls might think I'm gonna forget about you. Because I swear to you… that will *never* ever happen. I will come back here as much as I can to see you. I promise you that! You two will always, always hold a special place in my heart, and nothing or no one will ever change that."

John leaned his forehead onto Kristen's headstone and released every tear and every emotion in his body. When he finally composed himself, he stood up and motioned for Charlotte to come over. She mouthed the words, *Are you sure?* John nodded yes. As she approached closer, he reached out his hand. She clutched it tightly, then they both turned and faced the two headstones.

"Kristen… Hannah… this is Charlotte."

From the moment she watched John place the flowers on their graves, Charlotte, too, had started crying. She swiped her tears the best she could then looked down at their headstones.

"It's very nice to meet you… both of you. John has told me so much about you girls." She paused briefly. "I promise I'll take good care of him."

Over the next few minutes, they held hands and looked down in silence. Finally, John released his grip and knelt down in front of Hannah. With both hands on her headstone, he leaned over and kissed the top of it. He then did the same to Kristen's.

"I love you both so much. More than you'll ever know."

Charlotte placed her hand on his shoulder, then they slowly turned and walked away.

28

Despite their landlord's high-priced rent, finding a new buyer for the Wild Irish Rose was not only easy, but it was quite profitable as well. Between the profit from the sale and the extremely low price they bought the inn for, they had plenty of money left over to bring the old building and its property back to life. Julie was ecstatic to finally have a yard. So much so, she wasted no time hiring a landscaping company to rejuvenate the large lawn and its many flower beds.

John's luck, on the other hand, wasn't nearly as good when it came to money. He still owed a lot on the house, so even though he sold it for a decent price, there was very little profit left over. For now, this left him with one option: to live with Kevin and Julie at the inn. This allowed him to save money while he and Charlotte looked for a place of their own. John also used this time to help with the renovations for the big reopening of the Great Blue Heron Inn. And yes, there was no way Kevin and Julie were going to change the name. They wanted to honor not only the inn's past, but Janice as well. They still couldn't believe how low Janice sold the inn for.

"It was never about the money," Janice once told them. "I just needed to know this property would be in good hands, and I knew when I met you both that you were the perfect choice to carry on this very special place."

When they asked what she would do after the sale was complete, Janice breathed a sigh of relief and cryptically said, "Rest. It feels like

I've been watching over this place for an eternity… and now that it's in good hands again, it will be nice to spread my wings and fly away, so to speak."

As soon as the sale was finalized, and as soon as she handed over the keys to Kevin and Julie, Janice mysteriously disappeared from the island and was never heard from again. And it might be cliché, but Janice was gone but most certainly not forgotten, especially by those she had touched over the years. Julie redecorated the place in her own vision, but make no mistake about it, there was always something there that reminded them of Janice, especially when you saw a Great Blue Heron.

Less than three weeks after moving to Applewood, the island's magic held one more trick up its sleeve for John. Ever since the Evil Spirit and its Dark Waters had completely vanished, the weather on the island had returned to normal. Some would say, even better than normal. In between helping his brother with the renovations, John found time to do a few repairs over at William's house. He replaced some of the rotted trim, did a little exterior painting, and once a week he came and cut the grass. Unfortunately, the Galloways' trusty old mower didn't make it past the first cut before officially dying for good. Although there was a little sentimentality attached to it, John was more than fine with purchasing a brand-new high-powered mower.

John also replaced the rotted shed door and bought a shiny new padlock for it. When the yard was cut, and when the mower was locked up, John sat on the bed of his truck with an ice-cold Gatorade. Just as the last drop flowed down his gullet, a postal truck pulled into the driveway. A few seconds later, the driver approached with a large envelope in one hand and a clipboard in the other.

"How's it going?" John called out.

"Good, thanks."

"I'm sorry, but if you're looking for the Galloways, they don't live here anymore."

The driver looked down at his clipboard. "Actually, I'm looking for a John Mathews."

"What? Did you say John Mathews?"

"Yes, sir."

"Um… that's me."

"Excellent. I just need to see your ID real quick, and then you can sign for this."

Hesitantly, John pulled out his wallet and ID.

The driver quickly examined it and said, "Perfect. Just sign here, please."

"What is this?" John asked, signing his name. "And who's it from?"

The driver handed John a copy of the paper, followed by the large thick envelope.

"All the information should be on there. Have a nice day."

As the driver walked away, John didn't even respond. He was too busy looking at the mystery package. It didn't take long for him to rip it open and examine the contents. On top of a big stack of legal documents was a small white envelope with his name on it. He carefully opened it up and removed the letter inside.

John,

Well, I'm in sunny Savanah and loving it! My friend and I did some traveling this summer, and we are getting ready to go on a tropical cruise later this fall. I plan on doing a lot more traveling over the next few years. As hesitant as I was to move away from Chicago, I know I'm where I'm supposed to be right now. It was so hard to sell the place where William and I spent so much of our life together, but it was time. I've also been doing a lot of thinking about the place in Maine, and I think it's time to get rid of that as well. It's probably long overdue, actually.

I can't thank you enough for everything you have done for us. For me… for William… and for his parents. I'm also appreciative of everything you've done at the house, and that is why you've made my decision very easy. The house is yours,

John. If you want it, of course. The enclosed paperwork is just a legal formality. Once signed, the place is 100% yours free and clear.

Whatever you decide, I hope you find the happiness you seek. Trust me, it's out there. You just have to look hard enough, that's all.

All the best,

Rachel

John reread the letter two more times and did his best to decipher through some of the documents. When he was sure he hadn't misread or misunderstood it, he slowly placed the letter and papers on his truck and looked back over at the house and said, "Son of a bitch. It's mine. The house is mine."

29

John continued to help his brother and Julie get the inn ready to open, but he wasted no time moving his things into his new house, and he wasted even less time moving Charlotte's things in with him. Together, they had their very own place to do whatever they wanted with. They'd already taken care of painting the interior walls, so now they just needed to go out and buy some new furniture to make the house feel more like *their* home.

From the first day they moved in, John had his mind set on a secret renovation project. He waited until Charlotte went out of town for a weekend to see her brother before starting it. When she returned, he surprised her by transforming one of the bedrooms into her very own writing room. He turned one entire wall into a floor to ceiling bookshelf. He bought her the most comfortable (and expensive) ergonomic chair out there. He also hooked up speakers in each corner of the room, so she could listen to whatever she needed to inspire her.

John even paid attention to some of the smaller details. In the center of the room, he placed a gorgeous oriental rug that Julie had given him from the inn. He also added a small antique end table that Charlotte's mother had giving him. He placed Hope's favorite teddy bear on top of the table, tie dye shirt and all. For good luck, he added a bowl of Hope's crystals, which they found in the chest. And speaking of the chest, John lugged it upstairs and put it on the opposite wall of the bookcase. Little did he know at the time, the chest would become

Charlotte's lifeline to the Great American novel she was about to write. As perfect as the room was, the true centerpiece sat between the two windows of the back wall. It was a handcrafted oak desk that John had secretly been building for her since they moved in. In the top drawer he put everything a writer could want: pads of paper, pens, pencils, sticky notes, index cards, etc. The only thing sitting on top of the desk was William's trusty old typewriter. Charlotte had never met William before, but John was sure there was enough magic in the typewriter to inspire her future novels.

John also turned the gazebo outside into a mini writing retreat, especially useful in warmer weather. He strung white lights around the entire gazebo and arranged the interior for her utmost comfort. When Charlotte returned, she was blown away by his sweet and thoughtful gesture. Less than twenty-four hours later, she started putting both spaces to full use. As it turned out, Janice was right, Hope's chest provided more than a creative spark for Charlotte. From the moment that everything went down months earlier, Charlotte knew she needed to be the one to tell Hope's story… the true story of Medillia's Lament. She knew people would look at it as pure fiction, but that didn't really bother her—the story needed to be written.

Charlotte combed through each and every diary belonging to both Hope and her mother. She even read through Hope's father's notebooks, too, incorporating everything Hope had ever told her, including the story about the week Hope spent with her father back in 1981. Charlotte also included everything that had gone on between John, Kevin, herself, William and every other person who was part of the magic of Applewood.

After weeks and weeks of reading, note taking, and outlining, Charlotte was still left with a big question. Ironically, it was the same question Hope had asked herself for the past thirty years. What caused Hope's father to choose Applewood to reunite with his daughter that week? If he and Hope's mother had never been there before, then how did he know to take her there? It took jumping off the cliff for the whole truth to be revealed to Hope. Fortunately, Charlotte wouldn't need to go to such extremes to get the answer. She just needed to go to the wisest man she knew—Daniel.

Charlotte wanted to be as accurate as possible when it came to the Native American legends of the island. One evening after she and John had just finished dinner, Charlotte took a ride over to pick Daniel's brain on as many of these things as she could think of. He graciously invited her in and was eagerly willing to help. She explained what she was working on and told him she needed to know more details about Medillia's Lament. He basically reiterated everything he had shared with her, John and Kevin months earlier.

"This is exciting," Daniel said, leaning back in his wheelchair. "I'm very much looking forward to reading your masterpiece."

"I'm not sure about a masterpiece," Charlotte said. "I just think the world should hear about the Dark Waters and especially Medillia's Lament. And yes, I know that no one's gonna believe any of it really happened, but... but we know, right?"

"That we do," Daniel said with a wink and a grin.

He watched as Charlotte stood up and placed her notebook and pen back into her bag. "Thanks again for your help, Daniel. I thought there was another question I had for you, but now I can't remember it."

"You're very welcome, Charlotte." He pondered a second, rubbing his scruff with his fingers. "I'm not trying to tell you how to write your story, but I hope you plan on including the Legend of Lover's Leap."

"The Legend of Lover's Leap?"

"Don't tell me that you've lived here all your life and have never heard of it?"

"No, I've heard of it... sorta. Isn't it just about two teenage lovers who realized they couldn't be together, so they jumped off some giant ledge?"

Daniel covered his face with his hands and shook his head. "What are the schools teaching you here on the island?"

Charlotte giggled and said, "Well, to be fair, pretty much every state has some sort of Lover's Leap legend."

"True, but Applewood's Lover's Leap is the key to *everything* you're trying to write."

"Really?" she said, unsure if he was putting her on.

"I'll tell ya what, why don't you come back tomorrow, and I'll fill you in on Applewood's official Legend of Lover's Leap."

"Deal," she said, leaning down and giving him a big hug. She started to walk away but stopped short. "Oh, I remember what I wanted to ask you. Does the name *Medillia* have an English translation?"

With the widest of smiles, Daniel said, "It does. It means *Hope*."

"Of course it does," Charlotte said, beaming.

***

As promised, Charlotte returned the next day, and Daniel told her all about the Legend of Lover's Leap. Eventually, all the pieces fell into place, and all her questions were answered. Daniel was right; the Legend of Lover's Leap was the key to everything she was trying to write. Charlotte wasted no time. As soon as she got back home from Daniel's, she rushed upstairs to her new writing room, and that's just what she did—write. Unlike her past attempts, the words flowed easily and came to her faster than they ever had before. There were days when John barely saw her face. He used to think the best sound in the world was hearing the crowd loudly cheer after a Cubs victory, and while he still believed that, a very close second was hearing the rhythmic pecking of fingers on a typewriter—Charlotte's fingers—on William's typewriter.

Charlotte worked on her book for the entire winter, and when it was completely finished, she presented it to John to be its first reader.

364

Applewood – Maine's Magical Island

A novel by Charlotte Blaisdell

The story you're about to read is based on legends, folklore, and facts. I'll leave it up to you to determine which is which. All I can tell you is that truth, like beauty, is in the eye of the beholder. And although the following story may seem unbelievable, unrealistic, and at times, fantastical, I assure you it's 100% the truth… at least in my eyes.

The *real* story of Medillia's Lament will reveal to the world just how magical the island of Applewood, Maine truly is. A wise man once told me that it would be impossible to tell the story of Medillia's Lament without first telling you about the Legend of Lover's Leap, or more specifically, the love story between Ahanu and Maulian.

There have always been mysterious and magical elements to Applewood, which is what originally drew the Abenakis to the island in the first place. From the moment they arrived on the island, they felt the immense power of its magic. Not long after their village was settled, the chief sent a group of his strongest men to fully explore the island with hopes of finding the source of its magic.

Eventually, the men made their way to the small mountain in the center of the island. One of them came across what looked to be an entrance to a cave, but it was completely barricaded with large rocks. They were so sure the cave was where the magic resided that they all helped with the removal of the heavy rocks from the entrance. Once removed, they excitedly entered the cave. It wasn't long before their excitement turned to fear. The cave led them to the core of the island, and it was there that they came face to face with the Evil Spirit.

Just as quickly as they entered, the men rushed to exit the cave and to escape the Evil Spirit. They didn't stop running until they returned to their village on the outskirts of the island. Unfortunately, while they were in the cave, the Evil Spirit had sunk its black poison into the men.

In hysterics, the men explained to the chief exactly what they had encountered. The chief surmised that the Evil Spirit must have been banished and trapped in the cave, and unknowingly, his men had now freed it. It only got worse from there. Within twenty-four hours, the Evil Spirit's poison began to take hold of the men. Not only were their bodies in immense pain, but their minds were deteriorating as well. They heard voices, saw visions, and ultimately, they went crazy. Over the next week, the village witnessed the slow, excruciating death of each of the men. If that weren't bad enough, the poison appeared to be contagious, and anyone who had come in close contact with the men also became infected and suffered the same excruciating death.

By the time the chief figured out what was going on and had separated the sick from the healthy, nearly half the tribe was lost. The ones who survived were panic-stricken and wanted to flee the island, but the chief held firm. He still believed the island possessed magic, which had never been seen before. But he also knew it now possessed a dark, Evil Spirit. It was at that point he sent for the most powerful shaman in the northeast, hailing from the Penobscot tribe.

While they waited for the shaman's arrival, the chief forbade anyone to leave the village. After witnessing what had happened to half the tribe, no one dared to disobey the chief. Every waking hour, the Evil Spirit was on everyone's mind—everyone except Ahanu and Maulian. They were young Abenaki teenagers, who had fallen in love with each other months earlier.

Like most teenagers, they were certain that their love was the love of a lifetime. They were often seen walking hand in hand around the island. Each morning they would wake up early and head to the eastern-most side of the island to watch the sunrise together. They spent the rest of the day doing their tribal responsibilities before heading hand in hand to the west side of the island. There, they sat on the banks of the Alsigontekw River and watched the sunset together.

Also like most teenagers in love, Ahanu and Maulian thought with their hearts rather than their minds, which is what led them to disobey the chief. Each morning and night, the starry-eyed lovers continued to watch the sunrise and sunset together. As they snuck out of the tiny village, the last thing on their minds was the Evil Spirit. That all changed on the third morning. As usual, the couple headed to the apple orchid high above the cliffs of the Atlantic, which is now where Harbor Cove Park resides.

The sunrise that morning was so spectacular that Ahanu and Maulian were completely mesmerized. They had never seen the sky as colorful. They were so mesmerized that they didn't hear the Evil Spirit approaching them from behind. By the time they saw it, it was too late. The Evil Spirit surrounded and poisoned them just like the others. After the Evil Spirit disappeared, the young Abenaki teenagers knew they couldn't return to their village. Not only had they disobeyed their chief, but more importantly, they didn't want to spread the poisonous disease to the remaining members of their tribe.

After what seemed like forever, the couple stood up, looked into each other's eyes, and knew what they had to do. Ahanu took Maulian's hand, and they made their way to a giant ledge extending out beyond the cliff. With tears flowing down their cheeks, they vowed to be together forever. Through every afterlife and every reincarnation, they promised to find one another and fall in love all over again.

"You're not just the love of my life, but you're the love of all my lifetimes," Ahanu said to Maulian, as they grasped hands and stepped off the ledge.

It is said, their love was so pure and strong that in each and every afterlife moving forward, their vow proved sacred. Not only did they find one another, but they fell madly in love all over again. Unfortunately, even in the afterlife, the Evil Spirit's poison continued coursing through their bodies. Many centuries and many afterlives later, the couple knew their time was limited. They knew the Evil Spirit would eventually win. This time, however, there were no vows spoken—only prayers. The couple prayed for a miracle; a miracle to rid them of the poison and to defeat the Evil Spirit. The Gods took pity on the couple and granted their wish in the form of a beautiful baby girl. One who would bring hope back to Applewood and rid the island of the Evil Spirit once and for all...

The End

About The Author

Jody grew up in the Kittery/York area of southern Maine. He originally started out as a screenwriter. As of now, he has written nine feature-length screenplays ranging from dramas, to dramedies, to comedies. Not only did Jody grow up in Maine, but he makes it a point to utilize and represent his state as much as possible. From Maine's scenic rocky coast to its remotely pristine backwoods, to its eclectic characters; they all serve as backdrops and pay homage to his beloved state. His ultimate goal is not only to sell his scripts, but to have them filmed right here in the Great State of Maine.

Unfortunately, searching for the proper financing has been a long, tiring, and disheartening process. Feeling helpless in the whole "funding" process, Jody decided to reverse the typical Hollywood blueprint. That blueprint being: It's almost ALWAYS a novel that gets turned into a screenplay and not a screenplay which gets turned into a novel. Jody's thought process was simple: It's much easier to self-publish a book rather than self-finance a movie, and who knows, maybe, just maybe, this will be a screenplay that gets turned into a book only to eventually get turned back into a movie! But even if this wild idea never comes to fruition, at least by turning it into a novel, the *stories* themselves will be able to be enjoyed by the public. Whether it's two or two million people who buy his books, Jody is just happy that they are no longer collecting dust in a desk drawer.

Other books by Jody Clark

"Medillia's Lament"

"Medillia's Lament II – The Dark Waters

"Livin' on a Prayer – The Untold Tommy & Gina Story"

"The Wild Irish Rose"

The Soundtrack to My Life Trilogy
Book one – *"The Empty Beach"*
Book two – *"Between Hello and Goodbye"*
Book three – *"The Ring on the Sill"*

Available at

www.vacationlandbooks.com

I do most of my posting & promoting via my Facebook profile

Feel free to *friend* me!

Jody Clark (vacationlandbooks)